THE HIDDEN WORLD

THE HIDDEN WORLD

Paul Park

 A TOM DOHERTY ASSOCIATES BOOK
New York

THE HIDDEN WORLD

A Tor Book
Published by Tom Doherty Associates, LLC
175 Fifth Avenue
New York, NY 10010

www.tor-forge.com

Tor® is a registered trademark of Tom Doherty Associates, LLC.

Library of Congress Cataloging-in-Publication Data

Park, Paul, 1954–
    The hidden world / Paul Park.—1st ed.
        p. cm.
    "A Tom Doherty Associates Book."
    ISBN-13: 978-0-7653-1668-4
    ISBN-10: 0-7653-1668-4
    I. Title.
    PS3566.A6745H53 2008
    813'.54—dc22
                        2007047699

First Edition: April 2008

Printed in the United States of America

0 9 8 7 6 5 4 3 2 1

THIS BOOK IS FOR DEBORAH, WITH LOVE.

1

Rest and Recompense

1   *Miranda Popescu Dreams of Home*

TWO HUNDRED KILOMETERS to the north and east of Bucharest, in a farmhouse in the village of Stanesti-Jui, Miranda lay asleep. After dinner she had retired to her bedroom with a head cold. Now past midnight, propped up on the pillows, she lay with her mouth open. Then she turned onto her side and her dream changed.

It wasn't entirely a dream. That winter in her room she had become accustomed to the many intermediate states between sleeping and waking. She had been sick for much of the season, a lung infection that, without antibiotics, had lingered until the weather turned. Her hostess, the Condesa de Rougemont, and then later her mother, had dosed her with medicinals. She'd scarcely left her room. Of course she had undertaken several small journeys to the secret world, with the help of her secret tourmaline, Johannes Kepler's eye.

Now it was almost springtime, and she was feeling better. This particular journey had started with a daydream. She had sat with a French novel, her mind wandering. And as often happened, it had wandered back to the invented refuge that her aunt Aegypta Schenck von Schenck had made for her in Berkshire County, Massachusetts, where she had gone to high school.

She had lived with Stanley and Rachel, her adoptive parents, in the house on the college green in the middle of town.

Her best friend had been Andromeda Bailey, boyish and beautiful, her gray eyes spotted with blue and black and silver. Peter Gross had been in her class at school, and she had gotten to know him, too. They had spent some time together in the woods the summer Andromeda had gone to Europe. Often, as he sat cross-legged in the dirt or on a rock, he'd have a piece of a leaf or a twig in his brown hair. Often he'd have a blade of grass between his teeth. Sometimes he'd be playing his harmonica, a poor, private kind of music that she indulged. He only had the one hand. His right hand was missing because of a birth defect.

In those days all her knowledge of Roumania had come from dreams, fantasies, and a few stray memories. The facts she'd learned in school or on her own had been all lies or else distortions. The Communist dictator, Nicolae Ceausescu, the history of Eastern Europe—no, it had been the Baroness Nicola Ceausescu who had sent an emissary to bring her home to Bucharest. His name was Kevin Markasev, and he was famous here. He'd gone all that way to find her, and he had burned the book of her invented childhood in a fire on Christmas Hill above the art museum. Then morning came and the world was different. Peter and Andromeda were different, too.

Daydreaming in Stanesti-Jui, Miranda had found her way to Christmas Hill again, and she had climbed it in the dark. She had climbed back to the start of the story. The French novel lay in her lap, spine up, inverted. Three-quarters of the way through, already she could see the end, the denouement. It was reassuring and annoying to perceive it in the distance, the place where everything was sealed up in a circle and some kind of homecoming was possible, some journey or at least some reference to the beginning once again.

You'd go back, and you'd know something new. And you would take consolation from that new thing, a consolation that was phony and real at the same time.

So she indulged herself. She closed her eyes and imagined the dark night, the bonfire in the hummocks of grass on the hillside. The place was still there for her, and in a moment she could see it clearly, and Kevin

Markasev above her with the little book, her essential history, the entire story of her childhood, balanced in his hands. Only this time as he dropped it, she thought she might reach up to catch it, bat it away from the consuming fire. Andromeda was there, and Peter might come running down to help her, tripping and sliding down the slope. As she struggled with Kevin Markasev, he might pull him off her, chase him away. And she'd lie on her back. Maybe she'd have knocked her head against a stone. And Peter would be on his knees above her. "Are you all right?" he'd say, reaching to touch her face. "Are you all right?" he'd repeat, and she'd be happy to hear his voice, even though he might be implying some kind of weakness.

Of course I'm all right, she'd think, and then she'd say aloud, "I'm fine," which maybe she could make into the truth.

But the question was, if she had known then what she knew now, would she have wanted to preserve the book or to destroy it? Would she have been strong enough to hold out her bruised hands, accept the changing world and everything that was to come? In the dream she was not strong enough. Propped on pillows in her bed in Madame de Rougemont's farmhouse, she found herself muttering these words again: "I'm fine." Her French novel dropped to the floor.

She turned onto her side. Her daydream was no longer in her strict control. It had turned into an actual dream, a provisional dream only one step below consciousness. The three friends left Kevin Markasev where he lay stunned beside the burning fire. They left him and continued down the cow field, through the fences and the trees, until they reached the art museum parking lot at the bottom of the hill. There was some tension between them as they split up, each to walk home through the deserted predawn streets.

And when she reached her parents' house, the door was unlocked. She slipped inside as silently as she knew how. She could see from the front hall where Rachel had fallen asleep on the couch. She had waited up, which was comforting and irritating. She lay under the tartan blanket, curled up, mouth out of shape on the pillow. Sleep had cleaned her face; Miranda wouldn't wake her. Silent as a ghost, she climbed the stairs to her own room on the third floor, feeling wired and exhausted from the eventful night. In the bathroom on the landing she undressed, put on her PJs, flossed and brushed her teeth. Then she slipped into her cozy bed, cozy and private as this one in the farmhouse, on the slope of the mountain outside of town.

She fell asleep, and in her dream her aunt Aegypta came to her.

This was a different kind of dreaming, deeper and more powerful. It felt like being awake. Aegypta Schenck was dressed in a long coat trimmed with fox fur, and the little wicked heads hung down. She was wearing gloves, and a small pillbox hat was pinned to her gray hair. Her face was partly covered in a veil. "Ma petite chère," she said.

Miranda wouldn't let her start with that. She sat up in her bed, which in her dream was the one she actually occupied, in Stanesti-Jui. "Tell me," she said in English. "I was thinking about Peter Gross. Peter and Andromeda, my friends. Tell me, where are they?"

There was a pause. Miranda could see part of her aunt's face under the veil. Her lips were thin.

"Pieter de Graz is in Staro Selo with the Eleventh Mountaineers. There is a Turkish offensive in that area."

Miranda knew that much herself. She could see her aunt's lips, part of her nose. Her smile had no joy in it: "My dear girl. You will not fail to surprise me, the loyalty you give to these two men, your father's aides-de-camp. They were junior officers, and the ones closest to hand in a time of crisis. That is all. They were meant to protect you, at which task they have not distinguished themselves. Instead, you have saved de Graz's life more than once."

As sometimes happens in dreams, Miranda tried to speak but couldn't. "I am punished for my cowardice and my mistakes," continued her aunt. "I have been dead six years, and I am punished every day. In the book I gave you to take to Massachusetts, I described a war in Europe, a terrible war—do you remember? You asked me about it once."

Now she pulled her veil back, and Miranda could see her eyes. They had a yellow tinge. She went on: "It was my plan to give you a book in a language you didn't know, and as a grown woman you would learn to read it. Later you would follow the directives I had printed out, and with the coins I left in your possession you would find your way to Great Roumania. By yourself, you would find your way. I thought perhaps I would not live to see it—not that it mattered. But you would be wise with the wisdom from the book and your own life."

Fat chance, Miranda thought, and tried to speak. But she could not speak aloud.

"Then my enemies were planning my destruction," her aunt said, "and I didn't want to die. I thought of a new plan, and I goaded Nicola Ceausescu to send that boy to bring you home—prematurely, as it turned out. And now the coins were for me, so you could free me from tara mortilor. Blind Rodica and Gregor Splaa, who were my contingency, now supported the entire scheme, and they were too weak for that. And you were too young to be sensible when I met you in the land of the dead. There also you worried about de Graz and Prochenko, because of the damage they had suffered. It was not meant to be like this. Mixtures of people and animals from two worlds—what good are they now? As for me, I gambled my life and could not win it back. And I think this is the reason: I could not bear the thought of never seeing you again."

Because this was a dream, it could not capture the emotions of the real world. Her aunt Aegypta's voice was calm, her face almost expressionless. "Oh, my dear, you were too young. And you are still too young. Too young for these tools I have put into your hands. Too young to leave your friends behind and accept your fortune. Too young to listen to my guidance."

These words filled Miranda with an old frustration. How could I be too young? she thought. Her aunt had stolen away whole years, whole blocks of time, and yet still blamed her. And she was wrong—Miranda had done everything she wanted. How could she have done better, after all? Now Miranda could speak again, and so she totted up a list of her achievements. "The Germans have left Bucharest," she said. "The empress is dead. The Elector of Ratisbon is dead, his prisoners are free. Nicola Ceausescu is dead. . . ."

Silence. Then her aunt spoke again. "That is true. That is all true, though you are not responsible for all of it. But even if you were, you have not accomplished everything, and there is still much more. We have new enemies. Enemies without end. Bocu, Antonescu. And now these demons Nicola Ceausescu managed to unlock before she died—I meant them to serve you! I meant you to use them wisely, with my guidance. Instead they are infected with Nicola Ceausescu's hate, and they have brought the world into this war. So there are new tasks for us. It is an illusion if we reach a place of safety among the waves."

Miranda listened to the coarse, grainy whisper, which continued: "But you still have weapons, even though you might not understand how to use them. You have the power I have given you—your father's revolver and the black book. And the tourmaline, though you have managed to do something unexpected once again. Because of your stubbornness. But even so I think you must be able to learn. I have hope, and I have faith in you."

Miranda felt a surge of despondency. Because of my stubbornness, she thought. Then why was she so desperate to please? What should I do now? she almost asked. Tell me what to do, she almost asked. "Tell me," she asked instead. "Is anything left of what I left behind? You know, where I grew up in Massachusetts. That was a calm place in the waves."

And the smile on the ghost's face was softer now, touched with love, or else a kind of condescension. "Child," she said. "Every object has a symbol in the hidden world. Its counterpart."

A moment, and then she started again: "That town, those streets, those people—you might make a version for yourself in the land of the dead. A little corner for yourself in tara mortilor. Or you might search for it and find it in the hidden world. Scientists have quarreled on this subject. You might find it with the tools I've given you. Would you abandon everything for that? Everything that's yet to come? And if you did, it wouldn't be the same, of course. That place, it was your childhood. Who can say she has not done what you have done?"

There was some more of that kind of talk before Miranda woke in the same dark bedroom, the same bed where she had spent the last part of the dream. But in the dream she hadn't had this cold in her head, which filled up her sinuses as if with wadded cotton. Now awake, she found it hard to breathe until she sat up.

A lamp burned on the bedside table near her hand. There was a handkerchief beside the lamp, whose wick was turned down low. She blew her nose.

She did not disturb the woman curled on the settee under a plaid blanket. Rachel, her adoptive mother in the dream, also did not budge when Miranda had come in the door, climbed the creaking stairs.

The settee was in a bay of dark windows overlooking the vegetable garden. Miranda got out of bed, then crossed the bare floorboards. She stopped before an artist's easel. Clara Brancoveanu was skilled at drawing in charcoal and red pencil. During Miranda's illness she had occupied her time with a sketching pad. Most recently she had made a series of landscapes from the window: the back garden and the fields beyond, rising toward the forest and the mountainside.

Outside the glass it was gray night. Miranda turned her face toward the ticking clock. The hour before dawn.

She looked down at the woman's hair, carefully pinned into little wheels. She felt a mix of comfort and annoyance that was familiar. Ever since she had caught this cold, her mother had insisted on sleeping in her room, afraid of a recurrence of the pneumonia. Though what she could have done if it came back, Miranda wasn't sure. Hold her hand, she supposed. Bring her hot things to drink, as she had before. Hold the bowl for her to spit.

Even so, after these months of loving care it was still hard for Miranda to think this woman was her mother, her actual birth mother. Growing up in Massachusetts, she had resented Rachel the most when she was being too maternal. Sometimes, though, Rachel and Clara seemed to combine, unified by how she'd treated them. Unified also at moments like this, when they performed the same activity, occupied the same space—Clara Brancoveanu was propped on a little bolster in the arm of the settee. Her mouth was open and her breath came soft, a woman in her fifties, but prematurely old, with weak, sallow skin in the lamplight. Half her life a prisoner, she had been a beauty at one time. Miranda had seen a portrait in the People's Palace. And of course there was the sepia photograph in her locket.

She found she could still remember every word Aegypta Schenck had said, standing in this corner of the room in her dream. Now Miranda tiptoed out the door and down the hall, hoping everyone would stay asleep. She was still in her clothes, and in the cabinet at the bottom of the stairs she groped in the darkness for a coat. The two big mutts were there on the round rug. They stirred to greet her, pressing their faces into her hand.

They were named Lucius and Lionel. When she opened the bolt they scratched against the doorjamb, eager to get out.

First light was coming. There was fog in the fields behind the house, and in the paddock on the other side of the stone wall. She followed the path to the edge of the evergreens and then climbed up through the meadow. From time to time she would stop to clear her nose, using a technique Stanley had shown her on camping trips in Maine. You would put your thumb over each nostril in turn, then bend down into the bushes and exhale with your mouth closed. If you were dainty and careful, the spray wouldn't get on your clothes.

When she straightened up again her head was ringing. The air was cold and sharp as she sucked it in. She hadn't had much to eat the night before, and she still felt sort of terrible, her lungs delicate and easily exhausted. The dogs roamed away from her, appearing and disappearing in the mist.

She was working on the things Aegypta Schenck had said and whether they were true. Often when she walked by herself or sat up in her room, she would think about Peter and Andromeda and then stop thinking about them. At such moments her thoughts were like these two black dogs, superficially free. Yet always the dogs returned to her, reappeared to check on her, and they were never more than fifty yards away.

She had not seen either of her friends for months. Without a doubt, as her aunt had suggested, she had more pressing concerns. She was the white tyger of Roumania, and what she did or failed to do was important—even here, in this little village in the mountains. The country was at war, the Turks on one side and the Germans on the other. Colonel Victor Bocu had consolidated power in Bucharest after the death of Nicola Ceausescu, with the help of a fraudulent National Assembly. His Rezistenta Party had taken fifty-four percent of the first vote. When the Turks began to mobilize, Bocu had refused to listen to any of their demands, some of which were not unreasonable—the return of territories ceded under the Peace of Havsa in Prince Frederick's time.

Bocu had used the threat of war and then the war itself to justify his political position, which was unforgiveable. Doubtless he was an evil man, and doubtless the white tyger could find a way to destroy him, which was what Aegypta Schenck would have wanted or advised—doubtless, except Miranda was full of doubts. Destroying the wicked never seemed to change the world.

In the misty pasture Miranda paused and let the dogs come to her. It was easy for these subjects, important as they were, to disappear into abstraction.

She scanned the treetops, moisture on her face, worrying instead about Peter in the trenches and Andromeda wherever she was—these political issues were too hard to make real, except through the experience of people you cared about. They were her friends from Massachusetts, however much they had been battered and transformed. Without them she was abandoned, lost. But everybody had to break free, finally. Wasn't that what her aunt had said?

Aegypta Schenck had made no provision for Pieter de Graz and Sasha Prochenko, wasted no thought on what might happen to them once their purpose was accomplished. Now they had limped home: Peter Gross, Pieter de Graz, the ape and the scarlet bug. Prochenko, Andromeda, and the yellow dog. They had suffered for Miranda's sake. So maybe it was her duty to worry about them. And maybe that duty was as strong as what she owed to Great Roumania.

The mist hung round her at the top of the meadow. The dogs barged out of it and into it again. The house was out of sight. Miranda touched the golden bracelet at her wrist, and then she closed her eyes. In her mind she reached down and searched among the stones for the jewel, the tourmaline, her entry to the hidden world. The last time she had come this way, she had wrapped it in a sock and left it in a secure place, marked by a rock cairn. Now she found it and unwrapped it and held it in her hand. What had her aunt said about Berkshire County, Massachusetts, America? "You might search for it and find it in the hidden world. You might find it with the tools I've given you." The bright sun broke over her and drove the mist away.

Miranda was in a high meadow on a high mountain slope. She stood in the grass around her knees. It was springtime, and morning time, and the birds were singing. A brandywine bird was hidden in the grass. She knew its song. And above her she saw a big butterfly that was floating down, flapping wearily as if it had traveled a long way.

What a lovely spot! The sun was shining over the rock peaks. She had no doubt that in the grass with her, hidden there or maybe in that stand of birches, she would find the dog, the ape, the bug. They would share all this together and all danger, too.

As if conjured by the word, as she pushed through the grass she saw where it came to an end at a sort of a cliff. Below her the ground had been scooped out, a wound in the red and black earth. Smells came from it, a garbage dump here in this beautiful place, an uncovered pit that was so big she couldn't see the end of it. And there was movement down there in the garbage, a multitude of animals and creatures in a dump that receded into darkness as she looked.

Peter Gross was in the trenches in Staro Selo—God, she couldn't stand it. She laid down the jewel and the world shuddered to life again, the real world where she stood above Stanesti-Jui. But there too the sun had broken through a cleft in the high peaks. There too the mist had cleared, and she could see the town with its little railway station and the temple of Demeter with its turnip dome. She could see the farmhouse down below.

The dogs came to her and licked her hands, then ran off again. For several minutes she stood immobile on the slope. She remembered climbing up here with Andromeda the year before, after she'd escaped from Nicola Ceausescu and the People's Palace. It was one of the first mornings, and they had walked through the barley fields behind the house, then up the slope. In this same meadow they had looked down at the black-and-green farmhouse and the slate-roofed village around the temple, the railway and the road.

"Sort of takes you back," Andromeda had said in English.

At moments as they climbed, Miranda had been struck by how easy this felt, just like walking to school over Christmas Hill. At other times Andromeda seemed a stranger to her, untiring, unsweating, though she always kept her mouth open and spat from time to time into the grass. They scarcely spoke. Moment by moment it was as if they passed through alternating currents of familiarity and strangeness. Dressed in the same black suit and creamy linen for two days, Andromeda still looked stylish and well groomed. How beautiful she was, Miranda thought, not for the first time. Her skin seemed to glow, an effect of the morning sunlight in the fine, golden hair that seemed to cover her. Her teeth were white and shiny, disconcertingly large. She let her tongue loll out, then touched her lips. Nor did it matter if she was really someone else, some cavalry lieutenant or whatever. People were what they were. Everyone was a zoo inside if you could just scrape off the skin.

She'd left that evening or the next evening to take the night train back to Bucharest. "À bientôt," she'd said when the carriage came to the door. One thing Miranda had not discussed with her was Peter Gross or Pieter de Graz, and her feelings for one or both of them.

Now, alone with the dogs running back and forth, she remembered what he had looked like in the gazebo by the lake in the park under the plum-colored sky, the last time she had seen him. Nor did she understand, still, why they had had to separate, except because he'd wanted to. It was his choice, his decision. She had assumed he'd stay with her, and something would change, and they would . . . touch each other as they'd touched each other in the palace cell where they were prisoners. And that would be all right and even normal in some way, like something that was supposed to happen all along.

And she would feel—what? All she could see now was his dirty, brooding face, marked along his cheek with scabs or abrasions and made unfamiliar by the lantern's oblique glare in the little brick gazebo in the park. Certainly in her mind's eye he looked threatening and unappealing. But maybe that was normal too under the circumstances; who knew what normal was? This landscape of feelings, this really was the hidden world, stranger than a mountaintop or garbage pit. And she was no white tyger in that landscape, that was sure. This stuff had always made her crazy. Always she'd been hesitant and insecure. The boldest thing she'd ever done was to go up to Peter Gross beside the icehouse in the woods. And that was only possible because she'd pitied him and couldn't conceive of anything happening between them. How wrong she'd been!

2   *Staro Selo*

ON FRIDAY EVENINGS THE OFFICERS lit candles in the dugouts. From the Roumanian trenches you could see the glow. At sunset the Turkish guns would fall silent along the southern front from Balcik to Kula, a distance of four hundred kilometers.

General Antonescu and the Roumanian high command had thought at first to take advantage of the superstition of the enemy. They had begun several big assaults on Saturday mornings, especially in the sectors closest to the river. Interrupted in their meditations, the Turks had fought with murderous fury. Later the Roumanians, superstitious in their turn, would not budge from their positions for the entire Sabbath, fearful of the wrath, as they imagined, of an indignant God.

This became the routine in the first season of the war, a day of respite at the end of every week. The bombardments would stop on both sides of the line, and the men would climb out of the trenches with ringing ears. They would repair their works, search in the barbed wire and cold mud for the bodies of their friends. At dusk on Saturday the guns would open up, hesitant at first, just a few green flares and tracers taking range, and then it all would begin again.

One Friday night in March, a man stood in the communication trench behind a quiet section of the line. This was south of the town of Staro Selo, where there was a supply depot and a military hospital, as well as the battalion headquarters.

The man, a platoon leader from Theta Company, was not typical, because he had risen from the ranks. In the winter he had served first as a private soldier, later as an NCO. But during the most recent counterattack, the Eleventh Mountain Battalion had lost seventeen of its junior officers. The man had been promoted in the field to acting brevet captain, a rank that had not yet been either reconsidered or confirmed.

He was atypical in another way. His right hand had been amputated at the middle of his forearm, forcing him to wear a prosthetic steel hook, buckled with leather straps to the stump of his arm. This injury had preceded the beginning of the war, which made his presence in the army a cause for speculation. But as he had explained, an ape could have enlisted in the battalion during the first Turkish advance. No questions would have been asked.

The captain was a handsome man with curly brown hair and big, widely spaced white teeth. His name was Peter Gross. Now he stood listening in the deserted trench, a clean one, cut back and forth in a corkscrew pattern a hundred and fifty meters from the support lines. The telephone wires were fastened to the walls or else held safely overhead. The drainage sumps were marked in white and full of tiny frogs. Underfoot, the mud was dry.

Three weeks earlier the enemy had attacked under a creeping barrage, had driven the men back to the support trenches, almost to the town. But the Turks had not been able to sustain their progress. Isolated in their turn by the Roumanian artillery, caught in fortifications they themselves had blown to pieces, and which in any case were facing the wrong way, they withdrew. After two days of fighting, both armies had collapsed into their previous positions. The Eleventh Brasov Mountaineers, responsible for this section of the line, had lost almost five hundred men in forty-eight hours, most during the initial bombardment. Many had been buried alive.

Now, after a period of inactivity, it was as if none of that had ever occurred. The trench ran straight and clean. The world was peaceful in the overcast, misty night. The captain was almost invisible. He stood unnoticed in an angle of the wall, listening to the cheeping frogs. It was as if the entire battlefront were deserted, or else patrolled by ghosts.

Tomorrow the communication trenches would be full of soldiers bringing up supplies under shelter of the truce. Tonight, because of the impossibility of an attack, the discipline on this part of the line had been relaxed. The company commander, a martinet during the week, was on his twenty-four-hour bender. A line of light slid from the bottom of the dugout's corrugated iron door. The men were playing cards. Behind the captain on the slope, the machine-gun posts were empty. Covered in their tarpaulins and rubber capes, the men snored in their shelters, cut into the trench's inner wall.

Nothing stirred. There would be observers in the listening posts. Captain Gross stepped across to the traverse, a sandbagged buttress reinforced with timber at the level of his head. He climbed onto the fire steps and looked over the parapet. Nothing.

No time like the present. He put his hand over his heart so he could feel the outline of the envelope he kept there, tucked under his shirt—a ritual in these moments. He clambered up the stepladder over the top.

Then he was crawling on his belly over crusts of broken earth. After fifty meters he rose to his hand and knees.

The Turks had fortified positions in a wheat field, beyond the remains of a dirt road and a shattered line of trees. The land between the armies was a tormented strip of earth, in some places no more than a hundred meters wide. Peter Gross was interested in poetry, and at dangerous moments he would surrender to the poetical part of himself in order to achieve a kind of discipline. Tonight this no-man's-land was like a river to him, and he imagined a cold, furious stream that flowed down from the mountains to the sea, a metaphoric likeness to the Danube ten kilometers behind him, the border to Roumania, toward which the army now retreated in bloody fits and starts.

Now that he had left the trench, he could smell the river on the night wind. On his hand and knees in the stiff dirt, he imagined the silent torrent all around him. The land was more like water than earth, carved ridges of mud and circular depressions—whirlpools of stinking garbage. Surely now in March the snows were melting in the high mountains, and in the Vulcan

Mountains near Stanesti-Jui. Surely there was snow in the mountains where Miranda lived, away from all this. Now the spring rains had brought a devastating flood, had washed away boots and hats and pieces of buildings. People, too.

Here the stream broadened as it met the plain. It stretched half a kilometer to the flickering candles on the far bank. Here especially there were mounds of detritus: clumps of grass and straw, timbers, broken trees, all stitched together in ubiquitous barbed wire, which held the flotsam, he thought, like an abandoned fishing net.

Out of sight from both banks of the stream, he clambered to his feet. He recognized the place. He stood on the lip of a small dell, an oak tree in the middle. This was the exact location.

All was quiet here, as in the trenches. But there was no truce in no-man's-land, the broken strip of earth between the armies. Under cover of darkness, faces blackened with soot, Turks and Roumanians would patrol this ground, looking for their wounded and taking prisoners.

On Wednesday night Peter had taken six men on patrol. Past midnight they had encountered a Turkish wiring detail. One man was missing when they returned to the line, a farmer's son named Costache, eighteen years old. Peter had gone out again with two volunteers but had found nothing. The boy must have gotten lost; several hundred meters to the left of Theta Company's positions, someone was shot by snipers climbing back. He shouted in Roumanian, but by that time the sun had risen.

On Thursday they had listened to him calling out for water. On Thursday night Peter had tried to find him with the same two men, but they had been roughed up. Now, today, the boy hadn't made another sound. And Theta Company was pulled back in reserve. Even though it was Friday night and the guns were quiet, the company commander had refused permission for another attempt.

So Peter had had to come up the communications trench and try from another section of the line. It was easy to get lost. He recognized this tree. This was where they'd seen the Turks two nights before. Pistols and knives in the darkness for about a minute. That was all they could manage so close to the line. What a stupid waste.

All of a sudden it seemed crazy to him that he should think he'd find the boy alive, or even the boy's body—what could he do? There was no one here.

It hadn't rained for almost a week, and that was hopeful, wasn't it? Spring was coming; he could smell the spring. This was the Bulgar country, famous for its fogs. As he climbed from the dell, he saw he was closer to the Turkish lines than he had thought. No more than seventy meters. He could see the candles glimmer in the mist. He wiped his face and found it wet. A wet wind from the river and the marsh. Moisture glistened on his sleeve.

So it was good to have the candles as a point of reference. He put his back to them and picked his way over the wounded, pockmarked, cratered ground. He had a pair of clippers in his pocket, and he often had to stop to cut through the wire. It sagged from metal stakes that screwed into the earth—an African invention, he had heard.

He was moving toward a lantern burning in the lines, which indicated the Roumanian latrines. It and the corresponding Turkish light were never shelled, by mutual and silent understanding. Now it flickered in the mist, flickered and went out.

But the distances were short. It was important to find the right section of the trench, the right traverse. Omega Company held two hundred meters of the front. The CO was notorious for his laxness on Friday nights. And Peter knew some of the men.

He muttered a curse in the English language—had they blown out the lantern? Or was it hidden in the mist, which might still rise? All was in darkness, and he could feel the warm wind on his face. Behind him the Sabbath candles had gone out.

The barbed wire was around his waist. He sank to his knees, then pulled himself forward into a shallow crater. Without the light from the latrine, it was useless to blunder forward—should he wait for dawn? No, even before dawn the trenches would be full of men. Darkness was his only chance to get back to his tent unnoticed.

And so he crept forward into holes punched out of the earth by the crashing howitzers, the whining 75s. Many of them contained corpses, slimy or half eaten by the rats. What was the point of searching for one corpse among the thousands who had died here? Was it because of his own vanity, his reputation on the line? When the darkness cleared a little bit and he could see his reference lights, he would give up and go back.

He paused, lifted up his head. Why did he find it necessary to disregard his senior officers? Was he was hoping for some kind of wound or punishment, so he could escape this place? Or was he trying to punish himself, maybe, and to forget how he had left Miranda Popescu in Cismigiu Park in Bucharest, abandoned a duty as clear as anything in Staro Selo? Otherwise he would think about her all night long.

He had abandoned her. Now he was stuck here in the mud, trapped with a hundred thousand others. And there was nothing to be done, and so he continued onward on his hand and knees, because he was quite sure he was in the area where Costache had been hit. He was moving parallel to the trench, as far as he could judge. Here was a deep, broken shell hole, and he could smell the water at the bottom. Here he found his man, lying on his back at the top of the crater, asleep, unconscious, dead—he put his hand on his shoulder. He whispered in his ear.

And he was alive—he came awake and would have shouted, only Peter put his hand over his mouth. He was struggling as Peter pinned him, held him down with his right elbow on his neck, the steel hook in his face. Why, if he had this much strength, had he not called out to the men in the listening post so they could bring him in? And so Peter knew immediately this wasn't his boy at all—his hair was tight and curly, close to his scalp.

But was the man a Turk, a spy? After his first surprise, when he'd been startled out of sleep, he did not struggle or cry out. He lay tense and terrified under Peter's hook. And whether his eyes had adjusted or else some of the mist had cleared, now Peter could see he was hurt. His boot protruded at an angle, and he was grimacing and stiff with pain. Nor was he dressed in the green tunic of the Eleventh Mountaineers, but in the black uniform of another Transylvanian regiment, the Fifty-third Light Infantry. He had his service badge.

Peter let his hand roam over the man's body, ascertaining all this. Now he thought he could risk a flame, and so he brought his Turkish lighter from his pocket and flicked the wheel next to the man's cheek—just for a moment.

Men rubbed soot or burned cork on their faces when they went on these patrols. But this man was an African. Peter had heard a rumor there were soldiers under the protection of the noncombatant states that made this crossing. He had not believed it.

"Who are you?" he whispered next to the fellow's hairless cheek. He adjusted his elbow so the man could talk; he was small in any case, small-boned and weak. His voice, when it came, was soft and cultured, aristocratic. He spoke Roumanian without an accent.

"Oh my God," he whispered. "Thank God, I have been lying here. Dreams—I dreamt and told myself I must have fallen near my grandfather's farm in Sacele, and I have scratched myself in the wet briars. So many cows have come this way, the ground is broken up. I must have put my foot into a rabbit hole. Oh, I think I will die in this place. There is no excuse for me."

So: delirious. Sacele was a town near Brasov, north of Bucharest. The Count de Graz had had a hunting lodge near there.

Suddenly it seemed idiotic to Peter Gross that he was even here. To own or control the no-man's-land was an advantage mostly in the mind. But men died for it even when there was no fighting. Died or went mad. The colonel believed in these patrols because he thought they kept the soldiers sharp during periods of inactivity. He rarely visited the front line.

"What is your name?" Peter whispered.

"Janus Adira, sir, of the Fifty-third, Wolf Company. With dispatches. I ask you, is it possible to stay here on this hillside? If I call out, who will listen? Oh, but I will die in this place, brought down like an animal!"

Peter looked up at the sky. The light was changing, and there was evidence of a moon. Dispatches—what was he talking about? "Don't say anything," Peter said. "You'll be fine. You're not fifty meters from the trench. Morning comes, then you cry out. They'll bring you in under the truce."

"Ah, God, don't leave me. Don't say these things. You are Captain Gross, I recognize you. I've heard of you. Theta Company, from the Eleventh. They will shoot me or else hang me, because I am a brave man, an idealist and a student of liberty. This is not for my own sake!"

So he was a spy, Peter thought. No doubt under some kind of indirect protection. Officially, the Abyssinians were neutral in this war.

He raised his head above the crater's lip. He could see the latrine lantern now, back the way he'd come.

"Captain Gross, don't leave me," whispered Janus Adira. "If I lie here by myself—oh, God. At the university, sometimes we would argue these things. No, I would hear them argue these modern points of view, picked up from German texts. I thought I could believe them. I prayed to God I could believe them, that death was like a soft sleep—that's all."

He swallowed, started again. "My leg—I tell you I have broken my leg. Oh, it hurts, I tell you—I was saying the same things! Except the more beer I drank, the more I realized they were fools. Now I tell you I believe in everything, the hidden world, the country of the dead. What else is possible? In these trenches everyone has seen the cockroaches and vermin erupt out of the earth. So I wonder what kind of animal or insect will come from my own corpse, when I am lying below the gallows or against the wall?"

Peter cursed under his breath. It was bad luck the man had recognized him. Now as he tried to pull away, the corporal grabbed him by the sleeve. "Please, you must save me. They have given me directions to go to Chiselet, to the wreck of the Hephaestion. Please, I will pay you what you ask. Whatever you ask. I am not a traitor. . . ."

Tears were on his cheeks. Peter could see them now. The light was better. Damn it, he thought, the man would cry out if he left. He was sure to cry out.

He pressed his elbow against Adira's throat, cutting off the flow of words. God damn it. Adira had called him by his name—known his name and could identify him.

Now the man lay still. But what had he said about Chiselet and the Hephaestion? What did he know about that?

He turned Adira onto his side, watched him vomit in shock and pain. "Give me a break," Peter muttered, in English. But he had already decided to bring him in, for Costache's sake. He did not want to return empty-handed after a night like this. And so, because there was no other option, he gave up all attempt at secrecy or stealth. He dragged the soldier up and staggered to his feet. He pulled him up across his chest, crushed him against his chest, and the man was quiet at last. He was very small, very light. It was like carrying a child.

Peter climbed out of the crater and along the ridge, thrown up by the shell. Adira hung from his arms. Maybe he'd lost consciousness. Peter had given up the idea of sneaking or dissembling—it was too late for that. But he would trust the drunkenness of Omega Company's commander, and stagger back to the line toward the traverse where he'd started. He'd brazen it out, but as he came up to the trench, maybe he needn't have worried. A soldier saw him as he loomed out of the darkness—"Oh, it's Captain Gross. Good morning, sir."

Then later: "Should I bring a stretcher? Give him here. Trust me, sir."

"No, I'll take him back."

He climbed onto the traverse timber, crossing the trench as if over a five-centimeter bridge. The sky had gone gray, and he could see where he was going. So he strolled back toward the support line over the open ground, Adira in his arms. He walked parallel to the communication trench. "Hi, captain, where you going?" called a man from the machine gun post behind the line.

"I'll see you before dark."

This was agricultural land, or had been, all the way to Staro Selo. Ruined buildings—a farm. Past the third trench, Peter laid his burden in the mud behind the shelter of a stone wall. There had been an orchard here.

"Now," he said. "Tell me what you're doing."

Adira turned his face to the side.

"No more lies," Peter said. "Talk to me."

He squatted down and slid his hook into Adira's neck just above his breastbone. Delicately, with the point of his prosthesis, he unbuttoned the front of Adira's tunic. "I felt this before. I wonder what it is."

In the afternoon, Peter's company would return to the front line, and there were rumors of a push. He had no time to waste here, but he was curious about the envelope over Adira's heart—was it the same as his? A memento, a talisman, a good-luck charm? Peter didn't think so. With his left hand he unfolded it, opened it up. Underneath, tucked into Adira's undershirt was a wad of reichmarks. This was what the man had meant when he had talked about paying him.

The paper on the inside of the envelope was sky blue with threads of silk. There were pages of hieroglyphs drawn in gold. Andromeda might have been able to read them, Peter thought.

So: an African carrying messages from Africa. Under the bare trees in the dead, long grass, the world was calm. Corporal Adira, if that was really his name, was sniveling because of his broken leg. But even that was a hopeless little noise.

There were birds in the branches above Peter's head. And in the dawn light, on the hill south of the town he could see the battery come to life, the men pulling the howitzers out of their pens. It was quiet in that wood behind the line, the day-long hush before the evening thunder.

"Tell me what this says," he said.

"I—I don't know. It is from Abyssinia."

"I can see that. You don't know what it says?" Peter removed the wad of currency. "Where are you taking this?"

"To Brasov, sir. Dispatches. The money is for my sister and my mother. Not for myself—I swear it."

Peter wrinkled up his nose. "And you're from Abyssinia?"

"Yes. No. My father—"

"And you think this will help?"

"Yes. Yes I do. Yes, sir. Something must be done."

"I wonder."

Around them the day was gathering. The men on the hill were unwrapping the long muzzles of the 75-millimeter cannons.

Peter Gross looked up. "Thirty years ago, we marched through this country carrying rifled muskets with percussion caps. Now we have machine guns and grenades—from Africa, but they supply both sides. It's for the money, don't you think?"

"I don't know."

"That's what I think. It's too much money to resist."

They spoke in murmurs behind the ruined wall. The trees above them were full of little birds that suddenly took flight, turning all at once. Now a single long shaft of sunlight broke through the clouds.

Deep in the east, the light came slipping toward them over the broken fields and the remains of last year's harvest. "I'm going back," said Captain Gross. "I'll turn this over to my colonel. He'll send someone to pick you up."

"Please, sir, no. For the love of God. It's—it's about Chiselet. The accident at Chiselet. This is an investigation by the government in Addis Ababa—that's all. I swear to God."

Peter turned the papers over, examined the backs of them. "What do you know about Chiselet?"

"Nothing, sir—I'm just a messenger."

Peter laughed. "And not a good one. You're not the right man for this."

He dropped the wad of money in the dirt. The little man, still weeping, lying on his side, clutched at it feebly. "No, sir."

Peter got to his feet. He brushed off the knees of his trousers, stood for a moment squinting into the wide sun, sniffing at the air. From here, looking north toward the great river, you almost wouldn't know there was a war.

He turned and walked away through the orchard toward the communication trench. He would inform the military police after he'd returned to Theta Company. In the meantime he was being followed.

He recognized the scent first of all, an animal and human mixture. In cheap hotels across North Africa and the Levant, he'd gotten used to it. Now he sniffed it with an odd sense of nostalgia. Rank and appealing, heavy and light, there had been a time when it had disgusted him. Those also had been difficult days.

But difficult or not, now they seemed touched with gold, with the warm morning light that caressed every prewar memory, everything that had happened before the Turks had crossed the line. He turned and lifted up his nose, waiting for her to take shape somewhere in the dead weeds—dog, woman, or man. Standing over the idiotic spy, her name had occurred to him. Was that when he had first caught the scent? Maybe not, because he thought about her often, her and Miranda Popescu. Every hour, maybe more.

"Where are you?" he whispered.

"Behind you." Her harsh, queer voice. Maybe she crouched on the other side of the stone wall. But he heard her clearly. "Don't turn around," she said.

They spoke in English. "What do you want?"

"Just to see you, first of all. You're a hard man to find alone."

"I must go back," he said.

Then after a moment: "How is Miranda? Is she safe?"

She didn't answer him. "I have a favor to ask. For old times' sake. Past times in the Ninth Hussars."

They had served together under General Schenck von Schenck. Miranda's father. That's where they'd known each other first. So long ago, it seemed like the beginning of the world.

"Yes?"

"I know you're having trouble with conscriptions, all the Transylvanian battalions. I want to know if I could volunteer, and you could bring me in."

Now suddenly he remembered that old campaign, the sights and sounds conjured to life as if by a few harsh, toneless words. The smell of leather and horses when they were camping in the birch trees above Nova Zagora. Brandy around the fire. The view from the ridge when on horseback he had taken his men down. Not like now, cowering in a hole.

"You're crazy," he said.

Then, because she didn't answer, he went on. "We're not soldiers anymore. We're up against machines. Machines stuck in the mud. You know, like those *Terminator* movies."

It was too tempting not to make a little joke, to bring back something from the other past they shared, when they had been kids together in Berkshire County. And she laughed.

"No," he said again. "You're crazy."

She was laughing. "Please. Don't make this hard. I beg you. Think of that: I'm begging you. Take me as a private soldier under your command."

He understood it must be true—this must be hard for her to say. She had not loved him then, nor did she love him now. She'd been a lieutenant in the old days, Sasha Prochenko on a big white stallion, so dashing and romantic in his forest-green uniform, high boots, fawn-colored pants, so popular with the ladies, his blue eyes flecked with silver. And later at Mamaia Castle on the beach . . .

"No. This is not a place for you. It's not what we need. How could you pass the physical?"

When she said nothing, he continued. "Can you see yourself in a latrine with twenty men?"

That made her pause. "I had not thought you were so cruel."

He looked around. Her voice had changed, and she was closer. "What about your own physical exam?" she asked. "Or were you always Captain Hook?"

Then again: "I am begging you."

"No!" he cried, angry now. Morning had come. There was no time. "Wasn't it your job to stay with Miranda and protect her? Isn't that what we decided, what we agreed on in Cismigiu Park? I wish that was my job, not to die here in this place. This cesspit."

Now he could see her in the morning sunlight. She stood up on the other side of the wall. She climbed over between the tumbled stones. Always the dandy. Civilian clothes—her pants perfectly creased. She carried a silver-headed cane.

She had a way that both attracted and repulsed him. But he had seen no women for many months, and his heart lifted when he saw her. She was too exotic for mere beauty—her yellow hair under the slouch hat, the soft body hair that made her exposed skin seem to glow, the proud expression and strong features in which her animal nature, now, seemed to predominate. But the sharp, musky smell had disappeared. He was used to it already.

Though she was dressed as a man, and in spite of the dog or wolf that lurked inside of her, she looked more girlish or womanly than she ever had in Berkshire County. Her hair was longer now, curling down below her ears. "It doesn't seem so bad," she said, looking around at the quiet orchard, the guns on the hillside raising their muzzles to the sky.

"It's a beautiful sight," she persisted. "You'd better go. A girl can dream."

But now Peter wanted to stay a moment longer. "Promise me you'll go back to her. This is not the place for you. The Condesa de Rougemont—in Bucharest we had no choice except for her to take Miranda in. But do you remember her on the Hoosick riverbank? Young woman then, old lady now—the place stank of magic."

Andromeda gave him a blank look. She didn't remember. How could she remember? "I don't trust her," he went on. "No matter what Madame de Graz says. I wish I could—no . . . leave a message at the hospital. Will you do that? There's a corporal of the Fifty-third Light Infantry over in those trees. He's got a broken leg. And tell me," he continued. "What does this say?"

He thrust the envelope of hieroglyphs into her gloved hand. She didn't need to squint to read it. "This is a shopping list. Small arms."

"Sure," said Peter. "Is that all?"

"No, it's not all. Chiselet—do you remember Chiselet?"

She smiled, then went on. "You weren't yourself. Neither was I. But I saw those lead canisters in the baggage car. That's what they're talking about here."

Peter shrugged. Andromeda raised the paper to her nose and sniffed it. "They must have been blown up in the explosion," she said, "except for one. An Abyssinian in a gray suit. He crawled out to die south of the tracks. I took the suit, his money, and his watch. But I left the canister two hundred meters in the marsh—a dead oak tree. You could see from the embankment. Everything else was to the north."

Peter scratched his right forearm where the leather cuff chafed. He had his own memories of that day and the wreck of the Hephaestion. From there he'd gone to Mogosoaia, where he'd found Miranda Popescu. "Tell me," he said, though by now it was too late to listen, "how is everyone in Stanesti-Jui? How is she?"

He spoke the name of the village like a charm. It was impossible to send a letter, though he had written many, or else the same one over and over. "Tell me, is she safe?"

Andromeda smiled, cruel in her turn, he thought. Her teeth were sharp and numerous. "You'd better go." And then after a moment: "In any case, I've been in Bucharest."

"Don't tell me you haven't seen her!" Peter said. "Promise me you'll watch over her—is that too much to ask, while I am here? Inez de Rougemont—I saw her on the Hoosick River, dressed in Gypsy clothes. Since then I've told myself that was not real. Madame de Graz had vouched for her, her oldest friend. She talks about her in her letters, but how can I be sure? Promise me you'll go there now."

For a moment there was no irony or slyness in her face. But she was as he remembered her—his old comrade in arms.

"Give her this," he said. He unbuttoned the first buttons of his tunic, then took from an inside pocket the letter he rewrote every fourth day or so, whenever they pulled his platoon from the front line. He kept it over his heart, a piece of superstition. "'I have a rendezvous with Death,'" he quoted fiercely. "It's lucky I learned that one, isn't it?"

It had been a favorite poem of his mother's in Berkshire County, a battle poem from the First World War. Now he said it for effect, something Sasha Prochenko might be expected to understand.

Jealous, he supposed, she smiled at him. "It's true—you are the lucky one. I often think about what happened in Chiselet."

Standing in front of him, she took hold of his collar, brushed her fingers against his silver captain's bars. She held his letter in her other hand, along with the hieroglyphic message, which she'd refolded carefully, replaced in its envelope. "No, give it back," Peter said. "I changed my mind—it is not good for me to write to her. That's not what I promised to her father. I said I would protect her, not . . ."

His voice dribbled away. Andromeda supplied the rest. ". . . Care for her? It's not the worst thing."

Was she teasing him? Peter turned his head. He stood looking out over the field. "Madame de Graz told me not to write to her. She told me it was dangerous, because I was a wanted man. She told me the police were looking for me. I haven't seen any proof."

"I'll take your letter," said Andromeda.

"No—I don't want that," Peter said. He reached out for the two envelopes and she came to him. She tucked them into the inside pocket of his uniform. She patted him over his heart, buttoned him up.

Though he was uncomfortable to feel her so close, he did not step away or knock her hands away. He had refused her, after all, rejected her. Her animal scent came back to him, and he could smell the liquor on her breath.

He turned back toward the trench. It was only a couple of minutes later, after she was gone, that he realized she had picked his pocket, taken both envelopes—the letter to Miranda and the pages of hieroglyphs. She'd left him with nothing.

3 *Lieutenant Prochenko*

"I HAVE A RENDEZVOUS WITH DEATH" was published in a chapbook with a dozen other poems after the war. Edited by "a captain of the Eleventh," it included "Dolce et Decorum," "If I should Die," and even, "When I have Fears that I might Cease to be."

Lieutenant Prochenko, though, riding back to Bucharest in a second-class compartment, hadn't known what Peter was talking about. What kind of rendezvous? The lieutenant had never been a student of English poetry, either in his high school days in Massachusetts or at his boarding school in Chisinau.

He would have had no patience for Peter Gross's literary ambitions, even if he'd known about them. Caught in his own troubles as the train crept into the Gara de Nord, he had no inkling of events as they transpired: the second battle of Staro Selo. But already that night the Turks had used chlorine gas in their assault. An African invention, borne on the wind, it had killed hundreds on both sides.

Prochenko had heard the barrage from the station and for hours afterwards. Now, thankfully, they had passed beyond the thunder of the guns. Anyone with a map could see that Staro Selo was the fulcrum of the war, ten kilometers from the bridge at Tutrakan, another sixty to Bucharest. Captain Gross would win the Star of Hercules for what he already had accomplished in his trench full of poisoned, dying men.

Peering out the window at the city lights, Prochenko might have found himself consumed with jealous disappointment if he'd known. It had always been his habit to condescend to Peter Gross. But what could he do now? Every compartment, every station platform was full of men in uniform. All of them stared at him as if he were some kind of circus freak. At Vasilati he had given his seat to a man on crutches and gone to stand in the crowded corridor. There it was worse. Men pressed against him on either side as the train shuddered and swayed; couldn't they tell he was different from them? Perhaps they could—that was what was so painful. When the track attendant in Bucharest unlocked the doors and pulled down the steps, Prochenko stood against the black cold windows to let them all past. But there was still a crowd when he followed. There was always a crowd. Men were waiting at a tea stall on the platform, dressed in mud-brown sappers' uniforms, waiting for the train to take them south. He imagined what they were thinking as he strode through them in his calfskin boots, up the stairs and into the great hall of the station: weak heart, weak lungs, mentally deficient, a sodomite, perhaps. But if they only knew! Sometimes he was tempted to affect a limp or a damaged arm—no, he had too much pride for that. His wounds were on the inside.

And so he faked an easy, casual saunter. Under the gleaming mosaic dome he paused to light a cigarette, hooking his wolf's-head walking stick over his arm and stripping off his gloves. There was the row of itching bites along his wrist, where the demon had bitten him.

He checked the times for the train to Rimnicu at the departure board, the first part of his journey to the mountains—all those old women together, and Miranda. In his jacket's breast pocket he carried Peter Gross's letter, which he would bring to her. He was tempted to read it—why not? Lazy curiosity—he had his own adventures. He scratched the sores along his wrist, making them bleed under the soft white hair.

Hours to kill. The train wasn't till late morning. It was close to dawn. "Domnul—sir. Are you looking for something? Vous cherchez quelquechose?" The boy at the newspaper kiosk was talking to him. He had a sheep's big eyes.

Prochenko was looking for something. The world was falling apart. There was no news in the papers, but a clever man could see the shortages and misery in every story, even the most desperately optimistic. Elena Bocu-Bibescu, the president's wife, had hosted a grand cotillion in the People's Palace. In Poland, where the Germans and Russians fought each other in the endless woods, there was no progress of any kind.

He strode out into the piata and the street. God, hours to kill. And because this was Bucharest, the sapphire city with its marble buildings and blue-tiled domes, and because he had just seen Elena Bibescu's name in print, he knew the demon would find him. It was a question of time. A debutante's cotillion with only seventeen names—how sad that was! The first time he had attended an event like that, in the dress uniform of the Ninth Hussars, there had been three times that number—long-necked swans with white gloves up their arms. But that was more than twenty years ago.

He wore a light linen jacket and no overcoat, and in the raw, foggy hour before dawn he was not cold. On the contrary—he spat into the gutter. The train had been intolerable. Always when he was overheated, he found his mouth filling up with saliva. It wasn't normal; he was always a couple of degrees warmer than the rest.

For ten minutes the lieutenant strolled along the boulevard toward the center of town. These streets were deserted, dark. The shutters of the shops were closed. He would be easy to find. At a corner of the street under a portico he stopped to light another cigarette, a small, intermittent beacon, he supposed.

What should he do? What should he do now? Almost without thinking he drew the envelope of hieroglyphs out of his inside pocket—why had he stolen it? Just out of malice, he supposed, and because sometimes he imagined that in Chiselet might lie the key to his triple nature.

Now, disgusted with himself, he crumpled up the ornate pages, dropped them into the wet gutter. In fact he had no use for them. It was the other letter that concerned him, Peter's letter to Miranda Popescu. If Captain

Gross thought he could shame Prochenko into baby-sitting her in her mountain safe house, well, then maybe there was shame enough for both of them. And maybe Prochenko could bring Miranda something she cared about, something to share with her, some new piece of information. He wouldn't let Peter Gross humiliate him; he broke the seal, opened the envelope. He held the cigarette between his lips, and by the light of occasional matches he read Peter's schoolboy script—both he and Miranda wrote in the same childish cursive.

It was a love letter. It was not long. There was nothing poetical about it. Gray wolf, Prochenko thought.

But still, the letter filled him with emotion. And he would go to Rimnicu, and he would do what he had promised.

How strange it was, though, that he had to act as Peter Gross's proxy in this matter, protecting Miranda from threats he could not claim to understand—he had no independent recollection of events along the Hoosick riverbank. Vague wisps of color and distress: no, Peter's urgency had nothing to do with that. If, brooding at Staro Selo over the winter, he realized he had joined his regiment more out of panic than self-sacrifice or (God help him!) patriotism, now he was trapped just the same. Now, it was obvious from the letter, he was afraid he'd missed his chance to tell Miranda how he felt.

Carefully, almost reverently, Prochenko refolded the single page and slid it back into its envelope. He replaced it in his pocket, and then stood smoking his cigarette. He was expecting his own small manifestation of love. He didn't have long to wait. There it was above him in the round vault, perched on a protruding brick. It sat in a meditative pose, tiny fist under its chin, wings folded. Then it fell forward in a somersault, tumbling forward into the air, drifting down and down. Prochenko held his breath. He waited, a smile on his gray lips, and with his face inclined upward he let out a stream of smoke. Light and flimsy, the creature shied away, disturbed (as Prochenko imagined) by the small hot poisonous current of air.

"Go!" Prochenko said. "Vas-y! You know what I want."

The creature, a naked boy just a few centimeters tall, made kicking, swimming motions and flapped its evanescent wings. Buffeted by every change of air, it started on its way. As it rose into the pale sky, Prochenko wondered (not for the first time) how it could fly so fast, so far on its unsteady course. This he knew: By the time he had reached Tineretului Park and Belu Cemetery, it would have crossed the city to the Strada Italiana, to Elena Bibescu's house, or else found a way to reach her in the People's Palace.

And he had no intention of dawdling. Nor would he take a streetcar from the Piata Universitatii. But while the streets were still empty he would run the seven kilometers or so. It would feel good to run. He would not stop or draw breath. He would catch some pleasure from the strangeness of his body and arrive unwinded in an hour. Less than that, except he would take the long way round, find the empty industrial or residential streets. But first he stripped off his jacket, stripped off his boots and socks and tied them in a package underneath his arm, together with his stick and hat. His feet would be quick and clever on the cobblestones. He spat into the gutter, then started off down the alley toward the Dambovita River and the Promenade.

At such moments his body felt like a furnace to him, flaring and dirty, needing no stoking. But inside there was a metal that could not be rarefied, that separated often into its three component elements. How was it possible, he thought, that Peter Gross could have found a way to keep himself whole? He was lucky to have lost his arm.

How was it possible that Miranda had grown into a woman, while day by day Prochenko split apart? And yet in the beginning of this adventure he was the one who had found his way while they seemed helpless, even though his path was the most difficult. In time the separate parts of them had healed, and they had grown toward each other, too. What was in the love letter Peter Gross had given him? What was the feeling underneath the words? He thought he knew.

There was a mist on the river as he loped along the embankment. The still water cast up reflections of the narrow gothic houses, built in the previous century. Their stone façades were pitted with coal and charcoal smoke. The wrought-iron fence along the Promenade was stained and green. People came trudging down the streets, their scarves over their heads—a city of women and old men on their way to work. Special streetcars would take them out to the suburban factories for the morning shift.

Mouths agape, they turned to watch him as he ran past. If only they knew! He ran east along the Strada Lipscani, then turned south. By the time he reached the park, the light was in the sky.

What was Elena doing now? What excuses was she making to secretaries and servants? Would she come in the limousine? But it would take time! And he was glad to be here early; he crossed the street under the trees. She would know the place. They had met here several times in the previous year.

It was a pleasure, he admitted, to make her take such risks. Why should he be the only one? But he had learned to damage what he hated, damage what he loved. He was the one who had killed Nicola Ceausescu, after all, murdered her when she stood vulnerable and exposed outside her own apartment in the People's Palace.

At the time he had imagined doing what he did for the sake of Great Roumania, because the baroness had been an evil woman who had destroyed many with her schemes. Even so, because the czar loved her and the sultan might have learned to love her, perhaps she could have avoided this great war. And President Bocu was obviously worse, a criminal without a grain of sentiment.

Prochenko stood before the gates of Belu Cemetery under the trees. Almost canine in his obsession with his own guilt, he had come often to this place. The gate was locked, but he knew a hole behind the bushes where the wall was broken down.

First he found a park bench in a square of raked gravel. He wiped his bleeding feet, pulled on his boots. He swept his hair back from his forehead, affixed his hat at a precise angle, put on his jacket. And with his cane in his hand he climbed in among the headstones, once more a jaunty and dapper man about town. The light was breaking through the clouds.

No one who had seen him running through the streets, his tongue protruding over his bright teeth, would have recognized him now. And no one would think, to watch him stroll idly down the rows of tombs, that he knew where he was going. But in a corner of the wall under the linden trees, a new mausoleum had been built.

The first tomb in this plot belonged to the old Baron Ceausescu, once a deputy prime minister of Roumania, who had taken his own life fourteen years before. Loaded with debt, his widow had spared every expense. Not for him a grand celebration in the temple of his ancestors in Cluj. Instead she had trundled him in here under a simple stone that, nevertheless, took on a little dignity because of its surroundings now.

The baron had died penniless and bankrupt, estranged from his own family. Now beside him lay his only child, the dirt still rough over his grave. But the statue was eloquent, an image of Niobe weeping for her children. And in the stone face of the unfortunate mother, a careful observer could discern an echo of the baroness's beautiful features.

One of the stone hands reached out to a simple marker, cut with the young baron's name and dates—Felix Ceausescu, dead before his fifteenth birthday. But the other was thrown backward as if in a fit of grief, and the pointed finger indicated another stone, set against the bottom of the wall. There was no name or number there, and the lieutenant wondered whether there might come a time when no one would appreciate the significance of the gesture or the unmarked grave. How long would it take before all the witnesses to the events were dead? How long before it was impossible for any student of history to learn that the elaborate tomb of Kevin Markasev in Baneasa was empty, or else the wrong corpse was buried there under the wrong dates? No, the unfortunate boy lay here instead.

The lieutenant closed his eyes. Would there come a time, also, when no one but he would know the truth of how Nicola Ceausescu died? That while her proxy had destroyed itself on the stage of the Ambassadors, she had been savaged in her own suite of rooms in the People's Palace, torn apart, murdered by a wild beast?

At moments he could not but remember the sight of Kevin Markasev bleeding in his rented room in the Strada Camatei, beaten out of recognition by the baroness's hired assassin—though she had not paid him, doubtless. It was not her way. Doubtless also it was a kind of ironic masochism that had brought Prochenko here, made him choose this place for his rendezvous. What had Peter Gross said? "I have a rendezvous with Death."

To clear his mind of the bloody image, and to purge himself of any painful and embarrassing self-reflection, he turned now to the baroness's mausoleum. She had set herself apart from the other members of her family, away from the wall. There was a circle of gravel around the structure, and Prochenko sauntered around it, flicking at the pebbles with his cane. But little thoughts still picked at him: Why had he come here? Why had he sent that demon on its errand? Was there any part of what he did now that was motivated by love or loyalty? Or was he looking for people to suffer as he suffered? Sometimes he reassured himself by thinking he'd avenged Kevin Markasev after all, torn his murderer apart. But there was nothing noble in that either.

It calmed him and cooled him to admire the little tomb, designed by the baroness herself. She was a woman of many gifts. The drawings had been discovered after her death. They depicted a high, domed circular structure, decorated with fluted columns and alabaster screens. Delicate spires gave the exterior a spiky and forbidding look, which was softened by a pattern of carved marble, a motif that suggested flowers and vines and shaded bowers without actually representing them. All the ornamentation was abstract, a complicated shell that was more light and space and air than stone, but which still served to protect the image inside. It was a life-sized bronze casting of the baroness standing naked and erect, head high, arms at her sides, legs slightly spread—there was no art or coquetry in the pose. The artist had worked from a sheaf of photographic images that the baroness had made during the last year of her life, standing naked before the big box camera with the bulb under her toe. She had made many hundreds of exposures without sparing the most intimate parts of her body or making any attempt to flatter herself.

The photographs had not been reproduced or distributed. And the statue, though designed for public display, was perfectly concealed by the tomb's ornamentation. The archways that pierced the structure were too narrow, the screens that surrounded it too fine to admit more than an occasional stray glimpse of a shoulder, knee, eye, or hand. Some onlookers imagined a mournful expression, some an attitude of brazenness that matched the metal of the statue. But it was impossible not to take away an impression of constraint, of an animal inside a cage or a prisoner inside a cell, which was the baroness's intention, revealed in a letter that accompanied the design.

No, but it was lucky she had taken the photographs. Her dead body had been so damaged, no artist could have worked from it. Prochenko took no comfort from the fact, no comfort from reflecting on any of this. The doubts still snatched at him—why had he summoned Elena Bibescu to this place? Was it to express a feeling or a need? Or was it to demonstrate the forces that constrained or imprisoned her as well, imprisoned both of them? No, it was not generous, not kind to make her take such risks. The cemetery was public, after all. The gates would open at ten o'clock. But the tumbled section of the wall was not a secret.

No, he would not do this to her. He would remove his boots and run away. But he would leave something, perhaps a handkerchief or a glove here at the tomb where a marble plaque was set into the step: Nicola Ceausescu, and then a simple line indenture of a tiger. Many others, after all, had left their keepsakes here—flowers, candles, letters, coins.

He dropped the glove and turned away. But then he heard a voice behind him, "Oh!"

It was a habit she had, and he couldn't tell if it affected him or irritated him. But when she first saw him, and later when he kissed her, she gave at intervals a little breathless gasp, as if he'd pricked her or hurt her or deflated her suddenly. Now, ambushed when it had been his intention to run away, irritation was uppermost. He strode toward her through the tombstones down the gravel path. She must have taken the limousine.

"Oh, I had a premonition you were here. Oh, I'm so glad!"

A premonition? Was she trying to make a fool of him? She was wearing her hat and veil and long lavender coat. Without preamble he thrust his naked hand in through the buttons and opened it, crushing her to him, forcing the little gasp from her—there on the flushed skin over her collar bone, a row of bites.

But she was laughing as she submitted. She never pulled away. He lifted the veil, kissed her, covered her charming little mouth while she was trying to talk. "I can't stay. Just a minute," etc.

And was it possible to have her here among the graves, or else bring her back to the shelter of Ceausescu's tomb? He pulled her up the little slope while she was laughing and pretending to resist. Could he actually possess her here as thoroughly as his woman's body would allow? On the step beside the baroness's gravestone he pushed her down, pushed his hands beyond the slit in her skirt and into her underwear while she opened her mouth to him, leaned back, surrendered her breasts to his other hand. Her body was so cool and fresh and young. Part of him wanted to punish her for coming, for yielding to him against her best interests, which was neither fair nor good. (Had he always been like this? He couldn't remember. . . .) But there was another part that yearned to please her, and he supposed it was the combination that squeezed that little breathless gasp from her. She was not this way with everyone, not with her pig of a husband—"Beau-cul" as they called him in the graffiti near the river—how old was she? Scarcely twenty years!

"Oh, you're burning me," she said. "You have a fever."

She was used to it. Ever since the accident at Chiselet his flesh had been on fire. He burned like a dog in heat—something like that. And why was he even thinking about dogs? It was because he heard a barking dog, an Alsatian by the sound. It was barking by the wall. "Come with me," he muttered into her neck. It was obvious she had been followed.

Obvious, but not to her. "Oh," she said. He was pulling her up and she would not come; she was laughing as if this were a game. She had her arms around him. How could she be so stupid? He snarled at her and wrenched himself away. He would not be caught like this. Not in this trap. Though it was clear already that whatever happened, it would be his fault.

And he could smell them now, the oiled leather of their boots—Bocu's thugs from the Brancoveanu Artillery, a private regiment of bully-boys and torturers, whose barracks were in the city—he could smell them now, their frightened farts and dirty fingers. He could hear their shouts and whistles, and Elena heard them, too. "Go," she said. She got to her feet and tottered off down the row of stones without looking back, a brave girl, a champion who deserved better. And he—there was no place to go. They would have secured the outer circuit of the wall.

But he had some tricks up his sleeves. He was different from ordinary men, which was both a burden and a gift. No normal person could have fit between the slender columns of the baroness's tomb, slid in through the narrow arch. No one was so supple or so oddly jointed. But in just a dozen seconds he was in the hidden sanctuary, his body thrust against the bronze, naked statue. His nose was full of the stone and metal smell. He was straining to listen. Whoever it was had come into the cemetery and was guiding Elena back. Prochenko could hear the murmur of the conversation.

He was listening for the bark or the snuffle of the dog, not far away. He could hear Elena's voice now, and her husband's voice—he recognized it from the radio broadcasts, a forthright manly tenor. There was even some laughing as if at some small joke, which was Bocu's way. The posters on the boulevards showed him in poses that were not traditionally inspirational. He was always smiling, for one thing. A man in his fifties, powerfully built, with short hair and a gray moustache—he was not tall. Prochenko saw him in his mind's eye as he was straining to decipher the language of the dog, saw the amused, ironical expression that could not hide the coarseness and cruelty of his jaw and mouth, saw his gray or cream-colored uniform without any military insignia—where was the dog? Did someone have him on a short lead? There was a strangled desperation to the barking now, and Prochenko could hear him scratching at the steps of the tomb. The beast could smell him, he was sure.

No, there he was, there was his nose snuffling at the screen. So Prochenko spoke a word in a soft voice of command, a tone beyond the frequency of human ears; he scarcely had to make a sound. The beast knew who his master was. Suddenly there was a baffled whine, and the dog pulled away, ceased his barking, and Prochenko could hear the murmured conversation—Elena was going to pull it off! This was an unlikely place for a romantic assignation. It was not a hotel, or a restaurant, or a parked automobile. There were other more likely explanations for her presence, which were . . . he couldn't guess. But then he heard Colonel Bocu laugh and say, ". . . and what is this? Your glove?"

It was not her glove, Prochenko knew. It was a man's leather glove still damp with sweat.

He couldn't hear Elena's voice. But the man laughed again. ". . . no, no, I don't think so. Unless your hands have grown. We will see what Rex thinks of these. Rex, what is wrong with you? Thank you, Sergeant. Ah, you see here in the bushes we have found a walking stick, a hat, a linen coat, every part of a man except for one—where is he, please?"

He spoke Roumanian even to his wife. It was an element in his political program, the reintroduction of Roumanian at all levels of society, the prohibition of English and especially French. And his voice—tense, light, musical—was also compelling: "Oh no," he said, "no, I don't think so."

What would he do to her? Divorce her, send her away—it might be for the best. Maybe Prochenko's stupid selfishness and her stupid self-abnegation might have combined to locate a way forward that was better for both of them. Nothing tied him to this country, except for an as yet unrealized duty to Miranda Popescu.

A sharp intake of breath. A curious sucking sound.

"Sergeant, come. Give me a handkerchief. He must have jumped over the wall."

Prochenko laid his face against the cold metal buttocks of Nicola Ceausescu. He was listening to every sound. He was trying to make an image of the scene he couldn't see. Had she been on her knees before her husband, her lavender coat open and her throat exposed? Was Colonel Bocu able to appreciate the line of raised bumps where the demon had bitten her? Or was that what was impossible to forgive? Prochenko could feel the tickling along his own imprisoned arm, the creature scratching him, burrowing under his shirt—of course it had followed them here. The pain, when it came, would cause him to cry out, give himself away.

Always before when he had grabbed at it the demon had eluded him. It had been buffeted upward by the wind from his hand. Delicate and gossamer, it would drift upward to the ceiling. But here it was controlled in a small space, and he jabbed with his spread fingers using all his animal quickness—yes, success. He had it by something, its little arm or its little leg, and he tightened his grip, pulled it into his hand, and crushed it. He felt the breaking of its bones and its wet blood.

When the time came for him to extricate himself, he found his shirt was caught. He had to leave it behind. His boot was jammed between two columns, and his foot pulled easily away. He crept out into the morning. The sun was breaking through the clouds. Elena was still there where they had left her. Doubtless they were searching the adjoining streets for a man without a coat or hat, but they would return before the gates opened. Doubtless Bocu was speeding north in his automobile, leaving his wife behind, collapsed on the step of the baroness's mausoleum, her face immobile in a last little gasp of astonishment. There was a patch of blood over her breast as if her heart had broken.

And as the lieutenant prowled near her, touched his nose to the rim of her whorled ear, even slid out his long tongue to lick her cheek, he imagined a different source for her astonishment. It was not every day you saw a man become an animal under the bright, sweet, morning sun. Back and forth, back and forth next to her cooling body, while he felt himself grow hotter and hotter; he raised his mouth, his muzzle to the sky. And if at that moment what he felt was not exactly suffering, still he reassured himself that someone would suffer for what had happened here, what he had done, and it would not be he but someone else.

4 Miranda Popescu

THIS IS WHAT PETER'S LETTER SAID:

Dear Miranda, it's been dry weather for more than a week, which gives us something to be grateful for. Not much action either, just a routine to fill up the day, you know, like high school. Do you remember when Mr. Donati gave you detention for missing an assignment? I'm sure it was very unfair. Anyway, it was the first time we'd been in a classroom together since grade school, and I was very excited. You were so angry. You sat in the front row working away, not looking up from your French homework. I wish I knew then what I know now. I would have aced French for sure, though knowing me you never know. Anyway, you just sat there looking impatient, and you have this habit, you pull some of your hair back and hook it behind your ear so it won't fall in your face. I just sat there in the back row looking stupid I am sure. I had to read this stupid animal adventure book called Gray Wolf, *and I refused. I was reading good stuff with my mother after school. Do you remember the food in the cafeteria? Here we get bread and bacon and brandy before an attack, not the same. I think about you often, and I don't just mean every day. I know I must have confidence in the good intentions of Madame Inez de Rougemont, even though . . .*

Lieutenant Prochenko knew a love letter when he saw one. But he was familiar with the background and the references, which gave him an advantage. For Colonel Victor Bocu, the translated text was as perplexing as the original. He suspected a code. And he was intrigued by the name Miranda. It was obvious whom this letter was for. "Miranda P." was on the envelope.

On the evening following his wife's death, riding through the streets of Bucharest in the back of his limousine, Bocu perused the letter once again. It was not his first priority to hunt down refugees from the previous regime. Miranda Popescu—everyone knew this name. She had been the baroness's prisoner, caught up in some failed intrigue.

No, but it was more than that. It had been a political conspiracy, after all. It had involved the scattered followers of General Schenck von Schenck— old women, mostly. How stupid Elena had been!

Bocu could have overlooked adultery and treason, he suggested to himself. But his wife's stupidity had been a constant irritant and could not be forgiven. Her lover was quite obviously a spy. No, worse than that: a stupid, inept spy. Here were his passport and identity paper—efficient forgeries. Here was his ration card. Sasha Andromedes, his name purported to be. Here was his photograph. An effeminate face. Bocu had seen him before, he thought, in a hotel restaurant.

In the backseat of the Duesenberg he studied these documents one at a time. He squinted over them, held them up to the window, so he could see them illuminated in the fitful streetlights. Not just his coat—the fellow had left his trousers and his boots and shirt behind. But no one had seen him in the streets around the cemetery in the middle of the morning. What the devil! Bocu sat back, put his feet up on the plush banquette.

No, he was too trusting. He must not be distracted. This was a puzzle, a box he must unlock, not just for his own pride. Miranda Popescu was the key to it, perhaps. He must ask her what it meant. And, as it happened, he knew where to find her—a beautiful young woman, he had heard. Or maybe not—a man could dream. He pulled the unlit cigar from between his teeth and smiled.

Oh, he thought—but when he found Sasha Andromedes, or whatever his name was . . .

He went over some possibilities in a joking sort of way, and at the end of it he found himself in need of relaxation. Already he had had a busy day, a busy evening, a busy night. There had been meetings with ministers and generals and members of the assembly. And after dinner he had gone to see his mistress, a pouting girl even younger than his dead wife. As he lay in her arms, he wondered what he should do with her now, whether she'd expect something different. By the time he returned to the palace from her hotel, he'd already decided to dispose of her.

The Duesenberg turned into the Mycenaean Gate. The chauffeur opened up the door. Victor Bocu smiled, nodded to the saluting guards, and hurried up the steps into the enormous building. He took the elevator to his apartment, from which he'd already had Elena's clothes, jewelry, soaps and perfumes, and all other traces of her removed.

He was a sociable man. Friends from the army visited at midnight, and he sat up smoking cigars and drinking brandy. After they had gone he put on his jacket, retied his cravat. He picked up two clean glasses from the sideboard, two bottles of champagne, which he held by their crossed necks in his right hand. Exiting his apartment, he took the elevator down below the level of the street.

He'd decided he had an interest in Miranda Popescu. Not entirely for her own sake. She had been the Baroness Ceausescu's obsession, and the baroness was dead. But she was after all the only heiress to a defunct imperial dynasty that still commanded, he supposed, a nostalgic loyalty. He could make use of that. Any loyalty, of any kind, was tenuous among his political followers.

Besides that, he had his own needs. Urgently, more every hour, he found he needed the location of Sasha Andromedes. He couldn't get the fellow's long-jawed face out of his mind. When Bocu found him, he would make him beg for death.

The doors opened in a brick-lined corridor. There were guards among the flickering lanterns. Smiling, he ignored these men and their importunate saluting, their attempts at conversation. He passed the desk where a game of cards had been abandoned. But at the end of the corridor, he stopped.

"Please unlock this," he said to the fellow there.

A square glass window had been set into the door. A lantern glimmered on the other side. There was always supposed to be a light.

And as the man fumbled with the lock, he continued. "Do you find you have fewer keys in your pocket than a year ago?"

"Sir?"

"There was a time I had many keys. Recently. Now I have none. So I have an idea. The fewer keys you have, the more these doors stand open of their own accord."

The guard had several keys. He was searching for the right one. "Up to a point," continued Colonel Bocu. "When I was young, no doors were open, and I had no keys. So you could say my success consists of first accumulating them, then giving them away. But you must be approaching the maximum. When I see you again, I hope you have fewer than you have now."

"Sir, I hope so."

It was hard to get a smile out of these jailers. A little joke went a long way in these places, which were depressing as a matter of course. "I have good news for this particular prisoner," Bocu said.

Keys or not, maybe he should have sent a subordinate, one of the phalanx of efficient and dedicated fools he had accumulated recently. Or else one of his new friends—they were all his friends. But it was impossible to trust them with a private matter. "Thank you," he said, and the door stood open. "Please take this bottle. It's too heavy. You may drink to the time when you have fewer keys."

What would it take to get the man to smile? There is a tendency when a joke is unsuccessful to repeat it again and again. Bottle in one hand, keys in the other, the fellow made an attempt at a salute—a funny gesture. Bocu had no problem granting him a small guffaw. Then he turned his back.

Once inside the door, he placed the remaining bottle of champagne onto the table beside the lamp. He laid down the two glasses, turned up the wheel. As the flame came up he put his hands in his pocket. It was cold in here. But not, he saw as he looked around, otherwise uncomfortable. The prisoner was motionless in bed. He had blankets and a pillow.

There were some books on the desk, and a notebook, and two framed photographs. One showed a fat, middle-aged woman and her daughter—the prisoner's family. The other was a posed photograph from one of the Baroness Ceausescu's performances. She had signed her name. "To my old friend."

The colonel smiled. Nicola Ceausescu wore a metal headdress and a halter made of leather straps that crossed between her breasts, leaving her arms and shoulders bare. Lesser artists might have used a body stocking, especially at thirty-nine years old. Bocu had no doubt he could have smelled the odor of her maturity from the second row. He and Elena had had tickets to see her last performance, the night of her suicide on the boards of the Ambassadors. Who could have predicted he would never have another chance to see her naked backside?

There was the smell of a used chamber pot somewhere in the room. Bocu took a cigar from his inside pocket, clipped it, lit it at the flame. "Domnul Luckacz," he said after a pause.

He had the impression the man had been awake from the time the key had rattled in the door. Now he stirred, a bald man with a wasted, diminished face. Once, of course, he had been chief of the metropolitan police. That was during the German occupation, when the baroness lived in the People's Palace.

"Come," said Colonel Bocu. With the cigar between his teeth, he twisted off the cork from the bottle of champagne. "I want to ask you a question."

He pulled out one of the chairs and sat astride it backward. He made a gesture toward the other chair, and Luckacz raised his head. "Your excellency, I must inform you. And also I protest. I am not given any clothes."

His voice was ugly, marred by a Hungarian accent. Bocu laughed, then picked a shred of tobacco from between his teeth. He crossed his arms over the back of the chair. "We don't stand on ceremony here. Do you have any complaints?"

"Excellency, I am permitted nothing but underclothing!"

"But it's not as if you entertain. When it comes to me, I'm always having to choose a different shirt. And the cleaning bills . . ."

He smoked his cigar. Then he couldn't resist: "You must admit this is a convenience. No, I mean do you have any complaints. You remember why you're here."

"Yes, your excellency."

"It's because I asked you to do something. I gave you the responsibility."

"Yes."

"I asked you to arrest Madame Ceausescu and I gave you the men to do it. I specified the hour, not some other hour. Not some other day. You understand me?"

"Yes."

"Instead you made your own decisions, with the result that Nicola Ceausescu was able to escape her crimes, destroy herself in a public theater in this city. You understand that was not a fortunate result?"

"Yes."

"Then allow me to let bygones be bygones. Have some champagne."

He threw his cigar into the corner of the room. Then he poured the frothing liquor into the crystal flutes—two of a set that had belonged to Nicola Ceausescu, as it happened, a gift from the German ambassador. With a glass in each hand he went to sit on the metal bed, whose occupant had pulled himself upright. He sat cross-legged, huddled in his blankets.

"To your health. Now, I want you to remember what you said to me that day. It was about Mademoiselle Popescu, Miranda Popescu, von Schenck's daughter—do you remember? The baroness sent you on an errand, is that so?"

"Yes, your excellency."

"But you did not obey her—Domnul Luckacz, this is a custom with you! The baroness sent you to find this woman, this girl. She gave you an address, the name of a small town."

Luckacz groaned.

"Now I must ask you. I was remembering General von Schenck. I was thinking about his daughter. There are very few photographs of the general, but I found one. Let me show it to you."

Bocu drew a strip of photographic paper from the inside pocket of his coat. He angled it away from him so it would catch the lamplight. Von Schenck was posing with a group of officers, members of his staff. He had moved when the exposure was taken. His face was blurred and indistinct. The entire print was dark with age. The general had been dead for over twenty years.

But the faces of the younger officers had all come clear. Obviously they had been used to posing. "Do you recognize that man?" asked Bocu.

He lifted the champagne to his lips but did not drink. While the policeman examined the photograph, he replaced the glass on the little table.

Then he produced another document from his pocket, a folded ration card with a photograph attached.

"That is a person who calls himself Andromedes," said Radu Luckacz.

Bocu cocked his head. Luckacz's voice, nasal and foreign and therefore difficult to decipher, contained a trace of something—was it rage? The strip of paper was trembling in his hands.

"It is not his actual name," he went on.

"You astonish me. And is he an acquaintance of Mademoiselle Popescu? Is there a reason why he would be carrying a letter for her? You see in this exposure, the name is printed down below. Lieutenant Alexei Prochenko, Ninth Hussars. But you admit it is the same face on the ration card, the identical expression, clipped from another example of this same photograph. Don't you think so?"

Luckacz shrugged. The paper trembled.

"And if I were to look for this man, maybe I would look for Mademoiselle Popescu first. That would be logical. And maybe I would ask the help of someone who had no complaints. Someone who was eager to show he could be trusted. Especially if this was a private, secret matter. A personal matter—you have a fat wife and daughter in the city, don't you? Maybe you haven't seen them in several months, but they're still living at the same address. They are not permitted to go elsewhere."

Bocu smiled. Radu Luckacz, his face skeletal, turned to look at him. What was he thinking? He was hard to read. "Mademoiselle Popescu is a dangerous criminal," said the colonel. "Didn't I hear that somewhere? Didn't you tell me that?"

Radu Luckacz's lips were thin and bloodless. "She killed a policeman in Braila."

"Yes. So will you drink your champagne? And will you help me, do you think? Will you help me bring her back to Bucharest, to stand trial or at least answer our questions? There are a number of people who are interested in her, a beautiful woman, I suppose, the last of the Brancoveanus. At least I hope she is a beautiful woman—this is a duty you might owe to the republic. And you must tell me if you remember this name—Inez de Rougemont. I believe she was a figure in society."

The policeman shrugged. His face was expressionless. "She has been dead more than fifteen years."

Bocu smiled. "Maybe not so long. And so we come full circle. Will you tell me where to find this little town?"

EARLY THAT SAME MORNING in Stanesti-Jui, Miranda was on the mountainside. The dogs ran back and forth below her as she retraced her steps toward the farmhouse.

The Condesa de Rougemont had provided a refuge, not just for Miranda after she had escaped from the People's Palace, but for several others: Miranda's own mother, and even Jean-Baptiste, who had been the Baroness Ceausescu's steward.

Miranda was grateful. But she did not think that Inez de Rougemont was motivated only by generosity. No, she was another woman like Miranda's aunt, a dabbler in the hidden world, and someone who had dreams for Great Roumania. Miranda had seen her in a coven of strange women on Borgo Pass, a place that had been only partially a dream. If Miranda had not mentioned anything about that up to now, it was not because she hadn't thought about it. What could she say? "I saw you in Dracula's castle in the mountains, where you were dividing up the future of the world. I rode there on a Gypsy's back. . . ."—events that hadn't necessarily occurred in any normal sense.

Surely Madame de Rougemont should be the first to mention that, explain it. Without an explanation, what was there to say? It was not enough to know she was a friend of Madame de Graz—Peter's mother—and she lived in retirement in this mountain village, and she kept a number of connections from the old days.

When Miranda came down through the meadow into the garden, there was a light in the cowshed and the dogs scampered away. Miranda came in the front door and walked down the stone-flagged corridor. The fire was lit in the big kitchen, where there would be café au lait and slabs of dry toast.

Now that spring had come and she'd recovered from her illness, there were decisions to be made, explanations to be found. Perhaps Madame de Rougemont thought so, too, because she was sitting at the oak table near the window. In the half-light she seemed dowdy, her gray hair struggling to free itself. As always, she had some powder on her cheeks, some artificial color. Of these women, she was the one who worked to maintain an artificial connection to her youth. She wore lipstick. She was dressed in a flowered gown and a lace shawl.

She had been reading next to the window, and her eyes when she took off her spectacles were dark and bright. "You must not go out like that," she said. "I am pleased you're feeling better. But you must not go out by yourself."

Miranda shrugged. "Madame Ceausescu kept me locked in my room."

De Rougemont frowned. "I think we could chain you to the wall," she said. "You'd still be free."

Was she referring to the tourmaline, and Miranda's expeditions in the hidden world? She had poured a cup of coffee from the silver pot. Now she reached for the sugar bowl. "There is always part of this that is a game," she continued. "Let me remind you men are dying in Bulgaria and the Ukraine. It is hard to imagine it when we are sitting here."

Yes, it was hard to imagine. Miranda saw a furtive image of Peter's face as he had appeared to her in the brick gazebo in Cismigiu Park. She shook her head; what was remarkable, she thought, was how much sugar the old woman used. She had not noticed in the overheated kitchen on Borgo Pass. But now she watched, fascinated as de Rougemont poured milk into her big cup, then stirred in four—no, five—teaspoons of sugar. In the meantime, of course, she was completely right. "That's not what I meant," Miranda said. "I know I have a great deal to be thankful for."

This was not, however, what she felt, especially at that moment. She washed her hands in a basin of cold water with some yellow soap. The skin of her palms was chapped and raw.

Madame de Rougemont stood up. "The others will be coming," she said. "I want to talk with you alone." Carrying her coffee cup, she led Miranda down a different corridor into another room, a library with glass-faced shelves, furnished in a more elegant and cosmopolitan style than the rest of the house. There was a carpet on the stone floor and a table set for two.

She lit the petroleum lamp as Miranda came in, using a long wooden match that made her fingers, wrists, and forearms look unnaturally thin.

Miranda imagined she could snap them between her hands. She imagined them catching fire in some terrible accident and burning down to stumps.

But the condesa had been nothing but kind from the beginning. What was the source of Miranda's anxiety and irritation? She knew Madame de Rougemont would want to talk to her about the tourmaline, about the hidden world, about her father. Didn't she also want to talk about these things? Didn't she want to trust this woman who had been so kind?

Now the old lady moved from lamp to lamp. And maybe she felt some of the same anxiety, because she seemed so tired, dry, pallid, and brittle-boned. Her head was small and thin and bloodless, her lips red. "We don't have much of a table here," she confessed, shaking out her little flame. "But there is wine."

It was from Georgia, yellower than water, sweating in a glass bucket of ice. Breakfast was already served, bread and butter, cold beet soup, and parsnip salad. It was too much to eat, too much of the wrong things. Miranda blew her nose on her handkerchief and then sat down. She was thankful, at least, that she could smell the soup.

She felt a current of sadness in the still air, a sensation of loss that included many people, many things. She had come to this house with nothing, in borrowed clothes. How many times had she had to stop and start again?

"Come eat," said Madame de Rougemont as she sat down across the table and poured a glass of wine for both of them—who drank wine at breakfast? "It will give you strength for your journey. Do you still feel like a prisoner?"

Miranda thought she'd always been too easy to read. Andromeda wasn't like that, or even Peter, as it turned out. "I'll tell you this," she said in English. "If you've got an idea I'm going to help you fight some personal battle or something, I'm not interested."

De Rougemont smiled, a faint, wan expression. She answered in the same language. "Why would you think something like that?"

It was because Miranda could not fail to be aware of the tiger's-head bracelet on her wrist. Now it glinted in the lamplight next to the gray window. It made a noise as one gold bead moved against another. "Forgive me—someone always wants something. Why else would you keep me here?"

"I was a friend of your father. Madame de Graz and I were both friends of your father. That's why Pieter de Graz was on his staff."

No, don't say it, Miranda thought, but she did: "You remind me of your father in some ways. But there is something else from your mother's side. You understand your father was a modern man. He had his superstitions, of course, but even that was a substitute for something deeper. You must know I mean this in a technical sense. He had no interest in alchemy or conjuring. He was not like his sister, your aunt Aegypta. In many ways they were not . . . close."

"I had a dream about my aunt," Miranda interrupted. She thought she would introduce the subject of what had happened in the castle on Borgo Pass, broach it indirectly. "Do you remember once you told me how she wrote that book about America as an experiment? An exercise in moral philosophy, or a utopia, something like that? Then it was an afterthought to put me into it, to protect me. Two nights ago she told me that returning when I did, none of that was what she wanted. I was supposed to leave home, go to college, marry, have kids, die of old age—I don't know. The whole thing was supposed to be more gradual. I was supposed to be older, an adult. Which is why she hadn't given any thought to the consequences, or to what might happen to me or Peter or Andromeda—"

She stopped. It was a relief to talk about all that. But what the woman had remarked about her aunt and her father was beginning to penetrate. They were not close. How could they not have been close, or at least on the same side?

But Miranda was still in the middle of what she wanted to say. And so after a moment she continued. "I know you want me to be like him—my father. A hero. General Schenck von Schenck. Someone to grab hold of this world and force it to make sense. I know that's what my aunt Aegypta wanted. Your old pal. She gave me all kinds of letters and directions and clues and gifts. And you know what? I've failed at all of it. Things I tried on my own, things she told me to do . . ."

For some strange reason this felt good to say, although she didn't quite believe it. It was a relief just to be talking in the English language.

Madame de Rougemont interrupted with a faint, soft laugh. "Perhaps it takes a hero to fail so much," she said. "Besides, I don't think that you give yourself so much credit. An enemy of Great Roumania is dead because of you. And for a moment there was a truce in this terrible war."

She was talking about things from the hidden world. Actions Miranda had taken, choices Miranda had made—how had she known about all that? No, but it was important to remember she had her own secret access to these things.

Miranda reached out to touch her wine glass, and then paused. " 'Grab hold of this world,' " de Rougemont said. " 'Force it to make sense.' Isn't that what Nicola Ceausescu was attempting?"

She got to her feet, drifted a little way across the carpet. "Mademoiselle—I think there are a few things that you ought to know. "I knew your father . . . intimately. But I was not a friend to your aunt."

A bead of moisture slipped down the side of glass where Miranda had touched it. Yuck, she thought, if she was right about what this lady was implying. Then she let go of her reaction suddenly, hungry for what might come next.

"Mademoiselle Popescu—do you sometimes wonder why your father wanted that name for you? The most common name in all Roumania—it was not your mother's idea. Your father was a republican, according to the German model that he learned when he was young. Do you know what that means?"

"I . . . guess."

"It means he was not so interested in someone who would force things to make sense. He was interested in dull projects—land redistribution. Taxation reform. The abolition of hereditary titles. Not so much the glory of Great Roumania, or—God help us—the restoration of the Brancoveanu family. That was your aunt's design. That's why she killed him. No. These are things we cannot know for sure."

Miranda said nothing. As if just from touching the outside of the wineglass, she felt a little drunk. Inez de Rougemont moved back and forth across the carpet, rubbing her long hands as if they itched. Then she examined her painted nails. "That is why she took him from me," she amended. "Drugged his wine in Brasov—I don't know—when we were secretly engaged. Made him marry your mother—I can't prove any of that. These are more hard things to verify. It doesn't matter. I have had twenty-five years to say them to myself."

"But . . ."

"She wanted the pure Brancoveanu blood. The day after his wedding, he came to me."

"But . . ."

"I know what you want to know. Your father was arrested on a charge of treason. He was said to be plotting a separate negotiation with the German-speaking regions of Transylvania. That was a lie, I know it. But the documents were real enough. Baron Ceausescu believed in their authenticity, at least at first. You understand—I knew him, too. He was your father's oldest friend. Comrade in arms. This broke his heart."

Miranda had heard parts of the story from Captain Raevsky, Blind Rodica, and Gregor Splaa. Her father had died in prison after Ceausescu turned on him. "Where do you think those letters came from?" said Inez de Rougemont. "Who wrote them and forged your father's signature? Who abandoned your mother in Ratisbon hours after she gave birth to you—she could have brought her out. She wanted you all to herself. A weapon, I suppose. A hero, as you say, for Great Roumania."

These words, these revelations were delivered without any force as Madame de Rougemont moved around the room. Because it's all so old, Miranda thought. Who cares anymore? Clara Brancoveanu was asleep upstairs.

"Who stole your mother from you, and your father, and your childhood?" continued de Rougemont, as if she were discussing something not so very important.

Tears dripped down the outside of Miranda's glass under her finger. "I cannot prove these things, but they are true," said the woman. Her glass, close to Miranda's, had lipstick smears. "So it is not a terrible thing to fail or disappoint such a one. Great leaders, as we see, bring great wars."

Maybe all this was possible to listen to, Miranda thought, because it complemented something inside of her, a suspicion from long ago. At any rate, true or not, nothing was completely true. That's one thing she had learned. Baron Ceausescu might have had his heart broken, but he was still a bad man, from everything she'd heard. Aegypta Schenck might have done all these things, but she had loved Miranda, too. Or at least she had valued her and wanted to protect her. Tried and failed. What did love mean anyway?

"So. What gifts?" said Inez de Rougemont. She sat down again, put her sharp elbows onto the table. There was something clownish and hectic about the circle of blush on her cheek. When Miranda didn't respond, she continued, "You said your aunt gave you clues and gifts. I see the bracelet of Queen Miranda Brancoveanu. What else?"

"Well, there's my father's gun. Jean-Baptiste brought it from the palace. I told you . . ."

"Yes." De Rougemont sighed. "It would have been better if it had not fallen into Nicola Ceausescu's hands. Two of the secret chambers are already empty. And in the normal way, this was what she used to murder her own son, de Graz told me."

So this lady had seen Peter, Miranda thought. Where—at Cismigiu Park? What had he said? Had they spoken about her?

Though Inez de Rougemont lived here in hiding under an assumed name, she had often gone away on secret errands. Throughout the winter she was often gone for weeks at a time. Had she seen Peter and said nothing? What did it mean exactly, that the condesa and Miranda's father had been . . . intimate?

De Rougemont smiled. And it was as if she'd read Miranda's mind— "Madame Magda de Graz," she amended. "Who heard it from her son the chevalier. Whom I myself have never met. You do not trust me. Let me show you what I mean."

She fumbled underneath the embroidered placemat, and drew out something she must have hidden there just for this purpose: a photographic print. It showed a young woman dressed for a costume ball. Beside her was a man in military uniform—Miranda's father, she supposed. His face was indistinct, because he had shifted during the exposure.

The condesa stroked the edge of the photograph with her brittle finger. Her face took on a hungry, rapt expression. And everything that was sharp or dry or ugly in it nevertheless found its exact counterpart in the young woman's beautiful features.

"Then there were some smaller things I lost, money I spent," Miranda said, to change the subject. "I gave money to my friend Andromeda. Nothing's left."

De Rougemont shook her head. She covered the photograph with her white palm. "But that is not quite true. There is a reason why we are here. I was waiting for your health to improve."

Miranda said nothing. She was of two minds. Madame de Rougemont had plucked her out of danger, given her a home, probably saved her and her mother's life. An old friend of her father's—why did she feel so defensive and begrudging? It was obvious what they were talking about.

"It's an object, but you can't touch it or hold it," she admitted finally. "I've got it hidden."

"But this is quite a riddle. Where?"

Miranda didn't want to tell her. She thought in half an hour this woman had taken valuable things from her and given her nothing except beet soup and parsnips and some wine, none of which she'd tasted. "In my mind," she said, which seemed safe and ambiguous, and at the same time she was reaching down into the crevice in the rocks where she had kept the tourmaline. "I don't even know if it's real," she said, and for a moment she was digging around in the wet moss, heart in her mouth, because it was gone. But no, there it was in a different place. And when she touched it, held the pulsing, soft-skinned jewel in her hand, then something new shuddered to life inside of her.

Madame de Rougemont squinted across the table. Miranda could tell she knew something about what was going on. She was no fool. "What do you see?" she said.

Miranda stood on the hillside, the tourmaline clasped in her hand. In the hidden world her sinuses were not congested, and she took deep draughts of the cold air. But of course she was also in the farmhouse library among the glass-fronted shelves. She sat in an old wooden chair with a cane seat.

The mountains rose above her, and the sun was bright and harsh on her cheeks. She thought she could climb up the chute of rocks behind her, away and out of sight. It wasn't possible. The door to the library opened, and her mother stood there. "Miranda, comme j'étais inquiète—how worried I was. Are you all right?"

She came into the room and stood in the middle of the carpet. Her hair was tidy, curled up under tortoiseshell combs. She spoke in French, which was enough in itself to break the mood. "You left without waking me," she said. "How are you feeling? Would you like an aspirin? This is not proper food for you."

Ever since Felix Ceausescu's death, Miranda's mother wouldn't let her alone. "I'll ask Jean-Baptiste to bring hot broth and chamomile tea. What are you talking about? I can tell that I'm intruding."

Miranda dropped the tourmaline into the moss. She was relieved and grateful to see no trace of impatience on Inez de Rougemont's arch and brittle face. Her hand was on the photograph beside her plate, and now she slid her napkin over it. And everything about her seemed to soften as she spoke. "Clara, come in—of course, how silly of me. I thought we might need this breakfast for an expedition, but I was premature. Some chamomile tea—it would be lovely."

"What do you mean? Miranda is in no state to go outdoors." Clara Brancoveanu stood rubbing her hands together, her face full of anxiety. "Why don't you tell me anything? Please, I want to know."

Ever since Felix Ceausescu had died in her arms, bled to death on the stones outside the People's Palace, she had been intolerable. Miranda often found herself consumed with irritation, which made de Rougemont's gentleness even more impressive, she thought grudgingly. There was nothing in her voice but tenderness and concern—this for a woman, if Miranda had understood, who had married her lover, stolen him away.

"We were talking about Nicola Ceausescu," said Inez de Rougemont.

"Oh, and doubtless you were telling terrible things! You have no kindness for her. But I have told you many times how she saved us, freed us—me and Madame de Graz, when we were in prison. It was an act of kindness, and a day later she was dead—don't tell me that was a coincidence. But in this house all I hear is terrible accusations of murder and worse, things that no one can know for sure. . . ."

She was not capable of understanding even this, Miranda thought: that Nicola Ceausescu had murdered her own son. Now she stood in the middle of the room, rubbing her hands. Inez de Rougemont waited for her to stop speaking. "Clara, you're right," she said. "How could I disagree? It is not prudent to curse the dead."

5   *An Unexpected Visitor*

IT IS NOT WISE OR prudent to curse the dead, because the dead can hear us. Often they don't care. Many are able to lay down their grudges with their abandoned bodies. Many are able to forget their struggles and animosities. Nicola Ceausescu was not one of these.

People say the ghosts of suicides are especially dissatisfied, especially unquiet. Some of the thousands who had visited her catafalque in the nave of Cleopatra's temple, had reached past the velvet ropes to touch it and say a prayer, or had followed her coffin through the streets to Belu Cemetery, took a peculiar pleasure in imagining her among the restless dead. They saw her roaming the dark stages and concert halls in Bucharest or abroad, where she had seen so many triumphs. They saw her stalking the galleries of the People's Palace, or else lighting candles in the upper windows of her old house on Saltpetre Street. For years she had filled the little theaters of their hearts and heads. How could they think of her as vanished, gone?

They might have been thrilled to imagine the truth. The baroness's coffin had not contained her body, but only a small quantity of ectoplasmic slime. But they would have misinterpreted the cause: Nicola Ceausescu had not killed herself. She had not cut her own throat, as all the newspapers had reported, on the boards of the Ambassadors. She had not cheated the police as they reached out to arrest her for collaboration with the Germans and other more sinister and private crimes. The struggle between her self-love and self-hatred, always the secret of her artistic success, was too violent and elemental to have been resolved that way.

No, it had been a cold simulacrum that had collapsed onstage, animated from a distance. Nicola Ceausescu had died in the People's Palace, torn to pieces by a monster that was only partly human. She retained the burning rage of the murdered dead. Only two living persons were exempt from this. One of them was her loyal steward, Jean-Baptiste, who had found her despoiled body, wept over her, gathered her up, washed away the blood.

THE FOLLOWING AFTERNOON he was fussing in the kitchen. Just as Radu Luckacz boarded the train to Pitesti and Rimnicu, Jean-Baptiste came in through the double doors carrying toast and marmalade, some of which was on his sleeve.

Since the untasted breakfast of parsnips and white wine, the library had become Miranda's favorite room in the house. As Jean-Baptiste hovered above her, eager to speak, she put down her book.

"You don't have to bring me coffee and these things. You don't get paid for it. And it makes me uncomfortable."

"Miss, I do what pleases me. That's how you know I'm not your servant."

"Did Nicola Ceausescu pay you?"

"No. Sometimes I had to give her money in the old days."

He stood above her, still dressed in the baroness's personal livery, which he had worn the whole time Miranda was imprisoned in the People's Palace. Then she had thought his disheveled appearance in the ornate rooms had suggested some kind of ironic statement or attitude. Now she was less positive. His shirt had come untucked along one side. His jacket, decorated with threadbare scarlet piping, was too small, and pulled his narrow shoulders into a perpetual shrug—he was an old man with a high, bald forehead. He had shaved that morning for the first time in days, and had cut himself in several places. His Adam's apple showed a shiny new scab.

He dropped the plate onto the table and then stood above her as she nibbled at the toast. She thought it was the least she could do.

"What are you reading?" asked Jean-Baptiste.

"It's a history book."

"My mistress used to read poetry in the morning. She was a brilliant artist. There was no one like her."

"So you say."

Unexplored between them was the memory of Miranda's last night in the palace, when the baroness had forced her to read the palindromes in Isaac Newton's black book, and had fired her father's great revolver in the dark, releasing two powerful demons into the world. That night the baroness might have killed Jean-Baptiste, shot him or else had him shot. "She had an artist's temper," he continued lamely, picking at his nails.

After the baroness's death, he had come up from the city with the gun and the book, too. So it must have been somewhat on his mind, Miranda thought. Maybe the way he stood above her and praised the baroness now, under the circumstances that might have been part of the same ironic impulse. He and Miranda's mother never missed an opportunity to praise her. Stubbornly denying her worst crimes, they gave her the benefit of every doubt, though they lived in a house of people who had suffered from her malice.

"Yeah, that's great," Miranda said in English.

"Artists and geniuses are different from other people. Ordinary rules don't apply to them. Because they give us so much pleasure."

"I'll keep that in mind," she murmured.

The book she had been reading was about an earlier war, Miranda Brancoveanu's struggle against the Turks. This was Miranda's namesake, the first of the white tygers and the first person to wear the bracelet that now clattered wearily against her cider glass. And at least in this narration, it seemed as if she'd had an easier time. Whatever her tribulations, the victory had always seemed inevitable. And the forces of evil, the forces of good—all that was clear.

But maybe that was the thing about history. The pattern of events, of causes and effects, only was obvious when you looked backward. Nothing that happened had any predictive value. No doubt that white tyger, also, had been struggling in the dark.

Miranda closed the book, sipped the cider, nibbled the burned toast. Everything was murky now. Again Roumania fought the Turks, this time along an enormous battlefront south of the Danube River. But the Turks had mobilized against their wishes, according to some reports. They had been dragged into a war because of a secret treaty with the German Republic. When the Germans had occupied Bucharest, there had been no reason for this war.

And for a while there had even been a truce between Roumania and Russia—Miranda had had a hand in that, as Inez de Rougemont had acknowledged. But in almost her last official act, the Baroness Ceausescu had broken the truce in a spectacular double-cross, and peace had slipped away. Now the Germans still occupied the Bucovina and the Transylvanian oil fields, and there was a bloody stalemate along two gigantic fronts. The worst of everything had come to pass.

Needless to say, the first white tyger had had her own setbacks. From time to time, Miranda had read in her book, she had found places of refuge in the middle of some disaster. Once she had spent a winter here in these same mountains, prior to some new indomitable push.

And in those places of refuge, did she talk and think and argue about what should be done? Or was everything obvious and plain? Over the winter, during her illness, sitting up in bed to read Madame de Rougemont's books, Miranda could not fail to wonder what she was going to do next, after she was well—first things first, as Stanley, her adoptive father, might have said.

"She could be a model to us because of her passion. You must understand that."

Jean-Baptiste was still talking about Nicola Ceausescu. He stood beside the breakfast table with a teapot in his hands. His voice was anxious and aggressive, because he did not quite believe what he was saying, Miranda thought. If he believed it, why was it necessary to say it over and over? But a woman he loved was dead, that much was true.

And maybe she really could still be a model to us because of her passion. Maybe he was right about that. Miranda sighed, glanced out of the window at the long, dun fields. She had slipped out of the world into this village, but now it was time. Spring would be here soon, and she could walk into the mountain without coughing or losing breath. Even her cold had cleared up. For a week it had made her dull.

"You must seize hold of what you want," said Jean-Baptiste.

When she had first come to this world from Berkshire County, Miranda had pretended that she had a choice. She had believed or had attempted to believe she did not need to be concerned with all these problems, these people she didn't know, mothers and fathers she'd never met, intrigue that did not concern her. And when that turned out not to be true, she had thought that she could learn to dominate the world of guns and horses and heroes, because she was a princess of Great Roumania and the daughter of General Schenck von Schenck. When that led to disaster, she had retreated here, where what remained was access to the hidden world.

"Courage, that's what there is," said Jean-Baptiste. "That's what she showed me. . . ." What was he talking about? But it was true that Miranda had not used her strength, especially not here in this refuge. She had kept it secret and she had not shared it with the Condesa de Rougemont, who had saved her and protected her, protected her mother, too, a woman she had every reason to despise. Miranda had not thanked her. She had not given what she so obviously wanted.

The previous evening the condesa had left the house after supper, as she sometimes did. So when she next returned from wherever she was, from her own secret world, Miranda thought, maybe there was something to be done.

And it was not just because Miranda owed her something for her kindness. But maybe she could help Miranda to discover the strength of the white tyger, accomplish the task she had been brought here to perform. Which was—what? Oh, the usual. Peace. Stability. Justice, and the American Way. Though maybe those things would not turn out to mean what her aunt had intended—peace above all. Maybe her father's friend could be trusted, as she had never even tried to trust her own mother or Aegypta Schenck.

And as if conjured by her doubt, Princess Clara now appeared at the library door. "I thought I smelled some coffee. My, doesn't that look good," she said. But even in the middle of these banalities, her eyes were nervous, sad.

"Miranda, how are you feeling? You look flushed," she said. "Do you have room for us? We don't want to interrupt."

Damaged by suffering and her long imprisonment, as always she seemed close to tears. Behind her came Madame de Graz, up from Bucharest for a short visit; she had arrived that morning. Her shoulders were hunched, her back was bent from osteoporosis. Her eyes were milky with cataracts. She walked with a small limp, one hip higher than the other. But even so she moved with purpose and deliberation, a small woman with white hair and a thick neck. Physically frail, she gave an impression of mental energy that was different from the princess. Eschewing small talk, she marched into the room and sat at the long table. She unrolled the newspaper, the *Roumania Libera,* which had come up from the capital on the first train. She pressed the pages flat and then peered carefully at the headlines out of the sides of her eyes. It was her morning habit. She would not allow anyone to read to her.

Except for her adoptive grandmother in Colorado, Miranda had not spent much of her time around old ladies. But these three—four, if you counted the ghost of her aunt—she had gotten to know well, their little similarities and differences. All of them were joined to her and to each other by her absent father, General Schenck von Schenck—the lover, the wife, the sister, the political patron and confidante. Old vines hanging from a tree, and even when the tree was cut down they maintained some vestige of its absent shape, their static struggle.

"Here is the news from Staro Selo," came Magda de Graz's quavering voice. Miranda listened for a while. She knew that she and Madame de Graz were interested in the same piece of information, but they weren't likely to find it in the newspaper. If what the paper said was true, the war was almost over, almost won, the road almost open to Byzantium itself.

But there had been a victory. A great assault had been beaten off. Miranda glanced down at her book again, then closed it and sat for a while with her mother while Jean-Baptiste bustled around. Rude to the rest of them, he always treated Peter's mother with a dignified courtesy. The contrast made Miranda smile. In time she made excuses, said she would go lie down.

But she didn't, didn't feel like it. She didn't need to lie in bed worrying about Peter Gross. It was a bright day outside, and she wanted to take a walk, prepare herself for Madame de Rougemont's return. Her lungs were clear today, and she felt strong enough to climb up into the hidden world, up the chute in the rocks that she'd discovered, where the air was thin. She went out the big wooden door. The dogs came to her, and she set off along the edge of the field toward the evergreens in back of the house.

It was a bright, windy day. Clouds scurried over the mountain peaks, still capped in snow. The air was colder than she'd thought, but Miranda didn't want to go back for more clothes. Instead she hugged her arms and put her head down, kicking at the mud with her black boots. She found herself hurrying, stumbling away from the house as if she chased the dogs. In retrospect, later, she imagined she might have known where she was going. Or else below the level of conscious thought she had received some clue. The crows screamed and scattered across the field. Lucius and Lionel were investigating something at the edge of the trees. When they shied back, panicked and whimpering, she broke into a run.

She found Andromeda curled around herself in a nest of last year's pine needles. Her hindquarters were streaked with blood, and she was licking at herself with her long tongue. There were clumps of coarse hair in the hollow in the bank. Her face seemed bruised and malformed, and her eyes started open—gray with patches of blue and darker blue. Heart-struck, Miranda watched for a sign of recognition. The voice, when it came, was queer and airless, pushed out of shape by the distorted mouth: "Go away. Fuck you. Leave me alone."

Then: "Can't a girl get some privacy?"

Miranda, who had already turned her back, stood hugging her shoulders, as if to keep herself intact and untransformed. She raised her sleeve to wipe her face, wipe her eyes, before she turned around. "Hey."

"Hey."

Her friend lay curled up in the little hollow, her naked bottom streaked with red. Now, despite her words, she untucked her arms and legs and stretched out languorously, making no effort to hide herself. Her mouth opened and her tongue lolled out. She licked her shining teeth. Her whole body seemed to shine. Her hands and feet were filthy and abraded, black with grime.

"You don't look so good," Andromeda said. She yawned again, stretched her arms out straight. "I don't feel so good. What's for lunch?"

"Coffee, toast."

"Yuck." But then she smiled, got to her feet. "Sounds good. I had a rabbit yesterday—hey, stop that. You look all freaked out."

Miranda smiled. Then she turned to watch her mother stumbling across the field, fashionably attired in a fur-lined overcoat, and carrying a rolled-up bundle of tweed—Miranda's coat. "This is great," she murmured.

Already she had imagined smuggling Andromeda indoors up to her room. Already she'd been reminded forcibly of stuff they'd done when they were younger. Once Andromeda had gotten so drunk at a party she had almost passed out, and Miranda had had to drag her, giggling and laughing, upstairs in the house on Syndicate Road at two o'clock in the morning. Then as now, maybe it was appropriate that mothers should get involved, and that they should bring unlooked-for understanding. Andromeda's mother, after all, had known what it was like to have too much to drink.

"What happened to you?" said Princess Clara. "How could you come out without your coat? What's the matter with the dogs? They were barking to come in, and then they hid under the table—oh!"

"Mother," Miranda said. "You remember Lieutenant Prochenko."

"Ma'am." Andromeda stood up straight, arms at her sides. Miranda could see the deep, long scratches on her belly and her legs.

A flicker of anxiety crossed the princess's face. But then she closed her eyes and opened them. "Yes, of course. How do you do? Lieutenant, it's been a long time."

She kept her eyes fixed on Andromeda's face and head. And then she reached out her gloved hand. In her other arm she held the bundle of cloth. "I brought this for my daughter, but you might have a greater necessity."

"Madame la princesse."

Andromeda took the silk-lined tweed and swung it around her shoulders. Princess Clara grunted with relief. "I have not had the opportunity to thank you, lieutenant," she said, "for your loyalty to my daughter and the protection you gave her all those years when I was a prisoner in Ratisbon. A mother could not wish for more devotion over so much time."

She spoke carefully and slowly. Andromeda bowed her beautiful yellow head. Her hair was longer than Miranda had ever seen it. "I had a duty to your husband, ma'am."

"As did we all. But we were not all able to fulfill that duty. As for my daughter, you see how she's grown up. I could not be more proud and grateful."

So it was with her mother's help that Miranda brought Andromeda upstairs to her own room, bundled up, her face hidden, the dogs whining and whimpering on their beds under the grand piano. Miranda brought wet towels for her to clean herself, clean the blood out of her private parts ("Can you give me a little space here, for Pete's sake?"). Then she coaxed her into bed, and went downstairs to make sandwiches out of bread and meat. When she returned with a plate on a tray, as well as a cup of hard cider from the barrel, she was surprised and touched to see her mother had entered the room when she was gone. The princess was sitting on a stool beside the bed, talking in French about old times. When Miranda approached from the other side, Andromeda turned her head on the pillow and rolled her eyes, an expression so familiar and yet so faraway and gone, it almost hurt. Miranda smiled and hoped the princess hadn't seen; a minute later she stood up to take her leave.

"Oh, A.," Miranda said when the door closed.

Andromeda licked her lips. "Do I have a tale to tell," she said, also an expression from the long-ago time in Berkshire County where they'd been girls together. Then, half gleeful, half condescending, she would use it to introduce the story of some romantic escapade. Boys had always been crazy about her, and not just high school kids but college boys, and even men older than that on one memorable occasion. Then she had burst suddenly and uncharacteristically into tears, as she did now, led to them, maybe, by the same chain of reminiscence.

"Oh, it's okay," Miranda had said, then as now in her upstairs room, dragging her half out of bed to embrace her, and she'd been right. But now she didn't think she was. The tray that she had balanced on the coverlet fell to the floor. The cider spilled. Miranda could see the cuts under her hands, under the soft yellow hair, bleeding on the sheets.

The tears dried up. Andromeda pushed her away. Kneeling on her heels beside the bed, Miranda waited for her to start talking. But she didn't, and so Miranda changed the subject, rearranged the tray, picked up the cup. "Give me that," Andromeda said, and she reached down to seize the piece of beef from the plate. Scorning the bread, she brought the meat to her mouth, ripped into it.

"Something I don't understand," Miranda said, standing now, looking out the window at the mountain and the windy afternoon. "It was a dog at first, a yellow dog. Some kind of Labrador mix. Now that's changed."

"Sure. Haven't we all grown up a little bit?"

"But you're hurt."

Andromeda laughed, a sound and an expression unconnected to any kind of levity or joy. "Wolves, you know," she said. "They scratch at each other and they bleed all over the place. They do it when they—you know."

"What?"

"When they . . . you know."

"What are you talking about?"

Then she told Miranda about something else, a creature who had bitten her, a little demon on the wind, its wings as fine as spiderweb. It was the demon from the big revolver: It had bitten her along her arm and neck, and she hadn't been able to get her hand on it. But in some kind of enclosed space she had managed to pinch it between her fingers, crush it. "There was a lot of blood," she said. "I wiped my hands on my leg. I couldn't get it off. It had a perfume, or it made me bleed, you know, like an animal. Estrus, you know. I'd stop whenever there was a stream or a puddle all the way here. I'd try to wash away the stink, which brought them howling. All the way out of the city, or else through the woods. You used to tease me back at school. This was worse than that. Whatever."

"Oh, A." Miranda turned from the window, took a few steps toward her friend. But there was nothing in Andromeda's face that suggested she would welcome or accept any type of comfort or contact. She'd pulled back her thin lips to show her teeth.

Miranda had seen the little demon tumbling into the air off the barrel of her father's gun, a tiny figure of a naked boy. She'd said the words that had released it, while the Baroness Ceausescu pulled the trigger. There was another demon, too, a toad with a flap of skin under its fat arms, so it could fly or glide. Abcess, it was called. Where had it found its home, what section of muddy trench? Had it followed Peter Gross to Staro Selo?

She had thought obscurely she had helped release these dangers into the world, some kind of love, some kind of violence. But she had not imagined they would follow her friends, chase them down.

Abashed and guilty, she went to stand next to the window again. She watched the clouds blow over the mountain peaks. When she turned around, she saw Andromeda had gone to sleep as suddenly as an animal.

It was probably the best thing. Before she left, Miranda pulled down the sheets to examine the long scratches where scabs were already forming. She wondered if her mother had seen any of this, seen what was before her, when they had all stood together under the trees.

6 Luckacz Makes an Arrest

RADU LUCKACZ CHANGED TRAINS at Rimnicu to the narrow-gauge railway that led into the hills. One of the palace secretaries had telegraphed ahead, and the men were waiting for him on the platform. They were dressed in the pale uniforms of Bocu's Rezistenta party, as Luckacz was himself—baggy and drab, without any specific indication of rank, save for the discreet party badge on his lapel.

Rimnicu was on the border of the tara Romaneasa, the heartland of Great Roumania. It was still in Bocu's country, within his circle of control. The National Assembly, dominated by his political party, still had some influence here, though that would weaken as they moved into the mountains. The Carpathians and Transylvania belonged to General Antonescu and the army, except where the Germans had reoccupied the country north and east.

Hostility between the colonel and the general had lessened over time, smothered in the war effort and their mutual need. But it still burned dark and smoky in these border towns. The party cadres and off-duty policemen, recruited from the capital, moved uneasily along the station platform. A young officer of the Brancoveanu artillery had accompanied Luckacz from Bucharest—a narrow-chested braggart, like most of Bocu's private militia. Yet even he seemed to droop under the cold scrutiny of ordinary soldiers in their black and green uniforms, waiting for their trains.

Luckacz had his hands in his pockets. Then he took off his hat and wiped his bald head with his handkerchief as he stood under the signal board. He cast his mind forward to what he was going to do and why—it was not a question of personal revenge, he told himself. Nor was it an issue of Bocu's private, secret affairs, as he'd confided in the People's Palace—a personal favor for the president of the republic. Nor was it primarily a matter of Luckacz's own safety and ambition, or the safety of his wife and daughter, who were under Bocu's hand. There was no possibility that Luckacz ever could regain a semblance of his old rank—no, nothing like that. Still, it was good to be free in the open air.

It was a matter of principle. There was nest of traitors in Stanesti-Jui, aristocrats, republicans, and conjurers who could not be tolerated under present exigencies. The Baroness Ceausescu had given him the address, sent him on an errand, but he had failed her. Burdened with anger and jealousy, he had disobeyed her and been punished for it—he would not make that mistake again! But he would redeem himself by carrying out her last commands. If Andromedes was there, he would turn him over to Bocu's men. It was no concern of his. Anger and jealousy had made him lose his way.

No, he was after Miranda Popescu, the traitor's daughter, the alchemist's niece, who had killed a policeman. And the conspirators who had hidden her, refugees from the anti-conjuring laws and the collapse of von Schenck's political intrigues—these were the people he would bring back to Bucharest. He would act in the interest of his suffering country, as the Baroness Ceausescu would have wanted, and from heaven she would look down on him and forgive him for abandoning her, abandoning what he loved. Bocu had been right to seal him in that dungeon, which was not after all as bad as he'd deserved. Bocu had been right to give him time to purge himself, consider his mistakes.

And Luckacz would take the golden bracelet of the Brancoveanus from Miranda Popescu's wrist. And he would buy a little coffer from a jeweler, a miniature strongbox in golden filigree. He would take the bracelet to Nicola Ceausescu's tomb. He would lay down his offering among the flowers and candles, the simple keepsakes from all the people she had touched. And if Bocu took Sasha Andromedes, or Alexei Prochenko, or whatever his name was, and disemboweled him or tore his body into pieces, or set him up before a firing squad in the Piata Victoriei, Luckacz would make no effort to attend the ceremony. He would be with his wife and daughter. He would have better things to do.

Now, finally, the whistle blew, the little train steamed in.

IN STANESTI-JUI, ANDROMEDA was out of bed. Miranda had found clothes for her among the grooms. She stood in Miranda's room looking out the window, full of bravado that was about an inch thick; she wouldn't show her nose outside. But she would pace the floor or sit on the settee, wincing at every sound on the stairs. And she seemed to want to talk girl talk like the old days, as if they were still kids together in high school, or in Miranda's room in Stanley and Rachel's house. As if nothing had happened since—it seemed stupid to Miranda. Stupid and poignant at the same time. She knew why it was necessary. It disgusted her to find herself drawn in, especially when they talked about Peter Gross. "A certain you-know-who," Andromeda called him. "I had a letter from him. I had it in my coat pocket, but I lost it after I came back from Tutrakan. You know, Staro Selo."

"Did you see him?"

"Yes. He sent you this letter that he kept over his heart—it was really sweet. But I lost it in my clothes. I'm sorry."

Was he safe? How did he seem? What did he say? What was he like? Miranda thought. And then aloud, because she knew she wouldn't get a satisfactory answer to these questions: "What did the letter say?"

"I didn't read it! Besides, what do you care? Didn't he break up with you that night in the park? Cismigiu Park? Or did I get that wrong?"

"There was nothing to break up. . . ."

In these conversations, Miranda felt about as genuine as an actress onstage, rehearsing dialogue that could not express or uncover what she wanted to say. But if words and intonations failed her, still her emotions were real enough. Andromeda was jealous, she supposed. Jealous and sad—her beautiful eyes glanced nervously around the room. But then she gripped her hand, and said in another voice entirely, "I'm not telling you the truth.

There's more of Peter Gross in him than my old friend. You'll like him better now. We all have changed—how could we not have changed?"

After that she turned away and would not speak, even when Miranda coaxed her. She answered in monosyllables that faltered entirely, while Miranda made up her mind.

Steps must be taken. Full of a new determination to confide in Inez de Rougemont, she went downstairs.

Since their first conversation in the farmhouse library, Miranda had learned a good deal more about her hostess's life—from Madame de Graz, and, circumspectly, from her mother, and from her own inferences, and from the condesa herself: four separate pieces of information, which overlapped.

Before her love affair with Miranda's father, Inez de Rougemont had lived a life that had not satisfied her. Daughter of a banker, married to a Spanish diplomat, she had been a popular and fashionable hostess among the embassies and drawing rooms of the old regime. All that had ended with her surrender to Frederick Schenck von Schenck, who had introduced her to republican politics and, through his sister, to conjuring and alchemy.

But the general married Clara Brancoveanu, then died in prison on a fabricated charge. When Aegypta Schenck was first arrested and the conjurers rounded up, Madame de Rougemont found it impossible to return to any version of her former life. She manufactured her own death from a disfiguring disease. Then she retired to her secret farmhouse in the mountains, shortly after her obituary was printed in the Roumanian and foreign press.

Miranda had verified all this. She also understood that the condesa retained, even after fifteen years of isolation and the start of an enormous war, a web of duties and connections that often took her from the house. Some of her forays, Miranda guessed, must involve trips to the dream-landscape where they first met, meetings with Zuzana Knauss and Mrs. Chatterjee and Olga Karpov, efforts to reform the world.

Never, since Miranda had been in the house, had either of them spoken of that first meeting, in a place that, after all, did not exist. Out of some reticence or delicacy she didn't understand, Miranda had not spoken of it. But now Andromeda's arrival seemed to indicate a change in the weather and the time. The wounds and damage she'd sustained, the anxiety she'd brought with her from Staro Selo, now presaged a new urgency, a need for

Miranda to puzzle her way forward once again. The safety she had found here was quite obviously an illusion, a bubble in the stream.

In any case she had no right to safety, because of the suffering of her friends. That suffering had made a trail that led her to the misery of her own country, and to her place in it: She had failed to safeguard her father's pistol. One terrifying night in the People's Palace, Nicola Ceausescu had used it to release two secret messages into the world, communications of love and war.

All through the winter the Turkish and Roumanian authorities had predicted imminent victory, imminent peace, though they disagreed which side was closer to surrender. Now, after more than six months the war had collapsed into a kind of stalemate—the worst outcome of all, as Miranda had learned from Mr. Oats in ninth-grade history. So something must be done, if Miranda could manage it, some intervention in the hidden world.

So: a change, and maybe the condesa also sensed a change, for she was waiting for Miranda by the long table in the library. The black book and enormous revolver, which Jean-Baptiste had brought up from the city, were laid out on the slab of oak. Miranda scarcely glanced at them, because of her failure and the guilt she felt.

In time Madame de Rougemont got up and locked the door. She lit the lamps. It was evening time. Miranda sat in the tall chair, and they played a game that wasn't a game. They shared what they knew. Miranda said, "I didn't want to speak to you about these things, because they sounded stupid and because I didn't trust you. But now I know that trust is something I cannot afford. Why should I trust you, when you ask me to doubt the motives of my aunt? Everything I know—it doesn't matter. I believe we're searching for the same things."

"Wise girl. And that is?"

"'A cessation to the current hostilities,'" Miranda said, using a phrase from the *Roumania Libera*.

"All of them? Not just in Staro Selo?"

"All of them."

And in just a few more minutes they were ready to begin. "Before," Miranda said, "I meant I didn't know what I was doing. There was no—I don't know—volition, like a dream. I just did the things I did. Later I could see when I was in the world again. Things happened because of it. You know about this: A German general and a minister were dead. And that traitor Dysart and Dr. Theodore. And the Elector of Ratisbon. It's hard to feel responsible for them."

The tabletop was supported on two massive pedestals. There was no cloth on it, but the china and the glassware were delicate and fine. "I did things with no choice," Miranda said. "Maybe because of my aunt Aegypta. Now it's different. I'm in both places at the same time, and I'm awake in both places. Wanting things. Deciding things."

Madame de Rougemont walked to and fro beside the long table. Light, brittle-boned, she seemed to float from one side of the room to the other. "Because of Kepler's Eye."

"Yes."

"Describe it."

Miranda frowned. "They call it a jewel, but it's not like a jewel. It gives a little bit between my fingers. At nighttime there's a glow. I feel there's juice in it. Or blood."

"And it is in your hand?"

"Yes, now."

There was nothing in Miranda's hand. It lay empty, palm-up on the wooden arm of the chair. But on the hillside, as she'd said, there was the tourmaline clasped in her fingers and it seemed to throb as she climbed up.

"I've left the swamp behind," she said. "It's way below. This is another place. It's beautiful. Spring flowers. I don't know their names."

Yellow and lavender in the tall grass. She climbed up through a valley between two peaks, which she'd seen from far away. Sometimes she heard a trickle of water, or crossed a little stream. There were more rocks, and then the grass was shorter, coarser, growing in uneven tussocks as the way grew steep.

"Is there a path?"

"No path. No one has been here for a long time."

She said this, but up ahead there was a pile of little rocks. Once maybe they had formed a cairn. The land had closed in, and she was in a sort of a chute about twenty yards wide. She was in the right place, she knew. One rock wall was in shadow and one gleamed in the morning sun.

And it occurred to her even then that there might be some things she wanted to hold back and not describe. At first there was a simple reason: In the comfortable library, the curtains had been drawn to push away the darkness, which still seeped in around the edges. Sitting there, how was it possible to communicate in words the place where she was standing in the sun? Purple flowers in a crevice in the rocks—should she describe them? The stony peaks looming overhead, the ice mountains beyond them? And as she turned around to catch her breath, should she describe the valley she had left behind? The air was dark and thick down there. Creatures strove and struggled with the mud around their knees. Which part of this landscape was important? Which words would she use to make it real?

"How do you understand which way to climb?" asked Inez de Rougemont.

"I'm just going where I want."

She listened to the condesa's exasperated sniff: "This is a journey that has been described. Who do you think has left those piles of stones? No, you must follow the path he made, although it has been a long time. But when you find the place, then you will know."

Miranda didn't like to hear any of that. Every word the condesa had spoken, Miranda sensed a change in her, a little more desire in her voice, a little more greediness in this gray-haired woman, her father's friend—greed for knowledge, she hoped. De Rougemont didn't understand how difficult this was. Miranda wasn't even touching the tourmaline anymore. She'd slipped it into the pocket of her shirt, because more and more she had to use her hands in the steep chute, and the rocks were insecurely piled. She had to work even to breathe. Now every step brought her higher into a landscape where the air was thin and sharp and painful in her lungs, which had not recovered from her sickness. She knew that now.

Part of her wanted to stop, and it wasn't because the way was difficult. But the condesa wanted something, that was clear. Probably she hadn't told Miranda everything. Probably she also had held something back.

Miranda climbed the chute. There was always something greedy about this, she thought, this search for knowledge and secret power. No wonder her descriptions were sparse and stingy. Was she doing Inez de Rougemont a favor, offering her payment for room and board? Hand over hand in the thin air—the rocks had closed in around her and there was nothing to see. But even so, there was another part of her that wanted to keep moving, to discover . . . something. Something of her own. Here she was, though, trudging in the footsteps of some half-mad, long-dead philosopher—she was sure of the way now, even though she hadn't seen a mark or a cairn in a long time.

In the valley behind her there were hundreds of thousands of things. There was the long trough of the war from Kula to the sea. The little ape and the scarlet beetle struggled in the mud down there. All that she'd left behind. But maybe now she could look forward to a new terrain, purified of everything that had grown over and obscured the four essential elements of rock, water, light, and air.

The chute she was in began to level out, reveal a larger chunk of sky. The hummocks of grass came back, the little flowers. But every few steps, when she stopped with her lungs burning, she needed fewer words and a smaller vocabulary to describe it. Even so she found herself dissembling by holding back what she knew she could make clear. Who was this woman anyway?

"I'm at the top of the chute," she said begrudgingly, looking back. She turned around. "And, oh—"

"What?"

"Oh—"

"Tell me." Inez de Rougemont in her powder and rouge, in her old-fashioned yellow dress, paced back and forth along the library carpet.

"There's a building up ahead."

Maybe she shouldn't say anything at all, Miranda thought, sitting in her chair in the dark room. Up ahead there was a little tarn, its surface smooth and polished as a mirror. It lay at the bottom of a bowl of rocks, and on the far side the peak jutted up. Below it, a snowfield fell into the lake, and the flat boulders made a kind of promontory. It led to a stone tower, which rose out of the lake.

It was not high nor especially well made, Miranda saw when she came close. A path led through the scree, although in places it had slid into the lake. Miranda picked her way through the unsteady slope until she stood on firmer ground. And she could see part of the rock wall had collapsed.

"What is it?" said Inez de Rougemont. Miranda caught the sound of her impatience as her little bloodless gray head peered into the dark corners of the farmhouse library. The tower arch had fallen in, and the coping stones from the high wall. There was an inscription cut in the uneven surface of the rock: I. KEPLER FECIT.

"Please tell me," whispered Inez de Rougemont.

The tower seemed abandoned, but Miranda wondered whether there was something left alive, a brooding presence she could almost feel. She was not afraid, maybe because part of her was sitting in the safe black farmhouse far below. But it was possible the entire structure was waiting for this moment to collapse. She climbed in through the ruined stones and past a rusted iron doorway let into the rock. There was a stair to the top of the tower.

And maybe she should stop here, but she couldn't help herself. She was not immune to curiosity, which is another form of greediness. She had a sudden sense she didn't belong here, but still she labored up the stone steps. And when she stood on the stone platform above the lake, she could see many things. Above her the sun was blocked by the ice peak. Miranda could see stars in the sky. No, not stars but planets—Stanley had shown her the difference. Three or four were visible in the milky morning light.

She had the tourmaline clasped in her hand. From a new vantage point at the lip of the platform she could see far down the valley. She could see into the darker, thicker air. But there was no unusual detail. Maybe she needed some kind of telescope, a tool.

"Tell me what you see."

And she reported dutifully, begrudging every word. She did no justice to the immense cracked landscape, the splintered rock, the walls of ice. None of that was what de Rougemont wanted to hear. She was interested in patterns. She didn't care about the smell of the cold air.

"There's some kind of chamber underneath me. Locked like I told you. Maybe that—"

"No. It is where you are now. He described it in his letters. It is where he made his observations."

"Well, I'm not sure—"

"No, it must be there. Where you are standing. He described the place."

Leaning over the parapet, doubtful, skeptical, the tourmaline throbbing in her hand, she turned her back to the valley and looked up. The tarn lay in a bowl surrounded by ice peaks and rock walls. No trail led away from it. If Johannes Kepler had climbed past this place, Miranda couldn't see where he had gone. Maybe, she imagined, she would find a new path among the rocks, and she wouldn't even be able to turn back and see the valley anymore.

Part of her wanted to leave the stone platform and go onward, in spite of her foreboding. What had her aunt said about her home in Berkshire County? "That town, those streets, those people—you might search for it and find it in the hidden world."

But that was not the path of obligation, or the way to comfort Peter or Andromeda. To find that place, or even to search for it, was not a desire she would confess to Inez de Rougemont. No, she was in the here and now, looking toward the future. She looked up into the rock peaks.

But even so, she wanted to be silent. The words she had used to describe this place had diminished it somehow, stripped it of its beauty. She shivered, hugged her arms, drew the tourmaline up to her face, and then she saw what the condesa wanted.

It was in the little lake. When she peered over the broken edge of the parapet and down into the water, she realized she was looking at a map.

In the perfect light she could see under the water's surface. She could see all the boulders, rocks, and stones that formed the bottom of the lake. And not only was there no distortion, but everything—all of it—seemed unnaturally clear and focused, as if the layer of water functioned as a lens.

After a long silence, she described it to Inez de Rougemont, or else she half-described it. "It's like a map of Europe and the world. Then the boulders climb out of the water and they form the boundaries in North America, Southern Africa, and Japan, I guess—that's the banana-shaped sand beach. So from there it slopes down like the bottom of a bowl. Lowest in the middle is Bucharest and Great Roumania. Those blue pebbles are the sapphire domes of the old city."

"Where the time is deepest," murmured Inez de Rougemont.

Peter had told Miranda about the sinkhole in the Aegyptian desert, and she could see the line of it, reaching from the Nile to the Hudson. Maybe it was a piece of grass in the water, because there were living things deep in the lake, and things that floated on its surface, and currents and ripples and reflections, also, of clouds and overhanging cliffs. From the lip of the tower,

Miranda watched the surface move as if alive. That was what was so hard to describe. And at the same time she was conscious of some other living presence in the stones below her feet, as if she almost heard some grunting, whispering voice.

"It's like—oh . . ."

"What do you see?"

Miranda had the tourmaline in her hand, which sometimes appeared as a stone to her, and sometimes as a plum or a grape or something edible and full of juice. But maybe that was because she could not bear to imagine the truth. She was holding something that had come out of the brain of Johannes Kepler the alchemist, who had made this place for his own purpose.

Carefully, deliberately she laid the jewel down on the parapet. And then she found herself sitting in the wooden armchair in the darkened farmhouse library, her hands open and grasping. Inez de Rougemont walked back and forth, back and forth, her face as fierce and eager as a hawk or an eagle or a bird of prey, set to seize up every little word in her painted nails, devour every little phrase in her lipsticked mouth—Miranda couldn't stand it. Groping, blind, she put her hand out for the tourmaline again. It yielded under her fingers.

And there she stood on the stone tower with the planets above her, clustered together in the apex of the sky. The light was muted, the sun behind a cloud. Miranda looked down and saw a breath of air turn up the surface of the water north and east of Bucharest. She described it, because she understood what she was seeing—the great curve of the Russian advance, which had severed the German supply lines south of Minsk. But it had stalled now, stopped. And there were circular eddies where the armies had divided and sunk down in the mud.

Inez de Rougemont paused between the table and the armchair. Her eyes were staring, blind, yet she strained to see. "Tell me," she said, and Miranda told her about the seven small fish that issued now out of an underwater crevice—Russian dreadnoughts in the Black Sea. And then a line of enormous turtles on the dry land farther south. They were near the river in the middle of the line.

"You have discovered it," said Inez de Rougemont.

"What?"

"People said Johannes Kepler could predict the future. Tell me all of it. Follow the borders of Great Roumania."

Miranda found the mountain ranges and the Wallachian plain. "There's a tree trunk that's fallen to the bottom with all its broken branches—it's the Danube. And I can see the battle front with Turkey south of Chiselet."

Chiselet was where Peter and Andromeda had had their accident. Both of them separately had told her about that. The town was marked with a whirlpool, and dirty bubbles on the surface of the water. But on the south shore of the river, she could see the places where the water was churned up by the columns of horses and armored vehicles, she guessed—near Staro Selo and the Tutrakan bridge. That's where the turtles were.

In the library, Inez de Rougemont pulled from a low shelf a dusty atlas. She opened it, spread the book across Miranda's lap. "Mark what you see."

Head splitting, Miranda tried to think it out—first things first. Step by step. The condesa gave her a lump of graphite, which turned her fingers silver. She felt danger all around her, and it wasn't because of the Turks. But in the hidden world there was a cloudburst out of the cloudless sky, and the map disappeared into the lake, covered over by the stippled surface of the water.

"Do not stop."

"I can't see anything," Miranda said. She dropped the graphite to the carpet.

"Please, this is important. This might be a new method to break though. Some new machine, a strategy to cross the river. There is a rumor that the Abyssinians have abandoned their neutrality. This is information for Antonescu if we can reach him."

On the parapet, Miranda stared down into the map of Europe. The rain had stopped as soon as it had begun.

Because of its secret alliance with Germany, Turkey had mobilized and then attacked. This was after Nicola Ceausescu had let the Russian cavalry penetrate the German lines behind the Fedorivka Salient. And though an unofficial truce still held between the German and Roumanian Republics, elsewhere all of Europe had been drawn into the war, every country led by its alliances.

"So you must . . ."

Miranda didn't want to hear it. She'd lived in her aunt's book, studied the world wars in the ninth grade. If she'd learned anything from Mr. Oats, it was that these advances and assaults and counteroffensives meant nothing at all, or else nothing but slaughter. Victory was not to be found that way, not a victory that meant anything or did not lead to other wars—no doubt Aegypta Schenck had manufactured Mr. Oats to teach her this, make this point exactly. So that here upon this parapet, she would not be tempted to assume . . .

"Don't you see?" she said. "We can't win that way. It's an illusion."

"Yes, but we can lose."

Miranda considered the justice of this. If the Turks crossed the river in any kind of numbers, either by the open water or else by the bridge, with the bulk of the Roumanian army trapped on the south shore . . .

That was Peter's sector by the Tutrakan bridge.

But even if he weren't in danger, she would not decide between these competing claims, not now. The power was in her hands, and she would not use it to please one person or someone else. Instead she looked down at the map in the bottom of the pool, at the map over her knees, and forced them to coincide. She closed her eyes, sealing them together, and then she pulled herself away. She left the roof of the broken tower. The rain was a relief, but if she got soaked, she'd freeze. She looked for shelter underneath the stairway by the iron door.

"What do you see?"

"I don't see anything!" But then she told the condesa about the door, which was locked with a heavy bolt of iron. On the lintel above her head she saw some pictures scratched into the stone.

"But I think there's something in here. It's like a prison door. There's something alive in here. I can feel it."

"Stop."

These symbols scratched into the lintel, she remembered them from Edith Hamilton's *Mythology*—the mirror, and then a strange little round face. Once for about a week and a half, Andromeda had been interested in astrology.

In the darkened library, Miranda asked for a glass of water. Then she said, "Do you remember that lady? That French lady on Borgo Pass? She said a German alchemist had tricked some kind of spirit or a god—"

"Stop."

There was something in Madame de Rougemont's voice, some hint of menace, but also a strange wistfulness. She stood in the shadow behind the chair, and Miranda couldn't see her face. But there was no possibility at all that she would bring her something to drink.

So Miranda, parched and with an aching head, labored to stand up out of her chair. As she turned, she could sense some kind of movement. The door stood ominous and silent and solid in its stone frame; she had her hand on the bolt. But there was movement in the rubble of the broken wall.

This tower won't last forever, Miranda thought. Expedite the inevitable. She saw the movement of a small creature that hesitated when she turned to face it. Then it was gone.

The bolt ended in a ring. She tugged on it for a moment, banged it with the heel of her palm. Maybe something was suffering in there. How could she leave that big door closed behind her? She hammered at the bolt. It would not budge.

"Oh, stop," said Inez de Rougemont.

"Tell me what's in here!"

Something shifted in the rock wall, and Miranda left the door to look out through the fallen gap, not toward the lake but toward a field of rocks and tumbled scree under the shadow of the mountain.

Something was alive out there, or else not quite alive. She glanced back at the door. And when she turned again, she could see a man climbing toward her over the unsteady stones. When she watched him he stood still, but if she closed her eyes, or went back to the door, or fumbled with the water pitcher on the table in the library, she knew he'd take a few steps toward her, as if playing some ectoplasmic game of red light, green light. He was a ghost, she knew.

The rain had gone away, the rocks were dry. He stumbled toward her and she recognized him. He was dressed in expensive clothes, a little man with a ruined face, whom she'd last seen on he banks of the Hoosick River. He was the Elector of Ratisbon, Miranda knew—her old enemy. He had kept her mother prisoner inside his house.

And maybe all she'd have to do is flap her hands and he'd disperse, undone by a current of air. She went and tugged on the iron bolt a little more, but it was rusted shut; she was too weak. And as if conjured by that thought, she understood now she was vulnerable, and the nature of the danger had changed. It wasn't just the man in the cutaway suit. But there were little animals all around her in the crevices in the rocks. Above her the sky was going dark, though it was still midmorning.

"You've been lying to me," she said.

She was thinking about the photograph on the library table—Inez de Rougemont, young and beautiful, dressed à la paysanne. In her mind the soldier with the blurred face had been replaced by the Elector of Ratisbon, and she knew why. The last day she had spent in America, she had seen this apparition—this little man in his formal suit, his face ravaged with smallpox. And at the same time Peter had seen this woman, dressed in Gypsy clothes, and he had recognized her and known her name—told Miranda later when they'd spoken of that crazy day, the first time she had seen him in the People's Palace, when the doctors had cut off his hand—how could she have been too stupid to remember her name?

RADU LUCKACZ NOTICED the change in the weather as he walked up from the village along the dirt road. In the main square of Stanesti-Jui, looking up into the night sky, he had seen the stars, moonlight on snow peaks. The darkness was dry and fresh. But then in a moment the sky had clouded over and a mist had come, a thickness of the air. It clung to the torches Bocu's lieutenant had insisted on lighting. Looking back along the road, Luckacz saw each flame surrounded by a dull, glowing sphere. And he was immediately dispirited, because he recognized the effect of some unfair conjuring—it didn't matter. More men had joined them in the village in addition to the twenty who'd been with him on the train.

Bocu had insisted on this show of force. He was unsure of the extent of his power, Luckacz assumed, and whether the local police would obey him. There were just a few peasants in the house itself, peasants and servants and women, and maybe Sasha Andromedes. Everything else was superstition and stupidity. So this was where the Condesa de Rougemont had found refuge all these years! It had been fifteen years at least since the newspapers had reported her death.

This was a simple matter, and in the past it would have been unworthy of his personal attention. He paused to catch his breath. The torchlight shone on ditches full of wildflowers on both sides of the road. He rubbed his bald head and then replaced his hat. At the same time he stifled one of the gasping sobs that came over him from time to time as he remembered standing on the threshold of the amber gallery. The baroness had turned away from him, her hands over her breasts.

She had asked him to come here to this mountain village, and he had disobeyed her. Now she was dead. The road, a long dirt and gravel cul-de-sac, curved up to the farmhouse among the long-needled pines. There was dirt on his boots, the cuffs of his trousers. It looked now it might rain.

KNEADING THE STONES, STRETCHING her back, Miranda crouched down in the broken wall. Furry, blind, underground creatures moved among the rocks: badgers, rats, weasels, moles.

She went up on her hind legs against the door and hooked her hand through the iron ring. This would do it, she thought.

"For the love of God," said Inez de Rougemont.

It was a strange phrase under the circumstances. "I'm sick of this," Miranda said, standing by her chair in the farmhouse library. "All of you with your secret plans. What's the difference between you, except what side you're on?"

There really was a difference, and Miranda knew it. She persevered for the sake of the larger point, as Stanley might have said: "Don't you want to try something else? All of you, all of your struggling for wisdom and what's good. Where are we now—a world war? I know all about it. I read about it in my history class. Olga Karpov—"

"She betrayed us!"

"But there'll always be someone like that. Some part of you. That's what I mean. You have to ask yourself, 'What are you afraid of?'" Miranda asked herself aloud, to quiet her own fears.

Surely there was something in this little prison in the mountain pass, something sealed up by Johannes Kepler centuries before. And the world could be one way, or else it could be another way—the door was too heavy for her hand. But the paws of the white tyger could pull it from its frame.

Because she knew she had the strength, she stopped. "Certainty comes from weakness," Stanley had once said.

Now there were clouds over the sun, and a wind had come up out of nothing. The rain had blown away. Miranda felt a change of pressure in her ears. There was lightning, a momentary tree of light above her head, an explosion of thunder. She looked up to see a yellow hawk with its claws outstretched. There was a bald old crow among the rocks, and the hawk stooped down. But then it was caught up by the wind and overturned against the shuddering wall.

The ghost of Theodore von Geiss und Ratisbon had disappeared. But there were little animals among the rocks, small weak mammals that were the tyger's natural prey. They cringed and hid in the cracks and crevices, afraid of her smell, she imagined. Except for the bald crow that hopped down the slope—she followed it. But by the side of the small tarn she stopped, turned around in time to see a bolt of lightning strike the ruined platform where Johannes Kepler had once stood. Maybe some other force was trying to free the creature in the dark cell, or else destroy the tower. The air was full of ozone. Miranda turned downhill.

BOCU'S YOUNG LIEUTENANT HAD a sickly face, unpleasant in the torchlight. There was a hedge that separated the road from the fields, and the building loomed up suddenly in the dark mist. A single lantern burned on the ground floor, a diffuse flickering light, because the curtains in that room were drawn. "Someone is awake," murmured the lieutenant.

Luckacz had disliked him more every step they took. His teeth were stained and ragged when he smiled, as now. All the way from Bucharest, Luckacz had assumed these men were under his own control. Now suddenly he didn't think so. He had no official rank or position, after all. Why were all these men necessary for a simple investigation, a simple arrest?

On the train and again in the village station he had made his plan, which was to knock on the door with these fellows in reserve, to take away the possibility of resistance. But now he understood the lieutenant had a different plan. "What do you think?" whispered the lieutenant. "We will set the barns on fire. Then we'll have the light to shoot." The man beside him unstrapped his rifle, a new bolt-action carbine from North Africa.

Was he joking? Appalled, Luckacz raised his hand. "I will secure the house. Please wait," he said. But then there was a stroke of lightning and a crack of thunder above their heads, as if the weather were as disgusted as he was by these young men in their uniforms without insignia—were they soldiers or hired criminals?

Another flash of lightning, and the air stank and tingled. Some of the men threw down their torches. Oh, they were a fine, superstitious bunch, not one of them fit for army service or the metropolitan police.

And the rain came in a sudden burst. The lieutenant pulled the men into the trees on the other side of the road. The torches flickered, wan and wet. Afraid of a little rain, Luckacz thought, and he pulled the brim of his hat over his eyes, strode to the door, pounded on it, tried the bar. It wasn't even locked. He'd show Bocu's thugs what one man could do, one old man in the rain with nothing but a spring-loaded pistol in his pocket; he wouldn't even use it. No plan was necessary. A house full of women, and maybe a few fellows to help with the cows. No doubt they lived in a different structure.

But as he pushed open the door, a third bolt of lightning struck the house itself, the chimney or the ridgepole.

MIRANDA GAVE THE TOURMALINE a squeeze, then descended to the farm outside the mountain village of Stanesti-Jui, which had been caught in the same storm.

She imagined she would fall into her body with relief. But at first she couldn't tell the difference. Thunder broke above her head.

She came to herself in the darkened room. Her chair had toppled over. There was broken glass under her hand. Someone whimpered in the dark.

Maybe the house had been struck by lightning. If so, maybe it wasn't such a big deal. Nothing seemed to be on fire. The room was still intact. Miranda listened to the rain against the windows, and as her eyes cleared she saw the table had been overthrown. She remembered struggling to her feet, striving forward against all odds to find a glass of water. Had she done all this? She was surprised she'd had the strength to move such an enormous slab of wood.

The door hung on its hinges, the lock broken, the jamb splintered. Had someone broken it down? Now it swung open and the woman came in, Inez de Rougemont, carrying a glass lantern in her hand. Miranda remembered the diving hawk, remembered also the bald crow. Where was he? Maybe there. In the improved light she saw a man wedged beneath the table, the back of his bald head against the floorboards. He had a nosebleed, and was bleeding also from a gash behind his ear.

The condesa limped around the room, opening the curtains and the shades. Light-headed, Miranda knelt down beside the injured man. She recognized him, she thought.

She tried to push the table off him, but she was right. It was too heavy. She took a napkin from the floor and pressed it against the man's ear to stop the flow of blood. Once in America a neighbor's kid had hit her with a rake in the same spot. The wound was superficial, Stanley had said, though it had bled and bled.

Where had she seen this man before? She remembered when he started to speak, his voice harsh, nasal, foreign: "Miss Popescu, it is futile to resist. It is my duty to inform you that you are in a state of criminal apprehension, because of your complicity in the murder of Felix Ceausescu on the twelfth of Thermidor. I advise you to come quietly and not attempt to abscond, as you have been known to do. . . ."

This was Inspector Luckacz. She had seen him in Mogosoaia when she and Peter had given in to the police. Luckacz had had thick gray hair then and a black moustache. What had happened to him? It was not so long ago.

The rain crashed against the dark windows. Madame de Rougemont had put the lantern on a low table, turned up the flame in the glass chimney. Grimacing and limping, she came toward them. "I'll send Anton for the carriage," she said.

"No," Miranda said, "I'm sick of this."

She held the napkin against the man's bald head. "Why are you chasing me?" she asked as gently as she knew how, although her voice was trembling.

"Miss, I believe you must expect because of your connections to the former royal family of this country that our laws and natural laws do not apply to you. Even in this room here I see evidence of conjuring and prestidigitation. Though you might have used it to disarm me, and even if I give my life for it, still I must assure you that—"

He was interrupted by the Condesa de Rougemont's contemptuous grunt. "Let him alone. We must be gone from here, all of us, tonight. He won't have come alone."

"No, ma'am. There is no possibility to resist. The village boys were frightened of the lightning strike. But the house is surrounded. I have twenty-seven men, including several members of the Brancoveanu Artillery."

Inez de Rougemont paused at the doorway before going out. "Come with me," she said, but Miranda ignored her. Why should she pay attention to a woman who had lied to her? Or at least had not revealed a connection to her enemy—she felt sequestered and sheltered by the rain around the house, as if the effect of the big world might be muted here. Everything had always happened so fast. But now the inspector lay helpless, stunned. He stirred feebly under her hands, simultaneously rejecting and accepting her ministrations. There was a pitcher of water intact on the sideboard. She held a glass of water for him to drink.

Maybe he was lying about the twenty-seven men. But if the house was surrounded, he was the man she had to convince. "You know I had nothing to do with this."

Alone with Luckacz in the room, she wet another napkin. It was streaked with marmalade, so she found a clean corner to wipe under the policeman's nose. There was gray hair in his nostrils.

"I've defended myself against men who wanted to kill me," she said. "Peter, too."

The policeman flinched. The bump on his head was just beginning to rise. "Miss Popescu," he murmured in his dry, irritating voice. "You were with the Chevalier de Graz when he fired on Felix Ceausescu, the child of our national heroine."

At least this was true: Miranda had dragged the boy from his bed, dragged him down into the courtyard where he'd died. His blood had spread over the cobblestones.

"The Chevalier de Graz—"

"You don't really think that," she interrupted. "That woman murdered her own son. She shot him from the balcony."

"The Chevalier de Graz—"

"Are you insane? The boy was in my mother's arms."

She pressed the napkin against Luckacz's bald head. The cloth was saturated with blood, whose flow had lessened now. He continued in a whisper, his voice harsh and strained: "Miss Popescu, you must understand that you are not familiar with all types of firearms, as I am. And I must insist to you that in a circular space it is quite difficult to verify the source of this type of gunfire. There are echoes against the stone. . . ."

He was hopeless. He was like Captain Raevsky and Jean-Baptiste. What was it with these men? Besotted, she supposed. In love. A kind of love.

"You must reassure yourself we will dispose also of the Chevalier de Graz," continued Radu Luckacz. "He will not escape us. No escape is possible. None of this will arrive as a surprise to you, or to your associate Andromedes who—"

He grimaced, choked, could not continue. "Who?" Miranda asked.

"But you know this man! You must not lie to me! God help me!" Now suddenly he seemed in pain. His back arched off the floor, then subsided.

Miranda took her hands away from him. "I know the name. It's a little strange hearing you use it. I've known her since I was a child."

Miranda said this almost without thinking, though maybe she had meant to calm him, because it was clear he considered Andromeda a menace of some kind. But now he was even more agitated, his eyes wild and round as he turned toward her. His scalp started to bleed again.

"What are you saying? Is it true?"

"Hush, be quiet. Don't worry about—"

He grabbed hold of her hand. She pulled away; there was no reason to talk to him anymore. Where were Inez de Rougemont and the others? She didn't want to be alone with this man anymore. "That's enough," she said. "It's useless—"

BUT IT WASN'T USELESS. During the time he'd spent locked up in the People's Palace, some of the details of the baroness's last days had receded from him. Certain facts had been expunged, as if his guilt had wiped hers away. Now they all came back. All his suspicions—how could it have been true about Sasha Andromedes? "I have known her . . ."—what did it mean, this disgusting feminine pronoun? In the amber gallery Sasha Andromedes had been writhing on the floor. Yet he had been able to see her small breasts under her clothes. And if that was true, then was it also possible that Nicola

Ceausescu had murdered her own son and Kevin Markasev before him? Surely all of it was a disordered fantasy, invented to make Luckacz's betrayal seem less awful in the long, cold, naked nights inside his cell.

Now he lay on his back in the conjurer's library, the table overturned, Miranda Popescu kneeling over him. This was what one old man could do—it didn't matter. None of it mattered. Nothing had been right since Nicola Ceausescu died.

Now in the doorway he could see a man he recognized, the baroness's steward, Jean-Baptiste, still wearing his old jacket with the red lapels—what was he doing here? "Inspector Luckacz," he said now as he came into the room. "What is this?" he said, reaching down to grab hold of the Rezistenta badge, a cheap enamel pin in the shape of an eagle's foot. He ripped it away from Luckacz's coat, tossed it across the room.

Luckacz stared up at the steward's face as he bent over him, his astonished red-rimmed eyes. Was it possible this man had been his friend?

"There is nothing for you here," said Jean-Baptiste. "You must leave us alone." He was holding onto Luckacz's arms, pulling him to his feet, when the window broke and one of the short-barreled carbine rifles pushed in through the glass, pushed through the curtain, fired.

THE SHOT WAS LOUD in the enclosed space. And now suddenly the room was full of people. The wind from the broken window sucked at the lantern flame. The light, which had seemed sufficient for her and Inez de Rougemont, now could not separate the blundering, chaotic shapes. Miranda made no sense of it, and she was struggling to her feet when Jean-Baptiste collapsed. At first she didn't know what had happened. But he was hurt, and he pulled her down with him as he fell. She had her arms around his narrow shoulders, and his face was near her own. He hadn't shaved for a few days. His breath stank of anise or fennel, something like that.

She closed her eyes, groped in the darkness for the tourmaline. When she touched it, she found she was sitting in the upland pasture among the rocks below Johannes Kepler's tower. And it wasn't raining, and the dark clouds hurried overhead. She sat in a cold patch of sunlight on that windy hill, and she had a hedgehog on her lap in her cupped hands, curled up tight around its wound; it never would uncurl. "No," she said, "no, no," because she just couldn't stand this, not again.

In the dark, crowded library, she helped the old man down, laid him on his back. "You leave us—alone," he said again. In the high place in the hills Miranda saw the bald-headed crow close by her among the rocks, and a blind badger poking his nose out, and there were other creatures in the grass. She saw the ruined tower and the Elector of Ratisbon on the stone platform looking down.

"You—leave us." The room was full of shouts and stamping feet. There was a smell of oil or kerosene, and the smoke stung her eyes, too. Some idiot had brought a torch into the room. A burning drop fell to the carpet and was extinguished by someone's wet boot. But in the new light Miranda could see a soaked, bedraggled bunch of men in identical beige-brown suits, their carbines in their hands. A young man with a thin, greasy, pockmarked face was giving orders. The Condesa de Rougemont wasn't there, nor Anton, nor the other men from the farm. Madame de Graz wasn't there. But the men had caught Miranda's mother, dragged her out of bed; she was barefoot, dressed in her nightgown and nightcap. She had a man on either side of her. Their hands seemed huge on her elbows. She gave Miranda a timid smile as if to reassure her. And Miranda was reassured, because in another part of her mind she grasped hold of the tourmaline and felt the juice on her fingers. Soon she would get up and unsheathe her bright claws, rip these little men apart.

The greasy lieutenant with the yellow skin and the bad teeth was standing in the middle of the room, a pistol in his hand. He was talking to Radu Luckacz. "You. You're a disgrace. What made you think you had the stomach for this? This is men's work, not for babies, and I'll tell the chief about it. Why should we risk our necks for you?"

But then he noticed Miranda, and he brought his gun around. "So," he said. "The last of the Brancoveanus. I suppose it's time."

Then he was interrupted by two more men coming in, and they brought Andromeda between them and pushed her down onto the floor. She was dressed in some of Miranda's clothes, a shirt and trousers. She scrambled away from the muzzles of the carbines, crawling on her butt toward Miranda on the hearth, where she was kneeling over Jean-Baptiste. The old man's eyes were closed.

Andromeda seemed pretty calm under the circumstances. She yawned, let her tongue loll out. "This really sucks," she said.

The greasy man stood above her with his pistol out. Rain still dripped from the brim of his hat. "Domnul Andromedes," he said. "This is very good. You, we'll take this one back for the chief."

"I can't wait," murmured Andromeda.

Miranda closed her eyes. Now is the moment, she thought. Her fingers were slick with the juice. She sat among the rocks on the high mountain. She would lay the little hedgehog down among the dry stones, and she would let the beast come out of her. She would do it now.

In the secret world, the day had closed down, the mist come in. The valley and the peaks were hidden, the tower loomed out of the fog. Above her was the smell of ozone and the storm breaking. A rock fall in the pass sounded like gunfire.

She flexed her fingers.

"MADEMOISELLE," SAID THE soldier in the pale uniform. In the farmhouse library, he stood above her with his pistol out. Clara Brancoveanu heard a crack of thunder, and the rain against the windows. "Iorgu, Mihai, get the men outside. Take this gutless fool," he said, gesturing toward Inspector Luckacz—Clara recognized him from her time in Bucharest. "And this one," the man continued, kicking Lieutenant Prochenko with his muddy boot. "Then come back."

Someone pulled Prochenko to his feet, pulled him away. Miranda knelt by Jean-Baptiste in front of the dark fireplace. He lay on his back and his eyes were closed. Blood was on his shirt, but not much. There wasn't a lot of blood.

Clara watched the gun in the soldier's grip, watched it turn. She screamed, wrenched herself away from the big hands that held her by the elbows. She threw herself across the room, hiding Miranda's body with her own.

The torch had gone out, or had been taken out, leaving a layer of oily smoke. The door was crowded with people as they tried to leave, to give the

Rezistenta man the room to fire. But he did not, and when Clara looked up again, she saw his face transformed.

All the cruelty and purpose in it was replaced with fear, and she watched also, horrified and amazed, as Jean-Baptiste stirred and stretched and tottered to his feet. When he opened his mouth, Clara knew what she was hearing. She could not but recognize his hoarse, soft, well-remembered voice, which all of them had heard in theaters, or at political gatherings, or on wax recordings, or in the first scratchy and indistinct radio broadcasts from Bucharest that summer: "Oh, my friends. What have you done to me?"

Light came from a single lantern, flickering in the air from the broken window. The room seemed empty now, because the men in their pale suits had pushed themselves back against the walls or bookcases or glass-fronted cabinets, leaving the carpet open, a natural stage. "And what have you done to this good man?" said the voice out of Jean-Baptiste's clenched lips. "Look at him—he was my friend, faithful and loyal to the end of the entire tragedy—look at him now!" And Jean-Baptiste moved his hands down his dirty and disheveled shirt, stripped it away from his withered body; Clara had been wrong about the blood. But it had seeped into his trousers and his back was wet with it, and now his hands as he displayed himself, the angry lips of his wound. He did a little dance across the floor, and students of Nicola Ceausescu might have recognized a motif from the first act of Rafael Hoffman's *Madame Faust,* which she had performed to such acclaim in Petersburg in the old days. "Faithful to the end," she said, "and this is how he is rewarded, this man who took me into the old baron's house when I was just a girl. And helped me and cared for me in the days when I had nothing. Even when I lived in the People's Palace, he was the only one who never lied to me, who loved me for myself alone, my own self—not like some of the others here."

Two men had been pulling Radu Luckacz through the door, but now they left him, shrank away from him. Jean-Baptiste stepped lightly over the floor. He raised his bloody finger in a manner that was neither threatening nor accusatory. Instead he moved his hand in front of Luckacz's face, a gesture that was delicate and soft, almost as if he meant to caress the old policeman, who stared at him round-eyed. "You almost kept with me," she said. "You stumbled at the end, my old companion. But it heals my heart to see you, I promise. We played some tricks on the potato-eaters, you and I."

"Ma'am, I—"

"Shush, be quiet. This is a special night. Do not ruin it by talking—I will come for you, never fear. You and I will have our reckoning, but not tonight. Before we make amends, first we must feel our separation. But as for you, domnul. What about you?"

Lieutenant Prochenko stood beside the door, hands in his pockets, the back of his head against the yellow plaster. He opened his mouth, displaying all his teeth, but he said nothing. He was probably pretending, but he looked almost bored, Clara thought, and maybe Nicola Ceausescu thought so, too: "Oh, how you wound me. I mean in my heart, domnul—is that a terrible thing? When a woman surrenders her heart to you? And how is it that you could drop it, let it shatter like a piece of crystal? How is it possible to be so cruel? I tell you there was no damage to my body that did not come as a relief, because of what I suffered in my heart."

"You are such unbelievable dogshit," said Prochenko in English.

Jean-Baptiste flinched, and his high shoulders tensed. "I know you have suffered, too," he said. "Anyone can see it, the burden that you carry. I thought there was a way I could help you share it, or else let it drop. But you are proud, domnul—I understand that. I also know what it's like to be too proud!"

Prochenko yawned. Jean-Baptiste stared at him, then continued his circuit of the room. He squatted down over Clara and Miranda, reached out his bloody hands. "Here you are," he said. "I must confess I was a fool to think you were a threat to me. Let me see the bracelet—oh, it jingles. And so you must see I do not bear you any harm. Oh, I was in time! Why do you think these men are here, if not to shoot you like an animal and bury you in these woods? Why did they come so far if not for that? But if you live and you remember this night, remember also this is not for your sake. Your life, your death mean nothing to me."

And Jean-Baptiste moved his hand in front of Clara's face. "Not for you. But for you, madame la princesse, with my thanks. And my debt to you is paid—you were the first and last to hold my little Felix in her arms when he was bleeding on the stones of the Mycenaean theater. You could not save him as I have saved your daughter. . . ."

Horrified, Clara Brancoveanu watched the bloody hand reach out almost to caress her, touch her cheek. Miranda had sunk backward, closed her eyes. Her mother leaned against the wall, shrank away from the bloody fingers. And in the corner of the hearth, her hand fell on a pistol, her husband's old revolver, which Inez de Rougemont had stolen for herself.

There was no question of using it to protect herself from this ghost. In any case, she thought, Nicola Ceausescu did not mean her harm. Soon the phantom pulled itself erect again, swung around toward the men who had regrouped at the far wall. The yellow-faced Rezistenta man was holding out his own revolver, and now he fired it—once, twice. Jean-Baptiste never paused. But his expression changed, and his gentle, melancholy face turned dark with anger. Blood dripped from his ear.

Clara gripped her husband's pistol. She raised her other hand up to her face, and through her splayed fingers watched the old steward pull the poker and the tongs from the hearth stand, watched him raise them above his head.

Students of Nicola Ceausescu might have recognized the precise pose from the first act of *Madame Faust,* when the heroine gathers the two cavalry sabers from the floor, touches their tips together in an arc above her upturned face. The clean blades come together, a momentary hush before the carnage that precedes the curtain's fall. Now in the farmhouse library, Jean-Baptiste swung his poker in a circle. The clawed end caught in the nostril of one of Bocu's men, ripped a gash across his cheek while at the same time the sharp tongs came down.

11

The Brass Gates

7 · A Giant Walking

ONCE AGAIN ON SATURDAY there was an interval of quiet. In no sector of the line was it more welcome than in Staro Selo, where over the past week the Turks had managed to churn forward through the mud. There was fighting in the town itself. Several kilometers of trenches had been lost.

There had been speculation that for once the Turks would continue through the Sabbath. But on Friday night their guns went quiet, and the Roumanians pulled their own guns back. Men on both sides sobbed and cheered, climbed out of the mud to stand up straight, lift their faces to the rain. They lit fires in the dugouts, unwrapped their accordions and guitars. At numerous places Turkish soldiers came across with identical baskets of oranges and figs, an organized effort that managed to cause something genuine and unanticipated even so. Later the Turks staggered back across the no-man's-land, carrying half-empty bottles of schnapps.

Captain Gross's men were in reserve, and on Saturday morning he was called to battalion headquarters. This was in a farmhouse in a grove of poplars. He was in time for luncheon, which was not served to him. He stood where the secretary had directed him, and saluted as a parade of senior officers crossed the muddy floorboards and climbed the stairs. A dozen staff cars were drawn up in a field: long silver bonnets, little flags. The chauffeurs leaned against the doors to smoke their cigarettes. They helped push each other out of the mud.

Peter recognized the colonel, a small man with a bald forehead and a semicircle of white hair, who gave him a disgusted look as he strode past. After several hours a sergeant-major led him to a little room lined with cupboards, and heated with an enameled stove on bricks. There were wooden chairs, but he did not sit. The rain was intermittent on the narrow window over the drive.

Without preamble or announcement, a soldier came in and sat down next to the stove. He put his boots onto the grate.

He was an enormous man. His thick neck was ridged with muscle where it met his skull. His bald head shone as if it had been waxed and polished. He wore a dark green uniform without insignia, but Peter recognized him from photographs: General Ion Antonescu, commander of the Roumanian armies. He rocked back on his chair so that the front legs left the floor. "Tell me," he said, "why does a man refuse the Star of Hercules?"

"Sir?"

"You heard me."

The previous Monday, the company commander had put in Peter's name. On Wednesday he had withdrawn it, after Peter had requested it in writing.

"Sir, this is not a war of individuals. I said I would accept on behalf of my platoon."

Antonescu fetched some hazelnuts and a steel nutcracker from the pocket of his tunic. He cracked a nut and threw the shell into the grate. "Is that so?"

"Yes, sir."

"You are wrong. One man can win a battle by himself. I've seen it happen."

"Sir . . ."

"Don't talk to me. Heroes are different from good men, or even good soldiers. Real soldiers hate them, but they serve a purpose. I will send a photographer, and there will be a story in the newspaper. Is that understood? When I heard about this, I thought I had no use for one-armed officers like you. But I was wrong. I am sending you to Brasov."

"Sir?"

"Don't play the fool. My men deserve more than to be led by cripples. Cripples who will not follow the commands of their superiors. That is intolerable—direct orders! You will follow them now, by God. The Star of Hercules, or a court-martial—what were you doing in the no-man's-land, the night before the first assault? What have you to say to me? No, that is all. Have you ever heard of the Chevalier de Graz?"

"Sir?"

"Don't play the fool with me. You could be his son. He won a war for us on the wrestling ground on Sarayici Island. This was years ago."

"Sir, I am not the Chevalier de Graz."

"That is clear. But you will have to do. You will have the Order of Hercules and the thanks of a grateful nation. Do you understand me?"

"Sir."

"I have spoken to your colonel. We're pulling your men back for two weeks' restitution, anyway. The Eleventh has been shot to pieces. You will report to battalion headquarters in Brasov. It is your home."

"No—"

"It is your native place. You will not deny it in the newspapers."

All this time he had not looked at Peter, but had sat on the back legs of his chair, his boots propped on the grate. But now the wet leather started to smoke, and so he pushed himself away, rose to his feet. Peter looked up at his big, brutal face, whose expression nevertheless was complicated, and contained small elements of anxiety. "It is a matter of recruitment, and you are popular with the men. Otherwise there would be nothing to discuss. Count yourself lucky, Captain Gross—there's not much about you in the record. Peter Gross—I've heard your name before. In Bucharest, I think, before the change of government. Complicity in the murder of Felix Ceausescu—was that it?"

"Sir, it sounds to me as if that didn't matter anymore."

Small elements, now, of surprise and anger, but then Antonescu laughed. "Maybe you're right. De Graz's bastard son—we could at least hint at such a thing. I'll ask the liaison man. The adjutant will have your documents. . . ."

One hour later, Peter rode back toward Staro Selo in the back of a cart. His company was bivouacked in a field outside the wall, two rows of tents. But he asked to be left at the courthouse in the center of the town. Most of the wooden and brick structures had been destroyed in the barrage. Across the square, the courthouse was a smoking ruin. Though its dome had fallen, the stone temple was still intact. Light gleamed behind its broken windows, patched with pieces of oiled paper.

This was the field hospital for the region, a dismal place where Peter spent as much time as he could. All day they'd been evacuating patients in horse-drawn farm carts lined with hay, removing them to positions farther back. Peter had come from headquarters in one of these carts on its return trip; he had sat down on the wet bales. Now the cart joined a line of others waiting for more cargo along the north front of the building, while he climbed the steps on the other side, past the broken statue of the goddess of the harvest in the porch. Demeter of the wheat fields. She had lost her head, but still carried her bronze scythe, which struck Peter as ironic under the circumstances—a heavy, stupid piece of irony that matched his heavy mood.

Brasov—who wouldn't want to go to Brasov, two hundred kilometers away? And from there in his new capacity he could visit other villages up in the Vulcan Mountains. The general had confessed as much: No one cared about the death of Felix Ceausescu. Since the baroness's death, no doubt everyone had learned the truth, that she herself had shot him from the balcony overlooking the amphitheater. . . .

Maybe there was no longer any reason to keep away from Miranda Popescu. He looked around the porch, but his heart refused to lift. In Massachusetts years before, he had learned many poems about war. He had particularly liked long battle epics, written by Tennyson and others. But to please his mother he had learned some other kinds of poems, too. Even they served to romanticize the truth, though they were written by angry, wounded men:

What candles may be held to speed them all?
Not in the hands of boys, but in their eyes
Shall shine the holy glimmers of good-byes . . .

No, the rhythms were all wrong, the idiotic rhymes. How did it go?

What passing-bells for these who die as cattle?
Only the monstrous anger of the guns.
Only the stuttering rifles' rapid rattle . . .

No, absurd. Another way to glorify these deaths. There was nothing onomatopoeic about any of this here, under a gray stupid drizzle in the gray afternoon.

And the stench was intolerable. There was another cart in the stone porch where all the bedpans were emptied. It had almost disappeared in a mound of shit. Fully loaded, it was impossible to maneuver down the steps, so it was left up here. Fat, green-backed flies rose as he passed, a sign of spring, he supposed.

He went through the wooden postern into the nave. The pews were all gone, but some of the statues and paintings had remained, the tribulations of the goddess's life. A florid oil of her mourning over Persephone's tomb— no tears, but just a wise, pensive look. He could see it in the lantern light, and some long tapers were still burning over the prie-dieux. The side chapels were full of cots, or blankets laid out on the tiles. "Not in the hands of boys, but in their eyes." The boys turned their faces to him as he passed.

But the whole central part of the nave was empty now, the doctors and the patients gone. Peter's boots rang on the stones. Those left behind, he imagined, were the ones least likely to recover—gas victims, many of them, burned in their lungs. Or they were still bleeding through their bandages. But they watched him if their heads were uncovered—where were the orderlies, the nurses? Where were the men from Theta Company, whom he had seen laid here together at the base of this round column and then all the way back? Some had died, of course. He stopped a boy, fifteen years old, maybe, but with the white cuffs of the staff—"Where is Steiciuc and Dion? Where is Sabau? Where is . . . ?" but the boy knew nothing and was in a hurry. Peter let him go.

Some were left in the corner of the wall, wrapped up in blankets on the stone floor. Ioan Bratescu was there, eighteen years old, thin as a stick. A cup of water on the floor beside him—how could he eat? The whole top of his head was wrapped in grimy bandages, which covered his eyes and nose; Peter sat down beside him. He took the boy's hand in his left hand. More poetry occurred to him, a sad, stupid poem:

But Sir Richard bore in hand all his sick men from the land,
Men from something in something, very carefully and slow,
And he laid them in the ballast down below.

"Captain," whispered the boy.

He squeezed his hand. Peter gave him some water through a piece of reed, but he couldn't talk. He was too stupid with laudanum. But Peter talked to him anyway, and told him how they were being sent back to Brasov to wait for reinforcements—it wasn't true, of course. So far as Peter knew, he was the only one to go, the only one, also, who didn't have a mother or father or sister or brother or friend in the vicinity of Brasov. To him it was a town like any other.

Bratescu squeezed his hand. Across the chapel, a pile of blankets moved, and another face turned toward him, a man he recognized. It was the black man from the Fifty-third, the Abyssinian spy, still in his black uniform. What was he doing here? He had a broken leg. Even these butchers could reset a broken leg.

At intervals during the previous week, Peter had wondered what had happened to this man. For his part Peter had said nothing to his commanding officer, who disliked him anyway. Since Andromeda had stolen the hieroglyphs, there was no point, he'd told himself. He would have had to acknowledge where he'd been—for what? And of course the push had come that night.

"You are going to Brasov?"

"Yes."

"Brasov," repeated the man, the corporal from the Fifty-third, and the way he said it suggested a grand, perfect place, a shining city in the mountains, walls of spun sugar, narrow spires that reached the sky. Not, in any case, an ordinary provincial capital. "My grandfather had a dairy farm outside Sacele," he said. "That's by the stream. I used to go out in the mornings and spin round with my arms held out. I'd fall down and the sky would spin around. Not so long ago."

"How long?" Peter asked, uncurious.

"Oh, I was there last night."

Peter could believe it. He had seen these doctors with their teaspoons and syringes. Laudanum was what they knew. Laudanum and amputations. Now he saw the foreshortened leg, the weeping bandage, and his right arm ached. "Why didn't they take you?" he asked. "Was it because . . . ?"

"I have a fever," said the man.

He had a fever, but his teeth were chattering. Lying beside him, Bratescu squeezed Peter's left hand. His other arm itched and ached under the prosthesis, a phantom sympathy. "I don't mind," said the black man across the way. "I took a risk for peace. These others have risked everything for war, is that so different? But I am being punished. You don't think I am a traitor, Captain Gross?"

"No—"

"I've seen you come here for the others. You are famous here. I wanted you to stop for me. My spirit or my angel—I have prayed, isn't that foolish? We are in a temple, and I wonder what will come out of me. Men die, and there are vermin everywhere—maggots, lice, rats. Am I crazy to hope for something better? Do you think I am a traitor? I worry so much—"

He was delirious. Ioan Bratescu squeezed Peter's hand. "But I think God is good," murmured the corporal from the Fifty-third. "Not these stupid gods, but the God who hears our prayers. My friends would be ashamed to hear me talk like this. And yet here you are, going to Brasov on the next train. And I wonder if you will do something for me."

Peter wondered, too. "I don't know," he said.

"You see it's wrapped up in the bandage. It's the last place they'd look. I have seen them rob the dead; I don't want that. You could have robbed me yourself, or had me shot. You see I am sparing you the trouble—this is the price of my death, and I want you to bring it to my sister in Brasov, Chloe Adira in the Strada Cerbului. She and my mother have no one but me. Please, I think you are my angel or a ghost. Will you go to Chiselet and find this terrible weapon? Just you and no one else—it is not something for the soldiers. No, no—Brasov. Strada Cerbului—will you do this for me?"

Lying beside him, Ioan Bratescu squeezed Peter's hand, a soft, tiny pressure.

It was not true that Peter had no memory of Brasov, or of Sacele either. His father had had a hunting cabin in the hills. Sacele was a pretty place, a Transylvanian village on the east side of the stream.

His knees ached from squatting, and he longed to stand up straight. The temple was dark now. Dusk showed through the narrow windows. He had to go. He didn't want to get caught in the sunset.

But he was too late. Just a few guns at first, and Peter could imagine the high arc of the rockets. Then the thunder of the howitzers, a giant walking in the town. It wouldn't last long. An hour, maybe two. The attack would come at dawn.

With aching knees, he stayed for several minutes more. When an explosion shook Bratescu's fingers open, he removed his hand, rose to his feet. The corporal—Janus Adira, the name came back—had stretched his leg straight out across the gap. The bulge under the bandages was easy to see. The money was hot and damp. A stinking wad of reichmarks. There was a letter, too.

"You didn't betray me, did you?" said Janus Adira. "My angel—in the hospital I was expecting the police. And I asked myself—what happened to the message from Addis Ababa? Do you still have that letter? It cost my life. Promise me you'll see it is delivered. Chloe will know."

"I promise," Peter said, feeling foolish. God knew where the man's hieroglyphs were now. "I promise," he repeated as he stood up straight.

What had Antonescu said—that he had no room for cripples in his army? Other cripples were demobilized and sent home. Peter walked back to the porch without looking around. Where was Miranda now? What was she doing now? Would he see her soon?

He stood for a moment under the columns, looking at the fires. Then he turned up his collar, pulled down his cap, used his teeth to replace his glove. A priest or monk slipped from the doorway, took him by his right arm. "You can't go out in this."

The noise was deafening. "It's okay," Peter said in English. Then he ambled down the steps into the rain.

8 A Puncture Wound

RADU LUCKACZ RETURNED to the city in time for Elena Bocu-Bibescu's funeral, though he did not attend. The Rezistenta men—what remained of them—had been dispatched from Stanesti village and escorted as far as Rimnicu by a detachment of reserves. There they'd been permitted to re-claim their carbines from the baggage car, and immediately the lieutenant had put Luckacz under a sort of unofficial arrest. Once they had descended from the Gara de Nord, he'd brought him straight to the People's Palace.

There they had waited for a long time in an antechamber to one of the reception rooms on the ground floor. Luckacz sat in an uncomfortable armchair while the lieutenant paced the polished floor. Still aggrieved, he clapped his hands together, scratched at his thin sides, a dark expression on his narrow face. He did not look at Luckacz, who sat with his hands in his lap, wondering if he'd be put in the same cell as before, wondering if they'd let him keep his clothes this time.

He had lost his hair quite suddenly the year before. He had had to shave his black moustache. Now for the first time he felt an itching on his scalp and upper lip—there was some stubble there. It was eveningtime. Light flickered in the glass chimney.

Or was it possible he might be put to death because of what had occurred? The lieutenant hoped so, had hinted at it on the train. If you believed the rumors, one entire wing of the enormous palace had been broken up into interrogation cells, and there was talk of secret graveyards and mass graves.

He had not managed to see his wife or Katalin, had not even managed to send them a postal card. Surely there'd be no reprisals. He couldn't stand the thought of that.

Bocu made them wait. Luckacz sat back in his armchair in the overheated room. As often when he wanted to doze or fall asleep he thought about Nicola Ceausescu's face, brought it to mind in various moods and casts of light. Often his dreams would begin with her turning toward him acknowledging him, saying something. "Ah, my dear old friend."

Sometimes she would appear to him naked as he had last seen her on the boards of the Ambassadors, the blood dripping from her breasts. She had leapt over the smoking footlights as the crowd scattered and made way, until she had imprisoned him in his fauteuil. Her hands were on the armrests, and she leaned over him.

Or else sometimes she appeared in all her splendor, arrayed as if for battle in some perfect evening gown, her face as beautiful as Diana's or Cleopatra's or any of the warrior goddesses under their helmets of copper-colored hair. Now in Bocu's antechamber, as Luckacz fell asleep, she assumed the shape most poignant to him—as he'd last seen her in her chamber in the People's Palace, the small lines around her mouth and in the corners of her eyes. She had taken off her gold-rimmed spectacles to look at him. "How could you doubt me?" she said now. "How could you accuse me of these terrible crimes? How could I have harmed these boys—I loved them. I protected them. And is that what you actually think, that I lay down with a woman as if with a man?"

Sick with remorse, Luckacz opened his eyes. He had been startled by a noise. Colonel Bocu entered the room, laughing and chuckling, his cravat undone.

He had an unlit cigar between his teeth, which he removed, examined, and threw into the unlit grate. Shards of tobacco were in his teeth; he spat onto the hearth. It appeared he had been interrupted in the middle of a conversation. Lively companions, it appeared, had been abandoned on the other side of the swinging door.

"Don't get up. No, you'll appreciate this," he said, still laughing. "A man leaves his house the morning after his wedding night, and goes directly to a certain establishment, where he'd been known to visit before his marriage. And the proprietress, I suppose you'd call her, takes him into the parlor and tells him, 'Was it just as I said?' And he says . . ."

Like the last time Luckacz had seen him, he was carrying an open bottle of champagne and two glasses, all in his left hand. It was as if he had not put them down since then, though the wine itself was always for other people, Luckacz guessed—Bocu himself was never drunk. His sloppiness, his untied cravat—it was all part of a game he played.

He arranged the bottle and the glasses on a square table near the hearth. "'Practice makes adequate,'" he said. "Isn't that priceless?" The lamplight glinted on his square, even teeth as he turned toward them—"Now. Tell me what happened. A fiasco, as I understand."

Luckacz stared at the hat in his lap. Because he was a prisoner, he supposed he was not expected to respond. And the lieutenant seemed eager; he had leapt to his feet when Bocu entered the room. He had thin lips, bad teeth. "Chief, everything would have been perfect if we had followed our plan. But this fellow ruined everything. He gave away our positions when he barged in the door. He broke into the place, ruined the moment of surprise. I didn't even know where he was. When we finally stopped searching to approach the premises, the alarm had already been raised. The old woman had already managed to send a message to the village. It was bad luck that a company of infantry reserves . . ."

He was interrupted by Bocu's laugh. "Come, lieutenant, don't be so severe. Yes, I know. Antonescu has sent word we are not welcome even in Rimnicu from now on. What do you think of that? I swear, if this keeps up, you won't be able to wear your uniform outside your own water closet. Does that concern you?"

"Sir—"

"It's all right! You must be calm. We will prevail, you understand. Do you know why? Because we have the people on our side. These setbacks . . ."

He shrugged. As he was speaking, he had approached the young lieutenant to stand in front of him eye to eye. They were almost the same height, and Luckacz could see how terrified the young man was, the sheen of moisture on his skin. But now Bocu smiled again, and he reached out and grabbed hold of the lieutenant's shoulder with his big hand, squeezing him, catching him in an awkward half-embrace. "Don't worry! This man Andromedes, we will catch him another time. I have something planned."

He let his hand drop. The unfortunate lieutenant stepped back, brought his fingers to his forehead. "Sir, if I may, I'd like to volunteer—"

"Nonsense! Nonsense! You've made garbage out of this, and that's enough. And I can't spare the men—I'm joking!"

"Chief, I appreciate that. I want to say again that this was not my fault. This fellow—"

Looking at the colonel's face, Luckacz could tell the young man had made a mistake. "Not your fault?" Bocu asked, his voice suddenly cold. "May I remind you that Domnul Luckacz was once chief of the metropolitan police under Nicola Ceausescu and the German occupation of this city?"

"But that says everything! He was a traitor! A collaborator! How can you trust a man like this?"

Bocu tensed the muscles of his jaw, balled his hands into fists. "Maybe," he said softly. "But he was not too stupid to understand I wanted the Popescu girl alive, and her mother, too—a woman who is, I remind you, a heroine of Great Roumania and our struggle against foreign domination. And I am not so stupid as to not have kept an independent witness to these events. You meant to kill them—these defenseless women. Isn't it so?"

"Sir, I—"

How was it possible, Luckacz thought, that the lieutenant could have made such a mistake? Or was it only now that Bocu had reconsidered, changed his mind? He smiled again. "The Rezistenta does not fight against women. On the contrary, we embrace them. Luckacz is not so stupid that he doesn't understand I am a widower. Maybe you saw the flags at the station, the black crepe. A man like me—though I am shy to say it, I need women around me. This Popescu girl is heiress to the oldest family in Roumania, descended from gods, I seem to remember from my schoolboy days. Did you find her beautiful?"

"Chief, I—"

The young lieutenant was desperate now. Luckacz wiped his hands on the shapeless crown of his hat. Startled, he wondered what he should do or say—nothing, obviously. Miranda Popescu was a known fugitive, of course, wanted in connection with the murder of a policeman in Braila, never brought to trial. But did it matter? Obviously not. Bocu didn't care. History had turned the page.

"You did not find her beautiful?"

"Sir, I had no idea. If you had told me . . . It was not my fault!"

Again, a terrible mistake. This time Bocu was not forbearing. He tilted his head, an odd, wry expression on his face. "Lieutenant—this is what I heard. Nicola Ceausescu's steward—the man was sixty-five if he was a day. I heard he attacked you with a pair of tongs, killed some of your men in that farmhouse, chased the rest all down the drive. I heard you abandoned their corpses in a ditch where they were mauled by wild beasts. Their bodies lay in a ditch, bitten and mauled—is that your fault? You blame Antonescu's men, but they are not responsible for this. How many did I send with you? How many have returned? Just now their mothers and fathers have been asking me."

Suddenly he was in a rage. He reached out to clamp his powerful hand around the back of the lieutenant's neck, pulling him forward and off-balance. Luckacz rose to his feet, but it was too late to intervene. The lieutenant staggered and fell backward. Bocu seemed to have punched him once on his breast over his heart, and now he fell back onto the floor. He shuddered, sucked at the air, and now Luckacz could see the blood on his uniform where he'd been hit—not really so much blood.

It was like a conjuring trick. Bocu knelt over him, pushing his lank hair from his forehead. "Poor boy. Poor boy. There. It's all right. That's the end."

When he stood up he had a knife in his hand, an edgeless stiletto which he wiped on a handkerchief. How had he produced it so quickly? Did he have it hidden in his sleeve? He turned toward Luckacz. "This is unfortunate. I will never get used to it. My opinion is a man in my position is a coward to rely on others, some judge or court-martial. A man has a right to look me in the eye. Smell my breath. But I won't forget how terrible this is, terrible and cruel. So it serves a double purpose. A man in my position. Unlike you, this fellow had no family, of course. Otherwise . . ."

Bocu was quite obviously insane, Luckacz thought. He stood polishing the edgeless blade, grinding his teeth, his face furious. Then he smiled. "When I came in I thought I was rude to only bring two glasses. Now, you see . . ."

He dropped the knife onto the table as if it were suddenly too hot to hold. He poured two glasses of champagne, but did not drink. "Help me," he said, and Luckacz helped him pull down a curtain on one side of the antechamber, wrap the body in the heavy velvet cloth. "A man must do these things himself," Bocu said. "Otherwise you forget."

And when the corpse was stowed against the wall, he sat down with Luckacz on the settee. "Something is not right," he said. "Something is not right with this story of Jean-Baptiste, the demon steward with his tongs. I heard he was bleeding from a gunshot wound. So I must ask you. Inspector Luckacz, in your capacity as a policeman. What in hell happened in that place?"

"Your excellency, it is difficult—"

Bocu raised his hand. "Not another word. No excuses! This is a matter of your future, after all!"

Perhaps, Luckacz thought, they might put him in a different cell. Something above the surface of the ground. Something with a window.

And yet how was it that he still felt any loyalty to Nicola Ceausescu, who had betrayed him so shamefully with Sasha Andromedes or whatever his name was—he could not bear to think of her as a woman! How could he still feel any loyalty to someone who had murdered her own son, as well as that boy in the Strada Camatei? "Do you have an experience with ghosts?" he said at last.

Bocu laughed, an expulsion of breath. He clapped him on the shoulder. "You do amuse me, inspector—please, I must not interrupt!"

Sullenly, hesitantly, Luckacz tried to tell him what had happened. It was possible sometimes for dying soldiers on the battlefield to be possessed by something larger than themselves, some force or power that allowed them to perform feats of strength that were impossible—many scientists had observed this. And at certain moments, the body can be impervious to pain. Yes, it was true—Jean-Baptiste had murdered seven men, and he had bludgeoned the first two casualties at least with a pair of iron tongs. But after that he had picked up another weapon, a carbine with a fixed bayonet. . . .

But Jean-Baptiste was already dead! It was a different spirit that inhabited him. As he spoke, Luckacz listened mournfully to the sound of his own ugly and officious voice, while at the same time he was remembering the Baroness Ceausescu, how she had stood before him and whispered to him like a lover, "You stumbled at the end, my old companion. . . ." How could he express all that?

He tried. And at the end Bocu was staring at him, smiling. "I think we kept you locked away too long, my friend. I think you need some rest and quiet, and some country air."

Then he raised his hand, tilted his head as if listening for some sound outside the door. "Maybe listen to some music—hah! In the village bandstand."

And then his smile changed. "I understand you must have suffered much from your bad treatment. These are explanations from the past, while I look to the future." He gestured toward the dead lieutenant, wrapped in his cocoon—"This man failed me. So have a care! Go—now go! I am a busy man. Too busy for such foolishness."

Gripping his hat by the brim, Luckacz staggered to his feet. He moved toward the door, then paused. From Bocu's expression, it was impossible to believe this wasn't a cruel trick.

But when he looked back, he saw the colonel was laughing at him. He sprawled back on the settee, one hand raised, feet spread apart: "You will find I have not even interrupted your pension, with a supplement for various services!"

He rose suddenly to his feet, came toward Luckacz with his hand held out. He had cut himself with his own knife, Luckacz saw—just a beaded scratch along his forefinger. "You think I'm playing a game," he continued. "You tell yourself one man lives, another man dies—where's the justice in that? Then you console yourself—'He is arbitrary, like a tyrant!' I tell you, in the dark of night, lying next to your fat wife in your own bedroom, you must not even think these things." Again he indicated the lieutenant in the corner of the room.

He is mad, Luckacz thought, as he scuttled out the door. It was no comfort to imagine Bocu thought the same of him.

THE DEAD LIEUTENANT IN the antechamber had given one description of what had happened in the farmhouse library the night Jean-Baptiste had died. Radu Luckacz gave another. But all things have their analogue in the secret world. That night in Stanesti-Jui, needing to protect her mother and herself, Miranda had clenched the tourmaline in her right hand.

She had come to herself on the bare hillside underneath Johannes Kepler's tower. She was surrounded by ghosts and the spirit creatures of the Rezistenta soldiers, small animals that climbed out of the scree. But there was the Elector of Ratisbon in his cutaway frock coat, a silver derringer in his hands. And there was Nicola Ceausescu, crouched on a boulder with a strange flash of sunlight in her copper-colored hair. Elsewhere the storm was breaking and the sky stank of ozone and the wind blew the mist away.

Nicola Ceausescu's face was scarred and torn. When she raised herself up, Miranda saw she was naked.

And there was Aunt Aegypta climbing up the hill, dressed in her veil and fox-head stole, her gloved hand outstretched, shouting out some kind of warning or direction. Miranda didn't want to hear any of that. She had made up her mind what to do. In the farmhouse library, the lieutenant stood with his gun cocked. Miranda didn't have much time. She placed the tourmaline on a flat stone, gave it a little pat. She couldn't hold it in a tyger's claws.

When a tyger moves, the world surrounds her in a sphere of silence. Birds don't sing. Weaker beasts lie still. Except for her hunger, she might be happy to accept an illusion, that she is the only creature still alive. But it is her hunger that makes her stretch and move, and there were creatures in the rocks. She ripped open their refuges and found them. She tore into their backs and the rest ran shrieking away.

This was a matter of a few minutes. But when she looked up with her tyger's eyes, the world had changed.

She had an impression of a marmalade cat that crouched above her on the boulder in the light, its coat matted and seedy, its face split and ripped, its teeth missing or broken—she had seen this cat before! It was not a threat to her. Nor was the elector a threat, coiled among the rocks in his snake's shape.

What was happening in Stanesti-Jui? Miranda saw a little bird, a brandy-wine bird with iridescent feathers, pushed and buffeted by the wind in the pass. The snake had crawled down from the tower and was poised on a flat rock, its hooded head raised up, while the bird stooped and struck at it as if it had been a lizard or a worm in the hedge on a summer morning.

Could it be possible the bird thought it was protecting the tyger? There was no need! The snake rose up and struck, and the bird was in its mouth, caught by one wing.

And then the tyger was bounding up the slope, and with its heavy paw it crushed the snake, pulled it apart, freed the bird who fluttered down into a gap between the stones. And the tyger bit the snake's head off, ruined it so it would have no life or future in this world or any other. She pulled its flesh from its bones and then, unsated, looked down through the rockfall for the cat. But it had disappeared.

Miranda felt both tired and exhilarated. What was happening in Stanesti-Jui? What had she managed to accomplish there? Her mother and Andromeda—were they safe? She left the bird fluttering in its crack among the stones. She descended down to where she'd left the tourmaline.

By that time she had resumed her human shape. She had rebuttoned her clothes. She had found the stone where she had laid the jewel, hidden it for safekeeping. But when she came back it was gone.

She searched on her hands and knees in the waning light, combing through the grass. It couldn't have gone far. This was the rock—she was sure this was the rock. It was still damp, still slick with the jewel's grease.

Once before it had seemed to migrate under her fingers when she went to discover it again. But this was different. After fifteen minutes' search, she sat back on her heels. Someone had taken it, some animal or man. Was that why the Elector of Ratisbon had been spying on her from Kepler's tower? Was that why the marmalade cat was stalking through the rocks? She'd been an idiot.

The wind came up again and she was cold, her arms covered in gooseflesh.

She was wearing inside clothes, a linen shirt, wool trousers, boots. She fingered the bracelet on her wrist, then got to her feet. She ran her hands through her hair, combing it back. First things first.

The brandywine bird had disappeared. Miranda did not look for the corpse of the Elector of Ratisbon. It had fallen into a crease between the rocks, and all she could see was the ripped sleeve, the small white hand. The wind had blown the clouds away. The sky was full of stars.

Often Stanley had taken her to the observatory at the top of the science building, or else they'd just lain out in the backyard while he named the stars and planets and told her stuff—a long way away. She climbed up the slope again, over the rock slope where the little stream ran down out of the tarn. She washed the stains from her hands, washed her face, and then continued up toward the shelter of the tower. She didn't want to get much colder than she was, didn't relish the idea of sitting up outside the stone cell with the hidden creature in it—for how long? What were night and day in this place? She would wait for morning and she would search again.

But in the litter of broken masonry she found something she didn't remember, a pile of dry sticks. Stanley always said you should carry matches, but even he usually didn't. Her pockets were empty except for some silver coins.

She sat down in a crevice between some larger rocks and put her back against the wall. No, she couldn't stay here in this high, exposed place. She would rest, and she would see if she could summon up the tyger once again.

Because she was tired and alone, there was no reason to choose one moment rather than another. The stars moved overhead. And Miranda sat and thought about Stanley and Rachel and their house in Berkshire County. Or she thought about Peter Gross and Andromeda. These thoughts did not take the form of long chains of circumstance, stretching into the future and the past. They did not take the shape of decisions or possible decisions, or remembered circles of events. Instead she saw a sequence of disordered images laid down like playing cards—Rachel had a tarot deck. It was something like that. And at the same time there were wisps of unconnected feelings. She imagined herself in a space between worlds, between sleep and wakefulness. She saw a tower with the roaring beast inside. She saw the sun and moon together in the sky. She saw the map of the world, which disappeared when the wind disturbed its surface. She saw Peter in the brick gazebo in Cismigiu Park. She saw a flashing light before her eyes, an intermittent light in the darkness. She smelled Andromeda's rank breath, and then a sequence of other smells—barnyard smells, pig shit and churned earth. Rachel had belonged to an organic farm on Route 43, and sometimes in the summer Miranda had gone to collect huge masses of bok choi and exotic lettuce—Andromeda had come, too, though she pretty much only ate hamburgers. Once she had caused a stink by smoking a cigarette in the distribution center. Miranda could smell it now.

She saw the little light flashing in the rocks, and smelled the ordure and gunpowder and tobacco, and saw the old man materialize beside the wall, a cigarette between his lips, a lighter in his hand. He was thin and pale and dressed in formal clothes: a white waistcoat and wide, shiny lapels that were decorated with military ribbons and insignia, among them the eight-pointed Star of Roumania—she knew this man. She recognized him from his portrait in the People's Palace, his big eyebrows and delicate wide ears, his bald forehead and his face covered with fine wrinkles. He was the old baron, Felix Ceausescu, Nicola Ceausescu's dead husband, dead a long time.

She got up from the ground, put her hand out to keep him away. But he smiled, exhibited his splayed, gloved fingers, took a puff on his cigarette, ground it out under his heel. He started in at once: "Mademoiselle. This is a cold and lonely place for someone like yourself. Allow me—please? No? You understand who I am? Believe me, I mean you no harm, and in any case I am not strong enough. But I know what it means to feel cold, do you see?"

He reached out his hands and turned them, as if absorbing warmth from her. "No? But I can help. Please," he said, and he was kneeling down among the broken sticks, producing folded letters and envelopes and documents from the various pockets of his jacket. "There, you see? These are the official papers from your father's trial. And there are more where those came from—I have a supply! Never a lack of them—look!" He crumpled them in balls and pushed them down among the sticks, then lit them with his silver lighter, engraved with some heraldic device. The flames leapt up, blue at first.

Miranda was not reassured. She kept to her feet, watching, waiting. But the flames were a comfort, and the old ghost scarcely paid attention to her once it was started. He perched on the edge of a fallen chunk of masonry, drinking out of a silver flask and laying out some small meat pastries in his handkerchief on the corner of the stone. "Please," he said. "It's better, isn't it?"

And it was better, and it seemed to Miranda as if the firelight had made a little room around them, a room with walls and a ceiling defined by the reach of the light. A small, irregular-shaped room with one solid wall behind her. She leaned against it. And for a moment she imagined the dark chamber on the other side of the stone wall, where there was—something. Beyond the limit of sensation she could hear its weak breath, its furtive movement.

Baron Ceausescu turned to her, the firelight glowing on the ridges and stretched membranes of his ears. She wondered if he knew what she was thinking. "What is that, I wonder?" he said. "What is that sound? Johannes Kepler was the father of us all—the explorers, I mean. The father of alchemical conjuring. He built this place and put a lock on this door, and the world changed. The patterns came clear—no, that would be too much to say. Not clear, not accessible, but . . . possible to think. Do you understand?"

"No."

The baron smiled. His lips were dark. "Suppose there was a book in your father's house. And suppose your father used that book for everything he did, a complicated book of directives, like a cookery book, perhaps, and it is very difficult, perhaps in a foreign language. But your mother and your father understand it, because they understand the language and perhaps even wrote the book themselves, or parts of it. In addition, they are cleverer than you. But if you want to use the book, wouldn't you choose a moment when they were gone from home, or even you might lock them out, lock the door of their study or library, so you could examine this book?"

"I don't think so," said Miranda.

The baron had replaced his flask. He had laid out his pastries. And with one gloved hand he was fingering the points of silver star on his lapel—they must have been sharp. Miranda could see how the cloth on his fingertips was scored and pierced and bloody from what must have been his constant and obsessive habit. He smiled. "Then you're a fool. Once you get a taste for deciphering . . . But look! I have some food for you."

Miranda guessed he had never had any children. But wasn't the boy in the Mycenaean amphitheater, wasn't that his son? No, he must have died when young Felix was only a baby. He was not a man who could fool you, the way most fathers can. There was an eagerness, a greediness in the way he stared at her, the way he offered the six pastries on his handkerchief, laid out in a perfectly spaced line. And when she smiled, wrinkled her nose, a look of disappointment and anger contorted his thin features.

He had called her a fool. But she wasn't so stupid as to never have read any fairy stories or mythologies. Once Andromeda's cousin had spent a week in the house on Syndicate Road. He was just back from a trip to Thailand, and he told them stories about modern pirates who would sit next to you on some overnight bus, and want to talk English and be your friend, and give you food out of little containers. If you took it, or drank out of the bottles they offered, you woke up four days later in the hospital, robbed of everything. Just like Persephone in the land of the dead, Andromeda's mother had remarked.

"What are you doing here?" said the Baron Ceausescu. Now suddenly he was impatient: "You don't belong here. You don't deserve Magister Kepler's precious jewel—you don't deserve it. You are not one of us."

He threw the pastries aside and leapt at her, which was no surprise. She had been eyeing one of the burning sticks. She drew the stick out of the fire as he came at her. Nor did she feel afraid. He was an old man, after all. "Idiot!" he said. "Do you think I care about these things? Do you think they warm me, burn me? No, but I can feel the heat in your body, that much I can feel."

But he'd been right. He wasn't strong enough to overpower her, and whatever he claimed, the stick kept him at bay. Like everything else that happened to her in the hidden world, these events had an unreal quality that made them tolerable—this was not her actual self that was doing these things, facing these dangers. Her actual self—at least she hoped so—had chased the Rezistenta men out of the house. Her actual self had saved Andromeda's life. What was she doing now? Was she lying in bed? Relaxing or celebrating after a job well done? Or was she talking, moving, eating, sleeping, walking in the fields with the black dogs?

She backed away out of the half-circle of light. The ghost glared at her.

And as she threw the burning stick in his face, he staggered back. His patent-leather boots slipped on the rocks, and he fell down.

Once under shelter of darkness, she climbed down through the rocks to where the grass began. It was slippery with dew. Her clothes were wet. The moon was behind the peaks. But she could see the rock chute and the pine-clad slope. Better than that, she could see the lantern flickering below her where her aunt waited at the edge of the wood, wearing her old-fashioned velvet dress, lace collar, little fur hat, and her fox-fur stole with the fox heads hanging down. None of these ghosts was exactly dressed for the occasion.

"Hush," whispered Aegypta Schenck. She led Miranda into the trees. Miranda didn't recall this place from her ascent, this tangled patch of pines. The slope was more gradual than she remembered

The oil lantern was extinguished now, and her aunt had pressed her down into a hollow at the base of a tree, carved out of layers of pine needles and sticky with sap. Sure enough, soon they could see the baron coming toward them down the slope, his light feet clattering on the stones. He continued past them without stopping.

Miranda tried to move when he'd gone past, but her aunt still held her. She was a powerful woman with strong arms and shoulders under her old-lady clothes. Miranda remembered that, remembered struggling against her in Insula Calia, and lay still.

"The dead are easy to deceive," said Aegypta Schenck von Schenck.

"I'll keep that in mind."

"He's searching for Kepler's Eye," whispered Aegypta Schenck.

"No duh."

"What do you mean? Child—don't be impertinent."

But then she let her up, and Miranda pulled herself away. She supposed it was too much to expect a ghost to thank her, but even so—a little more kindness might have been appropriate. The brandywine bird had been caught in the elector's jaws.

Miranda looked away, looked into the dark branches above their heads, where another small body hung suspended. A woodchuck or a marten, one of the indiscriminate category of creatures that Stanley had called "wombats." Had the white tyger thrown him up there? She did not recognize this place. There was a wound over the creature's furry breast.

Aunt Aegypta didn't notice. "He was a suicide, like Ratisbon. They always come back here. They find it difficult to stay quiet in the land of the dead. This I know. It is difficult to leave the things you love. The plans you laid. So they hover here, still at the threshold. Still trying to influence events. They are victims of their own self-control. Their desire to control others, which lingers."

She'd released her grip, and they sat among the sticky roots of the tree. It occurred to Miranda that her aunt might have been talking about herself, or else partly about herself. In a literal sense she had planned her own death, prepared for it, goaded Nicola Ceausecu into murder. "He follows his wife," said Aegypta Schenck. "Always at a distance, because she will not let him come near. But he tries to protect her. I think it is for her sake that he searches for the jewel."

Miranda looked up at the pine marten in the tree. Now suddenly she guessed what had happened to the tourmaline. "He doesn't know she's already found it," she said.

Aunt Aegypta shrugged. She continued on as if she hadn't heard: "I have seen her up above here in the pass. She takes the shape of a cat sometimes. An orange cat. Half of her destroyed on the stage of the Ambassadors. The other half . . ." She frowned. "What did you say?"

It was lighter now. In this place, Miranda thought, perhaps the nights weren't as long. The sky was pearly. Her aunt sat with her skirt rucked up, her stockings torn and stained. What a joke, Miranda thought, to go through eternity like this. Aegypta Schenck had loved her horses, dogs, and guns. She'd lived alone by herself in a cabin in the woods, a strong woman with a coarse, mannish face, dark eyes that had that odd, yellowish cast. Now she frowned, peered at Miranda with her little eyes. Hanks of grayish hair had come loose from her long, U-shaped, tortoiseshell pins. The round hat was perched on the side of her head. The little veil hung down.

"Child, what did you say?"

Miranda hugged her arms across her chest. "I saw a cat just like that. I laid the tourmaline on a rock. It's gone now."

"Child, that is bad news." Aunt Aegypta's voice was even and she didn't sound upset.

Miranda turned to look at her. In an early memory, one of the few

Miranda had taken from Roumania to Berkshire County, her aunt had stood in these same clothes on the platform of Mogosoaia station in the snow. She had pressed the essential history into Miranda's hands, her expression full of anguish and regret.

But the little wicked fox heads had smiled at her. Now there was something else in Aunt Aegypta's face, a hint of satisfaction.

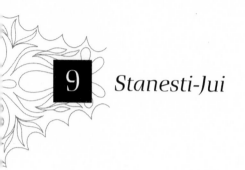

9 Stanesti-Jui

TIME IS NOT IDENTICAL in the hidden world, the passage of time, the duration of events. Down below, in the farmhouse in Stanesti-Jui, Miranda lay asleep. She had not woken since the night of the storm. Three women sat around her bed on the second floor. Lieutenant Prochenko was also there, dressed in borrowed clothes.

"How long has it been?" he asked.

Inez de Rougemont gave him a long look, but she said nothing. Magda de Graz raised her head. Back bent from osteoporosis, she sat perched on the edge of her armchair, a small woman who peered up at the rest of them through cataract-occluded eyes.

Her voice was tremulous and soft. "Lieutenant, we have told you we have no desire to listen to your questions or opinions. As far as it concerns myself, your welcome here is at an end. By your own admission you have led these ruffians to our door. By your own carelessness you have ruined a safe haven of fifteen years, as well as caused the death of an old man who never did you any harm. Can you not see the difference? My son the Chevalier de Graz, he left us in Bucharest because he found himself pursued. In Cismigiu Park. But you—"

Prochenko smiled. "It was your son's letter they found in my trousers' pocket. When I saw him in Staro Selo, he was the one who told me to come back."

"But these men were hunting you. Because of some carelessness or an adventure. Do you deny it?"

"Thirty hours," interrupted Clara Brancoveanu. She sat closest to the bedside on a low stool. She held her daughter's hand in her own hand, withered and soft at the same time. "Please don't argue. The lieutenant has been a faithful friend to us." She smiled shyly, hesitantly. "Domnul, for my part you are welcome here."

"I agree," said Inez de Rougemont. "We are too poor to send away our friends. A great deal needs to be done."

Earlier that day they had buried Jean-Baptiste on the hillside. Anton had fetched the cantor from the temple in the village. He had played the violin, and the plaintive noise had set the dogs to howling.

Jean-Baptiste was the only man they buried. Soldiers had already dragged away the bodies of the Rezistenta men, broken and torn. Bears, the sergeant had speculated. Bears had come out of the forest after the men were dead. But it had been a fiercer beast than that, the Condesa de Rougemont had told herself.

She had not been in the library when Jean-Baptiste had died. She'd seen nothing of what had happened. She'd been in the stables and had not returned until later. But she recognized the marks of the white tyger.

Now she sat in a chair in the corner of the bedroom, exhausted, leaning back. That morning she had sent away some of the men to look for another house in some other village—she hated the thought. Half her life she had spent fighting the same fight.

How was it possible she was still here after all these years, still holding the banner Frederick Schenck von Schenck had let slip from his hands? He was a man she'd loved without ever having possessed. And now the goal of a democratic republic in Roumania seemed further away than ever, further even than it had under the Empress Valeria or the German occupation.

Now Frederick's daughter had disappeared into the hidden world and not come back. Madame de Rougemont touched her fingers to the high bridge of her nose. How could she explain to Clara Brancoveanu what had happened, that she had sent the girl alone onto the mountain and had not guided her back down? How could she explain to Frederick in some imaginary conversation in her mind? How would she explain it to Zuzana Knauss and the others if they questioned her, in the castle on Borgo Pass or wherever else they might sit down together? She had not slept since the events of that night, since the death of Nicola Ceausescu's steward.

The Rezistenta man with the bad skin and foul breath had pulled his hired thugs away into the darkness of the house. Terrified of the murdered ghost, they had tried to take Prochenko and run away. Jean-Baptiste had pursued them, bleeding and shrieking, until he had collapsed on the threshold. But then something else had caught them in the dark, chased them down the road, dispersed them. Prochenko had come back limping and smiling, but that was all an act. He had drunk four glasses of brandy and then staggered up to bed.

It was not until she had already spoken with the soldiers and policemen from the village, and the body of the steward had been laid out in the stables, that Madame de Rougemont had come into the library again. Clara Brancoveanu was sitting on the hearth, her daughter's head in her lap. She'd looked up, bleary-eyed, in tears. "She won't wake up," she said.

But it was a strange kind of sleep, because sometimes Miranda almost woke. Sometimes she cried out, or rolled and struggled under the blankets. Now after thirty hours she lay quiet in her upstairs bed, her eyes open, her breath calm.

"We will find a use," murmured Inez de Rougemont. "There are ways he can redeem himself, I know."

She was talking about Lieutenant Prochenko and about herself as well. Prochenko paced back and forth scratching his hands. The condesa sighed. "There's a gun I must find. It is essential—did you see it on the table? It was in the room last night. If the Rezistenta made off with it, there will be a catastrophe. If they bring it to Bocu."

"I saw it," said the lieutenant. "The general's revolver."

"You understand what I am talking about? It was—"

"Of course. A big Webley-Doenitz, manufactured in the English style. It was not a standard bore—the bullets were made specially. The general used to wear it on his hip."

Madame Rougemont shook her head. "It has a different purpose now."

"Different to what?"

She was exhausted. Too tired to prevaricate: "Because of it—what should I say? You will not understand. There are two creatures from a secret place, brought here by force. One is almost like a butterfly, except it stings. The other will have grown by now because of the war. There must not be a third."

How could they understand? Clara goggled at her as if she'd lost her mind. Madame de Graz turned her head, squinting at her out of the corner of her eye, where she'd retained some vision. Only Prochenko seemed to find some meaning in her words. Why should that be so? Without a doubt she shouldn't even be discussing these things, not aloud. Not in front of these two women who were not entirely her friends, and in front of this strange hybrid of a man, conjured into being by Aegypta Schenck von Schenck.

But where was she to turn in her desperate hour? Her house—her refuge—had been discovered. She had found Isaac Newton's black book discarded in a corner of the room, but the gun had disappeared. And if she'd lost the girl as well—oh, it was too much to bear.

She remembered the last time she had seen Frederick in his cell at Jilava prison before his trial. She couldn't touch him, could not even touch his hands. But she had looked into his eyes and promised him and put her heart into the promise. Clara Brancoveanu was not there. She was home in bed in the middle of her pregnancy. The doctors had prescribed a regimen.

Lieutenant Prochenko shook his head. Somehow, the condesa thought, he knew what she was talking about. Now he came to squat beside her. He smelled like meat and blood and hair. "Madame," he said, "I understand it was wrong of me to come. I understand the trouble I have brought. But you must understand—this butterfly . . ."

He let his sleeve fall away from his delicate, hairy forearm. De Rougemont saw a line of scabs along his wrist, and then a larger sore—a puncture wound. "I have an interest in this."

"Lieutenant, if Bocu finds this gun—"

"Hush," he interrupted. "I have an interest. And there are other things I want to say to Colonel Bocu."

"Domnul," said Magda de Graz, peering at him out of the sides of her eyes. "There is also a letter for my son."

"Yes," continued Inez de Rougemont. "I believe the Turks have a new weapon in the Staro Selo district. I am wondering what to make if it—a line of turtles in the mud. If we could get this information to General Antonescu—"

It was idiotic, obviously, what she was saying. She was so tired. Magda de Graz blinked at her. Clara rubbed her eyes. Lieutenant Prochenko yawned. "I will retrieve your gun," he said. "Let's start with that."

He scratched at the sores on his wrist, pulled up his cuff. He stood up, yawned again, stretched. Clara Brancoveanu also rose, surrendered her place by her daughter's head. Miranda pulled away from her, clenched her hand into a fist. She groaned on the pillows.

"Lieutenant," said Princess Clara, and Madame de Rougemont was almost impressed by her quiet dignity, how she swallowed down her tears. "Lieutenant—I beg you will stay. You will not leave three old women and my sick girl? My husband trusted you, and I also—I am a beggar here, but everything I have is yours. You will not leave us?"

When Prochenko moved away from her, Inez de Rougemont felt a draft of new cold air. The warmth of his body had kept it from her. She watched his little bow, watched him take Princess Clara's hand, which she had offered him. "Ma'am," he said, "it's true these dogs are hunting me. I will come back when I can."

He gave her the name of a rooming house in Floreasca where he could be found. Then he went down on his knees beside Miranda's bed. Perhaps because he'd mentioned dogs, there seemed to the condesa something canine about the way he took Miranda's fingers, unclenched them, used them to rub his cheek, comb through his hair. Once again Madame de Rougemont was reminded of the last time she had said good-bye to Frederick Schenck in prison—she had not touched him. But she had tried to put her heart and every part of her body into her leave-taking, all without words.

Clara Brancoveanu began to cry. "What have you done?" she said, to no one in particular. "What have you done to my poor girl?"—words that tore de Rougemont between pity and vexation. When the lieutenant left the room, he took all the warmth with him, and so she followed him. She had already dispatched Anton to buy his ticket on the night train.

But she wanted to talk to him in private. She wanted to speak frankly.

The house had scarcely been her own since the terrible hour of Jean-Baptiste's death. Madame de Graz was making her own arrangements to return to Bucharest. She'd been clumping around the corridors, peering into every cupboard.

The condesa waited outside Prochenko's room until he reappeared. He was dressed for his journey in borrowed clothes that seemed to fit him perfectly, and which he had made stylish just by wearing them, just by turning up the collar of his jacket, looping a white scarf around his neck.

"Come," she said. She followed him outside.

Past midnight, she and Prochenko stood outside the farmhouse in the cold mountain air. They stood among the yew trees and juniper that grew between the barn and the road. The lieutenant smoked one of the cigarettes he had filched from Anton or else one of the grooms. His yellow hair curled over his collar. His handsome face, visible only by moonlight, gave the condesa an obscure kind of pleasure as she stood shivering in her overcoat, hands in the big pockets. "I couldn't question you in front of the others. I want to know what you have seen," she said.

He grimaced, expelled smoke between his teeth. He turned toward her with an odd expression. "It sounds ridiculous to say. But I suppose you are used to this. There's more to you than just an old lady living in the woods."

She smiled without joy. He took another puff of smoke. "Forgive me. What did I see? A naked manikin four centimeters tall. The wings bigger, big as my hand. Very delicate, disturbed by any current. It would bite me as I lay asleep or dozing—bite me or sting me. I showed you the scabs."

"And?"

He shrugged, dropped his cigarette end, ground it out under his boot heel. "It would find me. I would swat at it and it would move away. Once it got too close and I was able to grab it by its wing, put a stop to it."

This was good news. Hard to credit, but good news. "Really."

"I had its blood on me. I won't claim that was pleasant. But it hasn't come back."

And yet, why shouldn't it be possible to kill these things? They were physical manifestations, not spiritual ones. "I congratulate you. This is an achievement. But you are an unusual man. Anyone can see that. You won't take offense when I tell you . . ."

He laughed. "I won't take offense."

"It takes a special kind of man. Someone who can travel with these creatures in their same world. What would I call them? Demons, I suppose. Spirit demons. The next one will be harder. I won't pretend to you it is not dangerous to hunt."

Sometimes in waking dreams she would visit a place on the mountainside. Other women would be there. Their meetings had become less frequent since the war, but there was indirect communication also. In any case, they all agreed on this: "There will be no peace in Europe until this creature is discovered and destroyed. It is possible Bocu has found it, or he knows where it is. I don't know. But you must go to him first."

"Yes," said the lieutenant. "I'll ask him. I have something else to ask him, too."

"It is a powerful demon. Abcess is its name. It is red in color, and it will take the form of a toad. A winged toad. At the beginning they are small and weak, but it has grown, I'm sure. I will tell you something that is not literally true: It feeds on the blood and bodies of the dead."

Another cigarette was in Prochenko's mouth, so far unlit. "Huh," he said, and smiled, and she could see his big white teeth.

"Poisonous skin, I would imagine."

"Check," he said, which made no sense, until the countess realized he had switched from French to English. Even then the colloquialism was unknown to her. But he continued in the strange soft accent that he shared with Miranda Popescu and no one else, another misbegotten product, the condesa supposed, of Aegypta Schenck's reckless conjuring: "Bummer. I'll keep that in mind."

He lit a match. The flame didn't tremble, for the night was still. Inez de Rougemont saw, illuminated in the sudden light, the flash of his cold, pure, blue-gray eyes. "And the gun, of course," she reminded him. "Prince Frederick's revolver. Bocu must not have the gun."

THERE WAS NO CHANCE of that. The revolver was not thirty meters from where she stood. Luckacz and the Rezistenta men had not found it or stolen it or looked for it. Clara Brancoveanu was the person who had taken it. She had kept it under her nightgown, brought it upstairs, then hidden it behind a leather-bound edition of one of Madame Balzac's novels in Miranda's room, a line of books that stretched the length of the shelf.

The old-fashioned revolver had belonged to her dead husband. He had kept it as a memento from past days; it had been a gift from his father. And if sometimes he had displayed it, unloaded, on his belt during public appearances, he had never—so far as she knew—fired it or allowed it to be fired. It was too old, too heavy, too unwieldy, a symbol of his strength and purpose and ancestry, rather than a weapon.

Since Nicola Ceausescu had released her from the People's Palace, and since Magda de Graz and Jean-Baptiste had brought her to this refuge in Stanesti-Jui, Clara Brancoveanu had coveted this gun. The baroness's steward had kept it in his luggage, together with the black book that went with it. He had not shown these things to her, or offered them to her, even though the old revolver had been as personal to her husband as his shaving brush. In the only portrait he'd ever had the patience to sit for, it had lain at his right hand. But Jean-Baptiste had said nothing to her, and instead the steward had given it to Inez de Rougemont, who had snapped it up, cooed over it like a chicken over an egg—how dare she? And when the princess asked her, timidly, not even to keep it but to touch it, hold it, she had dismissed her like a servant.

That had been months ago, but it still irked her. Delicate in feeling as in body, Princess Clara had not permitted herself to think what many knew, that her husband had kept a lover both before and after his marriage. The notion scarcely crossed her mind. Besides, she was a beggar here in Stanesti-Jui, almost a prisoner, as she had been in Ratisbon and Bucharest. Dear Inez had been the soul of generosity, of course, but she was not a warm person. Often when she spoke to her, Clara could hear a sharpness in her voice, a sense of impatience or even condescension. And the princess had responded out of her own compliant nature, which was not unmixed with exasperated bitterness too subtle to be seen or felt or heard.

How dare the woman take up Frederick's gun, clutch it to her scrawny breast? What right did she have? And when Clara in her mild way had protested, the condesa had labored to explain as if to a child—the gun was not the same as it had been. Her husband's sister (whose own sharpness and impatience Inez de Rougemont sometimes brought to mind) had claimed it after his death, reconditioned it for some other use—all that was dark and mysterious, too esoteric for poor Clara, who hadn't had the benefit of a tutor in natural philosophy. It was true she'd been preoccupied with social engagements. Aegypta, at least, had been exempt from duties of that nature, because of her rude manner and unfortunate nose.

In Miranda's bedroom Princess Clara rubbed her hands together, then strayed, as she often did, to the mirror over the oak dresser. Just as often she turned quickly away, as now; she sank onto the stool beside Miranda's pillow, touched her daughter's forehead—would she never wake? How terrible this was! The doctor had come up from the village, but only because she had insisted. Dear Inez was impatient with all of her requests. Though she was right, as it turned out, because the man was useless, more a veterinarian than an accomplished practical physician—he was the first to admit it. And it was evident he thought there was something dark and murky and mysterious about this . . . accident (whatever it was), and doubtless also the condesa knew more than she was letting on. Clara had heard her whispering to Madame de Graz or else not bothering to even whisper, so convinced she was the princess would not understand.

Worse than that was the way dear Inez acted when she sat on this stool, the way she fussed and clucked over the mercury thermometer as if Miranda were her daughter, somehow. As if she were the only one who understood what needed to be done. But Clara wasn't as dense as they all thought. She had scarcely left Miranda's bedside, but when she did, when it was late at night and her daughter was deep asleep, she had slipped down to the library and lit a single candle so that she could study the black book in the locked glass case. She had seen where the condesa kept the key in the jackal-headed canopic jar she had first gone to when she knew the gun was missing. The jar was on the mantelpiece.

It had been during the first night of terrors when Miranda had fallen sick, when Bocu's men had murdered Jean-Baptiste, shot him through the window—all those terrifying events. The man had refused to die! Loyal to the end, he had held onto life long enough to chase away their enemies. He had been possessed, that was it—possessed by a malignant ghost that everyone else had been too blind to see! And in the meantime Princess Clara had scarcely known what she was doing. She had found the gun and snatched it up, found it where it had fallen on the hearth. But she would protect her daughter with her husband's pistol, though it was almost too heavy to lift. Later she had hidden it under her gown.

Now she sat on the stool beside Miranda's bed. She reached out sometimes to turn down the coverlet, adjust the bedsheet. There was a bowl of water on the stand, and from time to time she soaked a washcloth, squeezed it out, and used it to wipe Miranda's face, wipe the drool from her lips, give her something to drink. She had scarcely left her side except to lie down on the settee or forage in the library, and even that wasn't necessary anymore, since she had found Aegypta's letter.

She had changed the bed linen, stripped the sheets when Miranda wet them, and all those menial tasks had given her a fierce kind of pleasure. All those years she'd spent in Ratisbon as her daughter had grown up among strangers—now, changing her, making her comfortable, worrying and weeping over her, the princess was taking back some of that lost time.

"DÎTES-MOI," SAID PROCHENKO, outside in the cool spring air. "Tell me. Mademoiselle Popescu—where is she? Tell me where she is. Will it help her when I go do this . . . thing?"

The old woman stood in her unfashionable overcoat, hands in her pockets. Prochenko's night vision was preternaturally sharp, and he saw her face in the darkness, thin and bloodless, colorless except for her lipstick and the red indentations next to her thin nose, marks worn by the pads of her steel spectacles. Often her gray hair was pulled back from her face, anchored with combs, and you could see the contours of her small skull. But not tonight. She'd fixed it in a different style, a chignon or some such arrangement that might have been attractive on a younger woman.

In these past days she had seemed smaller to him, diminished with anxiety. These old women, and Miranda in some kind of coma—even if there had been no useful battle for him to fight, he could not have stayed here. He couldn't tolerate watching them sit their vigil over her as if waiting for her death. This Bocu—he would rip him to pieces, make him swallow his own entrails, string him up in the Piata Enescu with his testicles in his mouth. Or perhaps not. But he would do . . . something. Pieter de Graz wasn't the only one with a war to fight.

"I wonder," said Madame de Rougemont. "Did Mademoiselle Popescu ever tell you about a jewel she had, a tourmaline? Her aunt gave her several important gifts, powerful and complicated gifts. Frederick's pistol was just one. In some way they were . . . inappropriate for a girl her age, hard weapons, double-edged. I suppose Aegypta intended to be alive to guide her, help her, but of course that wasn't possible. And so here we are."

Prochenko had seen photographs and portraits of the Condesa de Rougemont as a young woman, when she had been Prince Frederick's mistress. He remembered her from a bal masqué at the Winter Keep, before the coronation of the Empress Valeria. And of course he'd seen some version of her on the Hoosick riverbank, dressed in Gypsy clothes. Staring with his dog's eyes, he had not remembered until Peter had reminded him later, in the time they spent together in North Africa. Then she had been a handsome woman—not in any obvious way. But she was lit with some kind of fire or spark or energy, which had dwindled now. She seemed cold and tired as she continued: "These are dangerous matters, full of risk. Aegypta Schenck was far more skilled than any of the rest of us. She was bolder, too—her niece takes after her. It was not for me to tell her to do this or to do that."

Then, "If she held it in her hand, she could come back, I think. The girl could never let it drop. But the white tyger, that was something else—you remember that night? One might be tempted to dismiss it as a fantasy, but these men were pulled down as they tried to run. And Mademoiselle Popescu, you remember—she lost consciousness."

But the lieutenant remembered Jean-Baptiste with his iron tongs and later with his carbine. He remembered Nicola Ceausescu speaking through him—Inez de Rougemont had not been in the room. So maybe she didn't know anything about it. Whatever, he thought. Then he spoke in English: "Miranda always had these crazy dreams."

His voice sounded unsteady even to himself. Madame de Rougemont turned her face to stare at him. "She will find it again—Kepler's Eye. It is a matter of looking properly. Perhaps she lost it among the rocks and stones or in the high grass. It is a matter of searching methodically, which is not her great gift. But it is essential, because of this information, these turtles she saw in Kepler's pool. I think this must be an offensive on the Turkish front, a way to cross the Danube with a new style of weapon. . . ."

"Whatever," said Prochenko. He took a last drag on his last cigarette, then dropped it to the dirt. "I've got to get my train. When she does wake up, tell her I asked about her. You know, for old times' sake. Tell her I said good-bye."

The old woman expected something more. She looked at him inquisitively, her head cocked to one side. You always wanted to leave them like that; he shrugged, took his borrowed gloves from the pocket of his borrowed jacket, turned up his borrowed collar, adjusted his borrowed scarf.

SHE WATCHED HIM WALK down the lane toward the village with his hands in his jacket pockets, his step jaunty, swaggering perhaps, and yet containing an admixture of feminine grace—he also was a lost young person, lost and unfortunate, carrying a burden that had been given to him regardless of his strength. For a moment she remembered Prince Frederick's aide-de-camp, always fastidiously dressed, though it was unclear what he did for money. All the soldiers and their women turned to stare at him whenever he had come into a room.

And then when he was out of sight she stood for a few minutes longer, looking up at the moon, postponing the time when she would go indoors, into the house that once had been a refuge against her enemies. She had scarcely realized how much she loved it, because of all the times she had chafed against its constraints, the diminished world it represented. But now a man had bled to death in the sanctuary of her library. The Rezistenta had found her and tracked her down. She must leave this place.

She made a circuit of the house and stood in the back garden looking up at the dim, flickering candlelight in Miranda's window. That also was painful to see. The girl's illness was a reproach to her—Frederick's daughter, whom she had not been able to protect. In the past she had made bargains with unsavory characters—enemies, she supposed—just to watch over the girl and keep her safe. She had gone to Massachusetts in the autumn leaves and snow. All of that had been for Frederick's sake.

It would be a lie to say she'd thought about him constantly since his death. It had been too long. But the girl took after him, had brought his ghostly presence back. Now she was on the high hillside below Kepler's tower. There was a war in Poland and the south. Prince Frederick's dream of a republican government was far away, mocked by Bocu and his miserable assembly. Tonight there were clouds overhead, snow on the peaks behind the house.

Miranda's window was closed. But Inez de Rougemont heard a muted explosion like a gunshot fired into a pillow. Then a scream.

And when she burst into the room, the dogs at her heels, she saw Clara Brancoveanu standing over the bed, her hands against her mouth. The Webley-Doenitz revolver lay on the rug where she had dropped it.

The dogs had been barking, but now they stopped. Something hung suspended over the bed, a flickering shape, a demon with a long tail. Black and shining, it twisted in a complicated repeating pattern above Miranda's head.

For a moment Madame de Rougemont thought of calling for Prochenko, but he was gone. He'd be in the village by now, or on the station platform. No one else, then. She stepped to the iron fireplace, picked up a poker.

Now she could see the shape more clearly as it twisted and turned back, a long black fish like a lamprey or an eel. It had no eyes, but a circular sucking mouth that was open now. The dogs whined and stumbled underfoot as she stepped forward, the barbed poker in her hand, though she didn't know what to do with it. Would the creature turn on her or else slip away, twist through the air, escape across the floor? Or would the metal pass through it as if it were a phantasm or a ghost? No, but it was solid, a living, sucking thing, and when Miranda turned her head, sighed in her sleep, another option showed itself. She yawned, opened her mouth, and the creature found a refuge. It vanished down the girl's red throat. Princess Clara burst into tears.

Inez de Rougemont let the tip of the poker sink to the floor. Then she went and sat on the stool next to Miranda's pillow, examining the girl while her mother flopped onto the rug, weeping, kneeling, wringing her hands. "Clara, be quiet," said the condesa. "Please, tell me what you've done."

But Clara couldn't help herself. She knelt weeping on the rug while the condesa studied Miranda's breathing, took her pulse, tried her forehead. The girl's condition didn't change. She still lay as if asleep.

Minutes passed. Miranda turned onto her side. Princess Clara's moans subsided and were still. The dogs lay on the floor. They were already forgetting what had happened.

"Which one was it?" asked de Rougemont finally.

"What?"

"Which one?" She looked around for the black book. "How did you know what to do?"

"It was in Aegypta's letters, copies of her letters. I just did what she told me, what she wrote down for Miranda. That's all I did."

It was sufficient, obviously. "Show me."

"Here," said Princess Clara. "It was the healing one, of course. I thought . . ."

"Clara, I don't care what you thought. Tell me what you did."

And then it came out. She couldn't read the text of the book itself. The English was too hard. None of it made any sense. She couldn't decipher any of the codes or much of the cramped writing. It didn't matter—she had found the letters in the back, pressed inside a section about raising corpses from the dead. "I recognized the penmanship," she said. "Aegypta had a double paper that she got from Italy for making copies—I remember it in Ratisbon. The first one I saw was something with my signature. She asked me to write something in the English language. She spoke to me about it before Miranda was even born. But already she was talking about a sanctuary in a foreign country. This was when I was still a guest in the elector's house, before he locked me into my room—she sent me a message, saying she had crossed the border with the invasion plans. And she asked me for letters that she could show Miranda as she grew. But the elector forbade it, forbade me ink and paper to write my only child—"

"Tell me what you did."

"Please, I'm getting to that! So Aegypta must have written one anyway, forged it and kept a duplicate. How could she do such a thing? All I wrote was about her and what she'd done—she made me sound so foolish. And then there was a letter from her, several letters. And then this one."

She rose to her feet and then crossed the room to the alcove where her easel stood. A candle burned there, and Madame de Rougemont noticed she'd been working on a charcoal sketch of Miranda as she lay asleep. But some handwritten pages were propped against the bar. Now she picked them up, leafed through them—one of the old letters she had found in the black book. The condesa had seen them there but had not read them. They had been tied in a lavender ribbon, slipped into a special envelope, the personal letters of a dead woman to her niece.

"You see they are duplicates—the ink still smears. Miranda must have seen them, but she didn't say anything to me. This one: *My dear niece, it is my pleasure to present you with this weapon that belonged to your father and his father, and which I know you will use wisely. This is the first of the treasures I have left you if there is a break in the rope and I am not there to guide your hands. First I tell you you must leave this place because it is not safe and full of robbers and murderers and spies. Here I must tell you what to do without delay. If the worst has happened and my enemies have buried me, then go to Insula Calia—*"

"Show me," said Inez de Rougemont. She had gotten up from her stool, and with trembling fingers she snatched the papers from Clara's hands. There it was on the second page. There were the incantations, culled from the black book. There were the diagrams, the small crude sketches of the imps, the directions in a language appropriate to a child or a young girl—the arrogance this represented! Magister Newton had spoken only of hypotheses! It was Aegypta Schenck who had rebuilt her brother's revolver, secreted these demons in the cylinder.

Magister Newton had hidden his results inside a crust of complication that was like a sealed box. But Aegypta Schenck had laid everything out, broken it apart for any first-degree adept or else someone with no training whatsoever. She had invented a mechanism that any fool could use. A few words as a primer, and then a tug on the stiff trigger—Miranda herself, obviously, had been too wise to fire this pistol.

But her mother, those were words to a different melody. And the condesa saw immediately what she had chosen. There was the sketch on the smeared page, the black, fringed, twisting eel. Mintbean first, Abscess next, and now Treacle. Three of the six demons had been released.

As Clara had suggested, the description mentioned healing, hope, and sustenance, all of which might sound like good things if you knew nothing or understood nothing at all about anything—these were ideas from long ago, when it was natural for doctors to bleed their patients dry.

Ah God, how would she explain this to Prince Frederick, when she met him in heaven or in hell? That none of this had been her fault? Or that Treacle in any case was preferable to Rotbottom, or Flimsie, or Thorpe, God forbid?

"I thought—"

"Be quiet, Clara, please."

But if you understood the rage of these creatures, plucked from the hidden world and then imprisoned in these tiny chambers—for how long? Years, certainly—more than a decade, certainly. She put the page aside. She took Miranda's hand again chafed her wrist, touched her neck, listened to her breathing. She pulled back her eyelid to see the rapid flutter of her pupil, which was unchanged. The girl was mumbling in her sleep.

Ah, God, the condesa asked herself: But was it possible she was mistaken? In the terror of the moment, was it possible she had inadequately witnessed what had happened? Was it possible the spirit had dissipated or vanished somewhere else, somewhere, anywhere in the wide world, leaving the girl untouched?

10 *The Living and the Dead*

AT AN ADJACENT MOMENT, on the hillside below Kepler's tower, an orange cat lay in the high grass. It had something in its mouth. It didn't move
or hide itself.

There was a rockfall in the glacier above the pass. Startled, the animal
leapt up, then continued down the hill. Nor did it hurry and then stop in
the forgetful manner of cats. But with an even, stiff-legged gait, it climbed
down through the grass and then the rocks.

Darkness came, but the animal kept moving. It did not stop and find a
sheltered place to rest, a hollow among the pine trees where it could curl up
and sleep. During the short, quick night it labored down, until it came into
the misty valley. This was a place without a sunrise, but the light came in
time. Many paths converged, then led away to separate villages.

At a crossroads marked with a rock cairn, the cat paused. It was an ugly
creature with a loose, striped coat. There were scabs on its knees and rump.
Its face was marked and scratched in many fights, one ear bitten out of
shape. Its lip was split, its sharp teeth broken.

But all this time it had held its treasure in its mouth. Now it spat it out.

The crossroads was a lonely place, two rutted footpaths in a dry waste. Fog had collected in a little bowl. There was no wind.

And if you chose this moment to look away, when you looked back the cat would have disappeared. In its place there would have stood a naked woman, or else partly clothed in fog. Beautifully formed, she was much mauled and damaged, like the cat. There were red wounds on her breasts and neck, holes made by a knife, self-inflicted. But her hands were cut and scratched where she had tried to defend herself against the dog or wolf, her face clawed and bitten, her copper-colored hair stiff with blood. Other marks were on her body like a cat's stripes in reverse, yellow and red against pale skin. They ran like seams of fire through the woman's flesh, over her thighs and buttocks, up her back. They divided her face into several parts, though the skin itself had reformed without any change in texture, any swelling or distortion. Even ripped apart she was a beautiful woman, as everyone but she had always said.

And a happy woman, too, at least according to the language of her gestures. In that cold, desolate place, surrounded by unmoving wraiths of fog, she gave a small performance, a little dance. Students of the dramatic arts might have recognized the triumphant solo of the whore and goddess Shamahat in Manolescu's *Gilgamesh le Roi,* before she immolates herself on Ishtar's altar. Reviews were mixed after the premiere in Berlin, though even the most angry critics praised the new seventeen-year-old prima donna of the company who, in the words of one, "brought a naked vulnerability to an otherwise bombastic role." Or she "snatched pathos out of bathos, lit an otherwise cold score on fire, and achieved a poignant delicacy in moments of the most savage and overwrought grandeur."

In the opera she danced with the heart of Enkidu clasped in her fist, the heart she had preserved out of his corpse. Through a trick of the light, in the middle of the dance the organ seemed to glow. Now too, twenty-three years later, the treasure changed in her outstretched hand, and in a moment it was not the soft piece of quasi-tissue that the cat had carried from the mountain. But it was something else.

The performance was over. Nicola Ceausescu stepped down off the rocks. She had the tourmaline clenched in her fist, and she wasted no more time. But she set off along the skein of paths that proliferated in this system of small valleys. She had left the mountainside. After several minutes the gate loomed out of the fog, the brass gate that marked the boundary to tara mortilor—the brass wall snaked over the hills. And the gate was different every time she crossed, sometimes a high triumphal arch, sometimes a forgotten postern, sometimes a gap in the broken wall, as now. But wherever it was and however you found it, once you stepped into the brass circle you were in a different landscape in the country of the dead. It is where we live in towns full of our dead friends and enemies, walk among streets we ourselves have laid out, climb the stairs in houses we have built, eat food we have grown or baked ourselves. Some of these towns are almost cities, full of counterfeited life. But some are small, deserted or abandoned. No one noticed the baroness as she stalked though the empty streets, climbed the cobblestones to the castle at the summit of the hill.

The town itself was picturesque. It commanded a small valley that was always full of fog, which gave the looming haystacks a melancholy, romantic aspect in the empty fields. The buildings were conceived in the manner of Italian hill towns, with pale stucco walls and flat terra-cotta roofs. The castle was a modest one with high, wooden ceilings, yellow or ocher-colored walls, stone floors covered with Turkish rugs that could be seen entire, because there was very little furniture.

The wooden door hung open and the baroness stalked the austere, undecorated rooms. In the street she had recovered herself, leather boots, tight trousers, loose shirt, long overcoat—often in her life she had dressed like a man. "Felix," she called out, "Felix," and he came to her. He was happy to see her, his face open with happiness, a young boy ten years old or so—it varied. "Maman," he said, "maman, I've missed you!" And he ran to her and squeezed his face against her chest. He was such a demonstrative child! He laughed and chattered. He didn't want to hear about her going away. But he looked up at her with bright, flashing eyes. No vestige of his father remained in his small face, though the old baron sometimes broke into the abandoned houses near the square. Sometimes he broke into the clock tower and set the bells to ringing. He wouldn't dare set foot in here.

"Go play in the garden," she said, and put the boy aside. "Maman will be back soon. Oh, but don't cry! You'll break my heart! I'll come back soon, and I'll bring a present for you. Just some little plaything, or a bicycle, or perhaps a book. You'll like that, you'll see."

Then she continued on into a farther room where the other boy sat listless in his cage, surrounded by all kinds of alchemical equipment. It was always dark in that low-ceilinged room. But his face brightened as she came to him, unlocked the padlocks as she always did, opened the bars and led him out—such a relief! He was weak and frail as always, and she led him to the daybed that was sometimes on one side of the room and sometimes on the other. And he was feverish, murmuring something that sounded like the name of a street, 351 Camatei—she didn't want to hear anything about that! Instead she laid him down, washed his face with the wet cloth that was at hand, fed him from the bowl of hot milk and buttered toast on the bedside table. She chafed his hands, pushed his hair from his damp forehead, revealing the strange marks on his temple, the soft, single eyebrow. This room had no windows and the only light came from the doorway, but it was better for him here while he was convalescing. Nor did she tell him she had to go even for a little while—she didn't want to worry him. Rest and time were what he needed and what she had to offer. Soon he would be strong enough to go outside, play with his little brother in the empty streets. She'd have to keep an eye out for the baron, though!

"Sleep now," she said, and pulled her hands away. The door on the other side of the room was open, and she walked toward it. This was the dark chamber, never lit. Past the threshold she was always stumbling and reaching out her hands, muttering some of the small charms she had learned from her husband's books. Filtered light could stretch in here sometimes, if it was a bright day outside. Sometimes that was enough to give the shadows shape and substance. Eyes straining, she reached out her hands. No, nothing, until she brought the tourmaline from the inside pocket of her overcoat, a stone that appeared now green now purple, and which glowed as if it were the source of a dim, uncertain light. And she was groping toward a shape she couldn't see, a shape that was made of shadow, indistinct, except she knew his features, knew his eyes, especially, that seemed to shine out of the darkness, beckoning her on—gray eyes with flecks of blue. They never changed.

LIEUTENANT SASHA PROCHENKO took the night train from Stanesti-Jui. As usual it was beyond crowded, forcing him into uncomfortable proximity with other men. The compartments and seats had been ripped out. There were no first- or second-class cars. Instead, wooden benches had been bolted to the floor.

The train stopped for no reason, and sometimes there were long delays. Men slouched against each other, asleep or half asleep. Prochenko was lucky enough to sit in the last row, so he could lean back against the wall. But the man on his left side had his head on his shoulder. Prochenko could smell the oil in his hair. Past three o'clock, they had not yet reached Rimnicu.

The car was full of smells: urine, tobacco, grease, coal dust, vomit, cabbages, potatoes, wine, raki, sweat, petroleum, even sperm. Unable to sleep, Prochenko filled the time by untwisting and separating all the braided strands. Sometimes he yawned, opened his mouth, let his long tongue spill out over his teeth, a process that sharpened his already acute senses. He could hear the watch ticking in the fob pocket of the old man whose long, unwashed hair lay on his shoulder. He could hear his soft, uneven breath, scarcely strong enough to press out through his teeth. But then there was a shuddering hiccup and the man was still.

Great, thought Prochenko after a minute. Why me, for crying out loud? There would be questions, unless he could slip away.

The train went creaking, slow. A long slow corner, and the man's head fell back. But then it seemed to move, return to Prochenko's shoulder, even press against it. Distasteful, but a kind of relief. The man's breathing, though, had not returned.

The lieutenant strained to hear it. After several minutes more, at the furthest limit of his perception he heard whispered words in a language, Prochenko imagined, the old man didn't know: "Ah, c'est toi! It is you."

The light was dim in the railway car. Suspended in wire niches, four oil lanterns showed their tiny flickering lines. Prochenko turned his head to see the old man peering up at him, his mouth gaping foolishly, pushed out of shape. He hadn't shaved in many days, never would again.

But underneath his rank sweat the lieutenant could perceive a different odor.

"How did you find me?"

He scarcely mouthed the words, but she heard him. "Ah," she whispered. "You are easy to find!"

The long, slow curve. "Now you've killed this stupid old man."

He could feel a shudder, perhaps a shrug. "There must be sacrifices."

"Yes, but never yours."

And then the train went faster, and there were clackety-clacks. "How could you know what I have suffered?" came the strange, airless voice. "Do not judge me. You and I are too much alike for that."

"I am not like you!"

"Do you not think so? But this is how we recognize each other, through our smells, through our eyes that do not change. But they peer out through a mask! If I take a shape where I can find it, whose fault is that? I was a living woman once—no more. You of all people must not reproach me."

As usual, what she said was not completely false. Though he scarcely remembered what she was talking about. Or he remembered chaotic sensations: the smell of blood, the splintering wood as he tore through the panel into the corridor on the third floor of the People's Palace. Miranda had used to laugh at his inability to recover dreams. It was a way to protect himself.

"I disgust you, I know," came the soft voice. "Now more than ever. How could it not be so? Once I dreamed—it doesn't matter now. But I will stay with you, remember that. I will watch over you. I will keep you out of harm. It is my gift."

Prochenko leaned his head back, closed his eyes. Great, just great, he thought. He listened to the sounds of the train as it bored through the dark.

NOT LONG AFTERWARDS, IN his apartment in the People's Palace, Victor Bocu staggered out of bed. Clothed in his undershirt and socks, he pressed himself against the wall beside the door, pressed his cheek into the ornate wallpaper. Unable to look away from the corpse on the bed, he fumbled for the doorknob, crossed the threshold into the antechamber and then crossed back, holding his camel-hair dressing gown, which he was too agitated to put on.

The girl lay on her back. She was twisted in the bedsheets, and one plump arm hung down. She was a dancer in the music halls, and he had rented her from one of the most fashionable brothels in the Strada Batistei, though she was not yet fifteen. And it was true when she arrived she had not been as he expected, had whimpered and called unconvincingly for her brother, even after he had doubled her fee. It was also true that he had lost his temper. But when he was convincing her, it was as if she changed under his hands, turned into some inhuman creature who had fought him off, pressed him down onto the bed, grabbed hold of him and might have broken his neck. As he gasped and floundered, it occurred to him his end had come, and that his enemies had succeeded in finding an assassin to best exploit his frailties—she was a devil, with a voice and a stink that seemed familiar. "What did you do to me?" she murmured. "What did you do? When you sent your soldiers to the Ambassadors that night, when you sent Radu Luckacz to arrest me, did you really think that would be an end to it?"

But at just the moment he was giving himself up, she collapsed across his body, dead.

11 *The House in the Strada Cerbului*

IN BUCHAREST, PETER BOARDED the train with a number of other soldiers. Magyars and German-speaking Saxons, they were headed home to Transylvania on leave. In the enormous smoky shed of the Gara de Nord, the train took hours to fill. It was the Szekely Star, made from cars that had been cannibalized from other railways and reconditioned for mass transport.

The line ran up the Prahova valley from Bucharest to Brasov, a distance of a hundred twenty kilometers. Scheduled for departure before dawn, it had steamed out of the station at the precise time, only to stop for several hours in the crossing yard. Afterward they made good time to Ploiesti across the plain, where they changed engines for the trip into the mountains. It was almost as if they had to cross a border to a different country, where the beige uniforms of the national railway and the Rezistenta were replaced with army green. This was Antonescu's land, under the peaks of the Bucegi Mountains and the Fagaras to the east.

It was evening before they reached Brasov. In the old days, the Count de Graz had kept a hunting cabin in the woods outside the town, and his son had shot bears in the autumn when the leaves fell. There had been fêtes and celebrations in the Stadthaus and the old citadel, none of which Peter Gross could remember now.

Or else he almost remembered, as if he'd once read an article in a society magazine—the fireworks for the Demeter festival, reflected in the surface of the Pool of Swans below the Trumpeter's Tower. He lingered by the delicate wrought-iron fence of the platform as the station cleared. He sniffed at the cold mountain air.

From where he stood he could see the streetcar terminus across the track and down the stairs. An officer scanned all the faces, looking for him, perhaps. With his pack on his back, he walked down to the other end of the platform, found the gate into the road, took the streetcar to the Piata Sfatului. He could walk from there to the regimental barracks in the Strada Castelului.

It was raining. The weather matched the mood of the entire nation away from the war, as far as he could see. As the streetcar came in through the brick gates of the town, he passed through streets that seemed stripped of all energy and color—no children played in the wet streets. One house in three looked unoccupied, and the curtains in the rest were drawn. Inside, as darkness fell, Peter imagined cheerless, silent meals of turnips and cabbages—the men exhausted, the children with their lesson books, the women upstairs in their rooms.

But Peter himself had nurtured a small hope since Staro Selo. Antonescu had no use for one-armed cripples. No one cared about the death of the baroness's son. No one was looking for Peter Gross or Miranda, either.

So how could he be unhappy, here, away from the front lines? And when he descended in the central square, he could see the streets were closed to carts and trucks and traffic, and the lamps were lit. Music spilled out of the doorways and across the slick cobblestones. Peter took shelter under a tin awning. He looked in through the diamond panes of some restaurant— Gypsy fiddlers and a woman dancing. Peter put his fingers to the glass, which throbbed to the music and the rhythmic stamp. In the shifting gap made by people's backs, he could see the Gypsy dancing with her skirt low around her hips, her hand above her head.

Yes, he had been grateful when General Antonescu plucked him from his regiment. He had been desperately grateful. But there was a price for everything and the price he'd paid was in this: a separation from his own experience and an introduction to a world of lies, of ordered principle and cause and effect, where men didn't cough their lungs out as they squatted in muddy latrines beneath the thunder of the guns. Maybe everyone above the rank of company commander lived in that other world of organized assaults and counterassaults, which was why talking to them was so surreal and strange—shaking hands with the politicians and the colonels. Now he was here, some kind of damaged metal soldier with his steel hook, his Star of Hercules. He was to find his regimental barracks where tomorrow he'd meet with the reporters from civilian and military magazines. He'd wear a dress uniform. He would be photographed. He would speak to new recruits, conscripts from these mountain villages. People had told him what to say.

How was it possible, in such circumstances, for him to recognize himself? Here was one way: In the bottom of his knapsack, in a crumpled pack of cigarettes, he had a wad of German reichmarks, which he would deliver to a certain address. This was a promise he had made to a dead man, a promise that made no more sense than anything else—a duty to a dead traitor or a dead spy. To be involved in any part of it, he supposed, was also an act of treachery.

The glass throbbed and tingled under his fingertips. The big wooden street door of the public house was already open. But now a lighter door opened as well, a screen or a barricade of wood and canvas that kept in the heat. Three people came out and stood under the awning, adjusting their overcoats—a man and woman and a boy. Smells came out with them—sour beer, and sawdust, and wet wood. By then they were aware of him, and even though he snatched his hand from the window and wiped his face with his damp cuff, still he could imagine the story he must represent, the crippled soldier coming home—if only that were it! If only his or any story could be summarized like that, as if it were a photograph or an illustration in a magazine! They clustered around him now, although the child hung back. But the man had big, thick, heavy eyebrows and a wrinkled face and a big beard. He groped self-consciously for Peter's left hand, gripped it in his big, hard palm, spoke to him in Hungarian, a language Peter barely knew. It didn't matter. It was all right, they must be saying, welcome home. What did they know about it? Peter had a sudden vision of his father's face, not the Count de Graz but the other one, alone in his house on White Oak Road.

He pulled his hand away, turned away from the public house, continued through the town. In the Strada Castelului he found his barracks, where the celebration had already started.

It wasn't until four days later that he managed to break off a chunk of time. By then the first of the newspaper articles had already appeared in the local press, together with a printed portrait. Already he was famous in the town, which complicated things. He had met the mayor, and the councilors, and the tribal chiefs, and the priests of Pan and the various mountain cults, and the representatives of the trade guilds.

But finally he was able to make excuses and slip away. He told the barracks commander he must visit some of the families of the men in Theta Company—men who'd died. The excuse was almost true, or true enough. He sent a message, and in the evening he found himself in among the streets surrounding the Piata Sfatului, a fashionable neighborhood of high, narrow houses with Baroque façades. He passed the mansion that had once belonged to Lucas Hirscher the vampire, then turned into a narrow, flagstoned lane where the houses were lower and older, built in the windowless Turkish style. Though the evening was mild, he wore an overcoat with cuffs long enough to cover his right arm. In the newspapers, many centimeters of ink had been wasted in descriptions of his hook, which had made him conspicuous around the town.

There was a small, circular park at the bottom of a cul-de-sac, a ring of gravel and a circular wooden bench under a tree, a beech tree with bare limbs and splotchy silver bark. A man sat in the waning light, a newspaper on his lap. Some pigeons had come to him. For a moment Peter imagined sitting next to him, studying the birds with him, maybe feeding them with crumbs from his pockets. But instead he found the address Janus Adira had given him in Staro Selo, and after sunset he climbed three stone steps to knock at a wooden door. The knocker was tarnished brass in the shape of a horse's head. The door was scarred and fissured, most recently painted black. The house was plain yellow stucco without any decoration or distinction, yet it maintained a solid dignity. The door was opened by a housekeeper in her apron and cap. Peter gave his name and rank, which had recently been confirmed.

And when the housekeeper returned, she led him back along a tiled corridor with closed doors on each side. The coarse plaster walls were painted yellow and dark green. There was no sound from the street, which was in any case a quiet one. But as they penetrated deeper into the house, Peter was aware of a soft music, a poignant simple melody played upon the pianoforte, and filtered through a series of closed doors. When the housekeeper led him into the receiving room, the sound broke off abruptly. The musician swiveled on her stool, then rose to her feet, a dark-skinned woman in her middle twenties, Peter guessed. Her dark, thick curls were loose around her shoulders, and she wore gold rings in her ears. Her clothes were stiff raw silk with the grain showing, a loose dress that was simple and unornamented, but which managed to suggest a kind of eastern exoticism, at least to Peter who stood speechless at the door. "Excuse me," she said. "It is *The White Tyger*. The funeral march—I have the sheet music from a Russian publisher—a work of genius, don't you think? And of course the composer, hounded to her death by this present government—she would never have led us into this war."

The housekeeper was gone. The woman came toward him, holding out her hand. "You must excuse me. I'm afraid I make no secret of my politics. We've had bad news. You've come about my brother, I suppose? I am Chloe Adira."

Her eyebrows were thick and black, her eyes lined with pencil. She had gold rings on her fingers, and her hand was cool. Peter stammered out his name, and she laughed. "I know—the famous Captain Gross. I have seen the posters in the market, though they do not do you justice. But I saw you were at Staro Selo—this is about my brother, isn't it? We received the letter yesterday, and the telegram the same day—you must forgive me. This is a terrible shock. He was in the university—a gifted boy—man, I suppose I must call him now. He was taking his degree in political philosophy, something like that, I think. Only now—forgive me."

"Please."

Peter still had hold of her hand. "Oh, you have come about him! Did you see him in the hospital? Will you tell me? You must forgive me, my mother—"

"Please."

"Will you come into the garden?" she asked. "Will you take supper with us? It is very simple, you understand."

The room was lit with candles in glass chimneys, or else in mirrored sconces on the wall. The walls were lined with painted portraits of men in uniform, women in long dresses. Chloe Adira's voice now trembled and was silent, but Peter also felt a rush of emotion that closed his throat. And he still grasped at the fingers of her left hand until she extricated them, showed him her pale palm. "Follow me."

Chloe Adira led the way into the garden at the center of the house, a rectangular courtyard open to the sky. It was surrounded by a gallery whose slender columns supported ornate wooden balconies, carved screens and shutters on the second floor. All was dark up there, but a servant lit lanterns in the garden as Peter followed his hostess along the covered gallery. She was barefoot, he saw.

It had been a long time, he thought, since he'd been alone anywhere with a woman his own age or what felt, at least, like his own age—how wonderful it was! Everything about her seemed important, every word or gesture full of meaning. He studied the fabric of her dress, which was slit in the back to revealed her bare calves. She stepped off the polished boards onto the grass that surrounded the tree in the middle of the courtyard, a tree with a bench under it. For a moment Peter was reminded of the pathetic old man with his unread newspaper, sitting in the little park outside the house. That tree seemed naked and exposed, this one intimate and protected. "You must come back in the summer when these pots are full of flowering plants and oranges—not since the war, of course. I want you to be comfortable. My husband was in Poland when Antonescu let the Russians through the Fedorivka Salient. I suppose he is a prisoner now. This was a great betrayal. Look, let me show you."

She turned and crossed her hands over her heart, then pulled a locket out of the top of her silk undershirt. She opened the clasp to show an officer from one of the Bessarabian regiments—they always wore a lot of braid.

Peter took the locket into his hand, conscious of how near she stood, conscious also of a fragrance that hung about her like the promised orange trees; she was a beautiful woman, with dark eyes, beautiful lips and teeth. "Sometimes I imagine him like this, alone in a strange country. And I would be grateful to anyone who showed him any kindness, took him into her home." She pulled the locket out of Peter's hand, stepped back—"It breaks my heart to think of him. And now this news about my brother."

Tears were in her eyes. But she put out her hand, its pale palm toward him, pale fingers outstretched. "Captain Gross, where are your people? Where is your home?"

"Satu Mare," said Peter, thinking of White Oak Road. "But my mother has a house near Lake Herastrau, in Bucharest."

"So, scattered. And is she the last one? Did you have brothers?"

Peter shrugged. He did not remember them. "My father was Prince Frederick's man—"

"So, a republican! They did not say so in the newspaper. I knew I could trust you, trust your face. Now you must tell me about Janus, I am strong enough. Here, sit here with me," she said, bringing him to the bench under the tree. "The letter came, but it told us nothing. Only that he'd died in hospital in Staro Selo while on transfer from his regiment. . . ."

She interrupted herself, then went on: "Satu Mare! But that's not what it said in the newspaper. They said you were from Arcus, north of here."

Peter shook his head. "My father had a hunting cabin—"

"No!" she said. "They did not say so. Your father was a farmer from the German villages. I read it. Now you must tell me, is the rest of it a lie? All those stories that make a woman's heart beat. I read you had taken a trench during a counterattack, and held it with thirty-five men. My father was a soldier, too, and my husband. . . ."

A glass lantern hung above them from the branch of the leafless tree. Her eyes were fierce in the lantern light. He found it mattered to him what she thought. How to explain? He remembered the noise above all, the noise and the smell, and the shouts of men whose names he knew—she rubbed her hands together in the chilly air. "How can I trust you? Why have you come here? You must not guess our secrets—"

"Here." He unbuttoned the brass buttons of his collar, and slid his fingers under his shirt. "I came to give you this, that's all. I won't stay."

For a moment as he said this, he caught a glimpse of Miranda's face, as if superimposed onto the face in front of him. But then the pale, open palm came toward him in a fragile, wilting gesture that was different from the language of Miranda's hands—she disappeared, as if Chloe Adira had moved her fingers through a breath of smoke.

The servant, a big man with a big beard, had returned with a metal tray, which he set clumsily on a low table. "Dumitru has made tea," said Chloe Adira. She gave Peter no more attention, while with trembling fingers she unsealed her brother's envelope. She didn't touch or count the banknotes. A faint expression of disgust passed over her, articulated in her eyebrows and her stiffening hands—then it was gone. She unfolded the pages of the letter, held them up to the light. For a moment her face was as still as a mask, and then it cracked apart and she was weeping, a shuddering sound that she tried to suppress and swallow down, which made it far more horrible—he leaned toward her and she put her palm up, holding him in place.

By the time she got to the last page, she had recovered some composure. "You must excuse me," she said. Peter sipped from a glass of sweet, Russian tea, watching her black eyeliner dissolve onto her cheeks. She raised a hand to her face, then frowned at her dark fingertips. "Please," she said, and she was gone from the bench. She stepped onto the wooden gallery, ran into the house, while Peter wondered what to do.

His glass was red with a motif of pointed arches etched in gold. Peter clasped his hand around it, warmed his fingers. He wondered if the old man in the hat was still sitting on his bench outside; then his hostess returned. She had washed her face, washed all her makeup away, and Peter could see she'd had some kind of color on her mouth, cosmetic powder on her cheeks. She looked different now.

Quiet and composed, she sat down next to him, her knees together. "He mentions you," she said. "He vouches for you. Now you must tell me what you know."

Peter didn't look at her. Instead he studied the etched glass in his hand. But he told her about finding Janus Adira in no-man's-land the day before the push. He told her about bringing him over the trench and back behind the line, leaving him in a field beside a stone wall in a ruined orchard; he had a broken leg. Peter told her about the money. He mentioned the page of hieroglyphs. A list of ordnance, Andromeda had said. Was it possible the letter could be traced to Brasov, to this house?

Maybe Chloe Adira wondered, too. "What became of that?" she asked, and Peter saw an anxious look pass over her face and disappear—everything was quick with her.

"A friend took it, a civilian. I sent him for a stretcher-man before I went back."

"Ah."

He told her about the last time he had seen her brother when the bombs were falling on Staro Selo. But there were no more tears in her. She shivered, rubbed her arms.

"My mother told me something," she interrupted. "After we saw the article in the newspaper. My mother is not easy in her mind, you understand. But she told me a piece of romance from the town, I suppose, about another hero from the Turkish wars who disappeared long ago. I suppose it is a rumor that intends for us to think that even in these modern times there is a guardian, a defender of Great Roumania, like Mother Demeter or Miranda Brancoveanu or like Hercules himself, when he fought the Amazons along the shores of the Black Sea near Varna as they say. But in these stories I see something mythological in you, and something frightening as well— I'm sorry. I apologize."

Peter placed his glass down on the metal tray on the low table under a bush that was just beginning to recover some kind of greenness. He had not expected to hear the name "Miranda" on this woman's lips.

He sat back, put his shoulders against the silver bark of the tree. He put the back of his head against the tree and closed his eyes. He felt exhausted, and he wondered how long he could sit here with Chloe Adira. She was silent beside him, and he listened to her breathing until it changed. Then he opened his eyes to see they weren't alone.

Someone had come out onto the balcony above them. Because the courtyard was small, she was not far away. Wrapped in a blanket or a quilt, she leaned over the wooden rail, peered down at them, an older woman with a soft, heavy body. Her hair was long, gray, unbrushed, unfastened, which gave her a wild look. "Dumitru told me you were here, but I had to see," she said, leaning as far as she could over the balustrade, reaching out one pudgy hand. The other kept the blanket closed over her chest.

"It is my mother," whispered Chloe Adira.

Then in a moment, because the gray-haired woman said nothing, she continued. "She has taken this so hard. He was her last boy. She is not herself—don't expect her to be herself. The doctor has given her morphine, but I'm afraid—"

"I know you!" said the woman on the balcony. "It is true what they say! You're the son, de Graz's youngest son. He had a hunting lodge in Sacele near my father's farm. I used to see you at the harvest festival before my marriage when I was fifteen. I know you—do you remember? When your horse lost a shoe outside our door?"

Peter closed his eyes again, just for a moment. No one yet in Brasov had told him this or any other story of the Chevalier de Graz. They had not spoken about it to his face. But now this old woman stood above him, accusing him—why did he feel so exposed? He rose to his feet as Chloe rose beside him: "Mother, please. Captain Gross is our guest. He has brought us news. . . ."

"But I know you," said the woman. "You came and stood in the kitchen. This was before the Turkish war and Nova Zagora, I remember. You ate an apple. You had a birthmark on your right hand—no, that's no good. You're crippled now, I see."

"You must forgive her," murmured Chloe Adira. "She thinks she's a girl again."

Now Dumitru appeared on the upper gallery and led the gray-haired woman back into the house. She had stood above them for not more than a minute, but everything had changed. Though he had no memory of the day, Peter found himself imagining the Chevalier de Graz standing in his riding boots on the tiled kitchen floor, legs spread, chewing an apple with his strong teeth while a straw-haired farm girl slipped out the double door. And it was some vestige of the Chevalier de Graz who followed Chloe Adira inside the house, caught up with her in an inside room. "You must excuse us," she murmured.

He put his hand out to touch her, and she raised her palm close to his own. They stood staring at each other in the little room. There were blue plaster walls, and the candles were lit. She said, "But it is clear to me that we must trust you, because we have no choice. No, please. Don't . . . move."

Then it all came in a rush. "I'll tell you what I know. There is a weapon in Great Roumania, a terrible weapon. It is from my father's country in Abyssinia and was brought here by Nicola Ceausescu on a train. Which was ambushed and blown up. And this weapon was not found. But my brother—don't you see how terrible it would be if Victor Bocu or Ion Antonescu got their hands on this device or this ingredient, whatever it is— you must see that. You must forgive him. You must forgive all of us."

Peter shrugged. "There is nothing to forgive." And then after a moment: "I was on the Hephaestion at Chiselet."

"Ah, God, how can that be so?"

"There was a baggage car in front of the train. We hit a barricade and Antonescu blew it up. It was on a raised embankment at the marsh's edge."

They murmured these things to each other in the place of endearments. She shook her head. "So—maybe you are a mythological creature. How can it be? Then there is no need to convince you."

He smiled at her. "I was there."

"Then you will help me, now my brother is gone. I don't know much. Only you must . . ."

Her palm was centimeters from his own. And now their hands touched, and pressed together, and their fingers interlocked.

"You must not think bad thoughts of me," she said after a little while. "Sometimes I imagine my husband in Poland, sometimes in a forest, or in the open fields. But he comes to a thatched cottage where a woman is living and waiting by herself. And he is hungry, and there's a fire in the stove. And maybe he is lost and alone, or maybe there are men chasing him, but she takes him in, makes him take off his wet coat. Sometimes I see it. She has yellow hair, and braids, perhaps. She has a bigger bosom, wider hips, perhaps—what do you think? But if she helps him and gives him comfort, what harm is there? I pray for strangers to be kind to him. And if she kisses him, what harm is there? I could not be jealous of such a one. I would thank her with my tears. Or if she takes him in her hands—ah, I would not expect her to be so bold. She never had an Abyssinian father, whose name she kept, and who taught her women mustn't tell such constant lies about what they want. . . ."

Just for a moment, again, Peter caught a glimpse of Miranda's face. How far away she seemed, in a mountain farmhouse he had never visited except in his imagination.

12 Topography

SHE WAS FARTHER from him than he thought. Dawn came in a few hours, a foggy dawn as Miranda and her aunt climbed down the hill. At the crossroads, Aegypta Schenck peered into the dirt. She had changed from her clothes, though Miranda had not seen her change. She had lost her long gloves, fox stole, lace collar, high-heeled shoes, small hat—all of the old lady's traveling attire that was part of Miranda's first memory of Roumania, at Mogosoaia station in the snow. Instead she'd put on the hunting clothes from the framed photograph in Mamaia Castle, wool shirt and breeches, dirty boots. She knelt in the dry dirt, examining the little footprints. Her hair was tucked up and fastened under a leather cap.

The cat had come here with wet feet. Miranda could smell something too, a tiny bitter smell. But when she went to pass the cairn, her aunt stood up. "Don't go that way. You cannot."

Miranda could see her face now in the soft gray light, her big features, yellow eyes, wrinkled cheeks and neck. She had no eyebrows, but there were a few untrimmed hairs around her mouth. Out of the hat and veil she looked both dignified and fierce. "You cannot go that way. We've lost her."

"Why not?"

She shrugged as if it irritated her even to be questioned. "The dead climb up this hill, up the back side. But they are not the only ones. It is unclaimed ground along the border. Down that valley, those paths to the left—that is their home. The road lies through a gate you cannot pass."

"And you?"

Miranda's aunt appeared to smile. "Do not worry about me. I have a home, never fear. A small house just for me, a long way from here. But there's nothing for you, nothing I can share while you are still a living woman."

It had not occurred to Miranda until that moment that she might have lost the tourmaline for good. She felt a sudden, stabbing wound of anger and despair. How could she have been so stupid? How could she have been so careless? How could this have happened?

Nothing was alive in that sandy bowl. They gray sky pressed down on them, a foggy ceiling a few feet above their heads. "Do you know what's happening in Stanesti-Jui?" Miranda cried. "My mother and Andromeda—can you tell me about them? Am I walking around, or talking there, or eating breakfast, or climbing the hill behind the house?"

The rim of the bowl was lost in fog. The crossroads marked the exact center, the pile of rocks. There was no wind, no water, not a blade of grass. No part of what was happening felt real. "What difference does it make?" Miranda said again. "Alive or dead, it's gone, slipped away. All those people and those things—isn't that what it feels like to die? That something slipped out of your fingers?"

She felt light-headed, parched. The fog seemed to have no moisture in it, the air no sustenance. Aegypta Schenck rubbed some sand between her palms, and with an expression half impatient and half pitying she reached out her hand, exhibited her cold flesh.

"It didn't feel that way to me," she said, "when my time came."

"Oh God," Miranda cried, "it's happening again! Is it happening again? Is this the second time I've lost everything? The fire burned up my book, and I put down my jewel, and each time I was to blame, my own stupid carelessness?"

Her aunt, evidently, had no intention of consoling her. "These things might be easier if you lived to an old age. If you lay in bed with your family around you. But in my house in Mogosoaia that was not my fate. I pray it will be yours. As for Stanesti-Jui, I believe you are asleep."

Aegypta Schenck was an intimidating woman, and she spoke with sincerity and confidence. On that indistinct frontier between the hidden world and tara mortilor, Miranda was desperate to be reassured. Empty and vacated, nevertheless she tried to smile.

THE CONNECTION TO HER body in Stanesti-Jui, in the farmhouse on the mountainside, had been severed when she lost the tourmaline. But she was capable of hope, because she had no other choice. So it was fortunate that she was spared the pain of watching herself come awake in her overheated bed.

The sheets were rank with sweat. But her fever had broken when her eyes opened and her body turned onto its side. "Comme j'ai rêvé," she said—"What a dream I had!"

During her illness, in the mornings when Clara Brancoveanu had watched over her, the first words out of her mouth had always been in English. Sometimes they were very coarse. Once Clara had asked the condesa for a translation, but she had only laughed.

"Comme j'ai rêvé!"—the phrase itself seemed peculiar to her mother. But she only permitted herself a momentary doubt. It was morning time, a bright, sunny morning. Miranda had been woken by the sun across her face. Now she smiled—she was a pretty girl when she smiled, though it had been too long!

The condesa had gone to bed hours before. Clara had stayed awake, hoping against hope, washing her daughter's face, chafing her hands. Aegypta's letter had promised healing, though the words, now that Clara thought about them, were portentous and ambiguous. What does it signify to attack and extirpate the causes of disease? How is it possible to eradicate suffering? How is such a thing accomplished? Is it worth the price, the risk?

But now Miranda was awake. And perhaps Aegypta hadn't know as much as she pretended, and perhaps the condesa's anxiety had been misplaced, her harsh words. Perhaps those old women weren't so clever after all.

And Clara Brancoveanu felt like weeping, she was so relieved. "How are you?" she asked, pulling back the coverlet, fussing with the pillows. In the evening she would take the carriage to the village and light eleven candles on the altar of the goddess of fertility, who had heard her prayers. Nor would she listen to any doubts or qualms, particularly since Miranda looked as contented as she had ever seen her, all marks of worry erased from her face as she smiled up at her from the damp bed.

"THAT'S MY BRAVE GIRL," said Aegypta Schenck. "I will keep you safe. In the meantime there is work to do."

Miranda's smile changed. "What do you mean?"

At the crossroads, Aegypta Schenck looked up at the absent sky. "Sometimes our duty is forced upon us."

She hesitated, then went on. "I did not bring you to Roumania to watch you stifle in your bed month after month in Stanesti-Jui. Inez de Rougemont was my brother's mistress, after all. She was not a friend to me. She would always meddle in what didn't concern her. I am not sorry to see you here out of her hands."

Oh God, Miranda thought. Then she spoke, trying with all her strength not to show emotion. "This was your plan?"

"Plans mean less than you think. It is opportunities that matter."

"Thanks. That's good to know. I'll salt that away."

"Child, don't be impertinent with me. It was not I who lost the jewel."

Her gray hair was streaked with yellow. Her expression was neither cruel nor kind. She couldn't control me in the real world, and so she brought me here, Miranda thought. But she could not deny the last thing her aunt had said, which made everything worse.

Aegypta Schenck continued: "Nicola Ceausescu has robbed you. That is clear. She has taken Kepler's Eye through the brass gates. I can't know what she plans to do with it. She has no flesh to return to. But she coveted it when she was alive. Perhaps that is enough."

She touched her hands together, cleaned her dirty palms on her shirt. "I will go find her," said Miranda.

"Child, you cannot. This is the boundary where all of us starve. I came here to lead you to your road, that's all."

They stood in the little barren bowl, rimmed with fog. They stared at each other. Aegypta Schenck didn't blink—could not, Miranda supposed.

Like a sudden surge of nausea, doubt and anger overwhelmed her and she turned away, started to run, following the little path of the cat and then the human footprints leading on, high-arched and delicate. Miranda staggered over them with her leather boots. It was important to remember Nicola Ceausescu was not tall or strong. These zombies and ghosts could be confronted, beaten, tricked like the stupid baron. Or else destroyed like the idiotic elector on the mountainside.

She'd taken her aunt by surprise. She found the path and continued south, downhill, jumping from rock to rock as the fog closed in. She gulped at the thin air, which seemed to have a metallic taste. "Lead you to your road"—she wouldn't be led like a donkey or a horse. There was no reason to trust anything her aunt said was true.

She felt the obstruction before she saw it. She heard it in a deadening of sound. And then the wall loomed out of the mist, an uneven cliff face, a metal barrier that reached a hundred feet above her into the clouds.

What she had said and thought and felt, what her aunt had said, their disagreement during which they had not raised their voices—all of it was in the mouth of the great gate that now rose suddenly above her between brazen towers. A sound seemed to come out of the earth, a frequency that hurt her ears as she stumbled and her aunt caught her from behind.

In her bed in Stanesti-Jui, Miranda had been smiling at her mother, a vacant expression on her face. But now she rolled into her pillow, sucking at the air, scratching at her sheets—a sudden seizure, and her mother knelt down over her and pried open her fingers, searched her mouth for her tongue, held her legs from shaking as she shouted for help. Miranda's eyes had rolled up in her head, her backbone had arched away from the mattress. But now she collapsed just as suddenly, her muscles soft as Aegypta Schenck dragged her away into the dirt and rocks until the gate had vanished as utterly and suddenly as it had first appeared. The wall was hidden in the mist. The sound was still. And Aegypta Schenck was weeping her cold tears over her, fussing over her just as her mother fussed and wept, until Miranda woke, rolled onto her side.

Later, sullen and submissive, she followed her aunt up the hill. "It was the wrong way," scolded Aegypta Schenck. "It was not the way for you, so close to the wall. It was a risk. Why must you always look backward, toward the past? How can you frighten me like this, punish me? Your way is east from here, forward, not back. Is that so difficult to understand? It is true for all of us. What is it about these past events that fascinates you? The tourmaline, that was a way to bring you here!"

They rose out of the clouds through the pine forest to the slippery grass below Kepler's tower. They passed the stone where the jewel had lain, where Miranda had set it down to become the white tyger. She raised her eyes, looked up at the ring of snowy mountains. The configuration of the peaks was different now. A rocky spire now jutted from the mountain above the tower.

"This has changed."

An impatient shrug. "Child, it remakes itself." Aegypta Schenck scratched her big nose and then continued: "Didn't I explain? Other people's experience is no use. Our own experience is no use. You might look over a high cliff and see the water. The next day nothing but a desert. Do you remember the ship that took you into tara mortilor, when you came to see me that first time?"

Miranda did remember. Now she imagined what might have been different if she had left Aegypta there, a bird in a cage. Would she be with Peter now? Would she be walking on the mountain above Stanesti-Jui?

The sun had crept over the high white ridge. They climbed the rest of the way into the pass, through the rockfall. The place was not so frightening in the sunlight. But the pool was dried up, the reflecting pool. It was just a bowl of cracked, dry mud.

"Maybe I should have broken this open while I had the chance," Miranda said. She circled the tower, laid her hand on the iron door underneath the stairs. "Expedite the inevitable."

"What?"

"'Expedite the inevitable.' That's what Stanley used to say."

"Who? I don't remember."

Miranda stood at the top of the world. "What do you mean?" she cried. "You made him tell me those things for a reason, didn't you? Step by step. First things first. Everything he told me . . ."

Miranda's aunt shook her head. "It is a vexed question. We always used to argue in the old days. I've told you more than once your life inside the book was different from anything we wrote. It grew from the inside, because of you. This is the fundamental question of all alchemical research: When you make something, are you creating something new? Or are you discovering something that already exists?"

The sun was on the spire of rock above the tower. Miranda took her hand off the iron ring. Stanley's little maxims and a hundred thousand other things, had they come out of her? Or were they just a way of leading her and keeping her along her road?

She stood in a perch of granite boulders. She could see the valley open under her feet as the sun rose and the light descended, not toward tara mortilor but east, down and down, a whole hidden world. Above her head, the light gleamed on the stones of Kepler's tower.

As the sun moved, every instant it revealed something new among the steep valleys sinking down. She looked out between two long arms of hills, which subsided into the distance. In that bright landscape she could see the river coiling toward the sea. She said: "So was Berkshire County something you invented or discovered?"

Behind her came her aunt's impatient, deflating gasp. "I do not think I would care so much about the future or existence of an invented place, a place I'd invented or caused others to invent. I do not think I would have sacrificed myself, everything, any chance of happiness—"

But if there was any reason to think it might be worth it to give up those things for the sake of an illusion, it was this: When Miranda first came to Roumania . . . No, not Roumania, but when she had first climbed down from Christmas Hill, she'd felt as if she'd passed from a false world to a true one, and not because anything was better or happier or else suddenly made sense—quite the opposite. No, the difference had been a matter of physical sensations, the intensity of colors, smells, sounds, all of which had faded over time. The warm air drifted up the valley, touched her face.

She said, "Am I right in thinking you can't follow me down there? Am I right in thinking that's the hidden world? Not just this borderland, as you call it—"

Another irritated gasp: "Child, you must not always look for guidance. A thousand men die every day along the southern front. Another thousand every day in Poland. It is time for you to get out of bed, climb down from this ridge. But I can't predict . . ."

Miranda glanced behind them toward tara mortilor. That valley was still in mist and shadow. Eastward, the sun had burned all that away. Rock cliffs turned black and brown, and then descended into forest.

"You might search for it and find it in the hidden world," her aunt had told her not so long ago. She'd been talking about Berkshire County.

"That's not what I meant," Miranda said now. She stood in the rocks below Kepler's tower. Whatever had moved inside the stone chamber was not moving now.

"I'll make you a deal," she said. "You can travel through those brass gates. You can pass through tara mortilor. Bring me the jewel, the tourmaline. Find it and bring it here to me."

And when her aunt replied nothing, she turned away and took her first steps downhill. "You've pulled me out of bed," she continued softly. "You've led me to my road. Step by step. What will I find? There is a war down here?"

She heard her aunt's voice diminish, because she hadn't followed her. "I will not quibble like a dressmaker."

But as she continued down through the granite boulders, and as the world remade itself, she heard an angry expulsion of breath beside her ear. She turned for the last time, and there behind her on the rocks stood Aegypta Schenck von Schenck in her old lady's velvet dress, the cruel fox heads hanging down, as they had at Mogosoaia in the snow.

"I will tell you," said the old woman. "You should need no excuse to be what you are, or do what is correct, or give your life for Great Roumania. But if there is a first step or a first place or something you should expedite, then I want you to rid the world of President Victor Bocu."

And it seemed to Miranda that her aunt was in fact, as it turned out, quibbling like a dressmaker or else agreeing to a bargain. She had already predicted what her aunt would ask of her, and she couldn't even listen as her Aegypta Schenck explained what she already knew: how Victor Bocu had taken control of the so-called National Assembly, a council of collaborators that had been founded under German auspices to advertise the supposed benefits of German democracy—a sham, obviously, and even more of a sham now because of its superficial legitimacy. . . .

Miranda knew all this. She found herself pretending to listen, while at the same time she was wondering how dressmakers had achieved their reputation for quibbling. And she was also wondering if she would find Peter Gross in this forest or this valley down below, and how he would have changed since she'd last seen him, and what form he would take, and whether she would even recognize him.

13 *Of Two Minds*

CLARA BRANCOVEANU SAT BY Miranda's bedside in Stanesti-Jui, wiping her face, stroking her hair. She was fearful of a new seizure. But the onset of Miranda's illness had been sudden, and now her recovery was just as quick; irritable after five minutes, she pushed her mother's hands away.

And after that she was content for several hours. Her mother had never known her in such high spirits. She seemed strong and full of energy, her old self from before her winter sickness and the worries and anxieties of the past few days. Anton brought her breakfast on a tray, but she refused to stay in bed. She paced back and forth with a hunk of buttered toast in her hand.

Watching her eat, Clara was almost able to convince herself that everything was all right. The black eel that had squeezed from the barrel of her husband's revolver had not been real. How could it have been real? No, it was a ghostly image that could not persist in this strong daylight.

And when Miranda went down by herself to the water closet on the ground floor, Clara was able to say to herself that she'd done something right for a change, that she'd been right to read Aegypta's letter, fire the gun. Inez's doleful warnings—what did she know? Doubtless she'd been jealous not to have broken the code herself, found the secret and the cure.

The princess was unable to deceive herself for very long. Miranda collapsed on the landing, and the servants had to carry her upstairs. She wasn't hurt or sick. But she wouldn't wake up, and she slept for another day, and her mother watched over her.

Sometimes she sank deep in slumber, and she lay immobile, scarcely breathing. At other times she seemed to rise quickly to the surface and struggle there, thrash about on the pillow until her mother came to her. Clara sat by her, held her hand until she was submerged again. Then she returned to the activity that consumed many of these hours. She had built a private altar against one wall beside the bookcase, a few candles on a stool, a bowl of incense. She had got some devotional literature from a woman in the village, and a small wooden carving of Demeter's wheat sheaves, arranged in a circle around the image of the waxing moon. Sometimes she would still draw at her easel—real and, for the first time, imagined landscapes, as well as portraits of Miranda as she lay asleep. These were obsessive, quick sketches that often reduced her to weeping. Then she would abandon them or cross them out, and flop down on her knees with her little prayer book. She would read the cycle of prayers that begins with the descent of Persephone, Demeter's daughter, to the land of the dead.

HER DEVOTION IRRITATED Inez de Rougemont. Anxious in their separate ways, the two women sometimes sat together in Miranda's room, kept vigil there. The village doctor had been useless. It was only in Bucharest that they could hope to find a specialist.

But that was suddenly possible. Much had changed since Madame de Rougemont's refuge had been discovered. And many of the changes had not been anticipated. She had received a letter from the office of the President of the Assembly, from Colonel Bocu himself, deploring the damage that had been done and offering restitution. He was astonished that his men had so far exceeded their authority, which was to arrest a fugitive named Prochenko, also known as Andromedes, on a charge of espionage. The Rezistenta men who had come to Stanesti-Jui had been part of a rogue group, and their leader had already been punished for his insubordination.

In fact, the colonel claimed, though he regretted the intrusion, it gave him an opportunity to invite the entire household back to the capital, where they would be welcomed with the dignity they deserved. Madame (formerly Princess) Brancoveanu was a famous patriot, a heroine of the long struggle against Germany. And the reputation of her husband had been officially rehabilitated by a voice vote in the National Assembly, as a progenitor of the republican movement and a hero of a previous war against the Turks. The colonel himself had read the proclamation into the record. And, if he might be permitted to insert a private sentiment, he was eager to meet Mademoiselle Popescu as well, the daughter of two patriots, and a young woman who had already captivated Bucharest with her beauty and her charm.

Madame de Rougemont (he claimed) had nothing to fear from the new government, which had repealed all of the Empress Valeria's anti-conjuring laws. It was the desire of the assembly to encourage all kinds of scientific or alchemical inquiry, to harness them for the glory of the nation. Etc., etc.— the letter was quite long.

Now, in Miranda's room, Inez de Rougemont stood up from the settee and went to stand next to the window. The sun was gone from the garden where the men were turning earth.

She listened to the muttered sounds of prayer, which she could hear from across the room, and which made her angry. Through her stupidity and carelessness, Clara had unlocked a scientific anomaly out of its cell, and now she tried to comfort herself with nonsense and religious superstition. She knelt on the floor, rubbing her hands in the candlelight, a puzzled smile on her soft face as she contemplated a problem that was all her fault.

As she turned, Madame de Rougemont caught a glimpse of her own face in the looking glass over the dresser. And she looked absurd—she could see she had put on too much cosmetic powder. But in the morning when she made her face, sometimes she could catch a glimpse of the woman Frederick had loved. He had planned to give her Spanish mother's name to his own daughter, as she'd requested. He'd laughed—"It doesn't matter. Why not? People will assume I've named her for Miranda Brancoveanu."

Almost her own daughter, then. As close to her own daughter as could be. And she had taken the girl in, protected her, kept her from harm, watched over her both here and in Aegypta Schenck's invented world— Clara had ruined all that.

Now Madame de Rougemont stood above her as she knelt on her cushion. "You are not helping her," she said.

When Clara opened her eyes, she continued. "It has been a long time since the gods could help us."

She pointed to the candles on the makeshift altar. "You looked at the black book. You tried to read it, didn't you? There's a story Newton tells about Johannes Kepler. He found a creature outside the brass gates. In the book it says he was able to seduce it with a mixture of honey and blood, which might not be true. But he lured it up a high hill into a place between two mountains. He built a stone tower and locked it in a stone chamber."

Dear Clara's face had taken on a panicked, bored expression. "Perhaps before that you could pray to God and God might answer," said Inez de Rougemont. "There were miracles that could be verified. The histories are full of them. Since then, nothing. Not a single visitation or answered prayer. Now we are left with science as a last resort."

But the princess, for all her weakness, had an irritating stubbornness. "I don't believe you," she said. Then later, "You will see."

AND SO CLARA BRANCOVEANU went and sat down on the stool beside Miranda's head. She held her hand and said the prayers to Persephone, who lived for months among the dead in winter-land. Dear Inez stood above them, glowering, scratching at her long, dry, tapered fingers, and she was the one who first noticed. Clara could concede such a thing—she had closed her eyes for just a moment, so as to better listen to her own prayer. But she opened them when Miranda's breathing changed, and she saw Inez's starved, painted face near her own. She could almost forgive the older woman's cruelty when she saw her expression change into observant hopefulness; Miranda turned onto her side. Her eyelids fluttered, and instantly she was awake. She sat up, started to talk—laugh, even, like a clockwork doll when you release the key.

"Ah, comme j'ai rêvé—but I am glad to be home again. This is my home from now forward, my own ugly, poky little house. And when I go away and come back, I will depend on you to keep it warm for me, warm and comfortable—I thank you! But there's no food in the pantry! You have been remiss!"

Observant hope, and yet Inez de Rougemont didn't understand. Clara understood. Perhaps she wasn't clever, and no doubt her education had been neglected. But she had studied her daughter's face during the past months. She had memorized every line and reproduced it in her sketch-book. "Lieutenant Andromedes," Miranda said. "I saw him on the train. But he'll come back here, won't he? He's left his luggage here! I believe he loves this ugly, stupid, rustic little house—such a relief to me, after I was prisoner in the People's Palace. Simple pleasures, though I believe the girl's lungs are not strong."

"She is feverish," whispered dear Inez—she didn't understand! Clara understood, and with the intuition she'd learned at her easel (she'd always been praised for her drawing, ever since she was a little girl) she could see Miranda's face had never managed this precise articulation. Now, as her daughter moved her hands, grimaced, rolled her eyes, Clara imagined she could feel every transient emotion, every gust of sensation in the room.

There was only one woman who had been able to command this effect, either on stage or in a private chamber. "I shall get used to these," she said, rubbing her bosom and pressing it together under the flimsy nightgown, and then running her hands down her rib cage to her waist. "Oh, and I have beautiful fingers now. I won't try to chew them or make them bleed! I shall wear gloves if it is necessary—look!"

She held up her wrist and gave her bracelet a shake, the golden tiger-head beads of Miranda Brancoveanu. "How it sparkles!" she said. "I did not think it would be so light!"

"Clara, will you pass me the thermometer?" asked Inez de Rougemont, because she didn't understand. Clara understood. But then she'd been close to Jean-Baptiste when he had jerked awake and pranced around the library like a broken puppet. She had seen the glint of his eyes, smelled the bitter, citric odor of his skin—all that was less noticeable now. Miranda's eyes were dark blue, what an artist might call cerulean, not too dissimilar a shade. And she hadn't bathed in days. She was a woman who perspired freely, and her bed smelled of perspiration. Her mother was sensitive to such things.

"Oh, but there is something in the larder," Miranda said. Her hair was spread out over the pillow. "I can feel it stirring now. Do you remember how Jean-Baptiste used to bring me eels steamed in wine, fat lampers from the Danube delta? They had round little mouths, and they were fat with the blood and juice of other fish. There's something like that here, or I would starve to death. Other houses—I can visit for a short time, but I must leave! An old man in a train, Bocu's little whore—I must leave after I consume the house. Burn it in a fever. But not here. Here I can stay. Because of these black eels. I have a craving for lampers from the old days."

Dear Inez loomed above her. "Clara, could you let me sit down?" she said—she didn't understand. She was the one who seemed feverish, and the circles of cosmetic powder gave her cheeks a hectic flush. Her penciled eyebrows came together when Miranda said, "I have the jewel, of course—my jewel, that I got from the Corellis. When the house is dark, I stand in the front hallway and raise it up. And it gives a light. And the light burns."

Then for the first time she turned her head on the pillow and looked her mother in the face. "Maman," she said, "will bring me something to eat? I'm so hungry, and it's not just lampers in the dark."

Because Miranda had never called her that before, not for this entire winter and entire spring—never called her "maman," or used that plaintive tone, Clara found herself murmuring, "Of course, dear. Whatever you might want."

14   *The Descent to Chiselet*

WHAT SHE WANTED and she wasn't getting from anyone else, what she was starving for, was the answers to her questions.

Or else as she climbed down through the rocks into the valley, Miranda discovered little pieces of answers, not in the hidden world, but in herself. In her travels with the tourmaline and since she'd lost it, she'd become used to a kind of dream-life, in which sensation and experience felt more than real. But in the high, thin air under Kepler's tower, the conscious part of thinking had seemed weak and starved, the part that depends on volition, and deliberate decisions, and consideration. All that returned to her as she climbed lower, down between the mountain's outstretched arms.

So the Baroness Ceausescu had stolen Kepler's Eye and taken it through the brass gates, where Miranda couldn't follow. And her aunt Aegypta would go after it, find it, steal it back, if Miranda brought her . . . something, some token or proof from the defeat of President Bocu.

Something she could hold in her hand, and she would bring it up the hill to the stone tower where the secret creature lurked inside its cell—so, a quest. The mystic jewel, the small token of enormous power: These were elements in the kind of story she had loved to read when she was sick in bed with a cold, or else on a summer afternoon in the icehouse in Berkshire County.

You might search for it and find it in the hidden world, Miranda thought. Somewhere up ahead she might come down from Christmas Hill and find the streets spread out beyond the art museum. And if she made them or found them, what difference would it make? What would be the difference, if Rachel and Stanley were waiting for her in the big house on the green?

But in Mogosoaia in the cave, when she had crawled into the secret world using the portal and the key her aunt had left for her, she'd found herself in Williamstown again. When she had fought the elector and killed him, she had found herself among the dark streets of her childhood. They were empty. The houses were open and abandoned. Nothing lived in them but bugs, and the orange cat, and the great coiling snake. Was that the limit of her creative power, here in the hidden world?

No, but she had grown since then, hadn't she? She had changed. But what if all her changing had the effect of taking her away, farther and farther into a new landscape she could not recognize. Now she was on a road into an unknown valley, a meandering path through green hills gnawed bare by goats or sheep.

At first she had been startled by what her aunt had said, that in the hidden world the land could move with her, because of her, though not, maybe, in a way she could control. Was it so different in the real world? Stanley, her adoptive father, had once told her how a dozen people could stand in the same place, look out over the same scene, and there would be no point of similarity in what they saw, no common shape or color or pattern or significance. Maybe he exaggerated for effect, but it was certainly true that even the same person could perceive the same thing differently on different days, according to her mood. Today, here, now there was a stone wall, a ruined house, its roof open to the sky.

She stopped beside it. Her boots kicked at the hard mud. A skein of paths led down from here, all leading in the same direction. This was her aunt's road, she thought, and she could follow it down to the tasks her aunt had set for her. If Miranda were to reach someplace or find something of her own, would it be along here? Yes perhaps, because in one sense she had already departed from her aunt's way, or else she'd laid her own way down on top of it.

When she had first climbed down from Chistmas Hill into the world, she had expressed her resentment like a child, pushing the old woman's hands away, rejecting her, refusing her comfort and her help. After Insula Calia that had changed, when Miranda had seen the ghost in the salt cave. And for some time she had needed guidance, asked for it, accepted it.

But now the world had changed again. Miranda had crushed the snake that held the bird in its mouth. She had the power to make bargains. She was the white tyger of Roumania. The road she traveled led not only to Bocu's death, but to Peter and to Berkshire County and the war's end.

She found herself walking in a light rain, dressed in woolen clothes that kept the moisture out. Homespun, she supposed. She had a kind of a hood that involved a lot of cloth around her neck—a cowl, she supposed. She'd always wondered what a cowl was.

So—a belted woolen tunic without buttons, and wool pants underneath. Russet and sienna and oatmeal: Stanley had always made fun of those names in J. Crew or L.L.Bean catalogues. But they were the colors of the long-ago, at least in stories, or at least to her. Now there were boys on the barren hillsides. The goats had rope collars with little clappers made of wood.

But like her aunt's book, this place was bigger than she knew, as she realized when she came down through the terraced fields. She passed men and boys spreading slurry on the famished earth—a mixture of manure and water, which the mules pulled in leaky wagons. Not planting season yet, though they broke the dirt with wooden hoes. No one looked at her.

So you made the world as you moved through it, although sometimes you'd never know, as when you were asleep. Even here, nothing felt under her control. But nothing surprised her either as she came into the village. It had stopped raining, but the sky was still heavy as she followed the muddy lanes downhill through rows of thatched stone cottages, mortared and faced in mud. There was sewage in the middle of the street, a little channel edged with stone. The wooden shutters were still closed in the afternoon and there was nobody around, until she came down to the well in the middle of the town. That's where the people were, a crowd on the stone steps of the church below the wooden cross. They were building a gallows in an open space, Miranda saw without surprise. She guessed what it was for. There was even a priest in a rough cassock—umber, loden, ocher? He had a rope of beads around his waist and a demented expression on his ugly face, and he was poking a stick through the bars of a wooden cage. Miranda knew what was inside. She knew what these peasants were thinking of hanging or burning or breaking on the wheel.

"What's she done?" she murmured to the man beside her, a gap-toothed simpleton with a big nose.

He answered in the antique Wallachian dialect that was current in these hills: "It's a bad case. She is pregnant from the devil that lives near Chiselet."

Chiselet was the site of explosion, where General Antonescu had blown up the train. Peter had told her about that. Andromeda, too.

"We have seen her on the mountain in the shape of a wolf," continued the man. How likely was that? Miranda thought. Life-destroying superstitions flourished in these parts, no matter what she did. She was the white tyger of Roumania, and with a strength that seemed more normal and less counterfeit every moment she spent here, she pushed through the crowd. She ignored their grumbling, even took a stubborn pleasure in provoking it as she elbowed them aside, trod on their bare feet with her expensive leather boots—goatskin, calfskin, suede? She pulled the stick out of the priest's hands, then stood against the cage with the people at her back. She listened to their anger, their uncertain muttering, while at the same time she stood with her hands against the bars, poles with the bark still on them, tied together with rough twine.

Andromeda lay on her back, her knees drawn up. "Hey," she said, "what took you?"

Miranda drew from her sleeve a little steel blade, the kind of steel these country people never saw up in these hills with their wooden tools and their brittle, shoddy iron. The steel handle was twisted in a braid; she cut the rope apart and pulled the cage open. The noise at her back was loud and furious; yet even before she turned around she could hear a complaining, thwarted tone in it. The priest grabbed at her arm and she shook him off. How dare he touch her? She put the blade away. She didn't need it. She stroked the wet bark of the cage, then turned and stripped the hood or cowl from her face. She stood bareheaded in front of them and listened to their shocked, defeated murmurs—"The white tyger, the white tyger." There was no golden bracelet around her wrist. There was no tyger's skin around her shoulders. She didn't need any of that. But they recognized her, pulled away from her, and some of the superstitious ones collapsed onto their knees.

"What have I always told you?" she said. "How many times before it splits your wooden skulls? And you," she told the drooling priest, "you should be ashamed of yourself."

Later they stayed in an inn halfway down the valley on the way to Chiselet. Andromeda's mood was better after a dinner in the private dining room and a bath—that is, a bucket of hot water in the outside privy. Then they lay on adjoining beds in Miranda's room, drinking Georgian wine out of teacups. "Oh, it was terrible," Andromeda said. "They chased me with dogs, hunted me down. I was much affronted, as they say in Victorian novels."

Miranda picked her nose. "Since when have you read a Victorian novel?"

"Hey," said Andromeda, fluttering her eyelashes. "This is your fantasy."

But it didn't feel like a fantasy. The sagging bed, the rough coverlet, the low ceiling. The candle in its mirrored sconce. Andromeda's curious face, her shining blue-gray eyes. In how much of every conversation, Miranda thought, are we really talking to ourselves?

"Besides," Andromeda said, "my father gave me *Tess of the D'Urbervilles* that summer we were in Turkey. You know how you read anything when you're on vacation. I think he was trying to send a message about promiscuity."

"Yes, I can see it really took."

"Hey. I never pretended I wasn't a slut."

Miranda considered this.

"And when I say 'slut,'" Andromeda went on, seeming to enjoy the word, "I'm talking technically. Not, you know, pejoratively."

Which was a line she must have gotten straight from her father along with the book. He was a philosophy professor in Berkeley, California. "Yeah, sure," Miranda said, just as her friend broke into tears.

LIEUTENANT SASHA PROCHENKO, formerly of the Ninth Hussars, formerly aide-de-camp to General Schenck von Schenck, stood under the mosaic vault of the Gara de Nord in Bucharest, beside the big, four-sided clock and the newspaper kiosk. He had a copy of the *Roumania Libera* in his gloved hands, and he was reading a small story on page seven, the police news. A music-hall dancer had been murdered, her body abandoned in the Piata Enescu. Until the previous year she had been a student at the Sisters' Academy in the Strada Julia. She must have been young—fourteen, perhaps.

Touched in a way he didn't understand, he rubbed a tear from his left eye, thinking of Elena Bibescu, who had deserved more than she'd received. The newspaper said nothing about how the girl had died. There was no mention of a single stab wound to the chest.

IN THE HALF-TIMBERED hotel on the way to Chiselet, Miranda rolled onto her friend's bed to hug her, touch her face. "Oh, A.," she said. "It's what I loved about you. What I admired. You don't just get to choose the parts you like."

The next day, she and Andromeda rode down the valley to the plain. Because she was the white tyger, she had claimed two piebald horses from the ostler, a mare and a gelding—she had taken the mare. Twice they had to cross the stream, the water leaping and crashing and gathering momentum for the marshlands, before it joined the great river down below.

The second time, Miranda pulled up in the middle of the stream, where it had spread over egg-shaped rocks. The water was quiet around the horse's hooves as it stopped to drink.

"Wait," Miranda said. "Doesn't this look familiar? Doesn't this look like that place where Hemlock Brook crosses Route Six?"

Andromeda wouldn't even turn her head. "You know, behind that restaurant?" Miranda went on, mentioning locations they had known in Berkshire County when they were girls. "What if we kept to this side of the stream? North of here—"

Andromeda made a gesture of annoyance as she pulled her horse around. Miranda followed her across the ford, south along the path. Her friend was right as usual. It would have been stupid to try to ride cross-country through the woods. Anyway, they might have gotten lost. Or else—no, it was stupid. She must have been mistaken, Miranda thought, as the trees gave out and they came down onto the flat.

And there it was all laid out for her. Out across the plain was the abandoned town of Chiselet, the embers still glowing from the fire, the smoky clouds bloodred above it. There was another fire burning over Staro Selo and the great bridge at Tutrakan. The smoke and flames were visible all day, at every turning of the road.

On the river's far bank the Turkish army waited to cross. They were building their great barges, each one round and heavy like a turtle's back. They were bringing up their diabolic engines of war, dragging them along the road from Africa.

The river folk had met them in the fens, Wallachian men-at-arms—free men and boys protecting their homes. Each one was worth fifty of the enemy. But the Turks pushed them backward step by bloody step, because of the force of their numbers and the power of their malice and the ingenuity of their machines. Degenerate, misbegotten, hideous, they marched under the shadow of the bridge. The air was full of smoke and fire, and their harsh and obscene screaming, which took the place of human speech.

In Chiselet, Miranda thought, the real world and the hidden world might intersect. In the afternoon she and Andromeda reached the hamlet of Faurei above Lake Mostistea and the marsh. They stayed at the round castle by the lake. Miranda was in the courtyard; she was tending to the horses when the Chevalier de Graz came through the gate. He was maimed from the battle with the Turks, his armor split and riven—Pieter One-hand, as the soldiers called him, the most famous knight in all Roumania, and still young. Still handsome, too, as Miranda saw when they unlaced his helm: dark curly hair, cheeks as dark as any Gypsy's, yet with a gray pallor underneath, because he'd lost so much blood. He lay back against the stones while his men stripped off his gauntlet, unbolted his breastplate, carried him up the outside staircase to his private room. He hadn't seen her, hadn't looked at her, hadn't opened his eyes. She stood in the courtyard with the curry bristle in her hands.

Later she saw the boys carrying the iron braziers, the bottled nostrums, the pots of leeches. Behind them the magi and the doctors climbed up the stairs—charlatans, all of them, of a particularly male kind, competitive in their bones, and jealous of the strength of other men. The aim of all their wisdom was to suck that strength away. She sent the castellan to put out their fires, chase them home, while at the same time she asked Andromeda how she should prepare herself, what clothes she should wear.

"The fewer the better." She shrugged. They were in Miranda's upstairs room.

"Don't be smart with me. Please. I need your help."

"Hey, I'm trying. You asked my opinion."

"I don't want to hear about it. You were with him for months, weren't you? All those nights in North Africa and Byzantium—don't tell me he never—"

"Never what?"

"Never—you know."

Andromeda laughed. "He's not my type." But there was something cold and melancholic in her face. "He's your type, evidently. Come on. I'll show you."

And so later, when everyone was asleep, Miranda climbed up to the top of the tower under the full moon. And the Danube coiled on the southern horizon, and the fire burned beyond it. Close at hand, the sky burned over Chiselet. Miranda wore a white robe like a tyger's skin—striped with gray— and she paced the gallery for almost an hour, looking out over her country. Then she slipped down the outside stairs until she stood outside Pieter's room. Men were in the antechamber, but they lay asleep. One stirred; she put her finger to her lips. Then she drew open the door and slipped inside.

A candle guttered on the table. Pieter lay in bed, moaning in his sleep. The coverlet was stained from his leaking bandage. Miranda let the robe fall from her shoulders.

AND IN THE HOUSE in the Strada Cerbului, Peter Gross lay dreaming. Moonlight stretched through the open shutters.

That night as usual he dreamed his chaotic dream of war. Voiceless and without images—heat, and color, and noise, and fear. Men retching in the mud. He lay on the lip of no-man's-land while the fires burned around him.

He dreamed without images, but only colors and sensations. The stink, the wet dirt in your mouth, and the concussive thunder. Crouching in a hole. Burning fire and the cold fog. Cowardice, shit, and cordite, and rotten meat. Tobacco smoke and brandy. No shapes or faces, no events. No beginning and no end.

But then the noise of the bombardment eased and ceased, as if the

Sabbath had finally come. Even in the dream his ears were ringing. And the darkness came, and the cool wind as the men stood down.

And his dream changed, and he was dreaming of Miranda, who stood above him and let her robe fall.

MOONLIGHT TOUCHED THEM, made the room bright. Moonlight over Lake Mostistea in the valley of Chiselet. She lay beside him. He stirred, opened his eyes. "Hey," she said.

"Hey."

She reached down to touch his lips with her knuckles, his unshaven cheeks. It was all so easy. Nothing to have worried about, or to worry about now.

"I'm thirsty," he said.

She poured some water from a ewer on a bedside table, which she hadn't noticed until that moment. Surely it had been there—every detail of the hidden world had a precision that made it seem more real than real. She sat up against the headboard, the sheet pulled up around her body. Surely in her own fantasy or dream she could reveal herself, show some square inches of flesh to him, expecially now when they had . . . been together like this, but no. What had her aunt Aegypta called this place? A landscape of the heart, something like that.

"Thanks," he said.

And because she could not help herself, she reminded herself where her body actually lay, in a farmhouse in Stanesti-Jui upon the mountainside. Because she'd lost the tourmaline she was cut off from it. She wondered if she was lying asleep, and if all that had happened since Inspector Luckacz broke in with his men had taken—what? Seconds, hours, days? Was she sitting up with the bedclothes wrapped around her? Was she laughing, eating, talking? Was Andromeda still there, or had she left?

But doubtless Peter was not there, was still in the trenches below Staro Selo, unless (was it possible?) her mother had gotten word to him. And maybe days had gone by, and maybe he had gotten leave to come up on the train, and maybe right now the two of them were playing out some version of this same scene, which is why it had seemed normal and unfraught—a word Andromeda had used to use in Berkshire County. No, it was impossible.

He put the silver cup onto the table. With his poor, maimed, bandaged arm he reached up to kiss her, and she allowed herself to be kissed. A landscape of the heart, and every object in this room she had created from her own desire, and the Chevalier de Graz, and every word they spoke, and everything they did.

So: a kiss. A little tongue, as Andromeda would have categorized it. And it was nice—why not? She felt the coarse sharp hair around his mouth prick at her lips in a way that was not unpleasant.

In the hidden world, she told herself, you didn't have to worry about doing the wrong thing. A little more tongue. And she suspected also, with a sudden suspicion that was stronger than knowledge, that the power and precision of her imagining had an effect on the real world as well, and that events there, still fluid and unformed, would seep into the mold she had created here. Not everyone could do this with her startled dreams and wants. Maybe she was the only one. This kiss was a premonition, she thought.

IN THE STRADA CERBULUI it was Miranda who had taken away Peter's nightmare, replaced it with another kind of dream. She had healed him by surrendering. But now the dream doubled as it disappeared, as Chloe Adira stirred, raised herself up, leaned over him, let her naked breasts brush against his chest. But he was not happy to wake, nor could he lose the sensation of being in two places at once.

At first he was not happy to wake up. But he responded to her as she reached for him, and teased him and tickled him. Later, he searched the intimate recesses of her body as if looking for something and not finding it—she didn't seem to care. She had strategies to prolong the search, stop and start it again in another place.

She kissed him as he lay on his back, then got up, as he supposed, to find the water closet. He turned away from her, rolled over, looked for his dream again.

Exhausted, he closed his eyes and there it was, miraculously, waiting for him. Miranda sat cross-legged on the bed, wrapped in a sheet up to her neck.

But because this dream was not just a gift to him, but also under his control, in bed was not the only place they were. But they sat together outside the icehouse in Williamstown, Massachusetts, on the flat stones above the little stream. His harmonica was in his lap. And she was talking just as she had in the old days, her forehead bunched and serious. She pushed back a strand of hair.

"How do you know what you are going to do?" she said. "I mean there are voices around you that tell you everything about it. And then inside voices that aren't so different, usually. Because the outside voices have sunk down in."

This was the kind of thing she would have said, and maybe she even did say it. Back then she would have been discussing her parents, or else what was going to happen after high school. Now in the dream she wasn't talking about those things anymore. Because everything that had happened since had changed her. He also had changed, and if his right hand was still gone, it was because he had had it and lost it. If he still could not play the instrument in his lap, it was because he had lost the skills of his right hand. So there he was again outside the icehouse, a journey that had taken him a long way.

"I know what you mean," he said, which also was different—he hadn't then, all the times he'd sat with her. He did now.

She looked up into the heads of the summer trees. "Oh, look," she said, and her face lightened and cleared. She made a gesture with her hand. He knew she saw something above them on the branch, a bird or a squirrel, something like that. But he was looking at her. He wanted to reach out with his left hand and touch her on her cheek and lips—he was almost close enough for that. And though he could still feel the fear that made such a thing impossible, in another part of the dream he knew she was there with him, sitting cross-legged above him on the messed-up bed, and all he had to do was look up to wherever she was pointing.

Later, he woke up alone. The dream had already receded from him, not the fact of it or the vividness of it. But he could not longer remember all the things they had talked about, the turns of their conversation. He lay in Chloe Adira's bed, or else in some other downstairs bedroom of her house on the Strada Cerbului. Morning light poked through the shutters, made a ladder on the floor.

Peter blinked. The walls were dark blue plaster and the ceiling was white. Framed photographs were on the wall beside the bed.

Peter turned his head. The painted walls were coarse and rough. They deadened sound. It was so quiet here. Street noise barely penetrated.

For days after he had left Staro Selo, his ears had rung and buzzed. But how astonishing it was to sleep in a bed like this! The mattress was hard, the sheet pulled into ridges. There was even a pleasant smell, a perfume that hid a darker odor.

An image of Miranda floated through his mind and disappeared, disturbed by the memory of how Chloe Adira had looked as she rolled away from him, stood up. A groggy gasp, and she had held the coverlet against her breasts. When she turned, he could see her bare back in the lamplight, the swell of her hips, her dark shoulders with the whorl of hair that curled down from the nape of her neck—that was something he knew about. It hadn't taken him long to learn.

She had left him, come back to bed, left him once more when he was asleep. Now he lay with his left hand behind his head, remembering also the way she had unbuckled his prosthetic, rubbed the chafed, sore, dimpled, tender stump of his missing hand. She had kissed it with her dark lips. Or was that Miranda in his dream?

On the train to Brasov he had been half-afraid he might not feel anything again. Thinking of the men he had left behind, he had imagined himself and all of them as victims of a long, slow-roasting fire. He imagined ridges of scar tissue forming on his ears, his eyelids, his nose, his mouth, his fingers, re-forming harder and sharper every time they were scraped away. He imagined himself deformed in an army of deformed men—it wasn't true. Now he lay bloated as if with exquisite sensation, his fingers as subtle as a pianist's as he moved his left hand over his face, pinched the bridge of his nose, felt the stubble on his cheeks. Time slowed.

He had duties later in the day. Hours from now. More than once the sergeant-colonel had suggested he go find a woman, and that's what he had done, hadn't he? Just what he said. What was Chloe Adira to him? What was he to her? She had a husband in Poland.

Peter had someone else as well. Miranda Popescu was in Stanesti-Jui, in the house of the Condesa de Rougemont. He had kept away from her—he was a wanted man, after all, suspected in the murder of Felix Ceausescu.

And by the time he realized no one cared about that, he was trapped at Staro Selo in the mud.

Now, lying on his back, he thought about the dream he'd had. Where was Miranda now? Had she forgiven him for the way he'd left her in Cismigiu Park? But if he could just leave this place, find her and ask her—what had General Antonescu said, that he had no use for cripples in his army? Peter rolled over, got out of bed.

If he couldn't find a way to visit her in Stanesti-Jui, maybe she could come to Brasov—he would write her. There was no reason not to. Andromeda must have already delivered the one letter. There was no hiding the contents of it now.

But he was in Chloe Adira's house. He got up to go in search of her, to find her and say good-bye. He wanted to be gone—out the door into the street; he didn't want to get trapped here like in the mud of Staro Selo. There was a linen robe decorated with chain-stitching, a style he associated with North Africa. It lay across the end of the bed. Maybe she'd left it for him. But he put on his clothes instead.

He heard voices in the corridor. There was an open doorway at the end of the passage. The passage was windowless and dark, but the shutters were open in the small square room beyond. Chloe stood there, framed in the light, talking to a man—the servant, Dumitru, who had served him tea the night before.

Peter thought to clear his throat or make a noise with his feet, but then he paused. Dumitru had a big chest and beard, and he was standing close to his mistress, glowering down at her. And though his precise expression was indistinct, the language of his body suggested a change from his surly deference the previous night—the deference had gone away. "Monsieur Janus was a fool," he said.

Then he grimaced. Except for the single French word, he spoke Roumanian with the German accent that was common in the town. "I suppose there is no choice what to do. They will know where he is gone. They will be watching the house, I think."

"It is not like that."

"Hah—I wonder. Why would Antonescu send this fellow out of all of them? What kind of spy will get his picture in the paper? And why would he . . . make this kind of occupation with madame—just a little recreation? Why not just knock down the door?"

Was it possible, thought Peter, that the man was right? Was it possible that Peter had been watched, or manipulated, or had the police after him? He wanted to say something to deny it, to announce his presence. But he was puzzled by the servant's truculence, curious also to know what Chloe Adira might say. He had no desire to cause trouble here. So he stood quiet in the darkness, his hook dangling from his hand. He had not strapped it on.

"It is not like that," Chloe repeated.

"Hah—what is it like? He came here with a letter from your brother. He came right to the door. Madame brought him in, and they talk about the war. Madame tells him about Chiselet. Just so—like that. Do you know who this man is?"

"Friend, everyone in Brasov knows who he is. He is Captain Gross from the Mountain Regiment. He's in the newspaper. I had to earn his trust," said Chloe Adira.

"I can see that," said Dumitru. "And so how many times did madame earn this trust? We have no use for services like that—"

She tried to slap him, but he caught her hand, pushed her away. Peter dropped his prosthesis and stepped toward them, angered by the look of brutal satisfaction on Dumitru's face—the man smiled. He was enjoying this.

"Oh, here's the hero," he said. "The wounded hero of Staro Selo." He stood in the middle of the hallway fumbling under his shirt for a weapon, a snub-nose Meriam—Peter saw when he drew it out—from Eritraea. Let him feel like a man, Peter thought. He had no intention of confronting him. His raised his hand, then took a few more steps to where Chloe stood. She was dressed in a long linen robe.

"You are finished, both of you," Dumitru said. "You are no use to us. You are dabblers in this, rich men and women—Monsieur Janus, too. You won't be with us when we march to Bucharest, I promise you. We will be boatmen and shift workers and farmers. We will be workers in the oil fields and mines. No Africans and no rich men—you will see."

After such a speech, Peter thought, he could have no intention of firing the pistol. Peter studied the man's heavy, bearded face, looking for clues.

With the gun at his waist, Dumitru backed through the doorway into the lighted room, then disappeared around a corner. Peter let him go. He listened to the clump of his footsteps, the muffled crash of the front door.

Chloe Adira was upset, and so he reached out his hand. When she came to him he held her close as she struggled gently in his arm. "Trust me," he murmured—what did he mean? Why should she? In what way was he deserving of her trust, or anybody's trust? She put her hands against his chest. He held her for a moment and then let her go.

But he couldn't leave her like this, now. Later, in the bedroom, they spoke about what had happened. Agitated, Chloe walked back and forth next to the bed while he stood by the shuttered window. She clapped her pale palms together, lightly, repeatedly, while she told him what she'd learned from her brother's letter, which he had written in the hospital, and which Peter had delivered with the reichmarks—"He broke his leg coming back from the Turkish lines. He stepped into a hole. He had delicate bones. He met a man who had crossed over from Constantinople, an Abyssinian, there between the armies. The hieroglyphs you took from him, that was a code. My brother told me what it said."

"He said he couldn't read it."

"Then he lied to you! Why would he tell you the truth? These are important subjects. As for that letter, don't tell me you have given it to the authorities. . . ."

Peter shook his head. Since the night before, he had tried not to think about these things. But now the question must be asked: What was the connection between this household and the wreck of the Hephaestion? He had wondered about it on the train to Brasov. Now, standing by the wooden shutter in this quiet room, he asked himself another question: What was he doing here? This was not just a matter of his duty to a fallen soldier. This was not just two lonely people reaching out to one another. What did Chloe Adira want from him?

He went to sit down on the bed. "Please don't speak," she said. "It is hard for me. Show me your hand."

He brought it up and opened it. "I will trust you because my brother trusted you," she said. "I will will trust you with my life and this house, because I have no choice—you heard what Dumitru said. I am so afraid."

He did not comfort her this time. He waited for her till she began: "I told you about the weapon in Chiselet. I know about it from my father."

She clapped her hands together, then continued. "You must have been a child, because it was before I was born. When Prince Frederick was attempting to form a government, then Abyssinia gave up its diplomatic and commercial ban—just for a few years, until the coronation of the empress. That was when my father was here as part of a trade delegation, and my mother was beautiful, although you wouldn't know it. But then he had to leave the country, and he could not take us with him, because of the miscegenation laws in Africa. He used to send us money—he still does, although with Janus's death . . ."

Peter listened. In fact he had not been a child when all this had occurred. Or rather, the Chevalier de Graz had not been a child, but a young officer. He had not been interested in politics. But Peter was interested now, in spite of his impatience, in spite of his desire to leave the house and not come back: ". . . So there is information that comes to us over the Turkish lines. Messages we pass on. My father is in the government in Addis Ababa. It has been many months since he first told us about the cargo of the Hephaestion, which he had tracked on behalf of his ministry—pitchblende from the Congo, as well as other more conventional weapons. These were things the Baroness Ceausescu meant to use against the Germans, and which she purchased from two retired officers—criminals, of course, who now live in Berlin. The pitchblende was incinerated, which might have caused some of the radiation sickness in that area—"

"I was there," murmured Peter.

"—in Chiselet. But there was something else."

All this time she had been speaking quickly, softly, swallowing between her sentences, clapping her palms together. "This was something so important and valuable, they sent a man, an engineer. His body was not found."

What was it Andromeda had said? When Peter had seen her in the orchard below Staro Selo: an Abyssinian fellow in a gray suit, south of the railway line. "Yes, I know. A dead oak tree in the marsh, two hundred meters south of the embankment. A lead-lined cylinder. What was in it?" he asked now.

"I—I don't know," she said. "It is hard to understand. But they are using poison gases in Bulgaria?"

"Yes." Men retching in the mud, he thought—an image rather than a sequence of words.

"This is like a poison gas, except it spreads like a disease. A germ that travels through the air. And it spreads from person to person, as it did across North Africa—oh, twenty years ago. Many died."

"And?"

"I—I don't know. The hieroglyphs are difficult, because they don't go word to word. And I didn't see them—this is what Janus wrote to me. I let you sleep when I was reading it, Dumitru and I—blood in your brain, and then it bursts out through your eyes and ears."

Men retching in the mud, Peter thought. Chloe Adira walked back and forth. "It is what my father told us," she went on. "The Germans accounted for every cylinder except one. So my father thought that someone like Bocu would use it as a weapon against the Turks. He might think it was a chance to win the war all in a moment. The chlorine gas, it kills men on both sides, doesn't it? This is like that. It cannot be so easily controlled."

She sat down beside him on the bed. She put her hands over her knees, then turned to face him. He closed his eyes. Men retching in the mud, and so he opened them. "My father says he is worried because Bocu will be desperate. There is a faction in my father's government that is supplying the Turks, giving them whatever they need. And so the military situation will get worse. . . ."

"I have a military duty here," Peter reminded her.

"Oh, but it is urgent. Now Dumitru—I'm afraid. . . . If the Turks cross the river east of Tutrakan . . ."

"Then the war is lost," Peter said. He shrugged. "The police searched Chiselet after the wreck. The Germans were there, too. This was a year ago."

"Oh, but it can't wait! Every cylinder but one—that's what my father says. The Turks also will find it if they cross the river below Staro Selo and the bridge. He said they have their barges in the water not ten kilometers from Chiselet—in hieroglyphs a picture corresponds to an idea. So there are turtles, he says, turtles with broad backs. And then an animal from Africa, a wild dog or a hyena with a long muzzle and enormous legs."

I've seen worse, Peter thought. But there was such anxiety in Chloe's face, he did not feel relieved. "You must help me," she said. "This canister of germs—you must bring it to me now that Dumitru has gone. You know where it is, by this oak tree! You must put it in my hand. I'll do the rest. I will send it to my father. You will be recompensed, and not just with money. You owe me this at least after last night."

She didn't know him very well, Peter thought. How could she know him well? Suddenly he was desperate to be gone. Was this the only reason she had taken him into her home? So she could seduce him and enlist him for some cause? Miranda's face occurred to him, not just for a moment, as before. But Miranda stayed with him when he left the house. She stayed with him in the street outside, and all the way back to the barracks in the Strada Castelului.

15 · A Landscape of Desire

IT WASN'T JUST that there were rumors in the city, because there were always rumors. The police investigation was perfunctory and brief, but the *Roumania Libera* was able to discover the name of the dead girl. In a series of small articles on page seven, one of the metropolitan reporters was able to track down her employers in the Strada Batistei, and to suggest that on the night in question she'd been seen getting into a government motorcar. The proximity of the body to the People's Palace was also mentioned, and there was a dark, irresponsible suggestion that this wasn't the first time. In the same issue there appeared an editorial letter on the subject of the modern demimonde, the collapse of public morals since the start of the hostilities, and the abuse of African cocaine in the University district. The victim's age was much discussed.

But the *Evenimentul Zilea* supported the government. It ran articles of its own, accusing its rival of defeatist speculation, antimilitarism, and pandering to the same prurience that it condemned. Its new masthead showed a stylized version of the Rezistenta claw, and in its own editorial letters it called for calm, and a new standard of professional dignity. When the offices of the *Libera* were ransacked and destroyed, it deplored the necessity. And when the minority political parties were outlawed and subsumed, it blamed the unfortunate exigencies of war.

In his private cabinet in the People's Palace, Victor Bocu sat with an unlit cigar between his fingers, the newspaper in his lap, unread. He had come from a special session of the National Assembly, where he had made a speech. It had been reprinted in the paper, broadcast on the radio. There was nothing in the pages of the *Evenimentul Zilea* that did not tell him what he already knew. There was no mention of a response from any representative of the military high command. What would Antonescu do now? He had no troops to spare, of course. And the Brancoveanu Artillery held the city.

Bocu's chamber had no windows, and inside it was neither day nor night. There was a decanter of Roumanian raki on his desk—none of these foreign extravagances for him. He unstoppered it, poured a small glass, smelled the bitter smell. He did not taste the liquid, which had a greasy look. Instead he scratched his scalp with big blunt fingers. "Come in," he said.

When the fellow was inside the door, he didn't turn around. "You'll forgive me if I don't get up," he said. "Maybe some gout, or rheumatism. Or else I broke my toe kicking these gentlemen in their backsides," he said, gesturing toward an article that described the dismissal of several ministers. "You've read the news," he said, laying the paper on the desk.

"Yes, your excellency."

Bocu turned to face him, an old man in a rumpled gray suit. "You don't look good," he said.

"Excellency, I am not able to discover why I am here. I comprehend I am no further use to you. But I was brought from my morning meal in my own house, and then obliged to wait—"

Bocu smiled. "How is your fat wife?"

"Sir—"

"Idiot! I don't require you to understand. You are here because I need you."

"Excellency, I—"

"Do not talk to me! It's been another fiasco. You are lucky I'm in a pleasant mood. But I want you to tell me one more time what happened in Stanesti-Jui and what you saw. The dead man who would not die, and spoke in the voice of a dead ghost . . ."

"Excellency, I—"

"I would have let you rot in Floreasca except for that. Will you tell me?"

"Excellency, I—"

"No, let me tell you. That man—that steward—was old and ugly, wasn't he? I saw him here in the old days—ugly, badly dressed. That's what surprises me. But then I thought—well, Inspector Luckacz is past his prime. I had never thought about it, whether old, useless, used-up people have an attraction for each other, search each other out—you and your Hungarian wife. Do you feel some kind of useless, used-up spark? Something compelling even so, something that might lead to violence. What do you think?"

Radu Luckacz was silent. He stood holding his hat by its soft, curled brim.

Bocu laid the copy of the newspaper on his desk. He aligned the pages with the corner of his blotter, then placed his hand on top as if to keep them there. "I remember a time not so long ago, when you were devoted to the artistry of Nicola Ceausescu. You were quite a 'fan.' Even if, like all loyal Roumanians, you ended up rejecting the decadent foreign influence in her work—I think that was a phrase you used. You yourself were born in Buda-Pest, I seem to remember. Maybe that makes you an expert. Even so—whatever you might think of Madame Ceausescu's artistic legacy, she was not the same kind of woman as a fat, gray-haired Hungarian in Floreasca. But then I thought, you are not the man you once were, either."

Bocu rose to his feet. He felt invigorated at moments like these. He felt as if his flesh had a different density from Luckacz's, from all these faded husks from the old regime. In the assembly he was like a man among ghosts, a ball among ninepins. But why? He was not tall, short, thin, fat, handsome, ugly, clever, stupid. And of course he was middle-aged, middle class—maybe it was the concentration of all that mediocrity that made him extraordinary in this modern world. A new kind of hero—whatever it was, the effect was entirely predictable by this time. Domnul Luckacz, former chief of police and in many ways the most powerful man in Bucharest under the German occupation, stood like a schoolboy, staring down at his shoes. "Tell me about Stanesti-Jui."

And the fellow told him, babbling about Miranda Popescu, babbling about the ghost of Nicola Ceausescu with the poker in her hand, chasing the men out of the house. "But how did you know?" Bocu asked. "How did you know who it was, in the corpse of this old man? Was it his smell, his voice?" he asked, because he was thinking about the actress who had died in his bed, and whose death had been reported in the *Roumania Libera*—he couldn't tell this old policeman about that! No, it had been a mistake even to bring him here. Unless . . .

He was still talking about these people, de Rougemont, Ceausescu, old names from the old days, old enemies. They could not hurt him, Bocu thought—not anymore. They did not matter anymore. Today he had spoken in the assembly. He had allowed every member a seat in his re-formed Rezistenta party, and they had stood up and applauded—they were desperate for the money. And the coalition ministers were all gone, departed like sheep or not even like sheep, because they hadn't even opened their mouths to complain. What was that compared to something that might or might not have happened in Stanesti-Jui, or in his own bedroom? Still he was curious—"What was it like? Did she speak to you? And finally, did she just collapse and die? Did you catch a glimpse of her face?"

"Excellency, I—"

"Oh, I don't know what I'm saying. What difference does it make? At least you must agree it was unnatural! Do you think so? What do you think? You must have heard, incidentally, about the repeal of the anti-conjuring statutes by voice vote in the assembly—there is no reason to dignify this kind of superstition by forbidding it. And of course it is better to flush these people out into the open."

"Excellency, I think—"

"But look at the time! I must change my clothes for supper. You're a good fellow after all, and we have something in common, you and I. You don't mind if I tease you?"

Bocu strode across the floor toward the policeman—just a few steps. The cabinet was a small room with ornate lacquered walls in the Chinese style. There were mirrors in ormolu frames. They augmented the colonel as he moved across the room—he felt fine, in perfect health, without a trace of gout or rheumatism, needless to say.

The lamplight flickered around him. He spread his legs, leaned his back against the closed door. With one hand he gestured into Luckacz's face with the unlit cigar, and with the other he untied his own cravat. Then he rocked himself forward as if unbalanced or drunk, so that he could reach out and squeeze the old man by his old, creased, hairy earlobe. "You're a good fellow," he repeated, "and I need good men. I am surrounded by fools. My valet is no longer with me, because I believe he spoke to one of the newspapers about my personal affairs—you would not make that mistake."

The old man flinched away. He was clever enough to know what was coming. Bocu let go of him. "I'd like the gray jacket with the velvet collar and a red cravat. Bring me an assortment. Your wife, have you sent word to her? In that old house in the Strada . . ."

"Yes, your excellency."

"Tomorrow the steward will find you something to wear. The household staff has some kind of official uniform. It is no concern of mine. But did I tell you? I got a response from Mademoiselle Popescu. A reply to my proposal. You'll be happy about that."

"Your excellency, I think—"

Bocu knew what he thought. He'd go on and on about it if Bocu let him. Miranda Popescu's criminality and the danger she represented were a fixed idea in him, a sign also of how hard it was for a dry old man to change with the times. To listen to him, Miranda Popescu and the Chevalier de Graz were at the center of every criminal enterprise in the entire country. Once a police inspector, now a valet in the People's Palace—it was a lesson to be learned! No, but his rigidity and prejudice, his utter lack of humor, had brought him to his present circumstances. The fellow couldn't even tell when he was being teased! Bocu would make none of these mistakes.

No, he would keep the old man with him, shield him from his enemies, forgive his failures—as a reminder to himself. No, the secret of remaining young was to surround yourself with beautiful young women. And if they'd been responsible for various crimes and deaths, that added spice to the brew.

Under present circumstances it was too dangerous to bring hired dancers or companions to the palace. Bocu had learned that lesson, obviously.

NO, MIRANDA POPESCU intrigued him. If at that moment he'd been able see into her bedroom in Stanesti-Jui, he might have been troubled also—preparations were underway. Miranda stood on the round rug, supervising a woman from the village who was packing the trunk. Already it was half-full of frocks and gowns and shawls and hose, which Madame de Rougemont had ordered from the catalogues of the Parisian dressmaker in Ploiesti, and which had been altered by a local woman in the village.

Sunlight slanted in the western windows. Holding some revealing piece of fabric to her waist, Miranda made a pirouette before the mirror, laughing with pleasure or else grimacing with distaste. Her mother couldn't predict what she was going to like—all of it seemed severe and modern and unornamented to Clara Brancoveanu. All of it was cut too close to the figure, as if the new style was to preserve as much cloth as possible, perhaps due to the war effort.

"Oh, maman," Miranda said. "What do you think of this one?"

Clara didn't like it at all, a silver dress cut to the knee. Below the waist, it left nothing to the imagination. Intended to be worn without a petticoat or even a slip, it was cut low over the bosom also, without any lace or voile to soften the line. If that wasn't enough, Miranda slid out of her dressing gown to judge the full effect. She stood before the mirror in her under-clothing as if the princess were no longer in the room, or the village woman, either—since when had Miranda been comfortable with servants and the work they did for her?

Clara Brancoveanu perched on the edge of a straight-backed chair beside the altar she had made. Even in the afternoon light, she had prepared a candle before the image of Demeter, who had also been scandalized by her errant daughter—no, that wasn't it. Miranda was a shy girl, modest in her person and uninterested in clothes. That was the shame of it. Left to herself she wore men's trousers, shirts buttoned to her neck. Clara had thought that too was unappealing and inappropriate. How she would have preferred it now!

Miranda twisted on her bare heel, showed her bare back, and for a moment her mother imagined that it was the body itself she was modeling before the mirror, shaking out the arms and legs, squinting at them sidewise, pursing her lips as if in disapproval—oh, but they might just suffice. At such times Miranda's face took on a gleeful, ironical expression, and her voice seemed tingled with sarcasm when she spoke: "I can't wait to return to the city. I've been so dull here. Do you remember those nights in the People's Palace? Colonel Bocu says there will be celebrations and festivals, because of the victory at Staro Selo—do you know we'd had a victory? You would scarcely know it from the newspapers or the way people talk. I can't wait to wear some of these things, though I'm afraid Ploiesti is still the provinces, after all. But at least they'll last me the first week until I look for something new."

Clara glanced at the pile of outfits on the floor and in the trunk—two dozen at least. "There should be enough," she murmured, sick to her stomach from worry and regret. It hurt her to remember how much Miranda had detested the People's Palace, how she'd felt a prisoner every moment, how firmly she'd resisted any effort to bring her out into society.

"Oh, I'll be so pleased to make the colonel's acquaintance. He will be able to introduce us to everyone we need to know. You've seen the photographs—he is not handsome, I suppose. But distinguished. But a trifle old."

"A trifle," murmured the princess. He was fifty-five at least. His father had been some species of successful tradesman in Bacau. He had gone to the military academy—that was something. Of course he had graduated into the artillery, which was reserved, her husband had always said, for the bottom third of the class.

"Is he married, do you think?"

"Um, a widower." Poor Elena Bibescu was scarcely in the ground. No doubt her funeral was one of the celebrations he'd referred to.

"Well, I suppose that's how a woman can hope to influence these great events, by introducing herself to the great men of history. That was what you did, I suppose, when you met my father."

The princess had slumped a little on her chair. Now she drew herself up, squared her shoulders. "I don't know," she said. But she did know: She had loved her husband. She remembered the first time she had seen him in

Kronstadt at the citadel, in his sky-blue uniform under the artificial flares, during the midwinter festival. His sister had introduced them, though Clara knew who he was already—they were cousins, after all. And besides that: All Roumania, all the world had known his name.

Oh, but it was not comparable. Sick with worry, Clara examined the image of the goddess between the pale candles. She tried to remember some of the words and diagrams in the black book and in Aegypta's letter. What kind of mother was she after all? Especially since, resist as she might, she could not but respond to this new Miranda when her face lit up with smiles, and when she said, "Dear maman," and squeezed her hand, and even embraced her on one high-spirited occasion. When she asked her for a mother's advice—none of these were things the old Miranda had ever done. And even though Clara knew there was nothing artless or sincere about these smiles, these words, still she was grateful for them. And even though she knew these gestures and embraces were as genuine as a puppet's, still she could not resist nourishing herself with them, because she had starved in silence for so long, when she was a prisoner in Ratisbon.

But she tore herself away, made her excuses, and went to look for Inez de Rougemont. Steps must be taken to end this farce, this masquerade. Her daughter was not responsible for her actions. She required a doctor's care.

She found dear Inez in the library. She was supervising Anton as he packed books into wooden crates. In contrast to Miranda, she was dressed in a frock that seemed antique even to the princess. She had an embroidered silk fichu over her shoulders in the Spanish style, Clara supposed: a black, fringed triangle over a red dress, which served to make her cheeks seem even redder than she had doubtless intended. Her hair was pulled back in a club at the nape of her neck.

And she was also in high spirits, eager to talk about the move, about what they'd do. She was gong to live with Madame de Graz in her house on Lake Herastrau. Miranda and the princess, of course, were going to stay at the palace, by Bocu's invitation: "You'll prefer it. I'm sure he himself has no idea how to make a table or what fork to use. But he'll have people to fix that for him. The formality of public office has a way of civilizing even a barbarian. And you'll be in no danger, obviously—he needs you. You can see it in the letter. He is trying to build a foundation of support, and for that he needs you and Miranda—a union, I suppose, of the new and the old, and a heroine, as he'll describe it, of the patriotic struggle. That's the happy thing about being a woman. You don't have to do anything, but only suffer for long enough. The world will come to you. Anton, here—take this one, and this."

She stood in the middle of the room, a load of books in her gloved hands. "I do not mean to alarm you. You must regard this as an opportunity. And now it is a chance to do something—don't you see? He is reaching out to us because he needs us; I have no illusions. But men can be transformed though their needs. Surely Frederick must have taught you that. You cannot wait for circumstances to be ideal. In any kind of politics, but especially the democratic kind, you work with what you have—that was the source of Frederick's strength. And that is the way a woman can exert power. You don't choose the men, but they choose you. Don't worry, I'll be there to tell you what to do."

Beau-cul, Clara thought, and reddened at the phrase, obscurely guilty in her heart of hearts. She did not like the way the condesa used her husband's given name. And what Inez had just said reminded her of what Miranda had also said—not Miranda, but the sprit that had taken over her body. How could these women be so cold? Clara had loved her husband. She had loved him.

It was her duty to protect her daughter, but what was she to do? "You don't think there'll be a danger?" she asked.

"Of course there'll be a danger!" said Inez de Rougemont. "Haven't you been listening? Isn't there a danger for the men at Staro Selo or the bridge? These are dangerous times. Perhaps I wouldn't even think of this, except there is a need to warn the military authorities. I believe there must be a new type of mechanical transport east of Tutrakan. An African invention—you must ask her about it! It is not a matter of her happiness or my happiness or yours."

Her voice broke. Then she went on. "Just look at what Miranda wants. She's made up her mind."

Uncertain, Clara Brancoveanu turned her back. Sometimes it was easier not to see people's faces. Now she could just listen to the condesa's voice, and it was clear to her the woman didn't believe what she was saying. This was a matter of a dream that Miranda didn't even remember anymore, apparently. Clara went to the window and stood looking into the kitchen garden. She could see where the glass had been repaired. The mullions had not yet been repainted. This was the window that had shattered on the night Jean-Baptiste had died.

He had bled to death there on the hearth, and Clara had stolen her husband's gun. How was a woman to protect herself? Terrible things had happened that night. Was she the only one who remembered? "I'm surprised to hear you say that," she said.

And then after a moment: "Anton," she continued, "will you excuse us?"

Something must be done. When the man was gone, she turned around. "You know she is not herself."

The condesa shrugged, smiled. How could she be so dense, so cavalier? Surely she cared about Miranda's health, Miranda's future.

"I know Miranda has not been well," she said. "Because of that unfortunate occurrence. But I believe she is stronger now, day by day. I have not done nothing while you prayed at your altar. I believe I can accept some credit."

"She is not herself," Clara repeated.

"Yes, of course. But whose fault is that? All that time she lay in bed she was fighting a battle, something we will never know. Now she has won, or almost won. You can see it in the way she sleeps—"

"Or doesn't sleep. She didn't sleep last night."

"I wouldn't worry about that. She has a lot of rest stored up."

"How can you laugh about it? How can you make a joke?"

It was because Inez de Rougemont had not seen Jean-Baptiste walking and talking in the library with his breast shot away. She had not been there. She had not heard his soft, harsh, woman's voice. If she had, she would not speak like this. "You know she needs a doctor's care," Clara continued. "Or an exorcist."

Dear Inez had put down her books. She wore wire-rimmed spectacles, and now she stripped them off. She rubbed her eyes, rubbed the bridge of her long noise.

"Really, Clara, why do you trouble your head with these things? They take years of study, and even then there is much we cannot claim to understand—"

"You didn't see him! You didn't see him chase those men away. You didn't hear him talking in Nicola Ceausescu's voice. Ask anyone!"

Exasperated, dear Inez scratched her unattractive chin. "You know there is no one I could ask except Miranda. Lieutenant Prochenko has gone away. And Miranda says nothing about this—Nicola Ceausescu is dead and buried. You should be happy that you did not harm your daughter more than you did."

"But I did harm her! I did her terrible harm!"

Inez de Rougemont pinched her nose, patted her cheek with her fingertips. She held her spectacles in her other hand. "Really," she said, "I don't understand you. We are leaving the day after tomorrow. If she needs a doctor we will find one in Bucharest. We will take her to a specialist in Floreasca. I am sure Magda de Graz has some names. We will take her to every specialist in the city, if you desire. We will do whatever needs to be done. Now, can it wait until then?"

It couldn't wait. Late that night, Clara was awakened by the sound of Miranda laughing and chattering in the adjoining room. There was a line of light under her door. Clara saw it as she came into the hall, carrying her candle, and at first she was tempted to knock. But then she hesitated, turned away, promising herself that she also would not flinch when the time came. She also would do what needed to be done.

THAT NIGHT THE FARMHOUSE went without sleep. Miranda laughed and chattered to herself, while her mother tossed and turned in her own white bed. But in a separate room at the front of the house, a peaked chamber overlooking the stables, Inez de Rougemont sat alone.

She was at her desk below the diamond-paned window. Toward dawn there was dry wind from the valley. It clattered through the pine trees, rattled the glass, pushed against the creaking house. At such moments the house seemed to the condesa to be capable of motion, breasting the elements, a ship under sail.

Whatever she had pretended to dear Clara, she was not glad to leave this house, this refuge, this room where she pursued her scientific researches. But they had no choice. Bocu's invitation could not be refused. Was it a terrible thing, therefore, to accept it?

Packing up her library earlier that day, she had been deliberately obtuse. She regretted that now. She had not wanted to confuse poor Clara, who annoyed her so. She had not wanted to remind Clara of her willful carelessness in the matter of the gun.

She had not wanted to, and yet she had. At the same time she had reminded herself of her far greater culpability—Prince Frederick's daughter had been under her care. Nor could she pretend to herself that Miranda hadn't changed, changed for the worse, changed in alarming ways. And if she could not believe in Clara's theory that the girl was possessed—if that seemed like ignorant and superstitious nonsense to her—it did not mean that something was not wrong.

But in Bucharest, perhaps, there would be people to consult, now that the anti-conjuring laws had been repealed. There was no one here.

As if to confirm this fact, she stood up from her uncomfortable chair—an alchemist's armchair from China, with a smooth horseshoe rail. She unlatched the casement, and drew it back. The wind blew the stacked-up papers from her desk, made a mess of her hair, blew out the candle—it didn't matter. She stood looking up at the far ridge above the town, the main thrust of the Vulcan Mountains. She scanned the icy, windswept peaks, looking for a glow, a glimmering. Somewhere, she thought, her friends met in secret; Zuzana Knauss from Germany, Jeanne Petite from France, and Mrs. Chatterjee from Bengal Bay. In their tiny and overheated refuge on Borgo Pass, they restitched and rearranged the torn fabric of Europe—the work was never done. At the same time they debated causes and effects, which grew out of their roots in the hidden world deep in the valley, a place they could not go.

For example, had Cornelius of Tyre been correct when he asserted a multitude of worlds, all expanding from a single point? In that case it was possible to imagine that Miranda might discover the lost places of her childhood just where she had left them, the people waiting for her there unscathed. Perhaps, for example, Miranda had already disappeared into that world and she was happy there. Perhaps this odd, immodest version of her that they were taking to Bucharest was some kind of simulacrum, animated (who knew?) through the effect of Treacle, the black eel. That was something to be wished, the condesa thought, if she could prove it. But even so, how could she take up her empty place again among the old women of the mountain, who had had such hopes that now, finally, they could achieve the solution to these mysteries, if they could hear about Miranda's travels from Miranda's lips?

No, she had failed in many things. And perhaps the core of it was this: She had not, when it was necessary, kept herself apart from evil men and women. It takes a peculiar kind of arrogance, she thought, to imagine you can use evil to do good. Now she shuddered to remember what she had said to dear, poor, innocent Clara Brancoveanu that same day, how they could use Colonel Bocu's interest in Miranda to accomplish . . . what? Something virtuous, no doubt, and something that could not be accomplished otherwise. And surely the condesa would not have used the girl herself, but only this soulless automaton that preened in her bedroom over her pile of clothes. She would not have used Frederick's daughter. . . .

And yet, in the past, she had not been too good for those kinds of bargains. When Miranda had first come to Great Roumania, she'd been there. When the Elector of Ratisbon had hunted the girl along the Hoosick riverbank, the Condesa de Rougemont had been there, disguised as an image from thirty years before, a painting from a wall, from a time when she'd been young and beautiful—the elector had not even been aware of it. No one had been aware of it except the Chevalier de Graz—no wonder it had been necessary to sequester him, and enlist Madame de Graz to help keep him away.

But that day on the riverbank she had protected Miranda, kept her from harm. Or else she couldn't quite remember—through the image in the painting, Ratisbon had been able to make use of her. But finally she had added her strength to his strength, and together they had brought Miranda safe across the ocean. He never could have managed it himself.

Before that she had traveled all the way to Berkshire County, Massachusetts, where Aegypta Schenck had kept her refuge—a weary way through the Port Authority Terminal. And she had even seen Miranda on the basketball court, and sent messages to Nicola Ceausescu, again without her knowledge. All that had been for the best, hadn't it?

But the price she'd paid was this: Miranda had not trusted her. She had not recognized her from Massachusetts, and had not seen her on the Hoosick riverbank, but even so she had not trusted her. And if the girl was lost now on the mountain below Kepler's tower, perhaps it was because of that distrust.

Shivering, alone, Inez de Rougemont latched the casement window, turned again into the dark, disordered room.

16 The Masquerade

SOME DAYS LATER in the city of Bucharest, Sasha Prochenko lay in bed at one o'clock in the afternoon. Drunk the night before, he had slept in his clothes. Now, looking up at the cracked ceiling, he wondered how he had found his way back to this small roominghouse in Floreasca, a sagging wooden structure at the end of a mud lane.

The streets of the city were dark after nine o'clock, because of the war effort. Many essential products were in short supply. The ministry had announced a general curfew, and required all householders to close their wooden shutters after sunset, or else seal up their windowpanes with canvas or oiled paper. Even without the curfew and the threat of a fine, people might have cowered inside their houses and kept their lamps dim, because of a new kind of danger. Closer to the front, Oltenita and Giurgiu had both been set on fire by Turkish airships, huge gas-inflated balloons, powered by some kind of internal-combustion motor. Appearing suddenly out of the night clouds, they had dropped incendiary bombs onto the wooden roofs.

So the streets were empty after dark, except for thieves and staggering drunks trying to find their way home, and except for the families of refugees who now lived under canvas in every public park or square. Every road to the battlefront was choked in both directions: men and equipment moving south, an army of refugees escaping north, carrying in wheelbarrows, suitcases, or cloth bundles the detritus of their lives.

But Prochenko had found his way back to the hotel, evidently. Now he lay on his back in his trousers and undershirt. He studied the mildewed splotches on the ceiling, which suggested various anatomical and vegetable shapes. The air was musky and sour. Clothes were strewn around. A chair lay on its side.

Prochenko had not unlatched the opaque shutter to the window over the street. Light came from the transom above the door. There was no meat to be had in the city; greasy turnip soup, the remains of some previous supper, had congealed in a broken dish on the floor. He must have upset it taking off his boots, upset the ashcan, too. He had no vodka and no cigarettes.

Since he had returned from Stanesti-Jui, he had lived inside this room like an animal inside its den. The money the condesa had given him was all gone. He had none left for the rent, which was exorbitant.

Thirsty, hungover, nauseated, he licked his pale lips. His hands couldn't stay still. He scratched at his scalp and armpits, wiped his mouth, smelled his long fingers. Then they were gone again, down around his lower body where he rubbed his crotch, the inside of his thighs. His hands made a circuit, returning always and forever to his upset stomach. He pulled up his undershirt, slid his long fingernails though the silver hair around his belly button, wondering what was happening inside, what kind of creature might be growning in there or—God help him—litter of small creatures. And though his stomach remained flat, still he felt bloated and distended, sick at heart.

He was a man who always tried to live in the present moment, to wake from dreams he couldn't remember, to leave the past behind him unexamined, foggily retained. He had come down from the condesa's farmhouse, trusting to a kind of hatred that had drawn him forward like a fragrance in the air. And that was all right, and there wasn't much to be done about it. The Brancoveanu Artillery was in the city. They had set up barricades around the People's Palace. Beau-cul never went anywhere without a motorcade and an armed guard.

So that was difficult. And the rest of it was also difficult, difficult to understand or even to remember. Difficult to maintain a sense of purpose. A creature, some kind of creature from another world—what did it smell like? Where could he find it? That other flying manikin had come to him, stung him over and over until he had caught it in his hand and crushed it, releasing a bloody stink that brought the dogs and wolves. But this other one, he guessed, was far away. If it fed on corpses, then it was south of the city in the front lines or at Staro Selo, where there were mountains of fresh corpses every day.

So it was all vague and all unsatisfactory. Pieter de Graz was in Brasov, Prochenko read in the newspaper; he was the toast of the town. The Turks were defeated daily on the road to the Tutrakan bridge. And Miranda and her mother were to be welcomed at the People's Palace, where there would be a celebration in their honor. Beau-cul had no use for the old feasts, Lupercalia and all that. He had invented new festivities unrelated to the old Roman calendar. This one was in praise of beauty, and was to involve a masked ball, a display of country dancing, and a beauty pageant, judged by the colonel himself.

Would it be possible, Prochenko thought, to cadge an invitation? Would it be possible to use some manner of disguise? He could wear a wolf's skin. He imagined himself in a wolf's shape, loping through the galleries—he had run that trail before, the night he'd released Nicola Ceausescu into tara mortilor, dragged her through the brass gates by her throat.

Miranda, obviously, had woken up. Miranda and her mother were in the city. What did that mean? Had they come of their free will? A naïve question—Bocu had a plan for them. One day he had sent his thugs to chase them from their refuge, even kill them. A week later he had advertised his idiotic bal masqué.

But it wasn't in the newspaper that he'd read the announcement. It wasn't in the same issue with the article about Captain Gross. Now he remembered, and when he did he sat up suddenly, swung his legs over the side of the bed. Now he remembered. Before dark he had watched a man put up a poster in the Calea Mosilor, an old man in a cloth cap.

Already drunk, Prochenko had watched him, a defeated old man with his bucket and paste, soaking the wall with a brush that seemed too large for his frail hand. Smoking his cigarette, Prochenko had waited until he was gone, then strolled across to street to read the proclamation from the new unity government. There were several older posters on this corner of the wall, along with some obscene graffiti. Prochenko read the recruitment notice for a new battalion named for Kevin Markasev the brave, hero of some former patriotic struggle. Male citizens between the ages of forty and fifty years—the war must be going worse than you might guess, Prochenko reflected, if you believed in the official news. In the meantime: Kevin Markasev. Prochenko brought his face to mind, his dark single eyebrow. The world was a peculiar place.

The next poster contained a list of deserters and wanted criminals. And the third was all for him. Prochenko found himself staring at a line drawing from an old photograph: a portrait, admirably precise. And a list of names and aliases: Sasha Andromedes, Alexei Prochenko, etc. There was notification of a reward.

The list of names did not include the one he'd used to register for this disgusting room. Thank God. The drawn portrait was worrisome, though. It was obvious the situation required a new kind of urgency, something you wouldn't necessarily have guessed, Prochenko thought, by looking at him now. But he got to his feet, staggered to the washbasin on its stand. There was some dirty water at the bottom of the bowl.

He would not let himself be hunted down in a dump like this, turned in to the authorities for a bucketful of the new and increasingly worthless Roumanian lei. Nor would he run to find some filthy refuge to conceal himself, or else wait to see whatever filthy, misbegotten or else stillborn beast came out of him. He was a man and he would die like a man, not like a dog or a sideshow freak. He was an officer of the Ninth Hussars, who had made his oath to General Schenck von Schenck in the old days. He was a man, and a brave man, and an officer of Great Roumania, but he could not tolerate . . . this. . . .

There was a knock at the door. Prochenko raised his head from the basin. The sound was a soft one, a furtive scratching. So he went to the door, unlatched it, opened it a crack. A woman stood on the landing, a tall girl in a white, embroidered dress. He didn't recognize her. She had a letter in her gloved hand.

He opened the door, gestured her inside; he didn't care about the mess, the smell. "What name did you ask for?"

"Domnul Andromedes, or else Prochenko—sir, it's on the envelope. Please, sir—you haven't dressed."

Oh, for Pete's sake. "What name did you tell to the concierge?"

"They hadn't heard of you until I gave them a description. The princess told me what to say."

He felt an urge to strangle her. "Princess Clara Brancoveanu," she went on. "I'm from the palace. I've been looking for you up and down the street."

She was a tall, bony girl with mouse-brown hair. He wanted to grab her nose, pull her ears. Instead he seized her by the wrist, yanked her inside so he could shut the door; she tried to twist her hand away. She was frightened, he could tell. "Please sir, your overshirt—"

"Did she give you any money for me?" He let go of her, pulled the envelope from her hand, tore it open. "I need an invitation for the bal masqué," he said. "Do you understand me?"

They spoke in French, which was discouraged in the palace and the city under the new government. The girl stood with her back to the wall; she wouldn't look at him. Nor was she reassured by the condition of the room. Prochenko could see her nostrils flare. He looked down at the pages in his hand, each embossed with a small crown.

Cher Monsieur, I am writing you because I don't know where to turn, and there is no one I can trust. I am more alone than I have ever felt, even since poor Felix's death, because Miranda has not improved, and she is worse than ever. You would not know it just to hear her speak a few words, or else dance across the floor. But a mother always knows, even a mother who has been remiss as I have been. It hurts me to say it. But is there any other explanation for the way these other women have turned against me and abandoned me? I thought I could trust them! But here we are in Bucharest, which is a city I cannot recognize. Sometimes I think I shall go mad. But I am sustained by my studies, and the hope that I might intervene. Come, and you will see what I intend! I think you only are in a state to understand me, and help us who depend on you for my late husband's sake. These few words in haste. The bearer is "a friend." Will you help us? C.

Prochenko folded the note up again. How useless it would be to lose his life for this nonsense! If he were as stupid as Princess Clara, he'd crush the pages into a ball, toss them into a corner for the police to find; they'd be here soon enough. Instead he slid them into his trousers' pocket, sat down on the mattress to pull on his boots.

But then he paused. He looked at the lace hem of the woman's plain-weave dress, embroidered in the Gypsy fashion. He looked at the woman's boots, hooked up the side.

"Go," he said. "Don't come here again. I won't be here. I will use the name Bailey, Andromeda Bailey—it's an English name. You can leave a letter at the post office in the Champs Elysées. Leave an invitation for the ball tomorrow night. Did you bring any money?"

"No."

"What use are you? Is there another message? Something else to say to me?"

He rose and stood in front of her. She was almost his height. She wouldn't look at him. She shook her head. "I am the chambermaid on the second floor. My mistress is staying in the Augustine apartments in the west façade."

"And Mademoiselle Popescu?"

She shrugged, and he lost patience. What was the point of her? "Go," he said. "Take the back stairs, the back way to the alley across the yards. Do not stop or give your name. Poste restante in the Elysian Fields."

The woman shook her head. Her nose was too large for her face. "My father said only the Brancoveanus could bring peace to Great Roumania," she said. "Otherwise it's all smashed to pieces. Princess Clara, she's so gentle with me. Not like the others—"

"Damn you, child, go. If Bocu's people find you here—"

That silenced her. Her mouth flapped open. He'd walked away from her while she was speaking, had opened the wooden shutter, peered outside into the lane. Already there were three policemen in plain clothes, waiting where the lane met the larger street. He could tell them anywhere. The concierge must have sent for them.

He had his balled-up shirt in his left hand, his balled-up jacket. And from the outside pocket he drew a pistol, a lion-mouth revolver from Abyssinia. He had bought it his first day in the city. Now he raised it up beside his cheek. The girl had taken too much time. He turned toward her, held up the gun. "Strip."

"Sir?"

"You heard me. Do it now. God help me, do not make me hurt you. You had your chance."

Now he left the window, went to stand with his back to the door. He threw the jacket and the shirt onto the bed. "Put those on."

"Sir—"

"By the balls of Dionysus, do as I say. Put these on, and go out the back way as I told you. Tuck up your hair under the hat."

While he spoke, he was pulling off his undershirt, unbuttoning his trousers, hopping on one leg as he drew them off. Horrified, the girl had turned her back, burst into tears. When he was naked, Prochenko stood behind her holding the gun where she could smell it. He helped her with the buttons down her back. He wanted all of it—the slip, the underdrawers, the boots and hose. "You want the Brancoveanus to return?" he asked, as gently as he could. "We have to make some sacrifices, you and me. We all have to surrender something to bring them home. You go tell the princess what you've done. She'll give you a jewel from her finger, I don't doubt."

Careful not to rip the cheap material, he drew the slip over her head, revealing her starved, spotted back. "Sir, if Bocu's men catch me dressed as a man, they'll—"

"God!" he whispered close to her ear. "Don't talk to me about it. The boots now—do as I say. No harm will come to you."

Furious because she was so modest and so slow, he tried to reassure her once again: "I'll give you time. What you fear—it is a certainty for me, when they force me to prove what I am. Afterwards, when they have me in the station, do you think they'll boast and say my skin was hot to the touch?"

These words gave him an obscure pleasure. Savage with impatience, he shrugged the slip over his shoulders, his right hand with the gun held high. How he hated her little fluttering hands, her weak attempts to hide herself and hide her eyes at the same time. He snatched her dress away, thrust his damp trousers into her hands.

Holding his clothes against her body, she turned away from him, collapsed against the wainscot and the bare boards of the floor. Humiliated beyond words, nevertheless she must have managed to catch a glimpse of him before the slip was down. "Oh," she murmured, the tears streaming down her face. "Oh, you are a woman, sir."

Prochenko pulled back his lips to show his glistening teeth. But when the dress was on, the hose pulled up, and he was sitting on the bed fumbling with the long boots and their hooks and buttons, he was able to swallow down his anger, still his breathing, calm himself. There was no reason to hurry. The men in the lane were waiting for instructions.

"Watch me from the window until you see them take me," he said. "Then do as I told you."

There was no hurry. He had several minutes to smooth down his layers of underclothes, lace up his boots, prepare himself like a knight preparing for battle. When he was a child his nurse had told him bedtime stories of the longago and faraway, when the knights would take their oaths in their white shifts, kneeling before dawn in the Temple of Mars.

He also had given his parole in the long-ago time. And this was no temple, but it would have to do. There was no mirror in the room, but he was confident when he stood up, when he arranged his yellow hair around his face, when he buttoned the white dress with the red embroidery, when he pulled on the white gloves, that he'd suffice. He would suffice in his purity and strength. And his clothes would be like armor, and they would protect him as he walked slowly down the stairs, along the corridor, as he pushed past the concierge and out into the street.

And for a moment he remembered Elena Bibescu at the mausoleum when she tottered forward to her death. "Here," he said to the girl. His voice was musical and light. "You see the safety clasp. I don't need this." He threw the revolver onto the bed.

EVERY VERSION OF THE hidden world is different, personal. In her version, Andromeda prepared for battle. This was not at Faurei Castle where Miranda had lain down with Pieter de Graz, healed him in an upstairs room. Nor was it at Chiselet or the great river, where the Turks were towing their enormous engines toward the open water, their enormous round barges like turtles' shells.

There was an enemy closer to hand. There was no reason to look beyond the borders of Great Roumania. In the heart of the country, the seat of government had been founded on a swamp that had not been drained. A monster had come out of the mud, a monster named Beau-cul—Goldenass. His standards showed a man defecating in the slime. Safe in his fortress in the swamp, he made waterspouts, thunder, and fog. From the battlements he drove his legion of toadies and pigs, who had kidnapped Mademoiselle Popescu as she lay asleep and vulnerable after her long night. They had brought her in through the mud gates of the fortress.

Only Andromeda remained to do battle with the monster. In the beginning of the afternoon, ambushed in her room, she sent the messenger away. "Go," she said, and then she climbed down to the boggy ground. She had no weapon to defend herself, but only a suit of white armor that did not belong to her.

"Miss, do you have papers, please? Here, sergeant, you won't believe it. Look at this. It's him all right."

How could she convince them otherwise? Without her armor, they would have shot her where she stood. But when she was in their power, and they had brought her to their hole, the white armor protected her by coming off. But it could not keep her from the knives and sticks of her attackers, who dragged her down into the mud and hurt her over and over before they let her go.

LATER, ACCORDING TO THE metropolitan report, a dangerous fugitive named Sasha Andromedes shot at two policemen in the alley behind the Floreasca roominghouse. A man who answered his description—linen jacket, dark shirt, slouch hat, gray trousers, leather boots—had been seen running down the Calea Mosilor. Then there was nothing. The scoundrel vanished while the officers, confused by a false resemblance, belabored a false clue. He left no trace. In the morning there were new posters in the streets, advertising this new crime and doubling the reward.

Lieutenant Prochenko, for this reason, did not change from his own disguise, the chambermaid's virginal and embroidered dress. After his hours in the Mosilor substation, he staggered out into the last light of the day, looking for someplace to wash. He walked down to the public water trough in Tineretului, then spent the night in Belu Cemetery among the graves. One of the officers had given him some money, an insult he had not refused.

With it he purchased a blanket, which was not enough to keep the chill away.

The next day—not too early—he went to the post office in the Elysian Fields. He gave his name as Andromeda Bailey and received an envelope. There was the printed invitation to the Festival of Beauty that same night. There was a pack of greasy banknotes, no worthless lei, but real reichmarks. The princess had scrawled a few words on her visiting card. Under her initial, "Ana" had added her name—the chambermaid, he supposed.

He took the money and he went to the women's baths in the Calea Victoriei, in the basement of the Venus temple. There, finally, he stripped off the poor girl's digusting clothes and underclothes. He spent many hours in the steam room with the towel wrapped around him. Then, dressed in a long bathrobe, he stalked up to the peristyle of the temple where the women had set up booths for manicures and pedicures. He spent his money at the shop inside the nave, buying new clothes for the masquerade. He had his hair arranged and styled. But he waved away the cosmeticians with their paints and powders, which were after all unnecessary; when they left him to inspect himself in the mirrors that adorned Venus's altar, he knew he had accomplished what he could. Even in his present mood, which was dark and furious, he could see he had transcended beauty, overshot it entirely. The other women in the sanctuary stood back to let him pass, and he stood as if alone before the icon of the goddess as she is represented there—naked by the forest pool, surrounded by animals who have come to gaze. And there is nothing adoring or angelic about their little faces. The beasts are jealous, hostile, as if she'd stolen something that belonged to them and they were half inclined, if they could summon up the courage, to destroy her, rip her apart. Perhaps one has tried already. She stands on the corpse of a silver wolf, who has reached up its paw to scratch her, and cover—as if accidentally—her pubic hair.

There is of course another reading of the old story. The goddess wears a wolf skin, and has removed it to wash herself in the reflective water. The painting, which still hangs there, is called *The Goddess and the Wolf*.

Prochenko's eyes were silver and blue, his hair yellow and streaked with silver, and he had silver freckles on his skin. He had not lost his winter pallor under the fine white hair that seemed to float above the exposed skin of his shoulders, the long muscles of his arms, and make them glow.

He wore a tight, sleeveless gown made out of black and silver goat's hair, brought at fabulous expense from the Russian province of Cashmere, a wool so long and fine it seemed to float around him, mix with his body hair in an effect that mimicked nakedness, at least from the waist up. He wore no jewelry of any kind, but an actual wolf skin, lined in raw red silk. And because many of the myths of Venus involved some species of transformation, and because many of the fashionable ladies of society had repaired to the temple to arrange themselves before the colonel's ball, the shop in the portico had stocked an assortment of animal disguises, including a feathered wolf's head that fitted over his cheeks and made his teeth seem sharp and white.

BUT IN THE HIDDEN world, in the middle of the morning Andromeda regained consciousness. She lay curled up around her wounds in the sharp grass. She'd been awakened by the south wind, which speckled her with ash and dust, and brought her also the acrid smells of war, of burning cottages and bodies. The wind troubled her soft hair, fanned her awake; she rolled onto her back and yawned, sniffed at the rank air, stretched out her tongue as if to taste it. When the change came over her, it spread from her nose backward over her cheeks, her brow, her ears, leaving only her eyes the way they'd been. Her muzzle lengthened, and the stiff coarse hair spread back, covering the soft pale under-fur.

She stretched, then yawned again. Along with the rags of clothes that had been left to her, she abandoned with her human shape all her contingencies and plans. All her memories and regrets—what a relief to leave them all behind! Stiff-legged, she crawled out from her refuge, then climbed down farther into the swamp itself, where the goldenass maintained his fortress.

IN THE PEOPLE'S PALACE, Victor Bocu was preparing for his masquerade. Radu Luckacz helped him with his costume. "I feel invigorated," Bocu said, examining himself in his dressing-room mirror. "I will enjoy the dancing. Do you want to know why?"

"Yes, your excellency."

"When you say 'yes, your excellency,' I presume you mean 'no, your excellency,' and vice versa. I reverse the phrases in my mind. It is because I don't care what you think. Do you understand me?"

"Yes, your excellency."

"I thought not. But I'll tell you anyway. I will enjoy the dancing because I used to be a dancing instructor at one time, thirty years ago. I am quite sure everyone who knows this is now dead—you are the only one. So if I read it or any reference to it in the newspaper, I will know where the information came from. Have you discovered what happened to my previous valet?"

"No, your excellency."

"I thought so. You still have the habits of a policeman, which is why I trust you in your important new job. I do not trust you, however, to help me with the right sleeve of my shirt," said Bocu, carefully arranging the folds of red and black embroidered cloth. You understand why not."

"No, your excellency."

"I thought so."

Victor Bocu was in a rare mood. The air in his dressing room was perfumed with the smell of his unlit cigar, his untasted glass of schnapps.

Radu Luckacz stood behind him. The old man was dressed in the palace livery. With a whiskbroom he brushed flecks of dandruff from his master's shirt, then tied the bandit's scarf over his close-cropped head. "I think you think you are being punished," Bocu remarked, "because you were unfaithful. I think you think you deserve your punishment. Soon you will be dead, you think, and in the land of the dead you will throw yourself at Nicola Ceausescu's feet, earn her forgiveness. Let me tell you," he said. "The reason I rewrote the anti-conjuring laws is to prove to men like you what's dead is dead. Here's another part of it, in case you think I'm too kind. Is it better to have my enemies scattered in secret through the villages? Or here in Bucharest under my hand—because they are deluded, these old women, doesn't mean they can't make trouble. But I believe I've pulled the fangs of this white tyger!"

Radu Luckacz stood behind his shoulder. Studying him in the mirror, Bocu guffawed. "It is absurd to think of Mademoiselle Popescu as any kind of tiger, after all. Or one can only hope. You, on the other hand, are very like a crow, I think—there is no suit of clothes you can't make dingy. Every time I see you, you look thinner and more miserable."

"Your excellency," croaked Luckacz, "we are talking about a dangerous criminal. I am convinced she murdered a policeman in Braila. . . ."

The colonel sighed.

THE STREETS OF BUCHAREST were dark as Sasha Prochenko walked up the Calea Victoriei.

It had rained while he was in the temple, and he stepped daintily through the mud. Beggars reached out their hands, Gypsy children came to the flaps of their canvas shelters, but he did not pause. He was faster on foot than the ladies who'd been with him in the Venus temple, stuck in their carriages and motorcars. A barouche had sunk to its axles at the corner of the Strada Eforiei, where a hole had opened up between the paving stones.

But on this night, in celebration of the victory at Staro Selo and the return of the lost princesses, the lamps were all lit in the Palace of the People and in the piata outside, where the carriages pulled up along the Hasmonaean Gate, looted from the sack of Jerusalem six hundred years before.

Prochenko had his invitation in his hand, but no one would have stopped him. Men and women pulled away from him to let him pass, then stared after him, muttering; he wore no cape or overcoat. And like any of the great predators of the forest, he was surrounded by a sphere of quiet that resolved itself in furious chattering when he had passed. Most of the guests had not yet donned their masks, which in any case were modest dominos on gilded sticks, and did not hide their faces. But Prochenko's silver wolf mask was fringed with peacock feathers.

A handsome guardsman offered his arm, and Prochenko swept into the gallery of mirrors, which led to the Bessarabian ballroom. Servants dressed as Cossacks poured Moldavian champagne. Two stories high, the entire enormous room had been rigged out in painted leather like the inside of a tribesman's tent. Victor Bocu stood on the dais in the middle of the dance floor, surrounded by his Gypsy orchestra. He wore red leather boots and leather trousers, a baldric with crossed pistols and cartridges, a black scarf knotted over his face and his round head. He peered out through embroidered eye-holes, a bandit or a captain of the steppes.

With him were the contestants from the beauty pageant, each representing a separate racial group or district of the country, each wearing a version of her distinctive native dress.

HE STOOD WITH THE girls on the dais in their idiotic clothes, the orchestra scraping away. Looking out over the crowd, he could see Miranda Popescu on one side of the hall—what a welcome surprise she had turned out to be! From what he'd heard, he'd expected some kind of ugly, gangling creature, awkward and shy. Her father had not been handsome, and the Brancoveanus were not a prepossessing family, to judge from the portraits which, after all, had been designed to please. No, this blood was tired, Bocu had thought, this aristocratic blood—though beguiling, obviously, to a man whose father had owned a shop: That was easy to understand. But Elena Bibescu had been stupid and faithless after all. As for the white tyger . . .

Colonel Bocu climbed down from the dais under the great chandelier. He had to push his way through the crowd, and it was possible that some of these idiots might not know who he was. But now a number of pierrots and scaramouches came to stand around him, ministers and secretaries, blocking his view of the Popescu girl—no, there she was. And it was not that she was beautiful. No one could claim she was beautiful.

"Sir, I thought that . . ."

Who was this idiotic fool in his sea boots and false moustache? It was Voineshti from the Treasury. What did he want? In the meantime Mademoiselle Popescu had disappeared. Bocu turned his head to search for the other one, the stranger in the wolf's mask. It was to be a night of surprises after all, and there were creatures in the forest he would hunt with Cupid's arrows. In the meantime, Voineshti nattered on. "Sir, it is only a question of time before . . ." God damn him! The old fool!

This scarf around Bocu's head, of course, did not make it easier for him to see. No, there she was—the wolf. Not for him, finally, the conventional vapid beauties on the dais. Give him something exotic, something unusual, as Elena—curse her—had been. And he could see that no one wanted to talk to the wolf girl. The women pulled away from her, the men didn't dare look at her—not that there were many men, of course. Except for the buffoons from the artillery, the colonel was as young as any fellow here.

"So on the first of the month . . . ," said Voineshti.

The colonel nodded his head. "Tell me," he said, "what do you think of Mademoiselle Popescu?"

The man shrugged. "Sir, she favors her father. . . ."

"Hah, I see. So you think her looks are a manifestation of her father's politics, maybe. You think her long neck is a function of the rights of the citizen—what was it—fifteen articles? You think her eyes reflect his wish for a deep-water port on the Adriatic, and her breasts the separation of religious and state policy—see the rift between them!"

These professional politicians, Bocu thought, all imagined he was crazy when he talked like this. Voineshti nodded sagely, his face a mask under his little fringed mask. His false whiskers did little to obscure his false teeth, his long thin face. Nor was he capable of seeing below the surface to the heart of things. When he looked at Miranda Popescu, the colonel imagined, all the old man saw was her black, straight hair, her small chin, wide forehead, and protruding ears. He was not capable of reading the proud grace of her gestures, or else understanding the delicate bravado of her movements as she made a little dancing shuffle across the floor. Nor could he appreciate her choice of clothes. She wore a dress that revealed everything that was beautiful in her, while hiding everything that was not. It was white, streaked with gray, cut to the border of immodesty, showing her pretty waist and legs. She wore a diamond and feldspar necklace that had once belonged to Nicola Ceaucescu. Her hair was pulled back from her face.

And of course, around her wrist was the gold bracelet of the Brancoveanus, a symbol of archaic feudalism, but beguiling even so! She made a little pirouette across the polished floor. The Gypsy violins and concertinas performed a complicated melody, which she anticipated with some complicated footwork in the most modern style, as if from some dance academy in Cairo or Damascus. Why, she danced as well as Nicola Ceausescu had herself! How odd that this exhausted family had still managed to produce one final blossom before it collapsed always and forever into obscurity. How lucky that all he had to do was reach out his hand for the flower to fall into it—that little dance step had been for him, he was convinced. Who else?

He stepped away from Voineshti and the others. But then he wasn't so sure after all, because the wolf and the tyger were together now, and it was the wolf who made a little answering figure, pulling back her silver gown to show her silver feet.

IN THE HIDDEN WORLD, and in the real world too, between the Tutrakan bridge and the village of Chiselet, the Danube breaks into a swamp that has from earliest recorded times provided a refuge for bandits and conjurers. This was where the monster had his fortress.

In that world, in Faurei Castle, where she had reached out to touch the Chevalier de Graz, and after she had kissed him as he lay asleep, Miranda discovered her own bed again in the early morning. Exhausted, she fell into a dream.

And in the dream she found herself surrounded not by her own men but by the enemy, a grinning throng of demons and familiars. And the golden-ass had changed her, turned her into an object of mockery for his own per-verted enjoyment. She had hated skirts and dresses her whole life, yet here she was forced to dance or exhibit herself in some tiny, white, slinky number that left her legs bare and the top of her chest uncovered. She found herself reduced to her mere body, her feet squeezed into shoes that crippled her, and that seemed to move and dance with a life of their own—that was the worst part. For instead of running from this place, covering herself up, she could hear herself laughing, hear the vapid question she asked, feel herself turn with her palms open at her waist, as if offering herself up.

Oh, this was terrible, after the frightening and perfect moments she had spent with Pieter in the upstairs room! Around her there were masks and animals, shadows and flames. Goldenass himself was there, a man who was neither tall nor short, fat nor thin. He wore a black scarf over his head, Zorro-fashion—she knew who he was. She recognized him by his laugh, his strong teeth glinting in the light as he spun away from the others, turned to meet her on the scorched ground.

Because she was the white tyger, sometimes she could see these ragged beggars in their spirit flesh, a circle of small animals that had joined to bring her down. She could have ripped apart one or a dozen, but not all these. In these moments the goldenass showed himself not as some obscene version of his name, but as a powerful beast, brick red and bloated, a winged dragon or else a slippery-fingered toad. In her own place, in her own skin she might have had nothing to fear.

Weakened and exhausted, she bowed her head. But here was help when she least expected it. Andromeda was here, and she had slipped in among these beasts in her own skin, as if in disguise. Surely the two of them—

—COULD ACCOMPLISH SOMETHING here, Prochenko thought. The Gypsies on the dais, quaint in their embroidered costumes, were making quite a racket. Men in high boots and long overcoats carried trays of champagne. But there was an open space between him and Miranda, whose dress was surprisingly risqué—much more so than Prochenko's own. It looked good on her, he had to admit.

"Hey," he said in English, when they got close. And then a few more words. It didn't take him long to see she didn't understand him, not long to recognize her acrid, citrus smell, not long, when he watched for it, to see the glint of violet in her eyes. His heart, having risen, now subsided in his chest. "Dog shit," he said. "C'est toi."

"Naturellement."

Now she'd grabbed hold of his arm. She recognized him, too. Disgusted, he pulled away. Was there never anything to hope for? Nothing to go right? Oh, but he would make this monster pay, Beau-cul, who now sauntered toward them over the floor. He was dressed like some Bessarabian chieftan. He had a smile on his odious face. Elena had deserved better. Great Roumania deserved better.

There was no liquor on his breath. He smelled like pepper, crushed in his strong teeth. "Mesdemoiselles," he said, the total of his French. He continued in Roumanian: "Si eu cum sa aleg intre voi? How can I choose between you? We men are only mortals, after all!"

What a clown. It disgusted Prochenko that he might have touched Elena's body, kissed her lips. And the lieutenant had no desire to converse with Nicola Ceausescu of all people. Instead he turned away, pulled away, noticing for the first time another woman—Ana the chambermaid—who stood gesticulating on the edge of the crowd. She wore the church clothes of a Transylvanian peasant with a voluminous white headdress—yards of cloth, out of which she peeped through a white domino. Prochenko recognized her nose, too big for her face.

"What is your name?" said the Bessarabian bandit.

"Andromeda," he answered as he smiled and slid away, probably not the wisest choice. But the dance floor was loud, and Beau-cul might not have heard; he smiled also, and then he turned back to the Baroness Ceausescu. No doubt he would exercise all his disgusting wiles to talk her into bed with him, then wish he hadn't.

"Follow me," Ana whispered. Away from the dancing floor, Prochenko had to push through the crowd. But they reached a door hidden behind a leather panel, away from the light. "I must thank you," said the girl. "I must thank you for the pistol."

"I wish you'd killed those men."

She shrugged, gave him a shy smile. "I didn't know what I was doing. I'd never fired such a thing. I broke a window on the second floor. They ran like kittens."

An odd phrase. "You look beautiful," the girl continued, breathless—what did she mean?

She groped for a door behind the curtains, and led him through a sequence of small rooms. Then there was a staircase that led to a small gallery above the dancing floor. There were chairs and a carved fretwork balustrade. Ropes of streamers led from it to the base of the chandelier. Princess Clara Brancoveanu stood with her hand on one of the wooden knobs, watching her daughter down below. The orchestra was playing a medley of Cossack folk tunes, including "Nights upon the Dnieper," which was a favorite that spring—a Cossack regiment had particularly distinguished itself at Staro Selo. But now they moved into the love theme from *The White Tyger*. It was appropriate, Prochenko thought, from several points of view.

The princess wore no mask. Her gown was simple and undecorated—tasteful, Prochenko thought. Her hair was piled onto her head, revealing her neck, the backs of her ears. The gallery sloped three steps down. Prochenko stayed in the shadow of the back wall. The chambermaid had disappeared.

"Lieutenant," said the princess. "I am glad you're here."

She didn't turn around. She stood with her hand on the balustrade not more than two meters distant. She didn't have to raise her voice. Prochenko remembered her as a foolish woman, easily flustered, easily made fun of. But she seemed calm tonight, overtaken, perhaps, by some of the same fatalism that had touched Prochenko on the dancing floor—calm and dignified. It occurred to him he had misjudged her. It was not foolishness that had sustained her through the years of her captivity, sustained her when Felix Ceausescu had bled to death in her arms, sustained her in her current excruciating pain—she must know.

She must. Below her the floor had emptied out, leaving a circle in the middle for the bandit chieftain and his lady love. The dowagers and the debutantes made a rhythm to the music, delicately clapping their gloved hands, rustling their small feet. And in the center Miranda swooned and spun, while the bandit turned around her, stamping out a complicated latticework of steps, then moving in to catch her when she subsided backward without looking—she might as well have a rose in her teeth, Prochenko thought. He remembered ballroom dancing in ninth grade gym, a brief craze because of some stupid movie, and an ordeal for him and Miranda both. "She dances very well," he said bitterly, now.

"It is not she."

No duh. "She is possessed by an evil spirit," the princess continued. In spite of the music and the sound of laughing and clapping, she didn't have to raise her voice, she was so close. Prochenko stood in the darkness, she in the light, and the light shone on her face—prematurely old, he thought, aged and softened from defeat, though she was smiling as she turned toward him, a false smile for whoever might be watching from below.

In profile she showed the proud nose of the Brancoveanus, which he had never particularly noticed on her face before. "I need to study how to cure her," she said. "I have a book. But I must get her away from this place. Madame de Rougemont is no help. We came together in the train. Oh, it was frightful—it was as if this spirit were imitating how my daughter used to talk, how she used to move her head, gesture with her hands. She was a great mimic, of course, an actress on the stage. The voice, everything was perfect. But she doesn't care if I know. When Madame de Rougemont wasn't looking she would put her tongue out—it amuses her. And she says she will stay in Bucharest. Farm life isn't for her, she says. She misses this great prison; I know how Miranda hated it, hated every minute she spent here. I learned to see it through her eyes."

"It's not the building that she misses," murmured Prochenko.

"No, of course not. She says she means to strangle him on their wedding night—she tells me these things! And then with the condesa and Madame de Graz she would use some turn of phrase only Miranda knew—they are living in Lake Herastrau. Even if she's joking about him, she means to run for the assembly, she says—oh, she is interested in the democratic rights of women!"

Down below, the music had changed. The bandit had one bare hand on Miranda's bare back as they turned together first to one side, then the other. "What about him?" Prochenko asked.

"Oh, isn't it obvious? She is von Schenck's daughter. My husband's daughter. The first martyr of the republic, murdered by Antonescu and the empress—what else could give legitimacy to this fraudulent government? Oh, but if Frederick were still alive—"

She smiled and nodded for the crowd. She showed a political sophistication that surprised Prochenko. Now, as he sometimes did, he remembered Prince Frederick at the window of the room in Mogosoaia, remembered the words of his oath to protect the princess and her unborn child, when he'd been a dissolute young lieutenant in the Ninth Hussars—the words had changed him. Here he was in his feathered mask. "Ma'am," he said, "you sent for me. Here I am. What must I do?"

He had not thought he would be asking her this question. Striding up the Calea Victoriei, he had thought he would find Miranda, find Inez de Rougemont. But he looked for Miranda now and didn't see her down below. The dancing was more general. The empty circle under the chandelier was now filled in.

"She won't listen to me," said Princess Clara. "But she might listen to you—both parts of her. Miranda had become your friend, of course. But am I right in thinking that Madame Ceausescu has a . . . fondness for you?"

Prochenko shrugged. "I'm not sure she likes to see me dressed like this."

And the princess's artificial smile, which she'd been displaying to the crowd, now for a moment seemed almost genuine. "You could be surprised. After all, this is a masquerade."

Then she continued. "I need you to convince her to come with you—some place where we can restrain her—Ana will help. And her brother, who works in the kitchen. I have been studying part of the book—how one could reverse certain effects. It is possible to perform what Magister Newton calls an exorcism—I need help with some of the English words. Your English is sufficient, isn't it?"

All this seemed so half-assed, it was almost poignant. "My English is just fine," Prochenko answered in that language. "It's, like, fluent." Then he returned to French: "C'est que—I'm surprised Madame de Rougemont isn't part of this. It would seem this might be more an area of her . . . special expertise."

And Clara Brancoveanu turned around, looked him in the face for the first time. "I cannot depend on her," she said, her voice trembling. "I want to know if I can depend on you."

"Ma'am," he said, obscurely touched.

"Thank you, lieutenant. Yours has been a long, thankless duty, I understand."

She stood with her hand on the baluster knob, dressed in her simple clothes. "Ma'am," he said. "Miranda—"

"We must search her out."

And she came up the steps and took his hand. Together they passed out through the curtains and the little door to where Ana was waiting in the corridor.

IN THE GOLDENASS'S SECRET fortress, the dance was over and the fight began. The circle of swamp creatures had closed in, while the wolf prowled its perimeter. Lizards, ferrets, jackrabbits, and snakes all pressed against each other, while every footfall disturbed hordes of seething insects. In the meantime the tyger had grappled with her enemy and pulled him from the circle, away from the crystal faerie lights that hung suspended in the trees. Once, because of the slime that gathered on his skin, the monster was able to twist away, pull free. But then the tyger hooked her claws into his back, a surface of scales, pimples, and blisters many layers thick. She could not dig down through it to release his blood or ichor, the fluid of his life. But still he howled with an agony that also sounded like pleasure, a grotesque simpering babble that burst out of him like some foul discharge.

They had stumbled out into the darkness, and the mud walls that constrained them had disappeared, and they were in the swamp itself, a mixture of effluent, sewage, and fresh water that bubbled unexpectedly to the surface in limpid pools. The mud was so deep, in some places it was thick with fossils, the calcified remains of other creatures that had struggled in these same waters, only to succumb to a common enemy. And the monster fought in a way that seemed to maximize this threat, searching always for deeper water or unstable ground, and stroking her or seizing hold of her with his repulsive, webbed, spatulate fingers. At the same time he secreted a poisonous liquid through special glands, which weakened her and made her numb.

Though she was stronger, better armed, always he found a way of twisting away from her so that her claws and teeth couldn't find anything to bite or scratch. At the same time she was filthy, hampered by the mud, and hampered also by another creature that now came out of the darkness, the monster's minion or henchman. He was a scarecrow, though at other times, as now, he appeared in his true or natural form, the crow he claimed to scare away, guard against—an ugly, immense, bald-headed, red-eyed bird. Help, she imagined, and help was with her—the wolf that had been her companion all her life, and now struggled to reach her as she fought on shifting ground. But the crow swerved to meet him with its claws outstretched, buffeting his face and snatching at his eyes.

"COME THIS WAY," said Ana, the chambermaid. "Follow me."

She led them through the servant's corridors, a labyrinth of little rooms and flights of steps and hallways that nestled inside the larger palace, unperceived, reached only by secret, designated portals, small doorways behind tapestries or under stairs. There was no light, but she carried a candle in a glass frame, which threw uncertain shadows. They climbed to the upper, private apartments and came out near Bocu's chamber, an ornate suite of rooms that had been furnished fifty years before in a massive, dark, faux-baroque style: carved cornices and low-relief paneling in oiled and polished wood. Axes and bayonets, arranged in roseate circles, decorated the walls. Radu Luckacz stood at the entrance, a crowlike, bald old man dressed in the gray livery of the palace staff. Prochenko could see him when he opened the door to the servant's antechamber—the old policeman who had hunted him in Stanesti-Jui. "You stay here," he told the princess. "I'll bring her back. Ana—we might need your brother now."

"Bless you, lieutenant," said Clara Brancoveanu, hands to her mouth.

He sauntered out into the hall. But these were not clothes that let you stride down the corridor, hands in your pockets, shoulders hunched, collar turned up to hide your face. No, this was another part of his nature, he thought as he spun in a half circle under the lamp, then tripped lightly down the long carpet past the wall covered with weapons—little steps, and his arms turned out to display his bosom or lack of it—chin up.

"Mademoiselle. The colonel is occupied at this present time," said the policeman, or inspector, or valet or whatever he was now. He also wore a costume that disguised his true abilities.

Under the feather mask, Prochenko's face was hot. He opened his mouth so he could sweat. A breathless giggle: "I believe I am expected. Please . . ."

"The colonel must not be disturbed," said the old man. His voice was harsh, and he spoke in a Hungarian accent.

A smile: "Do you think so?"

So Miranda was already inside. Radu Luckacz couldn't be happy about that. Unless he also had been bewitched by Nicola Ceausescu.

The doorway took up the entire end of the corridor, with false fluted pilasters and a mahogany pediment. The door itself was lined with russet leather and embossed in brass. Radu Luckacz stood with his gloved hands at his sides, a bald old man with a lined face and bloodshot eyes. He had been drinking, maybe. Prochenko took a step closer and the scent came clear— absinthe. The old man's upper lip was unshaved. He was attempting to grow a moustache. He had even used some paint or colored pencil to further the impression.

Prochenko took another step. He stripped off one of his long gloves and used his bare hand to pull back the skirt of his long gown, switch it back and forth, show his ankle. "The colonel is expecting me," he said. "He will be disappointed."

And he saw some doubt in the old man's eyes, red-rimmed with broken blood vessels. Once they had been blue. His eyebrows also had some paint in them.

"Mademoiselle—his directions were fully explicit. It is not possible I might have made a mistake. . . ."

But then the door opened. There wasn't much light inside. Bocu was there. He had taken off his mask, unbuttoned his shirt to show his hairy chest. He had an unopened bottle of muscadine in one hand. "What is this noise?" he said, more curious than angry, and when he saw Prochenko, he immediately smiled.

There was no drunkenness in him. He showed his square, strong teeth. "Mademoiselle," he said, "I think I must have died and gone to heaven. They say that heroes in the Elysian Fields don't have to choose between the things they want. That was what my mother said. She meant it as a reproach, but if she could see me now—or maybe not," he continued, laughing in the light from the corridor. "Please come in. Would you enjoy a glass of wine?"

Prochenko stepped over the threshold. At the last instant he turned to glance at Radu Luckacz, which was a mistake. He smelled the policeman's breath, saw again his moment of uncertainty. Too late. He looked away—too late. The old man had caught sight of his eyes through the feather-fringed holes of his mask. Luckacz had recognized his eyes.

And then his gloved hand came up, and Prochenko pulled back his head. But the policeman sunk his fingers into the soft feathers and snatched the mask away. The cord snapped. "Oaf," said Bocu, "what are you doing? Mademoiselle, please—"

He dropped the bottle of muscadine, which did not break. And he put his hand under Prochenko's elbow, pulled him into the darkened room.

"Your excellency," said Luckacz. "It is An—"

"Mademoiselle Andromeda, yes. Idiot—I know her name. We have been introduced." He closed the door in the policeman's face, then drew Prochenko into the dark bedchamber. "Mademoiselle, I must apologize. May I say I am not disappointed? Of course these masks are the first things we shall lose. You see I myself . . ." He gestured toward his head.

Miranda stood next to the enormous bed, a canopied four-poster with carved columns as thick as elephants' legs. And it was true—she wore no mask, except for the mask that was her entire body under these circumstances.

Light came from a lamp on a low table. As Prochenko stepped forward, he could hear a soft hiss from Miranda's lips. "So. It is you."

Bocu spoke from behind him. "You know each other? How delicious—"

"Oh, yes. We are old friends," Miranda said, her voice soft. She came to meet Prochenko in the middle of the floor, and she spoke as if they were alone in the room: "Je t'en prie—you must not think poorly of me. I was here to negotiate a bargain. I did not mean to seal it, not here, not ever— oh, you must not reproach me. It's just that there are things that I can still accomplish for the sake of Great Roumania."

"I'll bet."

"Tu ne me crois pas."

"Of course I do."

Miranda spoke in French, Prochenko in English, and if Bocu understood them, he gave no sign. "Sa nu va mai—none of this kind of talk," he said. "Dar trebuie—I must swear to you. I won't have this kind of talk. We are in Bucharest, in the People's Palace. Besieged on all sides. So we will speak to each other as Roumanians. But this will be a night to remember. . . ."

"Je te jure . . . ," said Miranda, as if he hadn't spoken. "I tell you there are many ways we have been able to misunderstand each other. Fate has kept us apart, and I have many regrets. So, so many regrets. But you must believe me, I have tried to please you in my own fashion. Everything I've done. Even this," she said, stretching out her arms, displaying not so much the small white dress as the body inside of it, "even this I chose for your sake, because I knew it pleased you. Miranda Popescu—am I right? She was a whore for you?"

Prochenko shook his head. But then he crossed the last few meters be- tween them, put his hands on her waist and drew her to him so he could whisper in her ear. "You must come with me."

He felt her trembling under his hands, one gloved, one bare. He listened to her short, soft breath. But then the leather door opened again, and light spilled in from the outside corridor, and Radu Luckacz was standing in the gap, his shadow spilling into the room; it was to be predicted. He wouldn't leave them alone. Probably he was fortified with another drink, maybe a weapon, too. "Excellency," he said. "I must insist for you to hear me out. I must insist that you discover a good look. It is Sasha Andromedes, whom you call Prochenko, I must insist."

And Victor Bocu, for all his faults, was a man of action. For several minutes he'd been standing on the carpet, with an expression on his face that moved between exasperation, amusement, impatience, and delight. Now that was gone in an instant, replaced with a tremor of recognition and a murderous fury that transformed him, seemed to swell him up with blood, so that his veins stood out on his face and hands and neck, and his skin turned dark and red. Then there was a strange, clicking sound and a stiletto appeared in his hands, a steel needle that appeared out of nowhere, that had killed, Prochenko had no doubt, Elena Bibescu at the tomb in Belu Cemetery.

Prochenko's hands were on Miranda's hips. He pushed her away, then turned to face his enemy just as the knife came toward him. Luckacz was behind him now. And Bocu leapt at him without any type of preamble, his compact, powerful body launched like a cannonball, the blade in his right hand. I will not die like this, Prochenko thought, looking for a weapon—he had seen it or half seen it as soon as he had entered the room, leaning up against a bureau in the corner, an ebony walking stick with a silver wolf's head. Had Bocu kept it in his bedroom since he had found it at the baroness's grave?

Luckacz also had a weapon, an old-fashioned battle-ax that he had pulled from one of the ornamental displays in the corridor. The old man was close behind with the ax above his head. But the colonel was closer, solid with rage, the stiletto in front of him, its point not more than a few centimeters from the breast of Prochenko's silver gown when Miranda grabbed his hand. A hiss escaped her. She fell on Bocu, bit him on the hand. "Assassins!" he roared. "To me!"

Then the stiletto was at Miranda's throat. Bocu fell on her; he was as strong as a dragon. Prochenko knelt under the falling ax; there was no time. He grabbed hold of the edgeless blade of the stiletto, twisted it from Bocu's hands. He slid his fingers into the monster's hair, greasy with pomade. He pulled back the monster's head, and with the point of the stiletto he searched for the artery below the ear, searched for the windpipe. He forced the blade through the thick neck until the point came out the other side, and the grunting and roaring was extinguished, and his hands were full of blood.

Miranda was unharmed. She lay on her back, dazed, and he saw the horror in her face; he knew what she was looking at. He was Sasha Prochenko of the Ninth Hussars. This was not his first fight. He knew that Radu Luckacz stood above him, his ax raised for another stroke. The stiletto was stuck in Bocu's neck, and he flung himself across Miranda's body as the blade came down. He twisted under it and reached for the wolf's-head walking stick in the corner of the room—too far.

IN THE HIDDEN WORLD, it was all done. The monster was in the pool, his bloated body turning and drifting as the blood spread away. He had died in his toad's shape, mauled and bitten by the wolf, his throat torn open. His tufted ear had been torn from his head. But the wolf also was hurt, her body savaged by the crow's steel beak, which in magic fashion had bit deep at the joint between the shoulder and the neck, and again under her armpit. Stunned, the bird had staggered under a bush and brooded there a dozen feet away.

But for Miranda and Andromeda the spell was broken, and she drew her friend's body to the bank, lifted her up beside a willow tree, smoothed her wet hair from her face. "Hey," she said.

There was a wind out of the swamp and a few drops of rain. Bruised clouds overhead, and a huge, sudden clap of thunder, so loud it disturbed the surface of the pool.

AND IN BUCHAREST, in the People's Palace, the windows shattered on the east side of the façade. Enemy zeppelins had flown from Ruse eighty kilometers away, where the Turks had their aerodrome. Lit up for the celebration, the palace drew them like a beacon in the dark.

Inside Victor Bocu's bedroom, the casement split and folded inward, spilling broken glass across the floor. The curtains blew back from the force of the concussion. Radu Luckacz, lying against a corner of the wall, could hear the drone of the foreign engines. Some of the houses on the other side of the piata had already caught fire, and by the light of the burning rooftops he could see the first bloated cigar-shaped airships blunder from the clouds.

The Turks dropped incendiary bombs as well as more conventional explosives. Luckacz could distinguish a great number of noises, as a man might, listening to an orchestra or a brass band, pick out the separate instruments: the crash of the detonations, the howl of the electric horns and the steam whistles, the thump of the motors as the zeppelins churned overhead. Then there were the anti-aircraft cannon opening up, and even at this distance, the clamor of individual shouts and screams.

But in the room itself there were more gentle noises. Propped up in a corner, he strained to listen to Mademoiselle Popescu's quiet sobs. He recognized the sound, the intonation. He'd heard it before, that soft abandoned hissing. He remembered from the night Felix Ceausescu died.

And with his eyes round as a bird's, by the light of the explosions, he watched the girl sitting with the corpse on her lap—Sasha Andromedes, dressed as a woman for the masquerade. Mademoiselle Popescu had pulled out the ax where it had lodged in his shoulder, bit into the bone. She pushed his yellow hair from his face.

Presently she lay back, as if she'd fainted or collapsed unconscious, or else fallen asleep. And even in the roaring wind, the blast of fire beyond the open window, Luckacz heard the chink of the golden bracelet. From where he was, he could see her chest rise and fall. But his eyes were round with terror, because he suspected what would happen. He had seen it before, or else some version of it in the farmhouse in Stanesti-Jui, which he had visited for one night in the rain. He had seen a corpse come back to life, and now he came aware of a small, spasmodic movement in the limbs of the dead man, the way a puppet, lying in a jumble on the floor, might come to life when someone touched its strings. In fits and starts he gathered to his feet, twitching and shuddering until he stood upright in his silver gown. He stepped away into an open section of the floor, where he stood erect among the shards of broken glass, the blood dripping from his arms.

Fire burned behind his head, framed in the split casement. Beyond him were the tracers' flare, the pounding cannonade, and now a larger explosion as one of the great ships caught fire. Luckacz could feel the heat on his face; he raised up his hand as if to push away the burning world outside the window. Then, instead, he strained to listen, strained to see, strained to understand: Students of Nicola Ceausescu, as Radu Luckacz had been in his own way, could recognize immediately the little dance that Ariadne dances on the beach. She gives the impression she has never danced before. And her movements, jerky, hesitant at first, then gather light and air and grace as she is touched by a fierce and angry God.

In the performance, Dionysus never comes onstage. But his presence is indicated by a thunderstorm—flashing lights and rolling drums that shake the theater. Here also there was changing weather in the piata, the crash of lightning here, too, and then a siren in the night. Sasha Andromedes spun in a circle. His gown spun open from his legs. Blood spattered from his fingers. Then he stopped on one foot, his hands above his head. His red mouth sagged open. "Radu," he said, "what have you done to me?"

There was thunder in the piata, and the burning fire. "Do not be afraid, Radu my friend—n'aie pas peur. I will see you again, I promise you. Je te promets."

Then he collapsed again as if the strings had been cut. Mademoiselle Popescu didn't stir. Nor did Radu Luckacz try to shift or budge, even when strangers came to take her away. A man dressed in the kitchen livery and a peasant woman in an embroidered dress, her head covered with several meters of white cloth. They bent down over Mademoiselle Popescu's body, lifted her up onto the man's shoulder—he was not more than a boy, really. He stumbled away with her, stumbled out the door.

The building shook, and there were shouts and alarms. But it wasn't for many minutes that Luckacz finally rose to his feet. He looked down at the body, Andromedes's corpse in its indecent disguise, lit with garish intermittent flashes from the window. Nor could he keep himself from bending over it, drawing up the skirt to see what might be underneath.

And there was Bocu's body also, collapsed in a wet pool, the knife still stuck in his throat. Bocu's ear had been cut from his head—had he done that? With the ax in his hand, he had slashed and slashed.

But there was no blood on Radu Luckacz. Horrified, he backed out the leather door and down the corridor, where he saw the servant's entrance was ajar. He found the marble stairs. No one paid attention to him. The building was on fire.

He found the gate, then walked out into the exploding piata. Once out of the city center he found streets of quiet houses in the dark. But the fire was spreading in the center of the city; Ibolya was awake. She wore her nightcap, the long gray braid down her back. She let him into the hall of his own house, the parlor decorated with Hungarian watercolors, the stair with its varnished wood.

"Radu," she said, "oh, Radu," and she took him in, gave him a bath and something to eat. His daughter was asleep upstairs. He wondered whether he should wake her, because he knew he didn't have much time, and the soldiers would come for him later that same day.

III

The Voyage Home

17 *The Hunting Lodge*

THE NEWS CAME TO BRASOV as to all Roumanian provincial towns: first by telegraph, in ominous words and phrases; second by wireless transmissions, full of static and bad information; third by train.

It might have been possible for an experienced politician or newspaper editor to tell the story in manner to inspire confidence. The damage from the air raid had not been catastrophic. Many of the enemy ships had been exploded or shot down.

Certainly it was true that the president of the National Assembly had been assassinated under scandalous and uncertain conditions—a shocking event, and one that justified some of the darkest rumors surrounding him. Because his corpse had been discovered in the same room with a murdered prostitute, only now it could be said: Colonel Victor Bocu was a tyrant who'd achieved his post through manipulation and chicanery. The fact of his death might presage a transition to republican rule in some more genuine form. And it might signal the reconciliation of a divided nation, beset as it was by outside enemies.

But there was no politician or editor to publish these ideas, though many discussed them privately, in artistic, military, religious, and intellectual circles. No word or action from the government, priesthood, or any source of organized authority dispelled the fog of anxious dread that settled over the country, more a product of emotion than of sense. The enemy had reached Bucharest for the first time in over three hundred years, when Sultan Ibrahim I had been defeated on the plains of Cernica outside the city walls. Colonel Bocu had been murdered in the People's Palace under circumstances that stank of treachery and conjuring. Among the people thought to be involved: a discontented subordinate (chief inspector of police under the Ceausescu government), and the last heiress of the Brancoveanu line. Only the former had been apprehended.

The attack on the capital could only draw attention to what everyone already knew: The enemy continued to advance on Staro Selo and the Tutrakan bridge. If they could cross the river there or just below it where the Danube split into the swamp, then Bucharest could no longer be defended, and the entire second army would be cut off on the wrong side of the river. The Turkish airships had demonstrated once and for all that the enemy had African support. There was talk of other devastating weapons, armored vehicles and barges. General Antonescu had announced so many victories that it was hard to think the fight was going well.

In Brasov, Peter listened to the rumors with the others. Antonescu would use the Eleventh Mountaineers to secure the capital. He would consolidate the power of the army in the new assembly, then let the regiment progress to Tutrakan.

Peter did not speculate about these things. His anxiety had a different source. In Chloe Adira's bed, in her house in the Strada Cerbului, he had dreamed a dream.

Afterward, that same day he had written a letter to Miranda in Stanesti-Jui, asking her to come to Brasov if she could. Or if she couldn't, then he would find a way to come to her. No one is looking for us, he'd said. We don't have to hide anymore.

For a week he had imagined her in her bedroom in the mountain farmhouse, which he had never seen. But every invented detail was clear in his mind—she would be standing by the window with his letter in her hand. What would she think? What would she feel?

Now it turned out she was already in Bucharest. The police were searching door to door. Fresh concerns for her safety now replaced his personal anxieties, which in any case he had no leisure to indulge. In the barracks on the Strada Castelului and on the parade grounds outside of town, the soldiers marched and drilled, marched and drilled. Peter's regimental duties required time and urgency. Following the census rolls and tax accounts, he rode with other officers into the villages. They gathered up the last conscripts, chased down the last deserters and resisters.

On the regiment's last day in Brasov he rode out, finally, to Sacele, east of the town, along the banks of the Tarlung River and the lake. This was a village of thatched houses on steep hillsides, where Chloe's mother's father had had a dairy farm. Peter had come here in late summer thirty years before, bear hunting with the Count de Graz.

He did not want the townspeople to recognize him from that time. In Brasov he'd begun to grow a beard, which itched. The day was bright and hot. He pulled his service cap over his eyes.

He rode a chestnut mare, a bad-tempered, skittish animal. Ahead on the dusty road was the leader of his team, Lieutenant-Major Crasnaru, a slender gray-haired man with gray moustaches that he waxed and curled. Corporal Sylva rode behind him, and when they reached the village they split up. They knew where they were going. Crasnaru dismounted before the white-washed temple of Osiris Jupiter, where the priest waited at the gate. Sylva and Peter had other errands in the farms along the river.

But Peter was alone when he rode up the rutted track to the high pasture. The fields were poor and stony. The farmer was growing barley, and a few cows grazed where the pine trees began. A brook fell from the mountain beside the stone wall. The farmer had built a shrine to Demeter of the wheat fields, a wooden pavilion a couple of feet tall, sheltering a crude stone image and a dish of wildflowers. They had been picked fresh that morning, though there was no one at the house.

Peter wiped the sweat out of his eyes. He stood for a moment beside the stream, scratching his chin and remembering the headless statue of the goddess in Staro Selo, and the wagonload of shit. And he was thinkng about Miranda—his letter had not reached her. She had been in Bucharest a full week. What had happened at the masked ball in the People's Palace?

If Antonescu brought the regiment to Bucharest, then he could find her there. If she was in trouble, then he could help her. He could hope there might be time for him to hold her in his arms and say—what? That he had had a long time to think about what Madame de Graz had told him in Cismigiu Park, about his duty to her father and to her.

No, he wouldn't have to tell her these things. He would show her. Re-energized, unsure, he replaced his cap and climbed up to the barn where he found them, the farmer and his two sons. They were standing in the hayloft, waiting. The light fell in strips through the uneven boards, catching them as if in a cage of light. Dust from the hay, touched by the sun, floated around their heads.

The old man sat on the bales. Beside him stood his older boy, dressed in overalls and a cloth cap, and leaning on a crutch. His right foot was bare. His left foot had been amputated at the middle of his shin, a common injury. He might have stepped on a mine during a counterattack.

The younger son stood behind his father and his brother, waiting.

Peter stood in the doorway, his eyes adjusting to the light. He didn't say anything. But in his mind's eye he saw Miranda standing in her bedroom, his letter in her hand.

After a moment he touched his steel prosthesis to his cap, turned his back, returned the way he had come. At the shrine he took a yellow flower, twirled it between his fingers—he would not play this role anymore, perform these shameful duties, hurt these lives.

He had a more important project. He would go to Bucharest. He would find a way to go. Maybe, by the time he returned to the billet that he shared with Major Crasnaru and a few others, the orders would have come. That would be the easy way. Then tomorrow he would reach the city. Antonescu had no use for cripples—with permission or without it, he would go first to Madame de Graz's house on Lake Herastrau.

Now he looked down over the valley. He had to account for at least an hour before he returned to Crasnaru with some made-up story. He let his memory run ahead of him. There was the rockfall where the cliff came down into the river. There was the track uphill into the woods, too steep for horses.

At first he didn't understand why he was searching for the place or what it meant to him. Even after he found it, thirty minutes later, he didn't understand. The hunting lodge meant nothing to him. It was wrecked and burned. The roof was broken in. Graffiti had been carved into the logs. The iron woodstove was gone. That was no surprise.

The lodge stood in a high meadow where the pines gave way to beeches and oaks. Under the trees, the ground was littered with the husks of acorns and beechnuts, which the bears love. The grass was around Peter's shins, and there were wildflowers here, too, the first of the year.

He had come here with his father almost thirty years before. And he had some foggy memories, he supposed. But as he stood there among the wildflowers, he was thinking about Miranda—what had she been doing in Bucharest? How could she have made the decision to return there? If he had been with her, he would have prevented her.

But now he understood—he had dreamed about her in the Strada Cerbului. He had seen the icehouse in his dream, and he had sat with her at the icehouse and they had talked like old friends. That's why he was here, now, he realized—he had no compelling interest in the childhood of the Chevalier de Graz. But this place brought him back to the icehouse where he and Miranda had first spoken. And maybe, when he'd discovered it in Williamstown in the woods beyond the baseball field, he'd gone back and back because it had reminded him of here: a little cabin at the forest's edge. And he had felt at home there, and Miranda had spoken to him as he squatted on the dam—where was Miranda now? Right now?

IN BRASOV, AS HE hoped, there were orders waiting. It was to be as everyone suspected. They were returning to Bucharest and then to the front line. Bucharest was far enough for him.

And there was a note from Chloe Adira. He had not seen her since he'd left her house. Nor had she written to him. But she sounded desperate now. So after supper he requested an hour's leave. He found his way to the Strada Cerbului to say good-bye.

He walked through the streets with his head full of pictures of Miranda, single moments from the past. The Hoosick River, the pebbles on the shore slimy with ice. He'd put up the pup tent, and she'd turned toward him, smiling, the light from the fire on her long neck and collarbone. She wore Blind Rodica's quilted coat. "Hurry up," she'd said, "I'm freezing."

Or in the woods in Mogosoaia. She had been asleep, wrapped in a gray shawl beaded with moisture. Curled up, her black hair hiding her face. He'd been standing above her, keeping watch.

Or in the brick pavilion in Cismigiu Park. What had he said? Why hadn't he gone with her as she wanted, as she expected? Hadn't that been his duty, as he had sworn it to her father—to protect her, keep her from harm? No, but he had surrendered that duty to Prochenko, who had screwed it up. There was no mention of him in the newspaper stories about Bocu.

Peter had pretended it was best for them to separate, that Miranda would be safer, because the police would chase him after Felix Ceausescu's death. He had spoken coldly and sincerely. In the lamplight he had seen the blood in her cheeks, seen her eyebrows come together.

Now he stood at Chloe Adira's door, his hand on the horse-head knocker. And the door opened, and Chloe's fat, sad mother stood on the threshold, her gray hair wild and unbrushed, a blanket around her shoulders though the evening was warm. "De Graz has come to call! De Graz has come to call!" she shrieked like a mindless parrot, until her daughter pulled her away.

The door shut before he could get inside, and Peter stood like a fool in the deserted street, wondering if he should stay. He'd caught a single glimpse of Chloe's face, her dark curls and heavy brows, her dark eyes lined with kohl—she was more beautiful than Miranda. Then the door was open again, and she stood alone, her pale palm outstretched. "My God, I'm so glad. I heard the news. I thought you'd already gone."

She was in her raw silk tunic, cut in an Aegyptian style. Gold glistened in her ears and on her fingers. She drew him up the steps and over the threshold, murmuring the whole time, "You must forgive me, I was so worried. You must excuse my mother."

When the door was closed and they stood together in the corridor, Peter wondered why he'd come. He wondered what to say to her. But it was she who solved the problem by pushing him away, turning her face away. "This is your last evening," she said, more a statement than a question.

The light was uncertain, a petroleum lamp in a corner niche.

"I've had a letter from my husband," said Chloe Adira. With a gesture of her hand, she directed Peter eyes to the end of the passageway. Her mother stood there, a bulky silhouette. "There will be a prisoner's exchange."

So that was that. "You must forgive her," Chloe said, still gesturing toward her mother with her pale palm. "She is distressed because the military police have been here—you remember Dumitru? Our servant—yes, of course. He must have told them. No, don't worry. My father can protect us even at long distances. There are many reasons why Antonescu won't offend the Abyssinian government."

All this time she'd scarcely looked him in the face. "This is why I sent for you," she said. "I must ask you—beg you—to consider what I want from you. Dumitru didn't tell them about Chiselet. There is still a chance. Only I'm afraid—I was afraid you'd gone."

Chloe was trembling. Her shoulders trembled, a motion augmented by the lamplight and the flickering tongue of flame. Now she hugged her arms across her breasts. "Come," she said, "come with me," and she turned through a narrow door on the right-hand side of the corridor. She bent forward as if her stomach hurt, hurried forward through the small square rooms that still confused him, until she brought him to the room where they first met. She had been playing the piano.

The plaster walls were painted yellow and dark blue. Candles burned in mirrored sconces. The piano's lid was down; she turned to face him.

"Chloe," he said.

But she raised her hand, showed him her spread fingers. "When are you leaving?"

He shrugged, and now she glanced at him. Her eyes were wet and full, increased by the dark liner. "I must tell you," she said. "I told you part of it—you have been to Chiselet! That is why Dumitru was so angry."

"I remember—"

"Please don't speak. This is hard for me. Show me your hand."

She'd said this before, not in this room but some other. He brought his left hand up and showed it to her, turned it over. But she ignored it, could not look at him as she continued, "I'm afraid of what Dumitru will try. He will find this thing, this cylinder. He means to set it off or release it—break it open in the Piata Enescu! Or in the Calea Victoriei in the middle of

Bucharest. Or in the Piata Revolutiei, because it would be a kind of revolution—there are people who would support such a thing. Or else they would use the threat of it, because they cannot comprehend. . . . The war would be lost, but it doesn't matter. It is not his war, he says. It's for rich people, this war—not for him."

Exasperated, Peter shook his head. "This does not concern me," he murmured, which was not true. Why was he angry? he asked himself. Was it possible he was disappointed, that he'd wanted something more personal from Chloe Adira? What had he expected—that she would try to say good-bye to him, hold his hand? And she would say—what? Some version of what he'd failed to tell Miranda in Cismigiu Park? But she didn't care about that. Her husband was coming home.

"Yes, it concerns you," she said. "It concerns all of us. It is because of you he knows where to look—I told him what you said. Two hundred meters in the swamp. By the dead oak tree. South of the embankment—do you see? Because you would not help me."

He stepped back, put up his hand. When he saw a furtive look of self-satisfaction pass over her face, he felt like striking her.

AND WHEN, STILL FURIOUS, he walked back through the streets of Brasov to his room at the outskirts of the town, he did not think about Miranda for at least an hour.

Nor would he have been reassured if he'd been able to see her at that moment. She was in the house of Ana Cassian and her family. Near the Museum of Municipal History, dilapidated, once-grand buildings had been broken up into apartment flats along the Bulevardul Republicii, which runs through the center of Bucharest. Miranda lay in a fourth floor room overlooking the noisy street. She lay on a straw pallet on the floor, beside an ornate, blocked-up fireplace. She was breathing, but she scarcely moved. Her eyes were closed. Her forehead was untroubled. Her mind was far away.

But in the hidden world she stood on the trampled plain of Chiselet, near where the Turks labored to cross the river with their engines. She carried in her hand a trophy, a flabby ear that she had severed from the monster's body as it lay bobbing in the dirty pool. She looked north and west toward the mountains, a long and weary way.

It had not taken more than a day for her to descend from the high pass and the hillside under Kepler's tower. But now the line of mountains scarcely showed on the horizon, and all around her stretched the featureless, empty plain. Maybe she could have predicted how the way up from that world was longer than the way down, and maybe she could have predicted that the land would change, would spread away under her feet. And there was no more inn or castle, and the Chevalier de Graz was gone. Andromeda was dead. She had buried her as best she could. Miranda was alone.

But she hoped her aunt was waiting for her at the top of the divide, or had pursued the tourmaline into tara mortilor. And she moved forward step by step.

18   *Peter Gross Returns to Town*

THE ELEVENTH BRASOV MOUNTAINEERS arrived in Bucharest five days after the death of President Bocu and the Turkish aerial attack. Some neighborhoods already had devolved into chaos, because there were no soldiers in the city, except for the Brancoveanu Artillery, the private militia of the Rezistenta party. Fearing reprisals, many of them took off their uniforms and joined the crowds, whose frustrations had spread through the streets.

The rioters pursued no strategy. Businesses were looted, the traditional scapegoats were hunted down: civil servants, government functionaries, aristocrats from the old regime, Jews, Gypsies, leaders of industrial concerns. Conjurers above all—recently pardoned and forced to register by President Bocu—were harrassed with something that approached discipline, because they were thought to be complicit in his death. Rumors had spread after the interrogation and subsequent suicide of the president's valet. The disgusting facts seemed to suggest no other explanation.

But more than anything the rioters possessed a moment of opportunity. General Antonescu was at the front, and it took several days for him to grasp the urgency of what was happening in the capital. In any case he had no troops available to reassert control, at least until the Eleventh Mountaineers arrived at Snagov Portal and the city wall.

But Peter Gross was no longer with them. The previous morning he'd left Brasov with the rest of the regiment. North of the city the Rezistenta had blown up the railway tracks near the village of Buftea. By the time Peter's train had crawled into the station, the regiment had already disappeared down the Snagov road.

Peter stayed with the support staff, with Lieutenant-Major Crasnaru and Sylva and some others from his team. In the afternoon they set up camp in the woods near the Colentina River. Peter shared a tent with Crasnaru, who had not spoken to him all day on the train—they had left Brasov before dawn—or before that since the trip to Sacele.

Even so, it seemed to Peter that the man was always with him, watching over him, guarding him. Crasnaru was in his sixties, a career officer with a scoured, wrinkled face that seemed both fierce and tired. His teeth were old and yellow under his waxed moustache, and that day he smelled of onions. Peter smelled onions around him all day long, because the man kept so close.

When it was half dark, Peter spread out his bedroll in the tent and lay down fully dressed. He unstrapped his steel prosthesis and laid it out. He could see the campfire beyond the canvas wall, and the major walking back and forth. The tent was a large one—a man could stand upright. In time, Crasnaru stood in the flap and looked down at him.

"We'll be in the city tomorrow," Peter said. "What do you think we'll find?"

Because of the man's unfriendliness, he did not expect a reply. So he was surprised to hear him laugh. "What makes you think you're going to Bucharest?"

"I assumed—"

"Is that why I'm your nursemaid tonight? I don't suppose. You'll be straight to Tutrakan."

The major was in silhouette against the firelight. Peter couldn't read his expression. "What do you mean? The orders—"

"What do you know about orders? Just for your convenience—it was not difficult, the duty I assigned to you. Well within a cripple's power. A few conscripts and deserters. I thought to use your reputation for the good of our regiment. Did you understand that?"

Peter rose up on his elbows. "Tell me what you mean."

"Don't answer me. Let me say I had to speak to the colonel about you, because I find you are unable to follow even these simple commands. It was no surprise to him. He told me about an Abyssinian agent in Brasov in the Strada Cerbului. Of course she is under the protection of a foreign government. And she is the wife of a hero of the Polish campaign. You should be ashamed. Is it too much for me to expect my officers not to be concerned in something like that?"

"Sir, I—"

"Don't talk to me. I would think you had more pride. What about old Tanda's son—the farmer?"

This was the boy Peter had been sent to collect in Sacele, the boy he'd seen in the barn with his crippled brother. "Sir, there was no one at the house. I tracked him to an empty cabin in the trees. He must have escaped onto the mountain."

"You're a liar! I had to bag him myself. He said you'd stood inside his barn, not six meters away. Now he's at the Tarlungeni subprefecture. They're not too proud to do their job—the great Captain Gross, who's been in all the newspapers! By God, I'll enjoy taking you down."

He wasn't enjoying anything about this, Peter thought. He was nervous or else frightened—his body stiff, his weight on the toes of his boots. With careful nonchalance, Peter lit a candle, twisted it into the mud floor.

Now he could see the man's features, his lined face and stringy gray hair. "So . . . ?" he said.

"So that's what I told them," answered Crasnaru. "This is not a matter of a court-martial or a reduction to the ranks. They've allowed you to represent the honor of the Eleventh Mountaineers, which means they cannot break you as you deserve. They'll find a way—you're a hero, see. You'll die a hero down in Tutrakan."

Crasnaru seemed to begrudge even this. "The colonel's got a story worked out. You might win another medal. It's for morale. The reputation of the army. My morale's never been higher."

He was lying, Peter knew: his brave words, his nervous gestures. And he wanted something. That was why he'd said all this, which was surely not part of the colonel's plan.

Crasnaru had an automatic pistol on his belt. Bravado and uncertainty—there was no reason for the man to be afraid of him, Peter thought, an unarmed cripple at his feet. But he was afraid, and now Peter guessed the reason. Crasnaru had followed him at Sacele. That's how he'd figured out about the farmer's son.

"You know my secret," Peter said.

He was watching the old man's body as a wrestler might, searching for advantage. Crasnaru's black eyes shone, ferocious in the candlelight. But at the same time he seemed eager to learn something, solve a mystery whose explanation he dreaded. Maybe he thought this was his only chance, before he had to turn Peter over to the military police.

In which case, Peter decided, something might be done. "You saw where I went."

"Don't play games with me! I had a bet with Filimon. That was the hunting cabin of the Count de Graz."

Then it all came out. He took a step into the tent, close enough for Peter to see the lines on his tired face, smell the onions. "By God," he said, "what story are you going to tell us now? Look at you—not a mark on you."

Peter let him go on: "Once I saw the Chevalier de Graz. He was with von Schenck and the cavalry. When did you ever see a dead horse-boy from either army? Look at you—not a mark! Do you think I've changed since then?"

He drew the pistol from his belt. Peter rose to his knees, then rolled onto the balls of his feet, his hand raised. "What are you doing?" he said.

But he did not think the man would fire the gun. Crasnaru would not lose control. There was something else in his face beside anger. Fear, perhaps, or awe. Even standing over him, two meters away, he couldn't quite look Peter in the eye.

"So what do we get?" said Lieutenant-Major Crasnaru. "One shitty world is good enough for the rest of us. You should see the alchemical laboratory that we found in the People's Palace, in Nicola Ceausescu's bedroom. Oh, but it takes years of study, I know. They didn't teach those sciences where I went to school. Now they've done in Bocu, everyone who stands against you. Who're they looking for? I'll tell you—the wife and daughter of General Schenck von Schenck! A conjurer named de Rougemont and her friend Magda de Graz! I hope they hang them!"

At first he had been shouting. But now his voice trailed away, as if his grievance was so hopeless and so old, it bored even himself. "Tell me the truth," he pleaded. "Where were you for these twenty years, while the rest of us got old?"

Peter spread the fingers of his hand, as if in supplication. He was in no danger, he decided. "Please, sir, what are you doing?" he repeated.

But Crasnaru didn't want to answer that question. He wanted to talk about the Chevalier de Graz. What would Peter say? That he had stopped in the village of Buftea, where in the old days there had been a hunting preserve along the Colentina River? This was on the opposite side from the Mogosoaia woods—he knew this place. Years before, he had pitched his tent in a hayfield fifty meters from here, close to this same fringe of trees.

Then he'd been on horseback, chasing stags. He'd been here with Prince Frederick in the old days, and had crossed the river at Constantin's Ford. The crossing would be harder in this season.

A wind from the river touched the canvas wall, made the candle flicker. The campfire outside had died down. Crasnaru wanted to know about the Chevalier de Graz. Peter would show him. All day Peter had been thinking about how to find his way to Bucharest, what he would do when he arrived there.

"Please, sir," he murmured, flexing the fingers of his left hand.

"Madame de Rougemont died of a tumor fifteen years ago," said Lieutenant-Major Crasnaru. "That was what was in the newspapers. My mother used to tell me stories when I was a child, and my wife told them to my son. Witches and warlocks and their schemes. They meet in secret places in the mountains. Soldiers march and politicians argue, but that's not where the power is. Do you think that's fair? That there's something else controls us, makes us do the things we do . . . ?"

He held the gun out in front of him, but he was already defeated. Hand held out, fingers splayed, Peter rose to his feet. He wondered if the man would let him go, walk out the door. The conjuring he spoke of, maybe it was not so complicated.

But then a shudder of hatred passed across his face, and the gun twitched in his hand. Peter sprang at him, knocked the barrel away. Crasnaru fell back against the canvas wall as the tent collapsed along that side. Peter hit him underneath the chin with the stump of his arm, and pulled the canvas over him as he struggled and flailed. The gun had not discharged.

Peter stood up through the tent flap. He disentangled himself, then stepped out past the fire pit and through the darkness and the little branches toward the river, which he could smell through the trees. He broke into a run. He knew where he was going: Constantin's Ford, where the river made a turn. It ran shallow over an abandoned stonework, marked on this side by the base of a ruined tower.

After three hundred meters through the woods, he came out on the bank. The river was wide and dark and quiet, full of the spring flood. There were no lights on the far bank, nothing but black forest. Upstream? Downstream? He guessed, then ran south as the woods came to life behind him. Lights and voices shouting. But he would find his way. He ran along the edge to the steep bank. The river was full and smooth, black under the black sky. Sometimes he slipped and fell.

In thirty minutes the abandoned tower rose out of the trees. Pinpricks of light shone through the trees. Peter slid off the bank and down into the rushing, silent stream, which rose above his knees. He groped under the water, found his footing, the stone dam or causeway under the surface.

Halfway across he climbed onto a rocky pier. Clinging to the rocks, he rested while the cold water slipped around him. Once he'd found the three flat stones and the cattails on the far shore, he told himself, he would follow the river downstream and approach the city from the north, one of a thousand other demobilized soldiers, fresh from the military hospital, perhaps. He would shave his new beard. No one would recognize him from those crappy rotogravures.

Once again his road had led him in a circle. But he would not stop in Mogosoaia or the woods. He would not visit any of those places from the previous year. He would not pass the grave of Aegypta Schenck—what for?

He would not find the stand of trees where he had said good-bye to Miranda. He would not penetrate the thicket where Ludu Rat-tooth had died, after she had seen the white tyger in the dark.

He wasn't the same man who had visited those places. He had changed. Now he stepped into the river again, and past the rocky pier the water was slower and shallower. He squelched among the rocks and under the dark trees.

He would follow the river downstream, keep to its bank. He'd make faster time that way. Night had come, and no one could see him in the dark, though men with torches searched the far shore. He would wait for a while until the lights went out.

But a man stood up and shouted, pointing. Crouching among the cattails where the bank was steep, Peter slipped and fell. He clattered down onto the stones. There were more shouts from across the river.

When he stood up again, they saw him. The bank was undercut, the stones unsteady. He grabbed hold of some roots and pulled himself up, amid cries from the far shore and a few gunshots. Maybe they had even seen where he had crossed, or else they'd known about it all along; he scrambled up the bank, pushed into the black undergrowth, where he stood among the little trees just for a moment.

But he could not follow the stream down to the city walls, not now. That was no longer possible. Instead he would break through the woods in a straight line until he found the fields of Mogosoaia and the lake.

Another gunshot, and he turned away into the shelter of the forest. At first he moved slowly, feeling his way. But the dark trees seemed to contain dangers that were conjured or animated out of the past—ape men, other creatures. After fifteen minutes he was hurrying as quickly as he could. He did not want to be in these same woods, which in any case he revisited constantly in his mind, and which had come to represent his failures and lost opportunities.

After half an hour he was almost running, just as he had on the Buftea side. The immature pine trees whipped at his face; he didn't want to be here. He couldn't understand what had prevented him from taking Miranda into his arms and kissing her in any one of a hundred moments in these woods.

Why had he let her escape from him in the brick gazebo in Cismigiu Park? Madame de Graz had reminded him of his duty to her father, the oath he'd sworn. But now he remembered listening to her with something that approached relief. He had not trusted Inez de Rougemont, but he had let her take Miranda to Stanesti-Jui, while he had run away south to the frontier, pretending to draw the hounds away. And he had gone to earth, and he had hidden there until the Turks crossed the line.

Out of breath, he paused among the trees. Figurative hounds—the Baroness Ceausescu's policemen and soldiers. But before that he had stopped underneath these massed, pale trees—yes, here he was exactly. This was the place. He couldn't avoid it, as it turned out. He had stopped here and embraced Miranda under this beech tree, and they had listened to the baying dogs. Then he had left her, because he had been a coward then as well. What if the two of them had crossed the stream together that night, by that same ford, and had come to Herastrau the other way?

No, he'd been afraid, and had taken refuge in his own kind of heroism. But surely he had changed, and if he had been able to go backward to the moment when they had stood together here in this swale, and then further back to Christmas Hill or even to the icehouse where they first had spoken, he would have known what to do. Two kinds of strength were now available to him, because Pieter de Graz and Peter Gross had made their peace at last.

People change and they don't change. Continuing on past the beech tree, past the thicket where Ludu Rat-tooth had seen the white tyger, he felt he was exploring and escaping the same landscape, a place he could not but inhabit in his mind. He walked and ran and shuffled through the woods and the open fields, and he would find the house at Lake Herastrau where de Graz's mother lived. There was a fig tree. Seven steps led to a door painted red. He would find Miranda there. At the same time he was possessed by an anxiety that would not stay away, that had another source—what had Crasnaru told him? The police were looking for accomplices to Bocu's murder. The crowd was hunting down the list of conjurers.

The police were looking for accomplices, and after tonight they would be looking for him, too. What he had told himself the year before—that keeping with Miranda would endanger her—was more true now than then. It didn't matter; he must reach the city. He could not afford to wait.

If he thought about Miranda now, if he punished himself for things he had not done, words he had not spoken, if he pictured to himself her black hair, big forehead, small chin, ears that stuck out, etc., etc., maybe all of that was a backward way of comforting himself, and quelling an anxiety that grew and gathered as he approached the city from the northwest side. Maybe that was a way to avoid grieving about what he was sure to find, and what he did find after the sun rose, as he stood outside the burned-out house for the first time in many, many years, however you wanted to reckon it.

There was the stone statue of Demeter with her empty bowl, standing at the bottom of the dirt road. There was the fig tree above his head, its leaves dry and singed. Seven steps to the door painted red, only it was gone. In the stink of the burning he could not smell the lake, nor see it over the rear of the house, which still rose like the back wall of a stage set. The front of the house was fallen in.

And like the back of a stage set, there was flowered paper on the rear wall, and intact pictures, and a glass-fronted cabinet full of books, and a doorway that led nowhere. The house stood in a block of peeling wooden houses with carved fretwork and wooden gutters. The fire had spread to the houses on both sides. Their roofs, though, had not collapsed.

And now his thoughts spread back to lick or touch the suburbs he'd been walking through since Mogosoaia, and which he'd scarcely noticed, so consumed he had been with worry and regret. Now as the sun finally rose into the dirty, heavy sky, he saw the long lines of warehouses he'd walked through in the dark, and then the silent streets. He had passed many houses that were burned like this one, fences broken down like this one. Barking dogs, and no sign of people anywhere, no lights in the windows before dawn. They were afraid of the soldiers, he guessed.

His thoughts spread backward into the damaged streets, then forward into the uncertain future. It was a way of neglecting the consumed and ruined present, protecting himself as he climbed up the broken steps, across the collapsed timbers of the porch. He stepped over the gap until he stood in Madame de Graz's sitting room among her broken piles of things.

There was shattered glass and plaster under his boots. He brushed the dust from an upholstered armchair and sat down in his damp trousers, staring at the wrecked piano and a viola or a violin that had been split in half across the back. Staring also at the remains of a framed photograph of himself, taken God knew how long ago, and yet still recognizable. So: a homecoming. But there was no one home.

The chair was weirdly comfortable, and he had come a long way. Soon he would get up and knock on the doors of neighboring houses, whose occupants might already be peering at him through the slats of their wooden shutters, surprised, maybe, to see him at his ease there, sitting as if on stage—a cramped domestic tragedy that had gotten out of hand. Soon he would get up, but in the meantime he sat staring at the broken picture in its broken frame, thinking now about the weapon Nicola Ceausescu had brought from Africa.

Prochenko had been with him when the baggage car exploded in Chiselet. Later, Prochenko had told him a story about an Abyssinian commercial traveler who had crawled into the swamp. And Peter had told Chloe Adira, who had told the lunatic, Dumitru. . . .

A dog came down the middle of the dirt road. Small, nondescript, it lifted its leg at the bottom of the fig tree. Peter wondered what it would be like to have a nose more sensitive than his—a thousand times or whatever it was. The stench was terrible, a rotted, charred, miasmic funk. But the dog didn't seem to notice and it soon went on, leaving Peter alone in his improbably undamaged chair, surrounded by piles of garbage and unable to look away from the image of his own face in the middle of this old-time, black-and-white portrait, as if he had dressed up in an old-time uniform in the concession booth of some traveling fair. The glass was broken, the frame propped at an angle against a fallen chunk of roof.

In time he took his boots off, squeezed out his filthy socks, examined his blisters, rubbed them with the stump of his right arm. The sun had risen into layers of saturated clouds—where was Miranda now? And what had happened here on the banks of this shallow, reedy lake, which he remembered could be seen from a veranda in the back of the house—what had happened here? How would he find Miranda and Madame de Graz, who had sat here in this chair, comforting herself with this posed photograph?

In time, after his socks had dried and stiffened, he had replaced them on his feet. Looking up, he saw a tall, skinny woman with a white, old-fashioned bonnet on her head. She came up the street and climbed the ruined steps.

She walked without any hesitation, stepping over the gaps in the charred floor. Maybe the bonnet served her in the way that blinders would a mule, directing her forward, eliminating distractions. She didn't pause, didn't seem to notice him as she passed a dozen feet away. Her clenched fists and determined movements suggested an anxiety that had been overcome, maybe with the bonnet's help; he couldn't see her face at all. But she marched past him toward the back wall with its undamaged wallpaper and glass-fronted cabinets. She stopped in front of one of them, unlocked it with a brass key—an action that seemed absurd to Peter in the midst of all that wreckage. He made a noise. She started back, almost lost her balance.

She turned to face him, and Peter could see her pointed nose and brown eyes, framed in the circle of the bonnet, which tied under her chin. She didn't say anything, but stared at him, as if too frightened to speak. These deserted neighborhoods, this no-man's-land was no place for her. But it wasn't fear he saw in her but rather an astonishment, and he realized she was staring at the photograph, which gave him sudden hope. "Where are they?" he said.

SO IT WAS JUST a couple of hours later that he climbed the stairs of Camil Cassian's fourth floor apartment on the Bulevardul Republicii, behind the Museum of Municipal History. Ana Cassian, after she had retrieved the book from Madame de Graz's cabinet, had been eager to escort him, grateful for his protection. Once they'd crossed the canal into Floreasca they were among the crowds: waves and receding eddies of old men, women, and children, their movements forceful and aimless, powerful and random, capable of knocking them forward, sucking them back. They heard rumors of fighting on the Ploiesti Road, but there was no gun- or cannon-fire, or any evidence of the militias or the police. The day was hot and wet and overcast.

The streets were empty of wheeled vehicles or even bicycles. A torrent of movement pushed Ana Cassian and Peter down the Bulevardul Republicii. But then they managed to step into the portico between the statues of Atlas supporting the hollowed-out hemisphere of the world; Peter had to grab hold of her long hand, pull her to shore. There he stood, sweating in his hot damp clothes, dripping in the sudden stasis as the people rushed by.

Peter caught his breath, eager to prolong the moment, for he was sick with anticipation. Ana had told him what to expect. But she could not prepare him for what he found upstairs in the room with the ornate mantelpiece. Miranda lay on a straw pallet between the windows, which had many small square panes. Madame de Graz was also there.

"Madame la comtesse," said Ana Cassian. "You see what I have found."

Peter sank down to the floor beside the bed. He did not look at the old lady—his mother—did it make sense to call her that? It was enough to be aware of her standing over him, leaning on a cane, her back bent with osteoporosis, her eyes white with cataracts—what could he say to her? This whole way from Herastrau he had been thinking about Miranda, wondering what had happened since he'd last seen her in Cismigiu Park the previous year, wondering if his memory was accurate, wondering what he'd think or feel.

For the time being, though, he would not have to share those feelings, nascent and unformed as they were. Miranda was asleep. Ana said she had not woken since the night of the aerial attack. On the way from Herastrau, she had told him what she knew about the masquerade in the People's Palace.

Ana's parents had decamped, taking everything of value from their rooms. Her brother had gone with them—they were staying with relatives or friends, or they had left the city. Grand though they might be, characters who had stumbled out of myths, these guests of their daughter were unwelcome and dangerous, Peter imagined. Camil Cassian was an inspector of drains in the central district.

There was nothing to sit on, just a few stools. Kneeling, Peter took Miranda's right hand in his left. No one said anything, though he was aware of Madame de Graz's intense presence. No doubt she had a lot to say and she would say it all, if not now then some other time.

After a few murmured pleasantries, Ana Cassian left them alone, went to another room to speak, he imagined, with Miranda's mother, who had never liked him, he recalled, either here or in Berkshire County. Madame de Graz didn't budge, a chaperone, he supposed, to make sure he didn't kiss or touch Miranda as she slept—he'd grasped hold of her hand. But he wasn't likely to do more than that, so exhausted he was, so flummoxed by his own feelings. Because his memory hadn't been accurate, he saw, or else Miranda had changed in the intervening months—she had been sick, Ana said. Sick and not herself.

Peter saw that it was true. Her face was worn and thin and showed the bones underneath. The circles around her eyes were like bruises. Her hair was oily and lank. Even in her sleep her face looked pinched, unrested. And if part of him was struck with pity (he also, he imagined, had changed in many ways—not for the best), part of him was on his guard. This was the moment, after all, when the prince discovered Sleeping Beauty in her glass casket, and at such moments physical impressions took on a symbolic value. And he could not but contrast her with Chloe Adira in her bed in Brasov, a bed that had felt as big as an entire country. Chloe Adira was a beautiful woman, the gold jewelry against her skin, the kohl around her eyes—where was she now? Had the police come to her house?

Peter examined for a moment the golden bracelet of the Brancoveanus on Miranda's wrist, then looked away. He glanced up at the wallpaper above the bed. Some pictures had been removed. He could see the pale squares.

How hot it was here, how stuffy! The windows were closed. Cries and yells came from the street. Clara Brancoveanu must have been hovering on the threshold of Miranda's room, because she flopped down beside him with a napkin, and with her own hands wiped the spit from her daughter's lips.

"Mais, cela suffit. . . ." Then she continued on in French: "You must not agitate her." So he pulled away, sat back on his boots.

"Madame la princesse," he said.

"Monsieur le chevalier."

She wore an old-fashioned gown that had spread out over the floor. She turned sideways to sit beside Miranda's pillow, placed her arm in a protective arch over Miranda's head.

Now someone else had come into the room. "You see it is difficult," said Inez de Rougemont, standing behind his head. "There is an obstruction. I needed a book from the library—I sent Ana for a book. Soon we must begin. Not . . . immediately."

He turned to face her. And he registered an impression of gray hair and painted cheeks. But then he found Miranda's hand again, gave her fingers what he hoped was a reassuring squeeze—the Condesa de Rougemont was an old woman with long fingers and thin bones. Her face was thin and sharp and colorless: pale hair, pale skin, pale eyes, which was why, he supposed, she put color in her cheeks and on her lips. She wore wire-rimmed spectacles that had worn into the sides of her sharp nose.

The rouge and powder seemed a kind of armature. Or else they were a vestige from the past, when she might have worn them more lightly. From his mnemonic archives Peter ordered two competing spools of film, two little loops, and one showed the pale, jerky image of a woman in a dark dress dancing at an officer's ball. She was laughing with her head thrown back. The other showed the phantasm that appeared to him along the Hoosick riverbank, wearing Gypsy clothes à la paysanne.

He'd keep his guard up. "What book?" he said, though Ana Cassian, returning from Herastrau, had carried under her arm the leather-bound volume she had taken from the glass-fronted cabinet. Along the way, also, she had told him what had happened: how, after her brother had carried Miranda to her parents' apartment, after the aerial attack on the city and the subsequent panic, after the president's valet had been arrested and condemned, the princess had sent him out again to retrieve the two old ladies in the house by the lake. They'd had scarcely fifteen minutes to pack. It was no wonder many things had been left behind to burn. "It is not as if she owed them anything. They'd been very stupid. The princess is a very generous woman," Ana had protested. It was one thing looking after the Brancoveanus. But after the two older women had moved in, Ana's parents had abandoned their own house.

Peter wondered if Inez de Rougemont was aware of that. "It is a scientific text," she said dismissively. From her stool in the corner, Madame de Graz glared at him through her white eyes. What was she thinking? Should he greet her, talk to her, inquire about her health?

Looking for help, he turned back to Miranda and her mother, who favored him, now, with a little smile. And it was possible the princess had forgiven him, or for her daughter's sake was willing to grant him another chance: "It's an exorcism," she murmured. "You will see. Inez doesn't believe me. You will see for yourself."

He shifted his weight, swiveled around until he sat beside Miranda on the pallet, his left arm across his body, his left hand grasping her right hand. He did not look at Madame de Graz. Now suddenly he remembered his own mother in Berkshire County, who had died of cancer years before.

Cries, shouts, and a muffled banging came up from the street. The lace curtains trembled. When would Miranda wake? When would she wake up for him? He could see a change in Clara Brancoveanu's expression, as if she had some sympathy. She was younger than these other women, her face softer and more tentative—a wonderful trait, he thought. "Hey," he said to Miranda.

"She cannot wake. There is an obstruction." Madame de Rougemont's voice was incisive. "Clara thinks there is a spirit that possesses her. I believe there is an obstacle that keeps her from herself, something conjured by Aegypta Schenck and released by dear Clara's carelessness—these are not simple matters. They require training. No one blames her, needless to say."

"You will see," murmured Clara Brancoveanu.

There was a bare wooden table against the inside wall. Madame de Rougemont had laid out the black, leather-bound book, opened it halfway through. From a bundle of papers she produced the black revolver of Frederick Schenck von Schenck.

What game was she playing? Peter remembered the big gun from long ago, when the general had worn it on his hip. Its long octagonal barrel, decorated with an inlaid pattern of leaves and thorns. Its plain bone handle—what was this old woman doing? It seemed too heavy for her hands and her thin wrists. She held it flat, not like a weapon but like some kind of ritual object. Then she laid it beside the black book. "There is nothing we can do for her," she said, gesturing toward Miranda. "Not yet. It is obvious she has not . . . found the means to return to us—this strength comes from inside herself. But in the meantime we must not be idle. We have decided to destroy these . . . creatures of Aegypta Schenck's which have done so much damage to ourselves and Great Roumania. . . ."

"She has decided," amended Clara Brancoveanu under her breath.

Peter squeezed Miranda's hand.

ALL THIS TIME MIRANDA had been laboring out of the hidden world, up into the mountains, toward Kepler's tower in the pass. She labored up as if through layers of consciousness, carrying the monster's ear, which was drying and curing in the sun. She was thinking about Peter Gross, and whether she would find him when she woke.

And at intervals she thought about her aunt Aegypta. She was wondering if she'd be true to her part of the bargain.

She need not have worried. On the far slope of the divide, Aegypta Schenck von Schenck stood at the brass gates of tara mortilor. She had climbed out of the pine forest, and passed the crossroads where she had spoken to her niece. But the landscape had receded. Day after day she had journeyed through the fog until the gates opened before her. This time they did not rise up to heaven, nor were they studded and buttressed and defended, nor did brass automata patrol the parapets, brass trumpets in their hands. Instead she came through a defile where seams of minerals rose to the surface of the rocks, zinc on one side, copper on the other—a degraded ore of little value. The cliffs rose above her as she found her narrow passage, a place where the cold stream ran beside the track, pulverized into dust by the millions of men and women who had passed this way, and over the dark water to the mountain.

The landscape was new to Aegypta Schenck, and yet she recognized it from the stories she had heard, the fabled mountain whose pits and seams had been exploited over hundreds of years. Whole slopes of it had been scraped clean, hollowed out, burrowed until the rock was worm-eaten and fragile, prone to cave-ins and collapses. But other slopes were still untouched, and there were hundreds of years left, and fabulous riches still to be exploited in the high, dry mountain air that burned the throat: not just silver and gold, but cheaper metals also.

The defile led her through a cleft and down into the town where the graveyard was, and all the miners who had died from the powder in their lungs. And the town itself was deserted—rows of square stone shacks with tin or tile roofs and floors of dust, untroubled by any bare footprint. But lines of ghosts still trudged into the mountain with their wheelbarrows and picks.

Princess Aegypta paused at the shrine at the top of the street. It was sacred to the gods of the upper air, a flat-roofed chapel lit with a single lantern. Small, crude clay figures stood in niches. Some had lost their arms and legs, or leaned drunkenly—Mercury, Mars, Venus, and a dozen others, each with his or her clay bowl of evaporating water. King Jesus of Nazareth was there, and Mary Magdalene.

And then she was on the causeway with the others. The mountain rose in front of her, its lower slope of tailings and slag, rising to its broken crown. The sky was gray, and there was a dusty, cold wind. As she rose higher, step by step, the landscape fell away, enormous, a dozen shades of red and brown and gray.

There were no trees or leaves or stems of grass. Nothing was alive. Princess Aegypta lagged behind. She wore her velvet dress with the fox-head collar. The veil over her face was caked with dust. Her feet were light on the crushed stones. There were numberless holes into the mountain, small claims worked by teams or families or even single individuals. By the time she reached the larger entrance at the top of the causeway, everyone had disappeared.

No, there was one old man. She had expected to see him there or some-where, an beggar with a broad-brimmed hat, always and forever caressing the eight-pointed Star of Roumania that hung around his neck—the old Baron Ceausescu, unable to break away. He reached out his gloved hand, but she didn't look at him. Instead she found the mouth of the tunnel, its lintel posts carved from the soft rock, and decorated with Diana's moon and stars, Venus's mirror, King Jesus's cross, on which he'd crucified the Roman generals. In the shadow of the doorway the light was gray and dim, but in-side it was brighter, the way lit with tiny acetylene lamps that were set into the rocks, and leered at her with tongues of flame. Beyond the threshold she could see a different altar near where the tunnel divided: the goddess of the underworld, and it was as she'd expected, a bronze statue of a naked woman, lovingly carved, and polished with the caresses of many hands un-til it shone.

Doubtless many of the corridors that curved and branched and sank and rose through the porous rock were following rich seams of minerals that di-rected their twisting paths. But there was one shaft that ran into the heart of the mountain, straight ahead and at a slight declivity. And there was no dust here, and the rock floor was polished smooth. And the way was lit not by torches but by another softer radiance from down below. The smooth walls glistened with reflected light, which caught at the deposits of un-mined crystals. Aeygpta continued onward, and the brandywine bird beat its wings faster and faster inside the cold chambers of her heart.

Then she heard a disturbance up ahead, a child's laughter. Felix Ceausescu—she knew it was he—came running toward her, a smile on his thin face; he was chasing a ball that gleamed under his foot, a sphere of pol-ished quartz. When he saw her, he gave a little exclamation of delight, grabbed hold of her gloved hand to pull her downward. "Maman," he cried out, then whispered, "Maman will be so pleased."

It was not inevitable. But when they came into the high chamber, the woman did seem pleased—pleased and angry and melancholy all at once, if you could judge these things by her expression, which was always under her control. She sat on a throne carved from a block of purple amethyst. She was naked and her legs were spread, her perfect body on display in the empty hall. Her flesh was seamed with gold like the flesh of the mountain itself, and her hair shone like copper.

Light came from globes of illuminated crystal around her head. In the soft light Princess Aegypta saw the boy was wounded, shot through the but-tons of his yellow pajamas. And to one side of the throne there was a cage with silver bars, and another boy lay inside, a boy with a swollen face; Aegypta recognized him even so, although they'd never met.

"I know why you've come," said Nicola Ceausescu.

She stepped down from her amethyst throne. She came toward Princess Aegypta with her hands outstretched, not to embrace her or to greet her but to pull her veil aside, adjust her fox-fur collar so she could see the marks of the cord that had choked her in Mogosoaia long before. Aegypta Schenck stepped back, watching the expression that troubled her—self-satisfaction? Despair? Or else a combination. Nicola Ceausescu turned on her bare heel, led her beyond the throne, into a smaller chamber hacked out of the rock and decorated as if for an expected guest. There was a bed, a basin on a stand, a table and stool, all of it made of the cold stone. Felix Ceausescu came in—"Whose room is this, maman?"—but Aegypta knew. It had been prepared and arranged for her brother's aide-de-camp, the handsome young officer of the Ninth Hussars, who was not there.

"Do you think he will come quickly? How long will he take?" asked

Nicola Ceausescu. But she didn't expect an answer. "I know why you're here," she said. Smiling a little, she moved her right hand around the different parts of her body, as if caressing herself—her breasts, her thighs. Nothing could be concealed there, but even so she wiggled her fingers like a conjurer, and at moments Princess Aegypta could see the jewel between them, glistening and winking and then disappearing. As a conjurer might amuse a child, she reached out to produce the jewel from behind Aegypta's ear. Then she brought it up to her own face—a purple and green gemstone, Kepler's Eye, which she now placed over her own. "I've got a chamber full of tourmalines. They mine them here," she said. "What's this one to me?"

Her expression was both mocking and indulgent, but now it changed, transformed by grief or else some sharp physical pain. "Ah, God," she said, "it took me years of searching to find it. I thought I would use it to look for my love in Bucharest, or else wherever he wandered under the sun and stars. How was I to know that he would come search for me here?"

She glanced around at the stone and crystal chamber, empty but for the three of them, the two women and the boy, who had skipped to the other side of the stone bed. "I took it from that girl—that whore, who did not understand its value—no, excuse me. She is your niece, I know. I've given you such suffering, I don't mean to cause you any more. I don't mean to insult her. She was traveling in the hidden world to do your work for you— yours and de Rougemont's—dutiful girl! Dry as dust, these political manipulations. Do not tell me love does not claim precedence. Not even death could sever us, I thought. And if sometimes he was cruel to me, I know what it's like, to be cruel! It was nothing I didn't deserve, hadn't earned ten times over—oh, I am sorry for what I've done to you. I apologize," she said, and with her left hand she reached a second time toward the welt around Aegypta's neck, half hidden by the fox-fur collar.

19 *The Amethyst Throne*

IN ANA CASSIAN'S FOURTH-FLOOR APARTMENT, the afternoon wore on. Peter had not budged from where he sat beside Miranda's bed. Sometimes he looked at her, examined her pale, thin face—how long had it been since she had eaten? Ana Cassian had brought food, bowls of watery soup, and Peter had been touched to see Miranda's mother try to feed her little spoonfuls. She would stroke Miranda's throat, encourage her to swallow in her sleep. Then with a napkin she'd wipe up the mess.

"You must learn to do this," she said to Peter. She gave him a hesitant, shy smile—what had changed? "She'll need someone to protect her after I'm gone."

What did she mean by that? With a growing sense of uneasiness, Peter watched Madame de Rougemont as she made her preparations. She'd arranged three hollow glass balls about twelve inches in diameter, balanced them in a line on the surface of the table. The glass was spotted, thick, and green. And there were two holes in each ball, one on either side. Each hole was surrounded by a heavy circular ridge where the soft glass, Peter supposed, had pulled from the glassblower's pipe.

Peter watched her fit the muzzle of the revolver into the holes one after another, so that it protruded into the middle of the sphere. "We must allow the pressure to escape," she said to Madame de Graz, who stood with her, leaning on her cane. "But not so as to let the creature go. Magister Newton has given his precise instructions."

She had prepared some melted pitch or tar, which Ana Cassian had brought from the kitchen in an enamel pot. The smell of it filled the room and made it hot—the windows were all closed. The curtains were drawn.

Peter squeezed Miranda's hand. Sometimes he thought he felt her move, return the pressure. He was sweating in his wool uniform, which was still damp. So many tedious little operations at the wooden table, and the two old ladies murmuring to each other as Inez de Rougemont slipped the muzzle of the gun in and out of the glass spheres. She could not intend to fire it, Peter told himself. He wasn't even sure it could be fired. The general, who'd had his superstitious side, had kept it as a talisman.

"You'll take care of her," said Clara Brancoveanu. "You have proved your loyalty, like your friend Lieutenant Prochenko."

What did she mean by that? Ana Cassian had told him about Prochenko's death. Prochenko . . . Prochenko—wouldn't the glass shatter even with a blank cartridge? But the gun appeared unloaded—what was the point of this?

"I'll take care of her," he said.

Inez de Rougemont was reading from the black book, and then suddenly, as if she'd mustered up her courage to do something dangerous, she thrust the barrel of the gun into one of the open spheres and pulled the trigger. There was a flash of light, the crash of a discharge, softer and more muffled than Peter anticipated; he started to his feet. Madame de Rougemont pulled the gun out of the hole and laid it on the table. She took a wooden spoonful of the tar and patched the smoking holes, her gestures quick but unhurried. She laid the sphere of glass into a nest of folded cloth, so that it wouldn't roll. Then she repeated this procedure with the other two spheres.

Now she stood with the last sphere in her hand. Peter could see movement in the swirling smoke inside of it, little struggling hands and feet. And there was no mistaking the triumph in her voice. "Rotbottom," she said.

"HOW COULD I GUESS," said Nicola Ceausescu, "that he would come look for me here among the dead? Do not think I meant him any harm! Please do not think ill of me. Domnul Andromedes was a young man, a handsome man with his gray eyes. I didn't care about that! But I felt he was the only honest man I knew, surrounded as I was with sycophants. An artist craves sincerity above all things! Honesty above all things. Andromedes could never punish me as much as I could hurt myself—not more, and you have no idea how I have suffered for what I've had to do. Because I think if only I had not used your niece's little body for my games, then he would not have gone to find her in Victor Bocu's bedroom—'Beau-cul,' we used to call him. But was I wrong to think I could entice him that way? I meant to offer him a present. Hadn't he loved the girl? I don't see why."

Seeing the distress on her face, little Felix had crossed the room again— "Is everything all right, maman?" he said. "What a pretty stone! May I touch it?"

And the baroness smiled a false smile. She shooed him away, sent him skipping out into the larger room so she and Aegypta Schenck could talk alone. "That is one of the ironies of the world," she philosophized. "You scheme and work for something. Then when you achieve it you don't need it anymore—I will not go to Roumania again. It has lost its . . . charm. It is full of . . . memories and regrets. Should I climb up to the mountain villages, the houses where I lived when I was young and innocent? Don't look at me! There was such a time! You have no right to judge me. Why should I prowl the corridors of the Ambassadors, or the National, or the People's Palace, thinking about what I could have done, or should have done? Should I go to Mogosoaia, where I burned you out of your little house? Or to Mary's cave, where I snatched your life away—you see I remember these things! Perhaps that's what you're counting on, that I would wish to make amends."

A shiver of suspicion passed over her beautiful features. "Is that what you thought?" she said, and shifted the jewel in her hand, wiggled her fingers as if preparing to make it disappear. "I owe you a great deal," she said, "but you have robbed me, too. Robbed me of everything, everything I loved, everything that made my life tolerable, you and your niece—what did he see in her? Andromedes—what does he see? Oh, sometimes I'm afraid that he will never come, and I will wait here forever, and he will stay on the hillside where he can look down and watch over her—was it just that she was young? Or inexperienced? Is that the most important quality, after all?"

Her eyes glittered, the same color as the jewel. "Or is it because she is a better woman than I am, not heartless, or selfish, or cruel, or a murderess. I tell you I was like her once! And I tell you also there are many ways to commit murder: Felix and Markasev—they died for her. For her sake, protecting her, or else because of choices that she made. Andromedes also, and behind her there was always you, the author of every piece of tragedy or bad luck in my unhappy life—you knew my artistic temperament! You goaded me to do what I did to you, mocked me with my hands around your throat—do you deny it? And now you have the impudence to beg me for my greatest treasure, the only treasure that remains to me. I suppose you think you can come into my house and take it because you are what you are, a princess of Great Roumania, and I am a poor peasant woman from the mountains, whose mother was a whore as everybody knows—this means nothing to you, the pain of ordinary people! It was my skill and destiny to give that pain a voice, dance it on the world's stage, while you sat in your darkened boxes, plotting your schemes. . . ."

She was in a rage. Her skin, white and pure as polished marble, now showed a roseate, agate glow. And the seams where the wolf had scratched and bitten her now burned like gold. She squeezed the tourmaline in her right hand, and she stepped forward with her other hand outstretched. She seized the princess by the neck as if she meant to murder her a second time. Aegypta Schenck fell backward through the entrance to the larger chamber, sprawled onto her knees behind the amethyst throne. "Never," whispered the baroness next to her ear.

"THEY WILL SUFFOCATE," said Inez de Rougemont, holding the glass sphere in her hand.

But at that moment, Miranda came awake. "Sweet Goddess," murmured Clara Brancoveanu. "Here it is again."

Peter turned back in time to see Miranda's eyes start open, see her throw the bedclothes off, swat her mother's hands away. "Never," she said, her voice hoarse and soft, unrecognizable after her long illness. "You will not steal this away from me."

She staggered to her feet, standing in her nightdress on the sweaty pallet, glaring at them, furious. "What have I to do with your plots and schemes?" she said.

Then it was as if she came alive to her surroundings, left whatever dream she'd brought with her into the room. "Princess," she said, "don't touch me."

She saw Peter for the first time, stepped down onto the floor in her bare feet. "Here I am," she said, "I'm your little whore. A perfect fit for the Chevalier de Graz," she said, touching her body as if offering herself up. She spoke in a soft, compelling voice he could not recognize in her small mouth, and he stepped back, horrified, away from her as with one quick gesture she shrugged the straps of her nightdress over her shoulders so that it fell down around her feet. Naked, she made a little pirouette across the floor. "What have you got for me? I'm hungry. Eels, are they? Lamprey eels—that's what I think."

Now she turned her attention to Inez de Rougemont. "What are you doing?" she hissed. "He will die like that." And she jumped forward with her hand held out, just as Peter recognized her voice at last, not from his direct experience. But he remembered the scratchy sound of a wax cylinder that one of the officers had played at Staro Selo in a portable machine— one of the recitatives from *The White Tyger,* which Nicola Ceausescu had recorded in the days before her death.

"Be careful, mademoiselle," said Inez de Rougemont.

She held the glass sphere above her head while Miranda reached for it, laughing now, it seemed to Peter—"What do I care? What do I care? It is my gift to you!" Peter seized her from behind, pulled her away, just as she succeeded in knocking the ball free. It rolled along the floor in a little trail of smoke, while at the same time Miranda collapsed backward in his arms.

"WHAT DO I CARE?" cried Nicola Ceausescu. But then the words faltered in her throat. Together she and Aegypta Schenck had fallen close to the silver cage, and Kevin Markasev had reached out through the bars. His swollen features were unreadable. His mouth was toothless, red. But he took hold of her neck. At the same time Felix had come back to stand above them as they rolled across the smooth floor. His pajamas had a bloody hole in them, and he had his ball of polished quartz in his hands. He raised it up, then let it fall onto his mother's head. She slumped away from him.

Aegypta Schenck had lost her hat, her dust-choked veil, her collar. She had collapsed onto her hands and knees. But now she crouched over the baroness's naked body, searching for the tourmaline, while at the same time Felix wept and wrung his hands—"Oh, maman, what have you done?"

The jewel had fallen away from Nicola Ceausescu as she fell, rolled away from her. The princess retrieved it and then found herself trapped, as the baroness grabbed at her legs. She had her fingernails in the filthy velvet, and she scratched at it until it ripped. Aegypta Schenck came free, not in the shape of the old woman outside Mary's cave in Mogosoaia, and not in the shape of the woman who had pressed *The Essential History* into Miranda's hands years before that, in the train station in the snow. It was a little bird with iridescent feathers that freed itself from the torn cloth, while a mangy old marmalade cat jumped after it, snatched at it as it leapt into the air. It had a nut or a berry in its claws, and it veered wildly through the chambers of the mine and the rocky tunnel before it found the entrance. And even when it burst into the light, the old baron in his beggar's clothes was there to snatch at her, grab at her, swat at her with his old hat before she darted up into the desiccated wind.

20   *The Bargain*

AT MOMENTS DURING HER JOURNEY, Miranda imagined climbing uphill toward Peter Gross. This was one of her strategies to force herself to
keep on going. She trudged step by step out of the deep recesses of the hidden world, up onto the rock pass and the border country below Kepler's
tower, where she was to meet her aunt. As she climbed higher, she thought
about Peter more and more. "I do not quibble like a dressmaker," she murmured to herself, a phrase that had become a talisman.

But at long last, as she clambered up out of the rocks, she was conscious
of a growing sense of disappointment. She paused among the granite boulders at the top of the pass—a way station, as she imagined, on the track to
what she wanted. So why should every step feel more dispiriting?

And when she saw her aunt Aegypta waiting for her as she had promised, she felt no happiness or relief. As she trudged up through the grass into
the rock pile, as she watched her aunt give a little wave with her gloved
hand, Miranda wondered what would happen now. If she took the tourmaline into her palm, if she came to herself in her bedroom in Stanesti-Jui or
wherever else her body might find itself (had she been moving and talking

and laughing and living this whole time?), would she discover a reality as insubstantial as a dream?

No—she would not let herself make that mistake. The sun was on the ridge of pinnacles above the tower. Aegypta Schenck came down to meet her through the rocks. She was dressed in her velvet dress and little hat, her fox collar—all of it ripped and muddy and askew. Miranda didn't ask. Miranda also had come a long way. And any urge to know was stifled when her aunt began to talk. She started in at once: "Oh, my dear child. Did you bring me what I wanted?"

Her coarse face, yellow eyes, thin lips, big nose—she was angry—she seemed angry. Miranda reached into her pocket for the token of success, the tip of the monster's withered and grimy ear, which she had brought from the plain of Chiselet. "I've done it," she said.

"Oh, my dear—"

Miranda's adoptive father in Massachusetts had once told her how it was possible to transfer your emotions onto others, observe in others what you were feeling. Love was like that, he suggested. And maybe anger, too— "I held him down while she ripped out his throat. Andromeda and me. She's dead, isn't she?"

Aunt Aegypta, standing in the rockfall, tried to arrange her collar, brush the dirt from her dress. "You mean Lieutenant Prochenko? I misjudged him. Oh my dear, it was a glorious victory."

"Good. I'm happy you think so. You have something for me."

"Yes—"

"Good." Miranda squinted up toward the tower at the top of the pass, the ramshackle tower that kept the world the way it was. "Because I'm not coming here again."

She held up the trophy, the monster's severed ear. Now she could see the tourmaline in her aunt's hand. The fingers of her glove were discolored from its juice. "Dear child, don't say that. I will want to see you."

Miranda was not surprised when her aunt closed her hand so that the jewel was hidden in her palm. "We have won a victory," she said. "But there is more."

"There is always more," Miranda said.

And perhaps her aunt could not decipher any kind of irony. Or perhaps she made a decision to take Miranda literally: "I did not say this would be easy. There are urgent tasks we must accomplish. I have kept my part of the bargain. But there is a dangerous weapon still in Chiselet."

I do not quibble like a dressmaker, thought Miranda. She felt a grim sense of presentiment as Aegypta Schenck went on: "This is something Nicola Ceausescu brought from Africa on the Hephaestion. Radioactive pitchblende from the Congo, as well as more conventional explosives—that was her intended cargo. But a faction of the Abyssinian government secreted something else, some canisters of a virus, which they called nepenthe after the Graecian panacea in the story. A cure-all, as Magister Newton might have said."

Miranda knew some of this story. She'd heard parts of it from Peter, parts from Andromeda. "The pitchblende was destroyed in the explosion," her aunt said. "The pitchblende and all the canisters but one. Most of the effects were mitigated in the conflagration, the ball of fire, which I witnessed from this mountaintop. But there was some sickness in the town. Some dementia."

She put her hand to her big nose. "I heard this from a commercial traveler in tara mortilor. The Elysian Fields—he came out of the mist. But he was wounded and could not defend himself against the wild animals in the marsh—this was on the south side of the railway near the dead oak tree. That will be the first place to start, though the location might be different from the way it was described. You must persevere, because it is something that would destroy a city such as Bucharest."

She might have known, Miranda told herself. Still, she found herself astonished without being surprised—astonished that her aunt would send her down again into the hidden world, after she'd expended so much labor to climb back up. "I would have told you before," said Aegypta Schenck, "—it was not urgent. Bocu was more urgent. But now something has happened, and I fear . . ."

How could she even ask, when Miranda had only just pulled herself up out of that parched, empty plain? How could she talk about these things so easily, as if it were nothing, what she asked? But aromatic smells drifted up the valley from the hidden world, and when she turned to look, Miranda saw she'd been mistaken—it was not so far. And the dale of Chiselet was beautiful and rich. She could even see the towers of Castle Faurei, where the Chevalier de Graz lay wounded. She could be there by evening.

Almost she was tempted to begin again. When she turned away from the valley, set her back against it, she found she had already taken a few steps down. She shook her head to clear her thoughts. "Give me my tourmaline," she said.

"Yes, I brought it. I do not forget my promises." And there it was in Aegypta Schenck's hand, in her discolored glove.

"Give it to me," Miranda said, and watched it disappear inside her aunt's clenched fist.

"There were a lot of books I used to read in Massachusetts," Miranda said. "Stories I suppose you gave me to prepare me. There was always something to be accomplished, and it was always difficult. People suffered. But at the end of the book it was all worth it, because the thing was finished and the story was over. That's not true here."

"No," her aunt admitted. "That's not true here."

"Tasks without end," Miranda said.

"Tasks without end."

Above them rose the high ice peaks. "Bring me the lead-lined canister from Chiselet," said Aegypta Schenck. There was some uncertainty, some desperation in her voice as she continued: "Then I will give you your jewel, if you still want it."

"I want it now."

The old woman shook her head. "Please, my child. I will make another bargain. It is your duty to bring me what I ask, for the sake of Great Roumania. But I will sell you something in return."

"Sell me?" Miranda paused. For a moment she closed her eyes. She stood near the top of the pass.

Now suddenly she imagined she could feel the hidden world re-form below her and behind her back. She imagined if she turned around, she would be able to see, north in the distance beyond Chiselet the range of the Taconic Hills, and maybe even the back side of Christmas Hill above the little valley and the little town.

She did not turn around to check. She took a few steps forward and reached out her hand. "That was not our bargain," she said.

"Besides," she pleaded, "these things must be accomplished in the real world. Don't you see? These interventions," she said, saying the words as they occurred to her. "Real people must accomplish these things. Not these tygers and these ghosts, as if they had some kind of right."

"Child," her aunt said, "there is a secret order to the world. Not everyone can know a secret. Look behind you."

But Miranda did not turn around. She raised her head and looked up toward the pass, where the sun glinted from Johannes Kepler's ramshackle tower. "The stone belongs to me."

Now she could see herself where the worlds come together and the paths branched down to Great Roumania, and Massachusetts, and the hidden countries, and the land of the dead. This was where the alchemist had built his tower, sealed up the creature that eats away the knowledge of these things. No, knowledge is too strong a word.

But that does not mean, because we guess and fail, that we cannot choose. Miranda took a few steps uphill toward where her aunt stood among the rocks. And when Aegypta Schenck tried to move away, it was not as a white tyger that Miranda sprang at her and forced her down, forced open her hand.

PETER FELT MIRANDA'S FINGERS move, uncurl of their own volition. Behind him, the old ladies were arguing. Inez de Rougemont was crooning over the ball that had fallen, rolled under the table. But it was made of a tougher stuff than glass, Peter decided. Now she held it up, unbroken. She replaced it in its folded nest of cloth.

After Miranda's seizure, Peter and her mother had guided her down into the bed. Reclothed, she lay back on the pillows, and Peter sat beside her, holding her hand. She had walked and talked and struggled for a minute or maybe even less—this event, painful and confusing as Peter had found it, seemed to have invigorated Clara Brancoveanu. Her voice was urgent and self-confident: "Dear Inez, for God's sake. You must agree with me now. You must see I'm right."

By contrast, Inez de Rougemont was diminished and unsure. She fussed with the glass balls, examined the surfaces before she turned away. "I agree there is some evidence," she said. "I will have to consider—"

"There's no time," interrupted Princess Clara. "This is killing her. Can't you see it?"

In that moment Peter was brought back to his mother's hospital room in Berkshire County, in the oncology center in Pittsfield, where he had sat beside her holding her hand, listening to his father talking to the doctors. He had tried to decipher her wishes by the pressure of her fingers—now he felt Miranda stir under his hand. Was this the beginning of another fit?

"I know you feel responsible," murmured the Condesa de Rougemont.

"Dear Inez—you must give me this chance."

Noises drifted up out of the street, horns and shouting. The stifling, shrouded little room was separate from all that, cut off in space and time. Outside, there was fighting in Tutrakan, Peter guessed, a big push on the southern front. And had the Eleventh Mountaineers entered the city from the Ploiesti Road? "What's wrong with her?" he asked.

No one paid attention. Or they answered him by talking to each other about something he cared about, as the doctors had in Berkshire County: "There is a risk," said Inez de Rougemont. "Not just to yourself. It is possible this demon has preserved the life of Mademoiselle Popescu to this point. This is why Magister Newton talks about its healing benefit. The purgative effect of the corresponding emotion. In which case, inadvertently, you might already have provided a service. You might already have prevented the parasitic spirit from destroying its host."

"This ghost, you mean. Ceausescu. You see now I was right."

"If you prefer," admitted Madame de Rougemont.

They kept on talking, the princess and the condesa. Peter listened. In time a new structure of information took shape in him, assembled like the array of petroleum lamps and glass pipettes that Ana Cassian now brought into the room, laid out in the center of the table.

There beside the three glass spheres lay the old-fashioned Webley-Doenitz, which had belonged to his commander, Miranda's father, General Schenck von Schenck. Useless as a modern weapon, it had been adapted for scientific purposes, redesigned to store and then release small emanations from another world. One of these had gotten loose, a parasitic worm or eel that had been described and named by Isaac Newton. It had found its way into Miranda, must be removed before it poisoned her.

But there was a disagreement. Sometimes the worm served a therapeutic purpose. A difficulty in translation had been enough to fool her mother when Miranda had first lain unconscious. The creature fed on other illnesses, especially those that involved a proliferation of cells, an explosion (one might say) of life. It choked off the supply of blood, secreted a black poison—Peter knew everything about this. Nor could he listen to the metaphysical applications (how the worm could achieve this in the body of the state as well, the tissue of the present time—the death of Colonel Bocu might be attributable . . .) because his mind was stuck in the past. A proliferation of cells was what his mother had died of. And she'd been treated with applications of black poison for the last eighteen months of her life.

So the information covered gaps in two separate narratives, one in the distant past, one in the recent past. Two kinds of love. Miranda had been taken over by a spirit while she lay asleep. But her unconsciousness had saved her, because there was nothing for the spirit to conquer and overwhelm—that was one theory. It was possible (in which case Clara Brancoveanu was unexpectedly justified) that the eel had weakened Miranda so the spirit could take up residence without killing her. And perhaps the eel was deadly enough to poison the spirit, drive it out.

Because of its healing properties. Because of its connection with a feeling—"detestation," as Madame de Rougemont called it—that sustains the weak. Although it was also possible that the worm or eel (called "Treacle," inexplicably) had attracted the spirit in the first place, called to it, even fed it—in which case "dear Clara" had made a blunder. Finally, it was possible that the existence of both "Treacle" and the evil spirit in Miranda's body were unrelated except coincidentally, in time.

It didn't matter. Peter was used to this kind of talk from his experiences in the oncology ward. There was a lot of confusion about the past, none about the future. No matter what had happened up to this point, only one option was now viable: The eel must be removed before it killed its host, choked her, starved her, poisoned her. The ghost (both ladies hoped) had finally been expelled through the application or removal of some mineral or stone or jewel. Miranda was herself again, and now the poison was attacking her.

As Peter listened, he imagined what might happen if whatever procedure they were talking about was a success. He would feel Miranda come awake under his hand. She would open her eyes, see him, react, smile.

"Hello," she might say, in English.

"Oh, life is a wonderful cycle of song," he might tell her, and then part of the rest.

No, there wouldn't be a lot of that. She might squeeze his fingers, look at him. There wouldn't be a lot to say. But he might find her face easy to read. And she would roll her eyes at the old ladies talking.

He tried not to think about her naked body, which he had seen, held briefly in his arms. Behind him he could feel the pressure of Madame de Graz's gaze, hear her labored breathing, and then her gruff, low voice: "She can't hear you." He realized he'd been murmuring aloud.

And Clara Brancoveanu was there, too. Embarrassed, Peter stood, surrendered his place to Miranda's mother. He'd scarcely spoken to Madame de Graz since he'd come into this room. He'd scarcely seen her since that night in Cismigiu Park, though he'd had letters in Staro Selo. "You have left your regiment," she said.

It was hard to explain. All this long day he had felt detached from what was happening around him, as if buffered by thoughts and feelings he could not describe. Half-formed memories of the oncology ward, his mother's hospital room—what could he say to this old woman, whom he scarcely knew? "I did what I thought was right"? What stupidity. And yet he could not tell her the truth about anything, scarcely knew it himself. He said, "I had a duty here."

She imagined or she hoped for another kind of intimacy, Peter thought. She stood beside him, her cane like a third leg. He asked her about Lake Herastrau, what had happened there. He told her what he had seen. She peered up at him out of the sides of her occluded eyes.

"I don't care about that. That house . . . was easy . . . to give up. But you have left your regiment."

What did she mean—that he had shamed her by coming here this way? Or that she didn't care about the house, or his honor, or anything except his safety?

"It is not easy for you," she murmured. She looked at him. But out of the sides of her eyes she was staring down at Miranda on the bed, and he deciphered what she meant. He had not been able abandon his feelings for Miranda, as she'd directed him in Cismigiu Park. That night she had spoken of his duty to the past, and the harm that he could cause, and how it was useless to want things you couldn't have.

He didn't want to hear any of that again. "Tell me about the creature that's inside of her. Tell me what you're doing now."

She peered at him out of her white, solid eyes. "It is best if it can be sequestered in one body and then burned. Not, of course, Mademoiselle Popescu. That is the point of this. That is how Madame de Rougemont has explained it."

The condesa had been laying out a line of beakers on the table. Now she came to stand beside them, interrupted them hurriedly: "We cannot let it out into the world," she said. "Because it could cause terrible damage. It could cause a war."

"A war," Peter repeated.

"A great war," amended the condesa without irony. "Sequestered in one person—well, you see. But we must be careful," she said, gesturing toward Miranda with her thin straight fingers.

Seated by the bed, Clara Brancoveanu gave Peter a shy smile. She did not seem to share the prejudices of Madame de Graz; she had changed her mind about him. His heart went out to her, a pretty, sad woman, prematurely aged. There was a generosity in her that he did not associate with Magda de Graz, arthritic and stiff with disappointment. Or Inez de Rougemont with her painted, powdered face. "I saw you on the riverbank," he murmured— a young woman then, not so long ago. Had she helped Miranda then, or harmed her? These things were hard to tease apart. He scarcely knew any of these women except Miranda, who might not wake.

Madame de Rougemont turned away. For the rest of the afternoon she avoided him, did not look at him. She busied herself in her experiment, as Ana Cassian taped butcher's paper over the windows. The day darkened and by the light of one of the new lamps, Madame de Graz showed him a page from a special supplement to the *Evenimentul Zilea,* a type of story that could only have appeared since the repeal of the anti-conjuring laws. It showed photographs from two investiture ceremonies, almost thirty years apart. It showed two posed portraits of the same young man, the Star of Hercules around his neck. ROUMANIA'S PROTECTOR, said the headline. Captain Peter Gross and the Chevalier de Graz.

What did she think about this? Peter wondered. Why did she show it to him? Since he had come to the apartment, Peter had sensed he was disappointing her. Almost to pass the time, to take his mind away, he set himself the task of comforting her while the princess sat with her daughter. Surely he was right not to intrude in that.

Madame de Rougemont assembled what was necessary for her experiment, a structure of glass tubes and alembics held in place with metal rods. She had removed it from the table where the glass balls lay in a row. She was building it again on the bare floor. And as the structure grew, Peter expressed his anxiety by attempting to mollify Madame de Graz, who would not even sit. Cramped, one hip higher than the other, she stood leaning on her cane.

She asked him questions about Staro Selo, and General Antonescu's strategy, and whether he'd heard rumors of the new Turkish machines. "Why did you leave your regiment?" she asked again. He told her about Brasov, and about the farmer's son in Sacele. "Do you think it right," she said, "that you should help him evade his responsibility? Now others will suffer in his place."

It was hopeless. She had kept Peter's photograph all those years in Herastrau, and yet he had no power to appease her. "When you went to Sacele," she asked him, "did you climb up to your father's cabin?"

He didn't answer her. He was reminded suddenly of Lieutenant-Major Crasnaru, who had followed him that day. And then later in Buftea—

Princess Clara sat beside Miranda's head. And every time she looked up, she smiled. She was kinder to Peter than he would have thought possible under these or any other circumstances. He thought he could remember the type of woman she had been before her husband's death, vain and proud and superficial. But she smiled at him as she tended to her daughter, wiped the sweat from her face and arms, gave her little sips of broth and wiped her mouth. In these small actions Peter recognized the tender industry that he had sometimes seen in temples or in churches, an impression that was strengthened by the makeshift shrine to Demeter and Persephone in a corner of the room: two wooden statues on a long stool draped in linen cloth, and a bowl of water between them, and a candle whose light grew brighter as it burned away and the day darkened.

So it was possible to change. And Peter recognized the busyness of an old priestess in a temple, whose forms and gestures also had a valedictory quality, as if this might be the last time Princess Clara Brancoveanu plumped up her daughter's pillows, wiped away her sweat, fed her with a wooden spoon while Peter watched. But he also recognized another kind of busyness as Inez de Rougemont assembled her scientific and alchemical instruments into a pile that rose three feet high in some places. There was to be some process of distilling, Peter guessed.

He was conscious, now, of a terrible anxiety. And he was reassured only when he was watching Princess Clara. She seemed joyful, almost, the way she wiped the sweat from Miranda's face, as if each trip to the altar of Persephone might be her last. So maybe there was something else he didn't understand. And maybe there was something between her and Madame de Graz and Madame de Rougemont, some agreement they were hiding from Ana Cassian, and Miranda, and him.

Again he found himself remembering Crasnaru in the Buftea tent. What had he said? They didn't teach these sciences where he had gone to school. Witches and warlocks with their secret plans—it wasn't fair to be manipulated in ways you couldn't understand. "There's something you're not telling me," Peter said to Madame de Graz. "Tell me what is happening."

But she didn't. Instead she told him a little story about an alchemist or conjurer who had locked a spirit or an animal inside a prison cell. "Yes, there is a hidden knowledge," she said, peering at him out of her white eyes. "But would it be more fair if the God were free?"

And for the first time she smiled at him. So—another type of wordless intimacy. It was as if she'd answered Crasnaru's unspoken question, as if she also were some kind of conjurer or sybil. Exasperated, he looked away, counting the moments until the tower of bottles and glass tubes was finished, and Inez de Rougemont stood poring over the diagrams and notes that were laid out over the tabletop.

It was time. The princess took from beside the little altar a notebook of pencil sketches, all of the same face. She leafed through them, aware that Peter was examining them, too. The ones of Miranda sleeping, as she was now, had a clarity and expressiveness that Peter could not but contrast to other sketches, the hurried and uncertain views of Miranda talking, moving acting, living. Doubtless it was harder to capture those things.

She shut the notebook, placed it by Miranda's pillow. "Adieu," she said, and leaned down over her daughter to embrace her. But then she grimaced, looked up at Peter, smiled. "Come," she said gesturing. And he imagined words in the wordless conversation he'd been sharing with the princess all afternoon, an intimation that even here he was not unwelcome, and his presence might be something of a relief.

So he knelt down, and Inez de Rougemont put her hand over his shoulder, almost touching him. She whispered in his ear. "You must hold her if she struggles. If she resists."

Then she bent to light the incense and the petroleum burners, siphon in the measured liquids while the pendulum marked time. Ana Cassian peered in at the door, her thin, plain face full of misgivings. So maybe she knew something. Maybe she knew something of what might happen. There was something hidden in the language of Princess Clara's body as she curled up next to Miranda's inert form.

In time, at what seemed to be a signal from Inez de Rougemont, she bent over her to kiss her daughter on the lips.

21 *The Exorcism*

AEGYPTA SCHENCK SAT in the rock pile below Kepler's tower. She had
barked her shin, ripped her stocking when she fell. Now she sat nursing her
split knee. Her clothes were torn and dirty, and her fox-head stole had
ripped, revealing the mark of the rope on her withered neck. She glared up
at Miranda with her pillbox hat, her veil awry. There was no pity or self-
pity in her yellow eyes. "Ungrateful child!"

Miranda stood above her with the tourmaline in her hand. This is what
I must do, she thought. Also: You made me do this. But she didn't say either
of these things. She found she didn't want to explain herself, didn't think
she could have if she'd tried. Nor did she want to tell comforting lies. I'll
be back. I'll see you again.

And so she took a few steps downhill in the evening sunlight. The sky
was clear above her head. There was ice in the high passes and on the rock
spires. The hidden world lay behind her and she turned away from it,
turned toward the rock chute.

"Oh child, don't leave me," said Aegypta Schenck. Miranda raised her
head, raised the tourmaline in a kind of salutation. Then she climbed down
through the rocks and her aunt did not follow her. When Miranda looked

back, finally, from the bottom of the slope, she saw the patch of her velvet dress against the rocks below the tower.

And in the waning light she climbed down through the pine forest, where there were martens and wombats and squirrels among the dead trunks. And they were quiet as she approached. They cowered in their burrows as she passed. She climbed down into the high meadow where there were wildflowers.

She gave the tourmaline a squeeze. It yielded in her hand, more and more like a ripe piece of fruit and not a stone, or like a tough little pouch of meat.

IN THE FOURTH-FLOOR apartment in the Bulevardul Republicii, light came from the candle on Demeter's altar. The petroleum lamps were lit, and colored fluids were bubbling in the beakers and alembics as the Condesa de Rougemont performed her alchemy.

In the hot, airless evening, the Princess Clara Brancoveanu lay with her daughter on the straw pallet. Isaac Newton's black book was open on the table. Beside it were the three glass balls in a line, and General Schenck von Schenck's big revolver. Inez de Rougemont murmured incantations while Madame de Graz leaned on her cane. Ana Cassian lingered in the doorway.

Peter sat beside Miranda on the pallet. But he had turned away from her, wanting to give her mother some small privacy as she bent over Miranda, touched her lips. He was staring at Ana Cassian, and it was in her expression that Peter first became aware that some terrible was happening. He saw the doubt in her thin face change into something else, some more violent emotion—he looked down toward Miranda. Clara Brancoveanu had raised herself on her right elbow, and in her right hand she held a beaker of some distillate that smelled like Vicks VapoRub. And with her left hand she was rubbing her mouth and lips with it, and then she bent down over Miranda and kissed her again.

This time it wasn't a little touch. She cried out, grunted through her nose, and her eyes started open—Miranda was still asleep. But now she was waking up, and she was coughing a little bit, and her mouth had something in it, maybe some new bile or vomit. Peter slid down next to her on the other side of the pallet. He grabbed hold of her hand. He leaned over her, so close that he could see, as the princess pulled away, the black eel like a rotten tongue protrude out of her mouth.

Now in an instant Peter understood Clara Brancoveanu's mood, the tender resolve of these last offices around her daughter's bed. Too late he realized as fact what he had half dismissed as metaphor, and what, if he'd been paying a different kind of attention, he might have been able to prevent. Horrified, he stretched out the stump of his right hand.

He could see the princess also had belated second thoughts, and her courage failed her. Eyes wide, desperate, she pulled away. But the eel was long enough to span the gap, a fat, blind, sucking fish that pushed its head into her mouth.

No one spoke. But Peter heard a soft, tearing hiss. He thought at first it was the sound the creature made, conjured from its refuge in Miranda's body. But then he realized the noise was in his own mouth as he twisted his hand from her clenched fingers, fell over her, grabbed hold of the black, fringed, slippery tail as it disappeared down the princess's throat. He coiled it between his fingers. And as the princess pulled away, he rose to his knees. The creature almost slid out of his hand. But he dug his fingernails into its tough hide. He squeezed with all his strength and dragged the eel backward inch by inch.

The hissing sound was louder now, mixed with the princess's grunt of pain. She was bleeding from the corners of her lips. The eel, sleek and slippery in one direction, was stubborn the other way. It had raised its circles of frilled spines. Peter's hand was bleeding, and he could not adjust his grip. He pressed the stump of his arm into the princess's face, and as she choked and screamed he pulled the eel out of her throat, then staggered up into the center of the room.

"Stupid fool," said Inez de Rougemont. She raised her hands as if she might strike him, while at the same time Madame de Graz glowered at him as if he were guilty of some mistake in etiquette—he had to get away from these women. He had to get Miranda away from them.

He backed away toward the door. The old ladies watched him as the eel turned in his hand, its mouth searching for purchase. He held its body at arm's length, but already it seemed to him as if the creature were distending, swelling under his fingers. What should he do now? He had acted on instinct. Nor had he asked himself whether he had the strength to kill this creature—what had Madame de Graz said? He could not let it loose into the world. It might cause a war.

"Fool," said Inez de Rougemont. "What are you doing?" Lines of sweat disturbed the powder on her cheeks; he could expect no help from her. Desperate, he turned back toward the bed, where Clara Brancoveanu lay gasping and choking.

He watched Miranda come awake. Her hand was fumbling for his, and when she didn't find it, she opened her eyes.

She sat up in the bed among the tangled sheets. "Peter," she said, and looked at him, and for a moment everything was still.

There was blood on Miranda's lips, and she spat. There was color in her famished cheeks as she looked around the room; the princess had collapsed away from her. She had fallen back on the pillows, straining for breath, her eyes wide and shot with blood. Drops of blood fell from her eyelids and her nose.

"Peter," Miranda said, and turned away from him. She bent down over her mother, and he could not see her face. He stood in the center of the room, the eel twisting up his forearm, the old ladies fussing and clucking; Peter raised the stump of his right arm to block them away. He felt a momentary gust of happiness, because he saw the exorcism had been successful. This was no wicked spirit, no ghost of a dead conjurer. But this was Miranda herself. He recognized her voice and the movement of her body as she crouched over her mother. He had not seen her since Cismigiu Park.

Now Madame de Graz clumped toward him, leaning on her cane. She stood in front of Peter with one hand held out. She let go of the cane, which clattered to the floor.

"My son," she said, "give it to me." She reached out her other hand. Her face was soft with acceptance and surrender; she opened her lips wide. The monster turned toward her, as if it smelt her with its sucking mouth.

Inez de Rougemont stood behind her with her hand on her shoulder. "It can be sequestered," she murmured. "Magister Newton says . . ."

But now Miranda got to her feet. Gasping and choking, her mother reached out to her, but she pushed her hands away. Then she stepped from the pallet to the floor. "You shut up," she said to the condesa. "You just shut up."

ON THE BORDER TO the hidden world, in the high meadow below the pass, Miranda stood among the wildflowers. She had the tourmaline in her hand. She looked down, and she was happy to recognize the little ape or monkey in a flattened circle of grass, where there'd been a struggle, perhaps, or a larger animal had lain down.

And because she also could feel the white tyger inside of her, and when she looked down she could see the beast scarcely restrained by her human skin, she was aware of Peter Gross in the dark apartment lit with oil lamps, where her mother lay on the pallet and reached out her hands. Miranda was aware of Peter Gross and the scarlet beetle, but in the hidden world she squatted down and put her hand on the ape's head. And his right arm ended in a stump, and in the wrinkled palm of his left hand he held some kind of worm or little viper that had twisted back to bite him. The expression on his small brown face was hopeful, as if he had a problem that was urgent but it could be solved—she was so glad to see him! And she reached out with her hand that nevertheless had the heavy claws of the tyger inside of it.

THE DEMON TWISTED IN Peter's hand so he could scarcely keep hold of it. Madame de Graz stood in front of him with her arms held out. She had made her decision. "My son," she said. "My son." But Miranda pushed by her and she might have fallen if Inez de Rougemont hadn't held her by the shoulder.

Miranda reached out toward the eel's head; it bit at her. "No," Peter told her. He tried to pull it away. But he could feel it swelling and shifting, and he could feel his grip loosening, and he knew he couldn't keep hold of it forever. Miranda reached under the turning neck; she grabbed the eel behind its mouth.

She locked her fingers below its gills, which spread out in a slimy black ruff—she'd seen these things before, Peter decided. She knew about these things. She had lived with this demon inside of her. She knew what to do. "Hold it away," Peter said. "Both hands."

They stood close together now, and they looked at each other without saying anything more. He dug his fingers into the creature's wet hide, while Miranda squeezed and throttled it. "They are weak at the beginning," said

Inez de Rougemont. "But they grow in strength." What did she know? She was rubbing her thin hands together while Madame de Graz stood with her mouth gaping wide—what did either of them know? In fact the creature seemed weaker now than it had a minute before, its movements slower and less furious. Maybe it could not live in the open air, Peter thought. Inez de Rougemont was wrong about it, maybe. Why did it search immediately for human hosts? Even now it tried to bite and suck at Miranda's hands.

"Keep it away," Peter said. He was with Miranda in the middle of the room. Miranda's mother lay on her back, gasping on the bed. Peter slid his hand up the length of the black eel, ripping his fingers on its outstretched spines, until his hand was with Miranda's hands. They looked at each other, and they held it as it throbbed and flailed and starved.

"You must . . . ," said Inez de Rougemont. "You must . . . ," and she told them what to do. But Peter wasn't listening, and he closed his hand around the creature's gills, and he could feel it weakening. In time they dropped it, weakened and diminished, to the floor. It wallowed on the floorboards until Inez de Rougemont pounced on it. Triumphant, she held it up in pair of tongs.

"I've got it," she said. "Don't be afraid."

Miranda pressed her face into Peter's shoulder, and he could feel her body against his body. He tried to imagine what she must be feeling, waking up into this chaos, not knowing where she was.

"Andromeda," she murmured. "Peter—Andromeda."

Madame de Graz clumped back to the pallet, where she sat down. Inez de Rougemont brought the eel to the table, and dropped it into some kind of chemical bath, where it rose to the surface, turned onto its back. She clapped her hands together. "Magister Newton . . . ," she continued, but Peter wasn't listening. He stood with Miranda in the middle of the room.

"Andromeda is dead," she told him, and he hugged her as best he could with his one bleeding hand. "How did I get here?" she asked him. He drew her away into a corner of the room, and he put his arm around her bare shoulder. Dressed in her nightgown, she stood beside him, and he told her a few bits and pieces of what he knew. He told her what he knew about Bocu's masquerade, and how she had come here. She was quiet, listening.

Madame de Graz had flopped down on the pallet beside the Princess Brancoveanu. Ana Cassian had disappeared.

The condesa, her gray hair disheveled, bowed her head over the table, clasped her hands as if in supplication. In the light from Demeter's candle, circles of red shone on her cheeks under her spectacles. This was not the same woman, Peter decided, who had come into the light of his fire beside the Hoosick River in the snow. She had been different then, younger, dressed in Gypsy clothes. A powerful, compelling figure—not like this frail old woman, painted like a clown. Now she turned toward them, turned around. "Child, is it a crime that I looked over you," she murmured, "took you in and your mother, too? Is it a crime I followed you and tried to protect you for your father's sake? Yes, I made compromises. Ratisbon, Ceausescu—no one has harmed you."

Miranda wasn't listening, Peter thought. Miranda didn't care. The old woman continued, because she could not help herself: "My child, I am so happy you've come back. I have such questions to ask you—where you have traveled. Questions . . . Questions. . . . All of us have questions."

Miranda wasn't paying attention. She looked at her mother on the bed. Inez de Rougemont put her hand out, turned back toward the table, fumbled with her glass spheres. "Oh," she said, "oh, oh," her face so full of defeat that Peter took a few steps toward her.

Now suddenly the condesa was in tears, and her long hands were trembling. And it wasn't because some half-remembered scheme had been uncovered. But she had grabbed up one of the glass balls, the one Nicola Ceausescu had knocked down. The others were in their little nests of cloth, still full of smoke, and Peter also could see the little shapes sprawled and collapsed inside—a creature with a fish's head, a coiled octopus.

But the third ball was empty. The condesa held it up. There was no smoke in it. There was a crack in the glass where the tar had been disturbed. There was a hole in the black, soft patch of tar.

"Oh," said the condesa—"oh." She was weeping, overcome. Madame de Graz sat on the bed with the Princess Brancoveanu; neither of them moved. Miranda went to them while Peter joined the condesa at the table. In the airless room, stinking of tar and sweat and conjuring, she pressed her hand down the page of the black book. "Which one?" she said. "Flimsie. Oh, please no."

"That doesn't sound too bad," Peter murmured.

The condesa smoothed her hand down the page, studying the diagrams. "You don't know," she said.

A little naked woman, Peter saw from the picture, hand-drawn in red on the spotted paper. "It's an infection. A disease," said the condesa. Watching her despair as she puzzled out the script of the black book, Peter caught some of her urgency. "It's a contagion," said the Condesa de Rougemont. "We cannot let it free. Oh, God—"

Miranda had sat down with her mother now, and was holding her hand. Peter thought he would not disturb them. "This will spread," continued Madame de Rougemont.

But how could the little creature get away? Peter took a lamp and searched the corners of the floor. He looked in the cupboards and the crevices, while at the same time he was beginning to imagine where the demon might go, the force that might draw it onward—not so far away.

It wasn't until Ana Cassian came in the door again that he realized what had happened, how the demon could have managed to escape. The girl had gone out for a doctor. Now she was back—she hadn't found one. "The streets are full," she said.

Breathless, she stood on the threshold, the empty stairwell behind her. "And the temples," she said. "The Turks have crossed the river below Tutrakan. They say from the suburbs you can hear the guns."

But Peter looked toward the pallet below the window, where Miranda sat with her mother. As he watched, he saw Madame de Graz lean over Clara Brancoveanu's body, close her eyes.

22   *In Chiselet*

IN THE MEADOW below Kepler's tower, Miranda stood among the wild-flowers. Peter Gross was with her, a scarlet bug lost in the high grass. A hummingbird darted among the blossoms and then disappeared. Lower down, at the bottom of the hill, the ground was wounded by the great trench of the war.

A little creek ran through the stinking piles of refuse. And there were turtles in the mud, she was sure. She could feel the presence of wild beasts on the far side, not these little animals in the trees and grass, but wolves hunting in a pack—she could smell them. No, not even wolves, but some exotic, deadly, African hybrid, hunting and scavenging far from home. Down in the great slough, the garbage pits at the bottom of the valley, they lingered at the dirty stream into her territory.

In the hidden world Miranda gave the tourmaline a squeeze. And in the fourth-floor apartment in the Bulevardul Republicii she stood not in the room where she had lain asleep, but in the adjoining room.

This was where the fugitives had laid out their belongings. She selected from one of the valises some of the clothes her mother had brought down from Stanesti-Jui. Indirect light spread from the doorway. Miranda stood against the wall, in darkness. She stripped off her nightgown, then dressed herself in the shirt and trousers and boots her mother had hated but had packed just the same.

She crossed into the kitchen, where there were sausages laid on the board. She picked one up and ripped into it, spitting out the casing. Peter stood at the threshold, the candlelight behind him. "It must have been the shock," he said. "She wasn't in any pain."

"Is that what they said?" She meant the others, Madame de Graz and the condesa.

Peter grimaced. "Not exactly. They said it was her choice. They said it's a blessing to give your life for your child."

Peter stood with his hand held out. "That sounds rehearsed," Miranda said.

"It was rehearsed. I can't believe I—"

Miranda shrugged. "You tried to save her."

Peter shook his head. "She told me to look after you."

Miranda said, "I woke up and I thought she was dying. I pictured her like Blind Rodica at the icehouse. Do you remember, with the candles around her head?"

"I remember."

"And now she's gone, and they are lighting the candles."

Peter nodded. Could he understand her? Could he understand what she was feeling when she scarcely knew herself? Here she was in Bucharest. And Bocu was dead, and Ludu Rat-tooth was dead, and Blind Rodica was gone and Clara Brancoveanu was gone, and Andromeda was gone.

They were all dead. Miranda shook the golden bracelet on her wrist. She took another bite of her sausage, spit out the casing. How long since she had eaten? The air was hot and close, a humid pressure on her skin.

In the hidden world she stood among the wildflowers, and in the failing light she could see animals crossing the river far below. And maybe the hummingbird was above her, and maybe the scarlet bug was somewhere with her in the grass. But they couldn't help her. In every essential way, she was alone. She stood hugging her arms, watching the animals among the garbage pits, observing their odd, powerful shoulders and enormous snouts, their little, vulnerable legs—top-heavy machines, they looked like, awkward and ungainly in the marshy ground.

"There was a hummingbird inside the room," Peter said. "It was caught next to the window, knocking against the glass. I pulled up the sash. It's gone now."

Miranda wiped her mouth. "A hummingbird. I guess that's right. I guess that was a change in her."

"I asked her what she was doing on the Hoosick," Peter said, meaning the condesa. "She said she was helping you. She was trying to help you. She never meant you any harm."

"Like she helped my mother," said Miranda.

Peter shook his head. "Don't think of it like that. Your mother—she had already made up her mind."

He was right—not that it helped, which was something Peter also seemed to understand. He was staring at her with an intent expression. What was he trying to say—that it was not necessary to blame someone, to feel better? She'd see about that.

In the meantime she was eager to get started, eager to leave the stifling apartment. She would climb down the hillside and down the stairs, the first steps on the road in front of her. "I never want to see either of them again," she said. She would shut the door on these old women in the other room, leave them behind.

Now suddenly it was as if she had broken through the last dark thickets into the open meadow, and all the tangled stratagems lay behind her. The road was straight, and in the real world Peter Gross would go with her, just as he'd gone with her over Christmas Hill so long before. He wasn't smiling, and there was no false encouragement in his face—he was growing a little beard!

"I like the beard," she said.

He scratched his chin.

"It's good to see you," she said.

He smiled.

"I missed you," she said.

He moved toward her, would have touched her, she thought. But Inez de Rougemont stood behind him in the doorway, and she was holding something. It was Miranda's father's gun, the same one she had used to shoot the policeman in Braila. Miranda didn't want or need it anymore. But the old woman broke it open, showed Peter how she'd reset the mechanism. She'd loaded it with ordinary bullets. She nodded and whispered, pointing with her long, brittle finger.

Peter shrugged, always an odd gesture with his missing hand. He tucked the revolver under his tunic, into the waistband of his wool pants. And maybe that was all right, because he had different enemies. He was not with her in the high meadow, or else she couldn't see him there. But here he was, standing at the door of the apartment on the Bulevardul Republicii.

"It's not for them anymore," Miranda said, meaning—vaguely—the people and powers that had brought her to this place. "And you?"

"Because of you," he said.

It didn't even matter that Madame de Rougemont was still there. He came to her and touched her hand. It was true what she had said—she had missed him very much.

But there was a way in which she scarcely knew him, because the past had been so long and complicated, and he had changed so much. And she had changed, she supposed, or at least her feelings had.

Behind Madame de Rougemont in the other room, Miranda's mother lay on the pallet and Madame de Graz stood over her, leaning on her cane. The candles were lit. But the door was open, and the chamber was unsealed. Miranda stood with Peter in the doorway. "I have to get out of here," she said.

"I'll come."

Of course he would. But it wasn't enough just to go out the door. Stanley, her adoptive father, had once told her it was more important to have a plan than to stick to it. And of course there'd been a plan all along. There was a place in the real world, a destination that corresponded to the bottom of the hill where the African hybrids had crossed the stream.

Now she tried to describe it to Peter, but he already knew. "It's just behind the lines," he said. "There's some kind of secret weapon hidden in the marsh. Beside the dead oak. Andromeda told me."

"Chiselet," Miranda said, grateful that he had known the name of it—the place her aunt Aegypta had laid out and determined for her, placed in her future, in the middle of her path.

She was grateful he was going with her, grateful he'd known where without being told. But there was no need for him to read her mind. "My aunt Aegypta told me about it," she said. "It was the last thing she wanted me to do."

She didn't have to go alone. It seemed unprecedented, a piece of luck. And the small pressure of his hand seemed lucky to her also—nothing heartfelt, not yet.

All her journeys in the hidden world she'd been alone, or else surrounded by versions of her friends that were not real. And as she climbed down the splintered steps of the old square stairwell, Miranda thought about how solitary her decisions had been up to this time—solitary, or else thrust on her by ghosts and other people she did not trust. Even if what she wanted was not so different from what those ghosts or people had demanded, still that was not the point. There was no reason to resist out of mere stubbornness. That was in the past as well. And there was every reason to choose freely what needed to be done: a series of desperate chances.

Up until now she had used her powers in the hidden world to destroy what craved to be destroyed. But surely it was more important to preserve things, keep them intact, not because they were perfect the way they were. What was the alternative to struggling forward with what you had? And to fight for these imperfect things required the rupture, finally, of your own container, the constraints that had protected you. She put her hand on the worn post at the bottom of the stairs, then stepped down through the archway past the Atlas statues, down into the street.

"Ana Cassian will take care of them," said Peter, behind her.

He meant the brown-haired woman whose name Miranda hadn't known. He meant the old women upstairs in the sealed rooms—Miranda wasn't anxious about them. "Hush," she said.

"They'll be safe till we get back," he continued. Why was he even talking about that? The way led forward, down the side of the dark boulevard, which was not so full of crowds as she expected. No one recognized them, the last of the Brancoveanus, the celebrated Captain Gross, as they pushed down the street. Their hands touched sometimes, their shoulders bumped.

Once he drew her toward him at the corner of the road. He put his hand against her back. For a moment he seemed strange to her—she scarcely knew him. But that was all right. There is a kind of ignorance that holds an expectation, as in the ordinary way a friend or an acquaintance or a stranger could become something new, on some special night when there was everything at stake.

"I had a dream about you," he said.

"Me, too," she said, remembering how she had touched him in the secret world, how she had kissed his lips.

"We were sitting at the icehouse," he said. "You were telling me about some things that you had done."

Someone you knew could become someone you didn't. Or else just as suddenly a boy could become a man. Peter Gross seemed like a man to her, his clipped brown hair, his beard cut close. Scratchy against her cheek. So: some trepidation also. Someone jostled against them. "We'll take this road," said Peter near her ear. "Then to the left at the corner."

There was the boulevard and the big crowds. Even though they spoke to no one else, still they were able to gather rumors as if out of the air. Rumors of collapse had come into the city on a wave of refugees. The bridge had fallen, the army south of the Danube was cut off, the war was lost. General Antonescu had been taken unaware. He had pulled back several regiments to squelch the riots in the city. Spies and traitors had sold their information to the Turks.

But above all there were rumors of the new armored machines that chewed through the barbed wire and ran across the trench, propelled by metal treads like a bicycle chain. Peter and Miranda knew an English word for them. The Abyssinians had named them after something else: some terrible huge creature from their country's highlands. Or a combination of creatures—part hyena and part lion. Miranda knew about those beasts as well.

This information came to them in half-heard snatches on the wind. But as they approached the Bessarabian Gate, the crowds grew less. Instead of words and voices, they listened to the sounds of the cathedral bells, the roar of trucks and private motorcars. What had the woman said? You could hear the cannons from the southern gates? Yet after an hour here they were, and they heard nothing.

"It will start again at dawn," Peter said. "Before dawn. You'll be able to hear it then. Not till then."

They came out through the old city wall. In this direction, they found themselves immediately among the onion fields—the dirt track over the dike, parallel to the main road. Southeast of Plataresti they found the seam Peter was looking for, the abandoned slot behind the front lines. These villages had been empty since the air attack on Bucharest.

"It's colder here," she said.

"Yes."

"You know the way?"

"Yes. Sure."

It was a relief just to walk together mile after mile, on the same road. He told her about Brasov and what he knew about Stanesti-Jui. "Where were you? What happened to you?" he said. And she found herself talking about the hidden world, and the high hill, and the tower, and the things that she had seen. She had not spoken to him about any of this before. Nor had she said anything to Andromeda, who had no patience for such things.

In the farmhouse library, in all her dealings with Madame de Rougemont she had felt such stinginess, as if she were afraid that something might be stolen from her, used against her. But not now. She told him how the tourmaline had come to her. She told him how she'd used it, and the mistakes she'd made. And in all this she imagined she was sharing not just the experience of the past weeks, but something more revealing, some internal landscape or topography. Because the secret world she talked about was different for every person. Even inside one person, moment by moment it would change as a sudden breeze pushed through the grass, and the clouds turned in the sky, and the seas and valleys shifted and transformed—she should know. She stood in that world with the jewel clasped in her hand.

"Hush," she said, and stopped in the middle of the dark road among the onion fields. "Do you hear something?"

"No."

But then he put his arms around her. Part of her was alone in a high meadow, and part of her was there with him. That felt like the bigger part, especially when the tears came out of her, tears for Rachel and Stanley and Andromeda, and Ludu Rat-tooth and Clara Brancoveanu and Aegypta

Schenck—a surge of feeling that she didn't explain to him. She didn't say anything about it. But this was where her tears fell, on the road to Chiselet, and after a while she wiped her nose on his shirt, took his hand, drew him onward.

They passed through Fundeni, Sohatu, and Nana on the Mostistea plain. These were deserted villages, collections of broken, ransacked hovels, grouped around a central shrine, or temple, or statue. Above them the sky was clear. Quite suddenly they could see the moon.

"You thirsty?"

"Yes."

They shared water from a stone trough and a public pump. They walked side by side along the dirt track through the fields. The main road went through larger towns, and once they saw the houses on fire on the other side of the embankment. Nana and Lucia and the track to Chiselet. The moon rose into a cloudless sky.

And by its light they could see what they'd been following: naked footprints in the dust. Maybe in the city there'd been nothing to see, on the cobblestones or the slate walks, just little wet patches where the demon had pulled itself along, tiny hesitant marks, easily lost, easily obscured. But the creature had increased among these villages in the dark. Now she had a child's footprints, and the traces she left were wet with slime.

"I think I know where she's going," Peter said, and their hands touched.

She didn't answer. These creatures, she thought, were his concern. He was carrying her father's gun, and he would track this demon and her mate—Miranda could rely on him. He had throttled Treacle in the upstairs room. Miranda couldn't help him, not here. She had her own task in another version of the world.

Past Lucia, larger still: a woman now. Miranda imagined her according to the description in the black book. Long, straw-colored hair. Pale, dimpled skin. For a long way she'd been dragging one foot. But now her steps were long, longer than Miranda's own. Soon the print of the heel and arch were lost, leaving only the toes. Something was calling her. Something was dragging her on.

Side by side with Peter Gross. Sometimes their shoulders bumped together. Now they could see the woman's footprints, they fell into a kind of silence. In the hidden world she climbed down the long meadow. In that world she'd always been a solitary creature. She stopped by the last tree.

For a moment she stood with the cool wind against her skin, listening to the grass seethe in the long light, the heads turning over. The sun lingered over the western peaks; the stars were not yet visible. But in the east, in the gap between two icy pinnacles, one of the planets glimmered into view—which one, she could not say. Stanley might have known, or not. Maybe she would see Stanley soon, if the worst came to the worst.

Below her, the hyena-lions lifted up their heavy, spotted heads. They were not afraid. Their little eyes, their strange long muzzles—they made muddy tracks in the long grass. Soon they would bark and yowl and roar.

AS IF BROUGHT TO him on the south wind, Peter smelled the antiseptic odor of the oncology ward at the Berkshire Medical Center, where his mother had lain. How tempting it was to think you could cut yourself loose from all that memory and regret—how tempting and how vain. These memories and regrets are who we are.

"What's that?" he said.

They were standing on the dike beyond the road. Miranda shook her head.

Before dawn, they came into the village of Chiselet. Miranda had never been there, Peter only once. There was the temple of Demeter with its turnip dome. There was the embankment and the railway line. The empty houses were lit with moonlight. They were twenty kilometers from Tu-trakan.

At this moment, the light on the thatched rooftops and whitewashed walls seemed beautiful to him, a calming pressure from above. There was an abandoned bicycle beside the ditch. Peter groped for Miranda's hand, then released it. Oddly and suddenly, he felt the presence of a small hope, because the direst rumors in the city had not been confirmed.

And because Miranda's presence, in what surely was the lull before the battle, changed what he felt. In Staro Selo and elsewhere, he had grown used to the dead, dull, boring calm before the storm. Those moments, more terrifying than the confusion of violence, required a kind of vacancy to even tolerate, a separation from yourself. That was not an option here, with

Miranda, on the outskirts of Chiselet. It was not emptiness that distracted him, but something else.

"This isn't so bad," he whispered.

She smiled. Footsore and exhausted, they walked down through the fields to the embankment. Because of the war, the railway line had been rebuilt and reinforced, a high gravel slope where Antonescu's partisans, fighting for the Empress Valeria, had blown up the tracks. The toppled coaches of the Hephaestion had been cleared away.

They would have to wait for dawn to search in the marshlands where the Abyssinian commercial traveler had crawled from the wreck. Or they could follow the spirit that had drawn them there, and would be searching also for the lead-lined canister. Or else the spirit knew already where it lay.

Dividing the marshland from the plain, the embankment was the highest hill in all that flat expanse. "This is all new," Peter said as they climbed up. Miranda didn't answer. If he was exhausted, he thought, what must she feel, woken out of how many days' sleep? Spoonfuls of broth and a single sausage—he was surprised she was still on her feet. And to have seen her mother die under such circumstances, to have held her in her arms—it was no wonder she moved forward like a sleepwalker, hands trembling, eyes almost closed. The moonlight fell on her black hair, pale skin.

Or else, he thought, she was in the hidden world that she'd described. If part of her was there with him, there was another part that climbed a higher hill, anticipated a separate fight. Dangers known to her alone—with a surge of unhappiness he realized he couldn't even guess what they might be, what form they'd take. And there was nothing he could do about them anyway. Or else one thing: He could offer the same comfort she provided him.

They stood together on the top of the embankment. He looked back toward her, back the way they'd come. Then he heard the guns come to life along the southern front—in Staro Selo, he guessed, and in Tutrakan. He turned, and he could see the flashes of light on the southern horizon, the star shells, the high flares. He saw the storm front, the thunder, the lightning, and the fire. He felt the crash of the big guns, which had haunted his dreams. He knew what was happening along the ground. He reached to touch Miranda's hand. Nor could he suppress a tiny hopefulness, again.

Wasn't it obvious? The Turks had failed to break through. The rumors in the city had been lies.

Even so he felt a weakness in his legs, a lurching pain inside his stomach—what was happening in Staro Selo? What was happening right now? Was there chlorine gas in the trench, or one of the new mustard gases from North Africa? Did the men lie huddled in the craters with their mouths full of dirt?

Part of him was there with them, but not the largest part. He stood on the embankment above the marsh, and from this distance he could even see a type of beauty in the crashing shells, muffled as they were, and far away. Inside the storm, a type of beauty and a small remembrance: Once with his mother and father he had visited an island off the Rhode Island shore, and on the Fourth of July they had stood on the beach, watching all the quiet fireworks displays rise from the mainland towns, sixteen miles away over the water.

He looked at Miranda, and her eyes were closed. What was she watching in the hidden world? Or else maybe she had felt a premonition, because when he turned back he saw he'd been mistaken—there was reason to fear the worst. In the predawn light he saw a shape above the marsh, a heavy floating shape. He heard the thump of the motors. Then it was over them, an enormous black shadow with its cables trailing down.

But the roar of the engines did not lessen as it passed. And from the top of the embankment, looking south and west toward Tutrakan, Peter could see what he had not known existed, a raised causeway through the marsh, straight as a yardstick from the river to the plain. And under the gray sky he could see a line of lights along that road, approaching at a speed that seemed impossible. These were the Turkish assault chariots, each with its long cannon and mounted machine guns. They'd crossed in barges below the bridge. They'd broken through the line, maybe because Antonescu had pulled back his soldiers to secure Bucharest. Or maybe this part of the front had always been lightly defended, because the river was wide and the marsh impenetrable.

But the causeway ran through a tunnel under the embankment, a quarter of a mile from where he stood. Even if this was the only place where the front was broken, when the Turks reached the plain they would spread east and west, sever the road to the Tutrakan bridge, roll up the line.

The airship throbbed above them. Miranda stood with her eyes closed. Already she seemed far from him in this catastrophe—what could one man do? He ran down the embankment and across the soggy ground, his left hand and the stump of his right arm raised. He shouted, then reached under his shirt to pull out Frederick Schenck von Schenck's revolver.

From the edge of the marsh he could no longer see the big tanks with their caterpillar treads. But he could hear them crashing through the trees. And there were aeroplanes, also—the first ones he had seen in this war—boxy, double-winged, their engines whining. He took a few steps into the marsh and sank over his boots, while at the same time he looked back to see if Miranda had followed him. He thought he could feel her behind him, close by. But when he turned, he saw he was mistaken.

A woman stood at the edge of the wet ground. She was smaller than Miranda, with long powerful arms and hanging breasts. She was fleshy and naked, her skin streaked with moisture, her hair long and stiff and straw-colored. And her face was not vicious or irate. She had a melancholy look, until she saw the gun in Peter's hand. Then she howled and came toward him.

The tanks were smashing through the trees as the road approached the railway line. He could see the burning lamps and the green flares laid down to mark the road. Shadows leapt out toward him through the small trees and undergrowth. And then something more substantial, another creature that seized him and pulled him down. It was big, bloated, red, stinking of blood.

It squatted above him now, more toad than human, its warty skin slick with grease. The woman was there, too, and she put her hand on its shoulder, pulling at the tufted hair. She pulled the creature onto its heels, and it turned toward her, distracted, so that Peter could twist away. He rolled over in the mud, slid through the reeds, and he peered back at them to where they stood at the water's edge. He watched their faces change and soften as they took each other in.

This was a marriage, he guessed, of demons kept too long apart, united not just in malevolence. Even now, aware of a common threat, they could not avoid glancing at each other, the red face noseless or else all nose, the white face dimpled with fat, streaked with moisture that ran down her chin.

On his knees in the mud, Peter raised the big gun. Maybe these creatures didn't understand its ordinary use. Maybe they understood it only as the engine of their long imprisonment—the wide red lips flapped open and the red eyes bulged. Awestruck, with shaking hands, Peter shot the straw-haired woman in the chest, all the time while he was looking into the red face. He watched it change, distort with wrath and anguish as the gun recoiled. Ears ringing, Peter tried to bring it around for another shot, while at the same time he could hear the war erupt around him as if conjured from the creature's rage: the boom of the long cannons, the chatter of the machine guns. Peter saw the flash of the explosions, and the ground trembled. When the heavy, spatulate, red fingers closed over his wrist, he twisted away, while at the same time launching himself forward with the last of his strength. He placed his head under the quivering red chin—an old wrestling move, which he'd last used on Sarayici Island long before. Then he reached up to dig his fingers into the staring, bulging eyes.

23 · A Glimpse of Home

IN THE HIDDEN WORLD, on the borderland, Miranda paused beside the lone tree at the top of the meadow. Below her at the forest's edge, the African beasts made creases in the high grass. They moved back and forth, gathering strength and confidence as more of them slipped over the stream.

Their shoulders were heavy and brutal, but their backs sloped down to small, spotted hindquarters. They scratched at the earth with paws that were almost hands. They raised their long muzzles. Their heads swiveled back and forth. They had no necks, and their eyes were small and round.

They were powerful beasts, but clumsy and disjointed, as if bred in a laboratory or constructed by machines. They moved back and forth, sinking down on their hind legs, while Miranda made her preparation, stripped off her clothes. Shivering, she hung her clothes from a low branch. In one of her pockets she'd buttoned up the tourmaline, which leaked blood or else some other fluid into the cloth.

She was not afraid. It was not fear that tempted her to unbutton the flap, take out the jewel again, abandon this place and this fight once and for all. She stood in the twilight in the tall grass and the little yellow flowers, and the fact that she was here did nothing to stanch or alter what she'd come to think—that the secret patterns of the world were not the most compelling ones, not any more, maybe not ever. The world could not be fixed this way. And even if it could, the separation from herself—tempting as that was as well—remained too bitter a price for a grown woman, after all.

But maybe one last time, because she had no choice . . .

And besides, now her fingers were too clumsy to reach up. When she dropped to the ground, her nails dragged holes in the thick bark, slashed at it as she regained her feet. She turned her heavy head, stretched out her legs under the tree. She kneaded the ground, carved holes in the turf, then turned downhill.

And the hybrid beasts ran back and forth, their little eyes gleaming in the last of the light. Above her head there was a sudden chatter of crows, and then one big vulture flying in a circle just below the clouds. The beasts were too stupid for courage or despair. They loped up to meet her in a single line. They cut a single line through the high grass.

DOWN BELOW, AT THE edge of the marsh, Peter struggled in the mud. All around him he could hear the crash of gunfire. One of the aeroplanes, circling above him, lost part of its wing, burst into flame. One of the assault chariots crashed off the causeway and tipped into the swamp not far away. Peter was close enough to see its cannon plow into the mud, its jointed tread spin uselessly and then break free, smashing down the saplings and the old dead trees. He was grappling with the demon, but as time went on he could feel it weakening, feel its fingers slip and loosen as he moved. As the noise of the explosions built around him, Peter felt his enemy grow weak, felt the disadvantage of his single hand grow less. He could gouge his fingers, now, into the flesh of its neck. And even though the poison on its skin burned and stifled him, still he felt himself grow used to it, felt, even, that it strengthened him as time went on.

And when the creature lay still, and he climbed out from underneath it, he found everything was done. The naked woman lay on her stomach, her yellow hair drifting in the shallow water.

Standing at the bottom of the embankment, he guessed or he imagined, as if some kind of breeze or emanation had touched him from the hidden world, that Miranda had survived this battle, too. In the sudden quiet of the marsh, despite his anxiety he sensed a premonition of greater silence and the end of the hostilities. At least that's what he told himself later when the news was confirmed: that he stood in the aftermath of a victory as total and as unexpected as Havsa Gap, when Frederick Schenck von Schenck had broken through the Turkish line.

Later the historians did their work and listed the Roumanian regiments that had taken part. But when the bells rang for thanksgiving in the temples, the priests at the altars would suggest a different story. The land itself had risen up against the invader, the tara Romaneasa itself. Turkish veterans of the debacle would describe the battle in the marshlands as if they had fought not men but some malignant spirit of barbarism—the ghost of Miranda Brancoveanu, perhaps—who had conjured the destruction of their enormous assault chariots, disabling them in the mud. This was combined with more ordinary recriminations, an official complaint to the Abyssinian government and an accusation of sabotage. But the treads of the monstrous machines had broken from the wheels, and their armor had not protected them. Many of the gun turrets had been punctured, ripped apart as if with giant claws.

Later, elements of the Roumanian Third Army would come from Calarasi on the train, would spread out through the marsh. But in the meantime, Peter staggered back the way he'd come, up the embankment. He found Miranda a little way along the track, collapsed above the tunnel where the causeway crossed the railway line.

She was fatigued, as he was. He sat down beside her, took her hand, and they both winced from the contact. Peter's uniform was saturated and torn, and he had lost the gun in the mud. He said a few words to Miranda, but she seemed stunned, unable to look him in the face. All in front of him along the causeway, the Turkish tanks lay scattered and destroyed. Along the horizon, the cannonade was still.

"Wow," Peter grunted. Who could explain it? He leaned toward her and let his forehead touch her head. She reached up to stroke his cheek.

Then he looked up to see the man walking toward them, stepping along the railroad ties in the middle of the track. Peter recognized his big, sloping shoulders, his black beard. It was Dumitru, Chloe Adira's servant or accomplice, dressed in a Cossack uniform and a lambskin cap, strolling along the track with a silver canister in his hand. If he was astonished at the wreckage in the marsh, if he was astonished to see Peter and Miranda on the embankment, he didn't show it.

"Captain Gross. So I was right," he said in his German-accented Roumanian. Then he drew his Meriam revolver without another word. Peter staggered up, reached out, knocked the gun to the side—the shot went wide. And though he was angry, desperate, and strong, still the man was not a specialist in these matters. In a moment Peter had grabbed the gun from him. Peter had knocked him down and knocked him down again. The man roared like a bull, grunted like a bear, but it was no use. Even with one hand, Peter had him. He fell on the man's big chest, holding the canister in his right armpit, the gun in his left hand.

"Captain Gross," said the man, "Captain Gross." Out of breath, his lungs deflated, he would have continued talking. But Peter heard another sound from behind him, and he looked back to see Miranda rise to her knees. She was clutching her side, and her hand came away with blood on it, and then she fell back on the grassy slope.

"Captain Gross," whispered Dumitru. "Open it," he said. "Nepenthe," he said. Peter took his gun by its barrel and clubbed him to what he hoped was unconsciousness. Though if he killed him it didn't matter; Peter knew what had happened.

ON THE BORDERS OF the hidden world, Miranda had labored to stand up. She had left the carcasses of the African dogs. Bleeding and weary, she climbed back up the hill to the lone tree where she had left her clothes. Hands slipping and fumbling, she dressed herself. She felt the bulge of the tourmaline in her stained pocket—never again.

Night was falling. Darkness had closed in around the ice mountains. She couldn't see into the valley. But she studied the wildflowers close at hand, their pretty heads, their colors bleached by darkness. Then she reached into her pocket and drew out the jewel, which throbbed under her fingers.

She would not go to where her own self couldn't follow. She would not go where Peter Gross couldn't follow her, even if he wanted—was that it? That was just one way to say it. She squeezed the jewel between her fingers till the blood or juice ran out, ran down her arm. She threw the empty remnant into the high grass, then tried to wipe her hand clean. She wiped her fingers on her shirt and watched the blood spread over her clothes and skin, while at the same time she heard the gunshot, felt the sudden crash of pain.

SHE CAME TO HERSELF on the embankment. She lay on her back, looking up at the sky. Peter knelt down over her and took her hand.

"Love is a thing that can never go wrong," she murmured, part of the poem he'd first told her years before.

"I've got it," he said, meaning the lead-lined cylinder, which lay beside him on the rail bed. "You'll be all right," he said. "You're not hurt," he said, which was a lie. The bullet had torn her under the arm. She was bleeding, but he had pressure on the wound.

"And I am the Queen of Roumania," she said—"I don't think so. That was always meant to be untrue. That was the point."

And she was fumbling with her bracelet as if she meant to pull it off. "Yes," he said, keeping her calm. No reason to disagree. She was in shock, he thought, that was all. Exhausted and in shock.

"It is true what they told you," Miranda said. "It will be true. I know it will be true." Then she closed her eyes—

—AND OPENED THEM.

She lay on a dark hillside. She propped herself up on her elbows. There was grass in her hair. She was sore and tired. Her hands and feet were all banged up.

Something given, something stripped away. She sat up slowly, hugged her knees. But it was late, too late to stay out on that hill in the moonlight and starlight—what time was it? She turned her head, her neck, her shoulders. There was the path up through the woods. She had to get home. Among the evergreens, birch saplings held out white, entreating arms. The last pale leaves of the year.

She got up, wiped off her knees, and climbed up through the woods to the ridge of the hill. At the place where the paths divided, there was the stone ruin, the empty tower among the trees, the door battered and intact—it would not be disturbed, at least not by her. She found the stone bench, then the path that branched off to the side, and it was only a matter of minutes before the land opened up, and she was in the high cow pasture.

What had her aunt told her? "You might search for it and find it in the land of the dead." Down below, the town was dark except for the street-lights. But there was the white block of the art museum, the parking lot; she paused. She could see the old stone wall, the barbed-wire fence at the bottom of the hill. Doubtless there would be some piece of brass down there, a coin or a slug someone had dropped, just to make a little, narrow gate for her to slip through into tara mortilor. Andromeda would be waiting for her there at the gap in the trees. Pale and ghostlike, she'd be sitting on a boulder in her gray T-shirt, rubbing her long bare legs.

Miranda would be glad to see her. Rachel and Stanley would be waiting with the fire laid. But Peter would not be anywhere, not in his little house on White Oak Road or anyplace in that dark town. And even though there was a force that was leading her downhill, a force that was suggesting she'd be comfortable there forever in her parents' house beside the green, still she had the strength to resist, to turn uphill again.

She touched the golden bracelet around her wrist. She climbed up through the hummocks of grass, the earth churned from the cows' hooves. At the top of the pasture where the woods began, where she and Peter had seen the little monkey that first time, Miranda went down on her hands and knees and then collapsed.

The pain in her side had gotten worse, and she closed her eyes and opened them, and there was Peter kneeling above her, pressing a wad of cloth into her side.

There she was on the embankment under the morning sky. There she was, sprawled out on the cinder rail bed outside the village of Chiselet. "Life is a marvelous cycle of song," she said. And then later: "Come on, help me. Help me up. Let's go get help."